THE INTIMIDATION OF FRANZ HELMER

By

Euan McAllen

Published by New Generation Publishing in 2014

Copyright © Euan McAllen 2014

First Edition

The author asserts the moral right under the Copyright, Designs and Patents Act 1988 to be identified as the author of this work.

All Rights reserved. No part of this publication may be reproduced, stored in a retrieval system or transmitted, in any form or by any means without the prior consent of the author, nor be otherwise circulated in any form of binding or cover other than that which it is published and without a similar condition being imposed on the subsequent purchaser.

www.newgeneration-publishing.com

 New Generation **Publishing**

THE WILD EAST

God is my land:
if I close my eyes the metal and machinery are gone
leaving only the song - of birds and bees
and the wind in the trees.
So gently I rock to the rhythm of the heat:
no thoughts to cloud my mind, no words to speak.
A minute in my life becomes a succulent feast
as I trace the detail of never ending landscape.
This is my genesis.
The sinking sun fills my head with faraway ambition.
I linger, and chill air sucks me dry.
I want to merge with the distant horizon.
I want to fly - else run as a child.
I humble myself and cry.
God is my land.

New Europe was off balance, ill at ease with itself, uncomfortable with its success. Europe had committed the sin of digesting a lie. The big lie sat on top of the truth. Truth was reduce to a commodity, and rationed, and tailored to suit need. In some parts - mainly the middle - it held its head up high, and boasted. In others it sank to its knees and clawed at the earth, begging for release. It was strong in the street while weak in the heart. Europe had a massive headache: too much wine, women, sex and song followed by too much anger, anguish, calamity and crime. It brought out the best in people – and blew them out of the water – else led them to do their worst. There were the best of intentions and the worst. There were the best of dreams and the worst of nightmares. Sometimes it was a lottery.

Democracies led by chance sat side by side with those led by dictators. Germany sat on top, smug, self-satisfied. Britain lumbered on, grumbling, clinging to its remaining empire as proof of greatness. France, fazed, turned inwards and declared itself above it all. It danced to its own tune, else wined and dined. Poland hung on while politically it continued to tear itself apart. And as for the Soviet Union? It had splintered into sharp pieces: little nations with little leaders and borders which changed with regular frequency. The lands of Russia were once again ruled by a succession of short-lived warlords, each swarming over the feast: in parts it was not ruled at all but simply left to ferment and agitate.

Section One: The Wild East

Germany led Europe even though Europe did not want to be led. In the name of peace and security its superior army watched its far Eastern border, and enjoyed the spectacle of a broken bear tearing itself to death. But it worked because the money flowed as goods and services were exchanged. It was a good time for some, a miserable time for others. The centre of gravity had shifted east, leaving the West to look over the fence.

In the German Ukraine a good German boy by the name of Franz Helmer was fast asleep. He was stuck in a dream, the kind that left him reeling. He was running around in the summer heat: across scorched earth, through standing columns of sunflowers. He was chasing and being chased by girls from his school: each one delicious; each one making him delirious. He tried to grab hold of Bridget. He tried to lift her skirt but he slipped in the mud and she vanished. Suddenly it was raining hard. Mud. There was always mud, and so much of it. And then she was back, picking him up and kissing him on the forehead, just like a mother; and again he was chasing her through the sunflowers under the summer sun. It made him want to bash his drum. And so he did, and he marched down the main street through the centre of town.

Suddenly he was in uniform and banging his drum to maintain the beat for the troopers as the locals looked on. A few - mostly elderly - saluted to be on the safe side. The local youths did not. Some, the more adventurous, laughed, their arms folded to state a position. Ahead of him marched his father, also in uniform. His was black, and had been worn in battle, and on it were pinned medals won in war. As usual Franz was impressed, and jealous, and fearful that he would never get the chance to match his father's achievements.

Franz marched down the hill, then back up it. Always the same hill. Always the same beat. He marched around in circles and bashed his drum ever louder. He never stopped marching. He was not permitted to stop marching. He had to bang his drum as hard as he could. And he had to salute. He always had to salute. And then the alarm clock exploded into life – right on time – to spoil it all. He rolled over and woke up, protesting his innocence.

Franz stared up at the ceiling, head numb. He had decided to wait things out. Occasionally he glanced at the clock to see how far he had pushed it. This time he lasted eighteen minutes before his mother's voice shot up the stairs. Frau Helmer knew how to shout.

"Franz! Where are you! Get down here!"

Eighteen minutes. It was a new record.

Franz slid out of bed and stretched, and threw cold water across his face from the bowl and jug provided. He did not bother with soap but

Section One: The Wild East

did bother to brush his teeth and comb his hair. After dressing he made sure he looked smart before leaving the room.

On the landing Franz glanced out of the window: winter was definitely history and spring was warming up. Conscious of the time he ran downstairs towards the front door, slowing to avoid crashing into his father. As always first thing in the morning his father was severe, unsettled; like a man with too much on his plate and unable to unload, or no place to unload. For Franz this was normality: mothers smiled in the morning; fathers did not.

Franz stopped and saluted his father as he clicked his heels. He made a point of speaking first: always with the formality that was demanded before and during the raising of the flag.

"Good morning Father."

"Morning Franz. Did you sleep well?"

"Yes Father."

"Good. Good." Franz Senior looked around. "Where's your mother?"

"Hurry up there mother!"

Franz had to pull her leg. He could not help it. He had to prove his worth. As usual she ignored it.

"Just coming!"

She appeared wiping her hands on a tea towel. Her husband protested.

"Why are you drying your hands?"

"Just washing up."

"Washing up? You don't have to wash anything up. Leave it to the staff."

She shook him off. "It doesn't matter. I'm done now."

Her husband understood order but not tidiness. He shook her off.

The three stepped outside into the raw razor-sharp daylight and cold air of early morning. A tractor could be heard working a field. The field, the tractor, the plough it pulled and the peasant who steered it: they all belonged to Herr Helmer. They were part of his kingdom and he was absolute ruler.

The Helmer family walked across the courtyard towards the flagpole, the son following closely on the heels of his father. A passive Frau Helmer walked a few paces behind. They watched as Franz Senior raised the flag, both wishing to be elsewhere. Once he had been thrilled. Now Franz found it boring. Frau Helmer was indifferent, as she always had been. Both wanted to be back inside, in the warm kitchen. Franz wanted to stuff his face with hot food and coffee.

Herr Helmer pulled on the rope with all his might and sense of duty.

Section One: The Wild East

For him the raising of the flag was of vital importance. It declared his presence in this remote corner of Germany and reasserted his authority. He watched his flag uncurl and catch the wind, to become a red stain on the landscape. He was the first to salute the swastika, and the last to lower his arm. His wife and son copied him. Duty had to be seen to be done before breakfast could be consumed. All three hastened back indoors. Even a fervent patriot like Herr Helmer was easily led away by the temptation of a hot hearty breakfast. Just as his son was growing taller he was growing fatter. One was growing up. The other was growing out. They could almost be in competition. In which case they would need a referee.

The consumption of breakfast was conducted with a reverence and passion which almost bordered on the religious. Breakfast was almost a holy affair. At the breakfast table the Helmer family was a tight unit. They ate together, as families were expected to eat in the great Greater Reich. Breakfast was the foundation stone for the rest of the day. All three observed the ceremony. Herr Helmer said grace and thanked the Fatherland, and the Fuehrer, and spared a thought for his wife and child while they sat in cold consideration. In his mind it was order and understanding: here there was no chaos or confusion over roles and responsibilities.

On a bad day Herr Helmer dominated the table with mother and son responding upon request. His talk wandered around the estate, the factory, his civil and judicial duties, the pain of Poland (of which he was mainly ignorant), and back again to the estate. Talk of the house was the sole preserve of Frau Helmer as she was responsible for its running. Most of the time Frau Helmer was happy with this arrangement.

Food was always served up by whichever member of staff was on duty. Today it was Aneta, a local girl. She rarely had much to say and when she did there was never anybody to say it to. In the last year she had grown up fast and now Franz could not help but watch her: in his mind he measured her for no reason; he just knew he had to take measurements. The fact that she was just a peasant did not bother him. She was not particularly attractive but she was youth, and sex and she worked for his father: that meant he had power over her. He had yet to abuse it. If not watching Aneta Franz would watch his father talking to himself, else his mother pretending to listen. He had leant to recognise the signs which revealed when she was miles away.

There was little place for debate at the breakfast table, and definitely no place for argument. Father spoke. Mother concluded. Else Mother spoke and Father concluded, or corrected. Most days breakfast ran

Section One: The Wild East

smoothly and healthy appetites were satisfied. Today was no exception. Franz almost nodded off until Father spoke to him and made an offer, point blank.

"I intend to check the northern perimeter tomorrow. You want to join me Franz?"

Franz didn't need to think twice. He saw adventure ahead. "Yes please Father."

Mother cut in. "Make it Wednesday when Franz has no school."

Herr Helmer waved his fork as he was forced to comply. "Wednesday. Of course."

Eating done, Franz excused himself, wishing to thrash his motorbike before church. Herr Helmer granted permission by sticking his fork up in the air - even though his son was already fleeing the room. Aneta had to jump aside.

The Helmer house was big. It was a feature and a fortress on a near featureless landscape. It distanced those on the inside from those on the outside. The house was home to the conqueror so it had to be nothing less than grand, triumphant, ambitious and of solid construction. It had to last a thousand years. The house had been designed by German genius: a standard design built to order by slave labour. The house was complimented by a surrounding network of landscaped gardens. Frau Helmer was extremely proud of them – not that she ever got her hands dirty. She instructed her army of gardeners then simply stood back to wait and inspect the results. Like her husband Frau Helmer could cross swords and come down hard on failure and laziness. Like her husband Frau Helmer had little time for the locals or their excuses. With regard to the peasants it was a case of avoiding muddled thinking and expression, and dismissing all presumption of polite interaction.

Elsewhere another alarm clock kicked in to send Lev crashing out of his violent dream. He awoke with a hangover and hit the source of his pain with his fist. The alarm fell silent but the clock carried on ticking. He wanted to carry on sleeping but his self-protection system kicked in and refused to allow such a thing to happen. Lev scrambled out of bed: he hadn't overslept, he was just in a rush to be elsewhere. He was always in a rush to be elsewhere even when there was nowhere else. Then he remembered it was Sunday and sat down on the edge of the bed. He rubbed away the sleep from his eyes. The dark bags were now a permanent feature.

He was forced to listen to the familiar sound of his dad asleep next door. One day his snoring would bring the house down, thought Lev - not in jest but as a vicious assault. He noticed his half-smoked cigarette sitting on the window shelf. He leaned across and put it in his mouth,

Section One: The Wild East

then had a change of heart and put it back. He looked at it, wishing it to grow back to its full length. He stood up and stretched out, and stumbled over his clothes which were strewn across the floor. The carpet was dirty but the clothes were dirtier still. He went rummaging for yesterday's underpants and found them.

If it wasn't the alarm clock then the smell of the house was his wakeup call. He crept downstairs, trying not to make a noise and wake his dad. But the creaking stairs gave him away. He froze as his dad rolled over, shouted out something unintelligible, then carried on snoring. Lev carried on down the stairs, to the kitchen which welcomed him with the stench of unwashed plates and pots. The cook come cleaner did not do weekends. He made himself a coffee and looked in the egg box for something to fry. The wooden box was handmade and delicately painted. His mother had made it. There were three eggs left. A visit to the henhouse could wait another day. Lev had come to hate those chickens - his dad's chickens. He wanted to strangle them. They sounded so bloody cheerful all the bloody time. Sometimes he wanted to strangle his dad.

Breakfast done, Lev had to get out: there were sounds of movement upstairs. He wrapped himself up in his sheepskin coat and stepped outside into the mud - just as his dad began to cough and retch. The noise of his sick body permeated the whole space which constituted the cramped living conditions. Lev kept his head down, as if afraid to look up and take in the view of the small squalid house he shared with the man he had now come to hate: so much so that sometimes it tore him apart just thinking about that man he had to call Papa. The bastard's awake at last, was Lev's passing thought as he headed out across town. And still he kept his head down, because that was where he was expected to keep it – and all in all that was the safest place.

Franz loved his motorbike. It gave him absolute freedom to roam, and roar. With it he could swallow up the Helmer estate in one session. Despite Mother's protestations he refused to wear a helmet and as Father sided with him on that one Mother was stuck. But she refused to stop trying. Franz drove fast round blind corners and even faster along the straight and narrow: he was impatient to get to places, or leave them. Franz felt invincible: he was soon to become a full citizen of the German Reich and then nothing could touch him. And all the land he could see for miles around, all the land he was driving through, would one day be his, to do with as he pleased. At times this thought fascinated him, though as a rule he was not fascinated by the countryside itself. It was just a big place full of crops and cows, peasants and mud. It lacked surprises. It only offered hard work.

Section One: The Wild East

Ahead Franz glimpsed estate workers strolling along as if without a care in the world. As if with one mind and body they stopped, turned and stepped to one side to let the German kid pass. They watched him fly past, as if calculating how many years he had left to live. And although they all knew exactly who he was, still they looked at him as if he was an alien presence, a dangerous tourist, or simply lost. The Helmer boy was not part of the natural landscape. He could never be that. He was a German settler. He was an intruder.

For Franz life was, in the main, mostly perfect: the only major hang-up being the fact that he had not yet slept with a girl. He had to lose his virginity, and soon: he had to be first in his class. There were other minor hang-ups: such as Father's habit of ignoring what he had to say; and Mother's habit of making a fuss and trying to control him. At least Father didn't try to control him - but he did have to be in charge, out in front, like he was still in uniform. Father was proud of his war service and rank, and Franz was determined – driven perhaps - to match it one day, or better it, when he signed up for National Service. If he was lucky, or if Father could pull a few strings, he might avoid the boredom of border patrol.

Franz drew up alongside the barbed wire fence which surrounded the remains of a village. It was deserted, defunct. He knew of a gap between wire and ground which allowed him to squeeze through. Crawling under the wire had once been a doddle: now he was bigger it was a challenge, but still possible and still worth the effort. The place fascinated him and because it was off-limits it gave him a kick. And it was the perfect antidote to the faultless, dust free, antiseptic Helmer house. Here he could throw bricks, kick away the plaster, and make bonfires. Here he could sit on a roof and shoot or spit for sport, prize being a slug of cheap vodka or a packet of cigarettes. Here he could chill out. Here he could take time out from the role of universal German hero - born to raise family and defend the borders of the Reich. Today Franz remained seated on his bike, engine off, and just looked around. Then, wiping his nose, he restarted his bike and sped off towards town. He was in need of diversion.

He found it at the football pitch on the outskirts of town. Kids, scrawny Ukrainians, were playing five-a-side. They were scruffy, dirty, almost feral. As always, despite looking undernourished, they were fit and fast, and they could scream and shout to high heaven. When they saw the German kid arrive the screaming and shouting collapsed to the odd outburst. But still they carried on playing football.

Franz killed his engine and settled down to watch. Occasionally a kid would glance across at him, to keep an eye on the threat. Franz

Section One: The Wild East

knew the rules and kept his distance. He could not join in. This was their game. This was the way things were, and always would be, and should be. This was normality, the law of nature: to be separate, distinct; to be superior at all times by acting superior at all times. (In his mind a difficult but not impossible task: if Father could pull it off then so could he.)

When boredom set in Franz kick-started his bike and flew. The sound of cylinders firing turned heads, and as he roared away he knew they were jealous. And that felt good - less so church service which was next on his plate. Attendance was obligatory on a Sunday and you could not be late. He needed to shower and change, and remember to smile. His clothes were soaked in sweat and his trousers were splattered with mud. But that had been half the fun of it.

◆

The Helmers attended church - as did all other German families in the area - as if their lives depended on it. Their church was a church for German patronage only. And its elite faith was purely for their consumption, for their sanity. The church was huge and on the outside it looked magnificent, and pristine, as if it was constantly scrubbed clean of dirt and dirty lies; for it was, in the time span of religious buildings, still a baby. If you stared up its walls towards the spire for too long it made you giddy with power or flattened you with feelings of inferiority. It imposed its authority on all those who approached it and put them in their place, if only until they walked away. For those who went further and stepped inside, it provided relief and reaffirmation of all those precious things which were held to be true, and absolute, and worth defending. For the local Germans it was a good place, perhaps the greatest place to be.

On the inside it was simple in design, sparse: it provided only the basic functions for worshippers, but the most important ones. It had a simple message to tell the world and that message was '*My flock might be the superior race but at heart they are a simple folk, with simple souls, simple needs, and a wish to make the world a better place for anyone willing to join up and join in. Even if you are not a member of the Volk room can be found for you: all you have to do is sing the song, march to the beat, and abide by the rules of National Socialism. (But not here, not in this place. This is their church. Go build your own.)*'

The Volk who gathered outside the church were well-dressed. Their eyes sparkled with intensity. Their cheeks were flushed with the heat of the moment. Most made a point of greeting Herr Helmer and paying

Section One: The Wild East

their respects: he was a magistrate. Soldiers – young and old, retired and active - saluted him.

Heil Hitler!

At times like this Franz felt good, superior even. He was part of his father: therefore the men were also saluting him. And he felt good inside church. There he was surrounded by his people, and there was safety in numbers. Secretly he was not into God or religion (and he suspected neither was his father) but this place was for him still the truth. And it was the same truth for all other Germans. And truth mattered – that's what he had been told at school. Above all else truth mattered. That was what he had been taught, over and over again, until his ears bled.

As always the show started on time and as one the congregation sat down to listen to the sermon. It sounded much like those which had gone before, except for references to 'spring', 'renewal', 'the new growing season', and any specific cause for celebration or condolence. When asked to kneel and pray for forgiveness Franz never prayed for himself – he saw no need to – and he did not pray for others. He did not know who the others were. Instead he made the right noises and the right moves and thought about lunch. He was hungry again.

Whilst Franz was rooted to the spot a few miles away Lev wandered the streets of his town; drifting; hugging himself when he took his hands out of his pockets; on the lookout for any opportunity or any danger, or anything of interest; open for trade; open to gossip; hoping to hook a good-looking girl; looking for a free kiss. At all times he stayed on the alert. He could fake a welcoming smile just as easily as an angry rebuff or an innocent denial. Like his brother he had learnt to manipulate his own emotions and those of others – that's not to say he could always control them. Far from it they could explode, and leave him feeling wasted. And like his brother he had come to realize, early on in his life, how important that was to do.

The town was in a permanent state of disrepair and disregard. Parts of it were still battered by war, else consigned to the Ghetto. The back streets stunk of rotting vegetables, dog shit, petrol, and unwashed bodies. Lev had learnt to turn his nose up and ignore it all. He just kept on walking, looking for somewhere to go, looking for his escape. The majority of its inhabitants either did not care or had given up caring – or had never learnt to care in the first place. They locked themselves away, in their heads if not in their homes. Community spirit had been crushed by the German jackboot and was bedevilled ever since. The minority who did care, and had the means to make a difference, were the ones who did good business with the Germans and so were locked

Section One: The Wild East

out by the majority. The two sides did not mix easily, and when they did it could turn nasty. For Lev this was all an irrelevance. He did not take any side except his own.

World weary, Lev stumbled across two kids fighting on a patch of grass. Perhaps they were fighting over it. He found it entertaining. Would the bigger, heavier kid win? Or would his smaller opponent, lighter on his feet and with a longer stretch, wear him down? Did he give a damn who won? No, he reminded himself. He walked on, past second-rate shops which sold third-rate products and past pokey cramped little cafes which gave stingy service, and which even aspired, laughably, to be restaurants. Being Sunday everything was closed of course. The town had history but on days like this the weather washed it all away, else buried it under a tonne of grey, leaving nothing to inspire. Lev could walk on, away from everything, towards nothing of his own making, but sooner or later he would end up back where he had started, at his dad's front door, none the wiser, none the richer.

Lev was approached by a man - barely into his twenties but already middle-aged - who offered for sale a carton of French cigarettes: 'as smoked in their capital, Paris' he boasted. Lev made it clear that he knew Paris was the capital of France and scoffed at the price. He walked on, expecting the man to hang on. The man did exactly that, and lowered his price twice. Battle won, business was done. By pretending not to have any loose change Lev made a little extra on the deal. The man withdrew less than happy and Lev continued on his way more than happy. It was as much a sale of happiness as a sale of goods. Lev made the usual mental note to hide his purchase from his dad. Before he arrived home he swapped two packets of cigarettes for a second-hand porno mag. It was in poor condition. Its pages had been crumpled up several times. And all the words were written in Turkish. Still, beggars could not be choosers.

Back home Lev was forced to eat lunch with his dad. Worse still he had to cook the meal: the two had to fend for themselves on Sundays and dad could not cook to save his life. The two had little to say to each other so it was mostly conducted in silence and dealt with as a necessary evil. Lev never got anything more than grudging recognition for his efforts. In contrast the evening meal was not a burden on him: dad always went out eating and drinking with his mates. Sometimes Lev would join him, just out of bloody-mindedness, just to break the sheer bloody boredom, and perhaps to uncover family secrets.

At church, business done, songs sung, Franz yearned to be gone but as always was forced to linger, and smile when addressed. Sometimes Franz would chat with some of the other boys. But that was rare.

Section One: The Wild East

There was no point: they all met at school four days a week and preferred to talk there, in private, away from the eyes and ears of prying parents. So any conversation he did make was, in the end, nothing more than the smallest of small talk, driven by the agenda of adults. Finally the Helmers headed home for Sunday lunch, the heart of which was a great big roast leg of lamb.

♦

Evening dinner, and the Helmers were joined by the local garrison commander and his not so beautiful wife. It was not for the first time and the event had become a classic ritual. The Wehrmacht colonel would arrive, bottle in hand; sometimes stone-cold sober, sometimes not; sometimes in uniform, sometimes not, either way bursting at the seams and bursting to get in. And his wife would be clinging to him, her arms locked around one of his as if to stop him escaping. The colonel would click his heels and salute if greeted by Herr or Frau Helmer, then grin; else struggle with his impatience if held waiting by a servant.

Franz had come to regard the colonel's wife as a comical figure. She would laugh for no reason. She would run her hand across her colonel's head as if inspecting his hair - what little he had left. She would comment on his height and his broad shoulders, repeatedly. And she always wore thick red lipstick and red nail varnish - never any other colour. His own mother, also a woman, rarely wore lipstick, and that confused Franz.

Sometimes the colonel would turn up on his horse, in riding breeches: no car, no wife and possibly, but only ever slightly, drunk. On these visits the ostentatious camaraderie would reach new heights and the two old soldiers would drink long into the night – aiming for breakfast as a wager but never making it. It was a stupid wager. Franz had never forgotten the time when he had once come down to breakfast and walked right into a storm: Mother, furious, was laying into the colonel (who was barely awake) while Father, equally furious (and also barely awake), was apologizing, profusely, and trying to get Mother to show the officer due respect. Franz found out later that the colonel had been caught groping one of her staff. The girl had been reduced to tears. Franz had wanted to laugh - and did, later.

That evening, like clockwork, the two men talked and drank their way towards dinner in Herr Helmer's private study while their women wandered the house. They stayed close, side by side, as if chained together; exploring, perhaps scheming. At regular intervals Frau

Section One: The Wild East

Helmer dipped in and out of the kitchen to check that all was well with the cooking. Even then the colonel's wife was by her side. Franz had concluded that the silly woman could never let his mother out of her sight once inside their house. And she never stopped talking, even when Mother was obviously pretending to listen. And she had no children. Franz did not regard the colonel's wife as a good German. He regarded her as a failure.

During all this time Franz was left to his own devices – which were few – and fewer when the TV channels shut down after 9 pm. Sometimes he was invited to join his father in the study where he would receive a stiff drink on the strict understanding that Mother didn't find out. No such luck tonight.

At the dinning table Franz suffered the constant attentions of the pompous man from the military. The colonel put the same questions as before and Franz responded as before. He never dared to cross swords: at all times the colonel, the most important soldier for hundreds of miles around, had to be given due respect, and seen to be in total control of every situation. The colonel enquired, yet again, whether young Franz (always 'young Franz') was looking forward to his national service?

"Yes Herr Oberst". Stupid question. Same answer. "It will be a privilege to put on the black uniform." Exact same words.

"It is still field grey, even in the Waffen-SS," replied the colonel, correcting him as before. "Black is only for officers."

"That's what I want."

Franz glanced at his father. 'Get this man off my back!' he pleaded but Franz Senior was a million miles away.

"And does the prospect of border patrol bother you?"

Franz wanted to scream: same question.

"No Herr Oberst. Father is showing me the ropes."

'Showing me the ropes.' The expression never failed to humour the colonel.

"Showing you the ropes! Excellent!"

The colonel thumped the table and laughed out loud, forcing Herr Helmer to join in. Like his son he never got the joke. The colonel's wife sniggered, almost like a child. Frau Helmer smiled coolly, feeling sorry for her son. For Franz the one good thing to come out of it all was that if Father and the colonel drank too much they would start to reminisce about the war - and that would grab his attention. He was enthralled by tales of military exercises, not-so-secret operations, lightening strikes and land grabs on a massive, almost poetic scale. And there was always talk about tanks; and how they rounded up

Section One: The Wild East

millions of Russians like one huge cattle drive; and how they sent that monster Stalin fleeing East, all the way to the Pacific, to be gobbled up by the Japanese. And there was also talk at the most personal level: tales of personal courage and comradeship; like dragging a soldier to safety, or giving a helping hand under fire to a man who had just lost an arm, or sharing that last cigarette while expecting death. American boys had their cowboys and indians, their cougars and wild mustangs. Franz had his Germans and Russians, his Panthers and Tigers.

The women might look bored but no matter, the men would carrying on talking: about the purity and greatness of the cause - the cause to rewrite the map of Eastern Europe in everybody's favour, except that of the evil Soviet Empire. The women never showed any inclination to join in so they were cut out. For them the war had been a faraway thing, conducted by angry violent men on both sides. That did not sit easy now in their domestic utopia. Secretly Frau Helmer hoped that her son - her only son - would aspire to something more than simple-minded soldiery, officer class or not.

Franz wished he had been there, in the thick of it, inside his father's tank; leading the charge, blowing up Russians; winning medals, saving Germany, getting the girl. Their talk, often exaggerated, made him believe that he had missed out on a unique experience, a never to be repeated, cataclysmic event – which it was, and which he had. And afterwards, alone in his bedroom brooding, it made him think he had to prove himself fit to be a Helmer.

♦

Monday meant school, that secure place built next to the garrison for the purpose of education: the three R's and a heavy injection of the fundamental principles of National Socialism. Franz was expected to listen, repeat, and remember. He was expected to stand to attention and salute when the teacher entered the classroom. He was not expected to question, or deny, or seek alternatives; and he never did. The classroom meant conformity, containment, control. It offered consistency and consolidation wrapped up in compulsion and conceit. You could not pick and choose. It was all or nothing. You had to be there from the start and you had to see it through to the end. Franz saw it through, four days a week, week in week out. He hungered after the best of what it had to offer: the sense of superiority and a place in the world. Most of the time he was a good student and listened hard: not always understanding but never feeling the need to be understood.

In the classroom the boys were locked together; by determination

Section One: The Wild East

and deceit; by cruel device; by boot camps, blisters and festival barbecues such that friendships were assumed, rarely made. They were taken for granted - often little more than devices to fill time as and when required. And Franz never felt better, more confident, than when he was dressed in his uniform of the Hitler Youth - the standard for school uniform throughout the Reich - and surrounded on all sides by the same. He worn his uniform with pride, with arrogance; and rarely with vague detachment. Its impact was too strong, too alluring; its vision too addictive, too exciting to ignore. It made him feel like a soldier.

In the classroom the boys were taught to feel strong, act with decency, and strive to be the very best. Nothing else would suffice. Nothing less would be tolerated. They were Aryans. They had German blood – the best blood - running through their veins. They were the nation's hope for the future. They were its investment. It had been made clear to them, time and time again, the burden their generation would have to bear for the sake of the next. The empire was surrounded by enemies: war was always possible and they would be called upon to defend it: the Fuehrer was counting on each and every one of them to do his duty, to take up the challenge of National Socialism and maintain its dynamic.

And the Fuehrer was always there, staring out from the front of class, over their heads and into the deep beyond; his face still youthful, still melodramatic, still intense; his eyes still piercing, still persuasive; his expression both self-serving and expecting to be served. His portrait hung on the wall in prime position above teacher's desk. It was a constant reminder of who was always in charge: teacher took second place; everybody took second place. It was impossible to hide from the great dictator: every time a boy looked up he was locked in, again; and he was hooked, again; and he had no idea why, again. It took strength of character or teacher's sharp voice to break away. Some days, when he was feeling low, Franz could not look up at the face. Sometimes the saviour of Germany was simply too much to take in.

When teacher spoke it was with ruthless dedication to his cause. Heads and hearts had to be knocked into shape, and made safe. He was a simple man: solid but stiff; single and superficial. His respect for the past was absolute, as was his belief in the future, as laid out by the Fuehrer. He didn't ask questions – except those stated in the national curriculum – and he was always smartly turned out, as was expected.

Come lunchtime Franz found himself surrounded and set upon: hemmed in by his promise of a grand party. His classmates had moved beyond impatience and were now harassing him for confirmation, and

Section One: The Wild East

invites. Franz had promised them a party, with every girl for miles around invited. Rashly he had even promised them beer, endless beer. One threw a piece of sausage at him. It missed.

Franz fell into a muddle. He couldn't give them what they wanted, a straight yes, and he did not want to say no. He was too proud to admit his dilemma so he turned away, pretending not to hear what was being said behind his back. Some classmates did not like this dismissive treatment and friendships snapped: Franz, the oldest boy in class, Franz the son of a soldier hero, was suddenly not playing ball. Some gestured, as if about to pounce on him, as pronouncing him no longer valued, no longer German. Most turned away in disgust and gave up. A few turned nasty and closed in: Bruno poked him in the back.

"You don't like us Franz? You promised us a big party Franz."

Franz had nothing to say to Bruno: Bruno was a devious shit.

"We're suppose to be his friends aren't we?"

"He doesn't treat us like we're his friends."

"More like Jews."

"Or gypsies, Ukrannies."

Franz could not construct a reply. His silence only served to condemn him. Bruno poked him hard again. Franz stood his ground, stared back, and clenched his cap. He had whipped it off his head. Their words had stung.

Bruno began to chant. "Jew. Jew. Jew."

Franz wanted to smack Bruno in the mouth but managed to restrain himself, just as he had been taught in class.

"Arsehole."

The two glared at each other. They wanted to fight but fighting was not permitted at school: between Germans it was considered unGerman. Günter stepped in and pulled Bruno away. Franz watched them go, twisting up his cap and hitting it against his leg, wishing that he had at least smacked Bruno across the cheek with it. Things lightened up when the girls broke up for lunch and flooded into the schoolyard: the boys turned their attentions to the opposite sex. Franz was left to his punishment: ejection from the group. He took it badly.

Surrounded by boys, the majority of girls huddled together in a defensive circle, keeping them out whilst urging them on; daring them to do their worst. The girls with bigger breasts and better looks struck out, flaunting their worth. It was a standoff and the boys were frustrated by it - it being the lack of access.

Meanwhile Franz was hurting and feeling demoted. It wasn't his fault he protested, to nobody. He sulked in a corner and watched a bunch of girls giggling. Wolfgang was saying something to make them

Section One: The Wild East

laugh. He thought they were laughing at him. He kicked stones across the schoolyard and looked away, preferring to stare up at the watch tower. He could see two soldiers. One was drawing on a cigarette. Like many times before he wondered what exactly they were on the look out for, and what they were guarding in the middle of town. It never occurred to him that, amongst other things, they were guarding the school and all its contents – which included him.

Franz wondered why Father had avoided all talk of his request: all he wanted was to have a big party on his big birthday. It wasn't as if the house wasn't big enough. It was huge. It wasn't as if there wasn't the staff. They were everywhere. It wasn't as if Father had to do anything except keep out of the way and not embarrass him.

After school, face still screwed up by a never-ending moment of disbelief, Franz was approached by Paula while he waited for the school bus. She had decided that Franz – the boy about to be a man - needed cheering up. She would treat him to a bit of kissing. She fancied him, so time to show it. Paula smiled. Franz tried to smile back and not smirk like an idiot. He only half succeeded, but the response was adequate, and sincere. Over the last year or so he had slowly become sexy and it was starting to drive her crazy, against all the rules. Paula talked - about nothing – and Franz listened - not caring much for what she had to say – whilst tugging his tie and fingering his shirt badge. Then she stopped talking. This alarmed him.

"What?" It was all he could say.

"Nothing." It was all she was prepared to say.

Paula rested her arm on his shoulder and fingered the hair at the back of his head. It was not greasy. It was blond and gorgeous.

"What?" Franz grew more alarmed, but in a comfortable way.

"You can kiss me if you like."

Her thinking was suddenly very clear. His was not. Franz didn't know if he wanted to kiss the girl, or if he should, or if he dared. Then Paula pulled him in closer and all his uncertainties fell away. A new beast, previously unknown, took command. It grabbed the girl around the waist and pulled her in. His lips didn't quite hit the intended target and he had to make an adjustment to properly connect. He kissed her furiously and had a massive erection to boot. And Paula felt it, and was impressed. The kissing was at full throttle and both came up gasping for air. All the lessons in class had not done the subject justice despite having covered every aspect over and over: love, sex, marriage; not making babies; making babies; raising children; managing the household; contributing to the Volk. The list had gone on and on. Big, heavy words but in the end this was what impressed.

Section One: The Wild East

The two were out of sight so Franz took things further. His hands travelled up and down her back and across her backside, then around to her front. He tried to squeeze a breast but the girl resisted, forcing his hand away. Undaunted Franz pushed a hand up one leg and under her skirt, to made contact with underwear. He was approaching the forbidden zone. Paula dithered, allowing him to get close, very close to the source of his fantasy. Then she remembered where she was and how she was. She slapped him away, saying a few harsh words to reinstate her dignity. She walked off pretending that she had been insulted. Franz was left standing as if holding the baby, confused and temporarily crippled by blood pressure. All in all it had turned out to be a very uncomfortable day. Later Franz sat alone at the back of the school bus, feeling hard done by.

While Franz had been staring down into books, or up at the blackboard, or at walls, or at girls outside, Lev had been stacking shelves and pulling pallets; unloading bags of cement and shifting sand; sawing wood and cutting glass; counting out fuses and weighing out nails; lugging tins of paint to checkout and beaming a broad smile as the customer handed over the cash; or staring at walls; or stealing a moment with a secret smoke. If the customer was German Lev took care to speak only when spoken to; to insist on carrying all purchases to the car; to wait for a tip and show overwhelming gratitude upon receiving one; to stand to attention as they drove off. The rule was: the Germans must never be hindered; their needs must always be satisfied. They were important, busy people, and always in a rush.

During comfort breaks Lev would sit, drink, chew food, and stare out of the window. The big blue sky was the perfect escape. The thick blankets of cloud proved worth the watch as they churned over, and tumbled along, and continuously changed shape; refusing to settle, always on the move. They could be white and bubbly; else flat and grey; else solid black, threatening slabs; else harmless twists of moist air. Whatever they were, the view outside was better than that inside: the same boxes, the same crates, the same prices; the same mess and muddle, the same stacking rules; the same rows, the same standoff. And with the same view came the same smells and the same sounds: but those didn't bother him as much. He had grown up with unhealthy smells all his life.

That evening Lev drifted home exhausted, feeling hard done by, and in no particular rush as he had nothing to go home to except supper and sleep. As usual the day had been long and tedious. He had laboured all day in the hardware store, bored to death; forced to fake good manners; forced to look cheerful for the Germans. He had come to loathe the

Section One: The Wild East

storekeeper: the fat man stank; the fat man was a bigot, a racist; the fat man knew nothing worth knowing. Worse still the fat man thought he owned him. And his worse crime? The fat man sided with the Germans. Sometimes, when he was sharpening knives, Lev felt like sticking one into the back of the storekeeper. But that would have probably got him the sack.

Lev hated his time there and refused to put his heart and soul into the work, only his time. But that was only part of it: another part of him was grudgingly grateful for the job – real, reliable jobs were hard to come by in his town - and to complicate matters further another part of him hated the fact that he had to thank his dad for the job – unexpected when it happened but typical of his dad. His dad dealt in secrets as a way of life. The storekeeper could do nothing except rant and rage: he hadn't given the upstart the job, so it wasn't his to take away. Sometimes the boy displayed nothing short of total contempt for his duties. And at those times the storekeeper wanted to smack him hard, or punch his nose – it looked Jewish. But he dare not lay a finger on the runt. The boy's father was a dangerous man. And Lev knew it.

Today, like previous days, Lev had managed to hold it together and not walk out, not hit the boss, not tell customers to go fuck themselves. And like previous days he walked home disappointed that he hadn't walked out, that he hadn't hit the boss, that he hadn't told customers to go fuck themselves. And when he got home he would either be relieved that his dad was out getting drunk, else disappointed that his dad was out getting drunk.

◆

Back home Franz dumped his bag and uniform, and all thoughts of school. He launched himself straight out of the house again – to go running with the dogs – pausing only for a quick beef sandwich – cut the way he liked it. Running with or after the dogs was a much needed form of relief, an excuse to go get lost. Franz ran after his German Shepherds else they ran after him. He threw sticks, as far as he could. They chased after them, as fast as they could. They never ignored him even when he ignored them. He jumped over puddles else steered his way around. His German Shepherds ploughed right on through. If Franz stopped for a piss his German Shepherds stopped for a piss. Farm workers paused to watch him pass by: some, the older ones, would never get used to the sight of a German running, and across his own land.

The light was fading fast and Franz could not run far. He stuck to

Section One: The Wild East

the main road through the estate and avoided the muddy country lanes. A circular route was not possible this time of year: he struck out, turned around, and headed back; shaking himself free of all his discomfort. Cold and crisp, Franz returned to the house dripping in sweat and splattered in mud. Ditto the dogs. They never failed to yank him out of his gloom: Franz adored his German Shepherds. At the kitchen backdoor Franz shouted for service. A servant came running, apologizing for his tardiness, and Franz handed over the dogs. They had to be washed and dried as did he: Franz stepped indoors to go have a hot bath. Washed and dried, Franz crashed out on a sofa and stared up at the ceiling. The room smelt of disinfectant and furniture polish. Everything had been cleaned to death and it all got up his nose. Why did everything have to be so clean? Wasn't a bit of dirt suppose to be good for you? That's what he had been taught at school.

Though his body was warm, relaxed, almost limp, Franz could not relax. The issue of the party persisted. It agitated his mind. Furiously he scratched his head and his balls. He kicked out at the end of the sofa. It was getting in the way: he could not straighten his legs. This party idea had turned into a real drag. It had become torture. It was killing him. Father was killing him. Franz shuffled his body into a new position and kicked out again at the sofa; this time leaving a skid mark on the nice shiny leather. It was a small victory, but heartfelt.

Feeling stiffness sinking in Franz pulled himself up and walked around in circles, stretching his arms and legs. His eyes fell on the drinks cabinet. The bottle of French cognac had finally been opened. He was tempted to try some - just a little. He looked around: the coast was clear. He opened the cabinet and carefully removed the bottle. He unscrewed the cap and took a small sip. It was a cheap thrill and it delighted. The cognac burned his mouth and throat but what was left behind proved its worth. He took another sip, this time gargling. Bad move: he began to cough violently and tears came to his eyes. Grasping the bottle Franz collapsed into the nearest chair. Unfortunately this made him visible from the door.

A sudden movement caught his eye. Aneta was watching him. His throat knotted. Was she judging him? Did she dare to judge him? Anger welled up inside. He wanted to hit her. He also wanted to kiss her. Most of all he wanted the bitch to stop looking at him as if there was something wrong with him. He stared her down with his best face – the one full of raw talent for raw hatred. Aneta got the message and was gone. Holding the bottle like a truncheon, Franz jumped up and bolted to the door to peer out: the girl was already halfway down the corridor, dragging behind her her bucket on wheels and clutching her

Section One: The Wild East

favourite mop. He thought the girl was running away from him until she stopped to wipe a large wall mirror, whereupon she glanced back at him, just the once. Franz couldn't be sure but the girl didn't look bothered. Hadn't he given her his dirtiest look possible? It had worked with Bruno, hadn't it? He returned to the drinks cabinet and replaced the bottle, leaving no trace of its disturbance. He squinted: the level in the bottle did not look as if it had changed.

For want of something to do Franz went to watch TV in the television room. The new television was the biggest piece of furniture in the room and Mother's pride and joy: she cleaned and polished it herself – staff were not allowed to touch it. He watched it begin to glow and slowed his breath as the grainy, black and white picture slowly expanded to fill the screen. Franz was disappointed. It was news on one channel - as always news about Poland Poland Poland and those bloody Poles – else something about farming on the other – bloody sheep, bloody cows, bloody pigs, bloody farmers. And the sports channel was closed down. Franz gave up and switched the set off.

Moving on to the main living room Franz fiddled with the radio dial, trying to pin down any good foreign radio; preferably the strange stuff which came out of America. He picked up something in Turkish, listened for a minute, then gave up and turned it off. He was bored again. He moved towards the mantelpiece: there was a game he hadn't played for ages - probably because such games were due for the bin. It was an impressive installation, as was the fireplace which it embraced. The fireplace was huge and meant to impress visitors, which it did. Franz took one quick look over his shoulder then began to adjust the objects stacked up along its length. He rearranged the order of medals and medallions, the trophies, and the little goblets of dried flowers. He adjusted the positions of photographs – family and military – so that they could not easily be seen. The changes were minor, just enough to see if they caught out his parents and got the servants into trouble. He did the same thing with his father's favourite armchair, moving is slightly further away from the side table where Father would place his glass of schnapps, cognac or vodka.

The noise of a fast approaching car snapped Franz to attention. It was Father's Mercedes, a large station wagon. Franz dashed to the window. The car skidded to a halt on the courtyard gravel and doors flew open. Herr Helmer eased himself out of one side. Penkin eased himself out of the other. Both walked quickly to the back of the car. But then they just stood there, facing each other, smoking. Franz watched his father steady himself against the car. Father looked

Section One: The Wild East

agitated. Penkin stuck his hands in his pockets. He looked devious, defensive. Then Herr Helmer exploded and Penkin took two steps back, to put himself just beyond spitting distance. Herr Helmer threw down his cigarette while Penkin hung on to his. It remained glued to his bottom lip. Franz became excited. He wanted to know what was going down. He wanted to see a fight.

The anger on Herr Helmer's face was opposed by agitation on Penkin's. Both faces were red. From where Franz stood there seemed to be no difference between the two men. Then Herr Helmer gestured with a slight movement of his hand and Penkin shuffled off, dismissed. Herr Helmer stormed off towards the house, knocking over a flowerpot as he approach the main entrance. Franz had an uncomfortable feeling: right now Father reminded him of the colonel. He heard the front door slam; next the sound of Father throwing down his jacket and keys; next the sound of Father crashing into a chair and kicking off his boots. Franz decided to keep his distance. Next he heard the fast light steps of Mother. Mother was rushing down the stairs. Next came an exchange of words: vaguely subservient versus vaguely dismissive – first one way then the other. Somehow, as always, his parents held it together.

Franz decided not to raise the question of his party, nor anything for that matter. Father would be in a better mood after dinner. He returned to his bedroom, fell on to his bed and tried to crush the question. But it would not be crushed. It returned to infuriate him: he had suffered dishonour at school because Father refused to answer a simple question. Could he not have a party on his big birthday? If not, why not? Exasperated, he went looking for his mother and found her measuring curtains in a spare room at the back of the house.

Hilda Helmer paid her son lip service. Refusing to be discouraged Franz hung around, both bored and bothered. Finally it occurred to her that something was up. She loosen her grip on her tape measure and watched the metal strip rewind itself at a furious speed. She sat down on the bed and looked up at her son.

"Something's wrong. What's wrong Franz."

Hilda Helmer sounded tired. It was a tired phrase: she had used those words so many times now they tired her out immediately they were spoken. Franz didn't answer: instead he stared at the curtains. What was wrong with them?

"What's wrong Franz. Come on I haven't got all day."

In truth, she did have all day. But it was a truth she was not prepared to face: she had convinced herself that she was busy all day long.

"Why can't I have a party. He won't let me have a party." Franz

Section One: The Wild East

blurted out his grievance then looked away, embarrassed that he had come crawling to his mother for assistance.

Mother was suspicious. "Is that what Father said?"

"No."

"So what did Father say?"

"Father hasn't said anything. That's the point." Franz had wanted to add the word 'stupid', but that would have been suicidal.

"Give him time."

"He's had time, plenty of time." Franz' voice began to croak with the utter injustice of it all.

"Father is a busy man. You know that. Be patient young man."

Franz looked down and scuffed the carpet.

"Don't do that."

Mother's words were sharp and Franz shrivelled up slightly. He backed away.

"Can you talk to him – when he's not busy."

"I'll speak to him." Her next question was automatic. "Was school good today?"

"OK."

"Have you done your homework?"

"No."

"Well go and do your homework."

Franz drew a heavy sigh in a deliberate act of theatrical contortion. "OK."

He left the room and Frau Helmer returned to the problem of her curtains. They did not match the new carpet. Once such a thing had not been a problem.

♦

Tuesday, a different day but the same morning: up early, wash, dress; raise the flag; salute. As the flag came down the postman arrived in his van: always punctual; always polite; only once a week. He handed over a bundle of post to Herr Helmer, tipped his cap and was gone. At breakfast Herr Helmer had a system. He examined the postmark of each envelope then opened it with his letter opener to inspect it (if it was a bill) or to read it (if it had something to say). Then he put it to one side or handed it to his wife.

Bills were obvious: Herr Helmer's face turned sour. Likewise business letters, legal documents, and requests for mediation or adjudication: they all drained the blood from his face. Today one envelope stood out: Herr Helmer paused, knitted his eyebrows, and put

Section One: The Wild East

it to one side. It was stiff and the colour of cream, and it had come all the way from Berlin. After disposing of the rest he returned to it and opened it slowly, cutting his way carefully through the paper with the precision and consideration of a heart surgeon. He took out a letter – also cream coloured – and unfolded it, now deep in concentration. He glanced at his wife who, now alerted, was watching him intently. Franz carried on eating at speed, oblivious to it all. A broad smile broke out across Herr Helmer's face - and Frau Helmer followed suit. (Broad smiles at breakfast time were a rare event.) Herr Helmer looked at his son, as if he had only just noticed his son was there, as if wondering what to do with him.

"Franz."

Franz looked up, spoon frozen in mid-air. Had he done something wrong?

"Father?"

"Read this."

Herr Helmer leaned forward and held out the letter. Franz looked at it, thinking it was some kind of trick, then reached out tentatively. Father had never shared his private correspondence with him before. He held it as if it had come into his possession illegally.

"Go on read it."

Franz began to read. Incredible. Franz looked up at his father. It was the most incredible news. His jaw dropped. Time stopped. Franz was stunned. Franz was speechless.

"Well say something Franz."

Franz could not say anything. He looked at his mother. She knew. He could tell straight away: yes she knew.

"Thanks." It was the most he could mumble.

"It's an early present for you."

Mother looked at Father and beamed. She was genuinely thrilled. She had something big to boast about. She looked back at her son. Her poor boy was struggling.

"That's why your father couldn't say anything about the party. He was waiting for this news."

Franz didn't care about his party now. The ground had shifted, like in an earthquake. Suddenly he lost his appetite. He didn't bother to finish the rest of the letter and pushed it away. His mother intercepted it and began to read it, biting her lower lip as she did so. Herr Helmer watched his wife. It had been a long time since he had seen her so animated, so intense.

"Can I be excused?"

Franz had to get out of the room. He had to breathe. Father waved

Section One: The Wild East

him away.

Franz grabbed a chunk of bread and was gone. He had trouble finding his balance: his head felt like a big lump of rock. He went weak at the knees and had to sit down. He was going to meet the Fuehrer. He was going to meet the Fuehrer. He, Franz Helmer, was going to meet the Fuehrer. The same piercing thought ricocheted around inside his head and made him feel sick. Fear began to sink in. Franz threw up his breakfast in the bathroom.

Now dreading school Franz waited for the school bus at the end of his drive. When it drew up he jumped aboard, kept his head down, and headed straight for a seat at the very back. He wanted to share his news but could not share. He wanted to boast but was still trying to cope. He stayed bottled up while desperate to burst open. He was a confused child again.

In class Franz sat preoccupied with the fact that he was now different, not part of the pack. He had special status, but special status he did not want. The teacher's voice faded into the background and he could only stare up at the Fuehrer. The Fuehrer had always been remote, far away, overwhelming on the news but never in the room. Now the Fuehrer was in the room and he was searching out Franz. Franz was the focus of all his undivided attention. Franz had only one ambition that day: to survive in one piece; to get through the day unnoticed; to get away at the first opportunity.

It was not to be. The headmaster spoiled everything. Out of the blue the headmaster tapped on the door and without pausing marched in, smiling, which was unusual. The teacher stood up smartly and likewise instructed class to put down their pens and stand to attention. The entire class jumped up. A few chairs toppled over.

"Herr Direktor wishes to speak to us."

"Sit down. Sit down."

The headmaster rushed forwards and took centre stage. His teacher nimbly stepped aside and was reduced to being a bystander in his own class. The headmaster picked out Franz and fixed him to the spot. Their eyes locked. The headmaster looked extremely pleased with himself. Franz looked the exact opposite. The headmaster pointed at him.

"I believe a round of applause is in order for Franz Helmer, son of the distinguished Herr Franz Helmer Senior."

All around boys turned and fixed themselves on Franz. He had nowhere to hide. He was in hell.

"Would you like to share your good news?"

Franz shook his head.

Section One: The Wild East

The headmaster looked positively bemused. "Very well."
He shared it instead.
There was no reaction, no applause. No one moved a muscle - though mouths did fall open.
"Come now. I believe a round of applause is in order for young Franz."
With that prompt Franz duly received a round of applause, muted though it was. The boys in this class were not used to applauding each other.
"Thank you," croaked Franz. Even muted applause was too much to handle.
The headmaster gave up. "Are there any questions?"
There were no questions – not yet anyway. Every boy was struck dumb.
In the schoolyard things were different: Franz was battered to death by questions which came thick and fast. But all he could say was that he didn't know anything – other than he was to meet him, yes him, the Fuehrer, on his birthday, yes on his birthday. So no party? No party. Drawing blanks the boys drifted away and Franz was left alone - though they continued to watch him. A few apologized for their behaviour the previous day, Bruno including. Franz accepted, graciously, as he had been taught to do: secretly he still wanted to punch Bruno in the face. Bruno clicked his heels and saluted. Yes, thought Franz, that Bruno is taking the piss. He threw him a dirty look but Bruno missed it.
When the girls appeared and were told they went wild. They surrounded Franz and fussed over him. They chattered at him, around him, through him; leaving him dizzy. They all wanted to know what was he going to say, what was he going to wear. Was he scared? And why him? Surely there were lots of boys sharing the same birthday as the Fuehrer? Some had to touch him. One rubbed his cheek and turned Franz red. Another followed suit. Paula wanted to hug him. Paula wanted to get him alone, to have him all to herself. And when Franz looked totally stressed out, on the point of collapse, she took his hand, squeezed it and led him away to a quiet corner. There she calmed him down, told him not to worry, and began kissing him ferociously. He took it on the chin.

◆

On the day of Border Patrol and his baptism of fire, Franz found himself relegated to the back seat of the station wagon. He felt

Section One: The Wild East

sidelined. Penkin was up front alongside his father, looking dangerous. Only the dogs in the back were more ignored. Franz was not happy. Border Patrol was not living up to expectation. It was missing something: something important, something romantic, something dangerous. So Franz stared out of the window at the bleak spring landscape which offered nothing except the promise of better times to come. It was an absolute constant: unchanging and unchallenging.

Herr Helmer drove at speed, wishing to execute his duties as quickly as possible but as diligently as possible. At this time in his life Herr Helmer wanted minimum fuss and bother. He wanted to enjoy life. Let others carry the burden of state. It hadn't always been so. Penkin did it because he got paid for doing it.

Franz began to vegetate - rot from within. Even the dogs gave up looking around and settled down to doze off. What conversation there was subtly changed over time. Initially it was wooden, straight-jacketed and in one direction deferential: reflecting as it did the master-servant, employer-employee relationship that existed between the two men. Slowly though it warmed up and transformed: the talk became more relaxed; it became the talk of buddies; it became the talk of history – personal history shared by these two men and no other. Franz caught the change and caught the conversation.

As the land rolled past the men remembered and reminisced, sometimes profoundly so. Besides the usual talk of the war of liberation there was also talk of the times which followed, and how the men had rebuilt their lives after victory and resettlement. Franz found it difficult to absorb, let alone put into context. Their talk was fragmented, disjointed, not intended for public consumption. It was gentle gossip, village gossip, pub talk. It was private talk between two men joined at the hip. A cigarette constantly passed between them - often many crucial words did not. Sometimes they steered too closely towards something best left forgotten and changed direction sharply. They could have been talking softly in a prison cell, afraid the guards might overhear. Franz drifted off and the Fuehrer crept back into his thoughts: again and again Franz had to kick him away, into the long grass. A bottle of brandy was passed around from time to time, and Franz received his fair share. That did cheer him up but he was still left hungry in the head.

The day was dull, in scope and attitude. The sky was overcast, the clouds grey and indistinct, some fused together. There was nothing to enthuse the traveller except the urge to not stand still - unlike the clouds which could not be bothered to move on. There was a tranquillity, a vacuum, based solely upon the lack of other people. All three were

Section One: The Wild East

used to a lack of crowds so it made no impact - what did make an impact was a herd of cattle who refused to budge from the middle of the road. Herr Helmer forced his way through slowly by repeatedly punching the car horn and swearing. Penkin and Franz both thought it funny: Franz openly, Penkin less so.

They passed little traffic: the place was still waking up after winter. There was a lorry transporting scrap metal. It may have been the residue of war – a reminder of the waste of war and the rubbish war produces. In time the scrap would reappear like brand new in fridges and washing machines; in toasters and ovens; in kitchen utensils, cars and streetlights, and the like. The lorry slowed for the German car to overtake. They passed three men on a motorbike and sidecar combo: one holding on to the driver; one holding on in the sidecar. Franz caught a glimpse of their faces: these were three young men who looked like miserable old sods, and who dressed like inmates. Once again his feeling of superiority was confirmed. They passed a few ploughed fields made ready for planting, and trees in bloom – peach and apricot were present. The trees in bloom were the one exception in the landscape: they definitively did cheer the place up – but only for those who wanted to be cheered up.

They passed the war cemetery but Herr Helmer did not slow. He did not even glance across at the entrance - a grand design build from great blocks of stone. Through its metal gates Franz glimpsed the remains of a Tiger tank sitting on a concrete circular base. It's backside had sunk down into the concrete. It front, turret and 88 mm gun pointed up to the sky. It pointed East. It was impressive, and Franz was always impressed whenever he saw it. There was nothing quite like seeing a Tiger in the wild.

Smoke issuing from a cottage chimney changed everything. The cottage was one of a number huddled together for companionship and protection. Penkin knew they had all been abandoned – forcibly cleared to be precise – years ago and Nature's encroachment was proof of that fact. The smoke was a red flag. The day would not be wasted. Penkin liked a good fight so he persuaded his boss to stop.

Herr Helmer ordered everybody out - quickly, quietly - and instructed his son to pay strict attention. Suddenly the three were an army unit out on patrol and for a time Herr Helmer would be in his element. Upon their release from captivity the dogs went wild until they were slapped down and silenced. Franz did not dare to speak. It was then that he received his first birthday present, and early. It was a brand new Luger pistol, and loaded. It came with a leather belt and holster. Franz was jubilant and thanked his father profusely. Penkin

Section One: The Wild East

was truly impressed and said so. He wished he could give his son a gun.

Herr Helmer motioned them back into strict silence and produced his own pistol which he checked meticulously. All was in order. Penkin was the odd man out: he carried no weapon. It was not allowed. Instead Herr Helmer issued him with one. That was allowed. Franz held his gun firm and waited for orders - just like he had been taught. He stood tall. Now he felt like he was a proper soldier, or an American cowboy about to chase after those damned indians.

Back to business: Franz was told to keep the dogs on a tight leash, keep them quiet, and to follow on behind. Side by side Herr Helmer and Penkin walked ahead down a lane, dense thickets either side; through mud and on towards the cottage in question. The whole place was dead, empty, and falling apart. The smoke continued to tempt them in towards a prize yet to be defined. Herr Helmer trod in some deep mud which nearly reached his ankle. It served to deepen his mood and turn the game into a tiresome chore.

Herr Helmer was a soldier again: that Franz saw clearly, concluding that this was the reason Father was acting moody. And Penkin also: Penkin was a soldier and freedom fighter again. Franz also caught that. He was not surprised to see the two move forward together as one, as comrades covering each other's arse. It was no secret that Penkin had fought alongside the Germans in the war. It was a lesser known fact that he had fought alongside Herr Helmer's panzer unit.

As the two men crept towards their target - the small cracked pieces of wood which made for a front door - Franz was ordered to hold well back and keep watch. Franz held his Luger steady. He was used to guns: he just wasn't used to owning his own gun – and not just any old gun but a quality, best of breed pistol. He had to find an excuse to wave it around at school. Back to business: Franz adopted a severe expression – copying his father - and looked around for anything to get his teeth into. The dogs played their part and did nothing but growl.

Suddenly it all began to happen, and furiously, without thought; and the tedium of a slow dull day was swept aside. There was no time to think, no time to measure, no time to adjust. Together Herr Helmer and Penkin kicked the door open and burst in across a bare floor. It was covered in dust, dirt, splinters, pieces of wood, and the squalor of transient inhabitation. For added effect the two men began to shout – anything that came to mind and sounded good. A man standing close to the fireplace – hugging it even - dropped his mug and froze. Opposite him a young woman – more a maturing girl - swatting on a cushion on a broken chair gaped in horror and dropped her plate of

Section One: The Wild East

food, and her fork. Cuts of meat skewered on a long stick of metal were spitting fat as they cooked. They sounded strangely domestic, welcoming even. It was a cruel lie.

Herr Helmer pointed his pistol at the enemy and waited for Penkin to speak, knowing that to start shouting again in German would be a wasted effort. (Also it was beneath him.) Penkin started shouting: first in Ukrainian then in Russian. The man, slightly drunk, started shouting back while the girl tried to shut him up. Penkin approached the man and pushed him away. The man nearly fell into the fire so he pushed back. More shouting ensued and the man picked up his stick of meat. He pointed it at Penkin, as if to scare him or skewer him. Then, remembering who was the greater enemy, he pointed it at the German.

Outside Franz heard the commotion but stayed fixed on the spot and on guard as instructed. He knew how important it was to follow orders. That was one of many golden rules he had been taught in school. This is it, he told himself. This is it. Get the bastards. He checked his safety catch was still off and begged for the chance to fire his new weapon legitimately. We are on border patrol, he reminded himself. Today I am a policeman, a soldier. Today I am at war with those who threaten our state and our way of life. We cannot give way. We must not give way. We cannot give ground. We must be ruthless. We are expected to be ruthless. Those words had been dropped into his head by both his father and the state. I will make the Fatherland proud of me, thought Franz.

Penkin tried to pat the girl on the head and rub her hair but was kicked away by the man. The man seemed to have a death wish. Herr Helmer smirked. It was good, and right, that Penkin was kept in his place. He began barking orders and the man stared back at the pompous German, and laughed. Then the man turned on Penkin again and shouted something. It was not a compliment.

"What did he say!" shouted Herr Helmer. He could not stand being laughed at.

"He called you a stupid German pig who's stolen our land," replied Penkin, happy to be helpful. (He was being slightly inventive in translation.)

Herr Helmer stormed forward and smashed his pistol into the enemy's face whilst simultaneously thumping him in the stomach. The man collapsed onto the floor and the girl lunged forward to shield him, and to pray. For follow up Herr Helmer stamped on his head. The man would not get up now. And he would not be smiling away his troubles for a long time. He was a headless chicken.

"Come on let's get out of here. The army can deal with this mess."

31

Section One: The Wild East

Herr Helmer could not be bothered to arrest a couple of vagrants, or illegal immigrants, or gypsies, or whatever. It made for too much paperwork. He produced two sets of handcuffs and dumped them on Penkin.

"Put these on them. Quick."

Penkin did as commanded while his boss watched, and on the way out he recovered the stick of meat. He examined it: some of it was still clean.

Meanwhile Franz was elsewhere: he had heard the noise of movement through undergrowth at the back of the cottage and had gone looking for a fight. He regarded himself as invincible. The dogs thought likewise and were straining at the lead, begging to do their worst: Franz warmed to the idea when he set eyes upon a dirty, dishevelled man stumbling towards the cottage. The man looked confused. He was clutching an armful of small logs to his chest. He looked every bit an illegal alien. The man saw just a boy, walking his dogs - until that is Franz raised his pistol and ordered the enemy to halt and raise his arms. He was playing it by the book.

The man spoke but Franz did not understand. He assumed it was Russian. He was stuck. The man was also stuck. He dropped his logs - now very heavy - and decided to turn and run. He got no further than tripping over. It made him feel stupid in front of the crazy German boy. Franz, seeing his excuse, let loose his dogs. They deserved it, he thought. They had earned their bit of fun.

The dogs bolted forward and rounded on their quarry. For a few minutes they not family dogs but wild beasts on the kill. The man, terrified, covered his head with his arms and kept it buried in the dirt. Franz moved in and stood over his catch: proud, pistol pointing, just like in the movies. He swore, just the once, and the two sides stayed locked together in a deadly embrace: dogs on the verge of tearing the man apart but restrained from doing so by unknown forces; Franz wishing he could fire his gun. He so dearly wanted to pull the trigger, just to feel what it was like. The stalemate was unlocked by his father: he told his son to relax and lower his pistol. Easier said than done: Franz was on a high, almost in Heaven. His father had to calm him down.

The catch was handcuffed, then pushed and pulled inside, to be seated next to his accomplices. All three suspects were told to shut up and not move on pain of death. It was high theatre of the lowest kind, but it worked. Back outside, the heat of the moment having evaporated, Herr Helmer was impatient to get home. He had done his bit for country. Penkin was still on a high, as was Franz, as were the dogs.

Section One: The Wild East

And Penkin had meat to chew on - which he did not share despite the protests of the dogs.

Using his portable, army issue radio Herr Helmer contacted his local base and passed on the news of his catch. Being who he was he was promised immediate backup. All three had to hang around until the troops turned up. They finished off the brandy. Franz took the odd peek at their prisoners through a small window of cracked glass, still interested. Not that there was anything to see: just the sight of three badly dressed, crushed souls. The girl was crying. The men were not. They were just stony faced. Franz wanted them to play the part a bit better, put more life into it.

Nearly a whole hour passed before the soldiers arrived, which left Herr Helmer fuming. He made his discontent clear to the commanding officer but the man just politely shrugged it off and got to work. On the journey home Herr Helmer didn't speak: it was left to Penkin to ask Franz if he had enjoyed his day out.

Franz was forced answer the intrusive question. "Yes."

And he hadn't been afraid?

"No."

And he would come again?

"Of course."

Franz replied through gritted teeth, by now back to staring out of the window, but with hand on a brand new holster. He didn't like Penkin addressing him with such familiarity - and Father was no help: he was focused on getting home fast without crashing. He wanted his dinner and beer. He had a belly to fill. It had been a long day and secretly Herr Helmer loathed Border Patrol. It was a waste of his precious time and energy. Having Penkin along for the ride just about made it acceptable. Unfortunately appearances and attitudes had to be maintained and a good example set – especially as his son was watching him today.

♦

Later that day Franz hung out on his favourite rooftop at the place he had nicknamed the deserted village. He liked killing time on the roof. It gave him space. It cut him off. It was an escape, a place to dump the sludge that built up inside his head in a continuous flow. The day remained dull and overcast. He pointed his gun at the odd moving target but did not fire. He did not want to waste his bullets on pointless pursuits. He wanted to waste them on something better. Franz looked around: deep down he knew it had never been a village. It was a camp,

Section One: The Wild East

a camp now shut down. And he knew it was not to be talked about, ever. But he could live with that.

He heard a noise but was not disturbed: it was a familiar noise, the noise of somebody slowly climbing the ladder to the roof. He knew who it was and lowered his gun. A head appeared. It was Lev, and he was gripping a bottle of cheap Bulgarian white wine close to his chest, afraid it might spill – even though the top was screwed on tight. The sight of the bottle cheered up Franz greatly. Lev smelt bad but Franz forgave him. Lev was welcomed company. Franz tilted his cap back to get a better view.

"Hi."

"Hi."

Lev looked around, as if taking a reading, then sat down, satisfied; satisfied that secrecy was being maintained. The two sat in silence and shared the bottle: content to chew on nothing more than fresh air and enduring silence. Lev shared his cigarette and in return Franz shared his bar of chocolate. It was Belgium chocolate – actually from Belgium for a change – a country with which the Fatherland had a very neat relationship. They tossed bricks over the roof and listened to them smash below. They were up a mountain. The world was far below. They could not be reached.

Neither cared if the other had nothing to say. The view more than compensated. Finally though Franz did speak – be it in broken pieces. At first he didn't think Lev was listening: all that changed when he mentioned the Fuehrer. Lev's mouth fell open and he was blown away, temporarily off the planet. He plucked his cigarette from his mouth.

"Shit, your great Fuehrer wants to meet you?"

"That's right."

"Why? Why you? How does he know you?"

"We share the same birthday."

"And what's that?"

"April twenty. Everybody knows that."

"I don't."

"Well you should."

"Well I don't - anyway what are you going to say to him?"

Franz looked across sharp, face twisted up. "Say to him?"

"You have to say something to him. He's your bloody Fuehrer!"

"Why?" Franz began to tremble.

"Cos you have to."

"What? What do I have to say?"

"I don't know. How do you do?"

"Don't be stupid."

Section One: The Wild East

Lev's nostrils flared.

"Sorry. Don't be silly."

Over time Franz had learnt that 'silly' was a word he could use on Lev. 'Stupid' was not. The two fell back into silence – an awkward one this time. Then Lev noticed the pistol and its shiny new holster lying the other side of Franz.

"A new gun? Your own gun?"

"He gave it to me."

"Can I hold it?"

"If you must."

Franz picked it up and held it out like a piece of bread for a starving mouth. Lev took hold of it, delicately, like a piece of gold.

"Can I fire it?"

"No."

"Go on. I'll give you the rest of my cigarettes."

"OK. Just the once."

"That's two cigarettes."

Lev took off the safety catch and pointed the pistol at a window – one of the few remaining which still supported glass – and fired. The noise of glass shattering made Franz jump up to look around.

"That was stupid."

"No it wasn't. Sit down. No one comes here except us you know that."

Franz was not convinced. Lev savoured the weight and feel of the pistol before handing it back for safekeeping.

"It feels good."

"I know. It's the best. And it's mine."

Lev jumped back to the more important subject to hand. "Where are you seeing him?"

"Berlin."

"When?"

"On the day."

"When do you leave?"

"Not sure yet. May try and go early. Visit Bridget if she'll let me."

"There'll be crowds. Mega crowds, all cheering. And you'll be in the thick of it."

"Shit."

"Practice your marching – so you don't fall over on the day."

"Shit." Franz tossed aside his cigarette. "Shit."

He began to breath too quickly - too deeply. Lev, worried, put a hand on his mate's shoulder.

"You OK?"

Section One: The Wild East

"No."

"Relax."

"Easy for you to say."

"Relax!"

"I can't!" Franz began to panic as his body began to shake.

"Try!" Lev held out his bottle. "Here. Drink."

Franz grabbed the bottle and drank. Slowly he managed to return to something approaching the norm.

"Don't think about it. Just get through it. Be famous for ten minutes."

Franz nodded. The words made sense. Lev, for all his rough edges and peasant stock, could always produce good advice. No boy at school could ever do that.

"How's the job."

"Crap. Will you bring me that book next time?"

"Sorry. Forgot."

"Write it down when you get home."

Franz sniffed. Lev was sounding like his mother. "OK."

It was a book about the last two hundred years of European history. It had bored Franz but Lev was fascinated when he heard of its existence: he could not accept it being left unread on some bedroom shelf. He wanted an education. Anything would do.

The honesty of their friendship prompted the next question from Franz:

"Has he hit you recently?"

"No. He won't dare now."

Now it was Lev's turn. "Have you slept with a girl yet?"

"Perhaps."

"Perhaps?"

"No," conceded Franz.

"What time is it?"

Franz held out his wrist watch to Lev.

"I better go."

"No I better go." Franz felt himself getting drunk.

"Cheers then." Lev raised his bottle. "Until next time."

"Next time."

Franz began to climb down the ladder, slipped, and almost fell. He grabbed on and yelled out - just a little. Lev jumped up to come to his rescue but it wasn't needed. Franz was holding on.

"Twat."

"Just slipped." Franz looked down. A mean wild dog was on the prowl. "Shit."

Section One: The Wild East

"What?"

"Dog. But I've got my Luger." He continued his climb down.

On hitting the ground he brushed the dirt from his trousers and adjusted his cap, only then did he pulled out his gun and threatened the dog. The dog growled and moved on. It was on the lookout for anything alive or dead it could eat. Franz was too big to kill. Lev wished them both luck and sat back down, now deciding to finish the bottle before heading home.

◆

The next day Franz stood shivering in the wind as he saluted the swastika. Today it did not look dangerous or powerful, or poetic. He could have been saluting an old blanket or waiting for a train. A sickness had descended upon Franz, more of the mind than the body. It wrapped him up in a grotesque reality, one based upon a recurring nightmare: that he would stumble and fall; that he would have nothing to say; that he would be late; that he would be too early; that he would faint; that he would wet himself; that he would find the whole thing stupid and laugh out loud; that the Fuehrer, an old man, would bend over and kiss him on the forehead then force him to salute the whole wide world. Frau Helmer spotted the signs and sent him back to bed. No school today.

Aneta brought him refreshments and cleaned up his room. Franz watched her: sometimes like an employer, sometimes like a stalker; sometimes like a big cat, sometimes like a small boy. He tried to make her talk, but it was like trying to extract water from stone. He even shared his great news, interested to see her reaction - or to impress. She gave her congratulations, politely, but her lack of surprise revealed the fact that she already knew. (News travelled through the house and beyond in mysterious ways.) Worse of all she did not make eye contact. That tested him to the limit. Franz wanted to jump out of bed and shake - and rattle - the stubborn girl into submission. But he didn't: he dismissed her instead.

Mother checked up on him once. Father did not. Franz gave nothing away. Pride, a condition inflating within him at an astronomical rate, did not allow it. The fact that he would not give her an answer did not seem to bother her like it used to and she quickly moved on to more important matters. Franz took this as a slight.

The minutes became hours. The hours dragged on and stretched the day out towards a grotesque infinity with no end in sight. Franz did not like all this time: too much time for introspection. It was not right. At

Section One: The Wild East

one point, desperate, parents off the premises, Franz wandered into their bedroom and upon discovering nothing, wandered on further into their dressing room and the walk-in wardrobe beyond. There he found his father's old uniform hanging neatly, washed and ready for the next war to begin. It had been ages since he had last seen it. He had to touch it. It felt smooth. He had to smell it. It smelt clean. He had to take possession of it. He had to try it on.

It fitted him remarkably well. He was now slightly taller than his father and, being slimmer, was a better fit. He had no middle-aged spread. It went to his head. He marched around and barked orders. He saluted himself in the mirror. He addressed the troops. He reported success on the battlefield. And at the end of his outburst he sat down feeling stupid, but purged, and still dreading that special moment to come – less special, more like unbearable. Franz removed the uniform and flattened out the creases before replacing it back on its hanger. He wanted his own uniform and his own sense of occasion, on his terms. He left the room to wander the house and grounds, and to catch Aneta when he could. She had become his perfect piece of shit.

He could not settle. His problem buzzed like a bee inside his head. Now the pain came from not being able to tackle it, grab it and squash it dead. Then, while staring out of his bedroom window across the gardens he was struck by an obvious solution: ask Father to let him off the hook. What was the worse that could happen? Answer: Father would say no. Franz held on to that thought for the rest of the day.

◆

The same raging thought was still with Franz when his father arrived home, and sat at the dinner table, and talked tonnes while eating himself stupid. He was still holding on to it while his father poured himself a drink and retreated to his study. Then, clutching it even tighter lest he drop it, Franz summoned up his reserves of energy and courage and knocked on the study door. (Franz knew he had courage because he had been told a thousand times that he was a brave boy.)

Herr Helmer said 'come in' in his own special way: he sounded both inviting and institutionalised, relaxed and regimental, brisk and brittle. He was shuffling papers. He looked important. He peered up from his desk. He didn't frown but neither did he smile. He just wanted his son to state the purpose of the interruption. Only when his son gave no hint that he intended to speak did Herr Helmer grow impatient. At this point in his life Herr Helmer preferred things to be straightforward. He had known chaos and confusion once – and had even killed for it, and

Section One: The Wild East

more. Now he preferred the alternative.
"Well?"
"Father?"
"Well what?"
Franz glanced around the room. It was never allowed to be tidied. It was permanently littered with piles of papers, and box files, and other office paraphernalia; and here and there were the spoils of war. There were less books than Franz imagined – would not a noble place like Father's study have lots of books? – and far more in the way of clutter. Come to think of it, he had yet to catch Father reading a book for pleasure. Franz shifted position when his father barked again.
"Come on Franz I'm busy."
Still Franz could not speak. He had had the initiative stolen from him.
"Feeling better? You can make school tomorrow?"
"Not sure."
"Not sure?"
Father's voice changed: the discipline had returned. He was not happy with vague responses. It reflected badly on him.
"Well let your mother know first thing tomorrow. And if you are well enough, get on that bus."
"Yes Father."
Satisfied, Herr Helmer looked down and Franz watched him pull and push papers around his desk. He did not seem to know what to do with them. Read them? Bin them? File them away somewhere as read? Sign them and return them? Turn them into paper aeroplanes? Realising that he was being watched by his son who didn't want to leave the room, Herr Helmer paused and waited for him to say his next thing - hopefully that thing which was on his mind. The boy didn't, which aggravated the situation further.
"Well have you got something to say or not? Is there something you want to ask me?"
Franz tipped his head slightly and almost whispered his response. He was retreating into a haze.
"Yes."
That simple short little word crawled out of his throat. Suddenly it was far from easy. It was closer to hell.
"Well what then? Spit it out."
Herr Helmer was an officer again, in the Waffen-SS, and he had no time for this. He preferred tanks. Tanks didn't talk back.
"May I . . ." Franz looked up at the ceiling. "Can I . . ."
"Can you what?"

Section One: The Wild East

Franz took the plunge and jumped into the freezing cold water. "Can I give it a miss."

There, he had said it. He clamped his lower lip between his teeth and tried not to catch his father's eye. But Father hadn't caught on yet.

"Give what a miss?"

Franz would have to spell it out, a chore he was dreading.

"It. The trip."

"The trip?"

A shadow descended across Herr Helmer's face. The room suddenly felt cold and Franz began to shiver, inside and out. He wanted to run and hide. Father stared at him, drilling a hole into his head.

"The trip to Berlin? You don't want to go to Berlin? Are you mad?"

"No," croaked Franz.

Herr Helmer would not stand for it. He looked down at his paperwork in disgust.

"You're going."

Now, eyes off him, Franz found himself able to talk back, if only a little at a time.

"Why?"

"Why?"

A ferocious roar developed from below, the expression of absolute conviction. For a moment Herr Helmer thought his son was just being plain stupid. He looked at the boy, curious for a second, mad for much longer. No. His son could not be plain stupid. Such a thing was unacceptable. No, his son was being bloody-minded – a bloody-minded teenager - and that was equally unacceptable.

"Because it's the greatest honour possible. And it's your birthday – his birthday. It's a treat, a present, a duty to perform."

Franz's heart sank: the word 'duty' had slipped into the conversation. That was always a show stopper. But he had been taught to fight so he would fight back.

Herr Helmer banged the table with his fist.

"You will see our Fuehrer!"

He went on to spell it out.

"You will be best dressed, in uniform! You will greet him when he greets you! If he asks you a question you will reply with a positive, enthusiastic answer!"

Franz began to feel faint. Father saw his eyelids droop and banged the table again. The ashtray nearly took off. A photograph moved. Herr Helmer tried to lower his voice back down to an acceptable level

Section One: The Wild East

but only got half way.

"You will see the Fuehrer. That is the end of the matter. There is no place for cowardice or cold feet in my house. We went to a lot of trouble to make this happen."

Franz, defeated and wishing to withdrawn, wanted to cry, in private. He had to get out to lick his wounds.

"I understand Father. My apologies Father. May I leave now?"

Herr Helmer looked down again, never one for too much eye contact, and waved his son away.

"Yes. Go."

Franz fled, with a lump in his throat, a lump in his head, and lumps seemingly spreading out across the entire surface of his body: lumps up and down his arms and legs; lumps across the back of his neck. He felt like a freak, a circus animal, a headless chicken. He went back to his room and collapsed on to his bed, head buried in the pillow. He kept repeating to himself, over and over, that to meet the Fuehrer - the greatest man alive, the greatest man in the land - was no bad thing. The opposite in fact: it had to be a good thing. Surely?

◆

Lev was stretched out on his bed reading a stolen magazine. It was something to do with jet engines and how they worked. He had hoped to find it interesting, illuminating. He didn't, but that didn't stop him reading it. The rhythmic, familiar sound of his hamster spinning its wheel for its life proved more interesting. Unannounced and uninvited, Penkin popped his head round the door. Lev did not look up. He could smell him. Penkin wanted to invade his room, his private space. Penkin wanted to know what was going on in every part of his house. The notice on the bedroom door was always ignored.

"What are you reading?"

Lev gave his same old tired reply. "A magazine."

It was obvious, wasn't it?

"About what?"

"About jet engines."

Now Lev hoped he would go away, curiosity satisfied.

"Jet engines? Planes?"

"Yes."

"Why?"

Why not, thought Lev. "To learn how they work."

Penkin chuckled. "Learn. You always want to learn something. Is this the next thing to learn?"

Section One: The Wild East

Lev had taken enough and rolled over, so Penkin withdrew, damage done. Soon after Lev tossed the offending magazine into the corner of the room. It was proving to be too much of a struggle. He looked around his room, his small room: there was only the hamster, still hammering away on its wheel, still running for its life. It was happy. It never went hungry - too much to eat. It never went cold. It got plenty of sleep - too little to do. He wanted to get angry at something and there was only the hamster, running on the spot. He had felt for his hamster once - his friend once - now it just bored him. And it would keep turning that bloody wheel for no purpose. Round and round going nowhere. Going nowhere. Nowhere to go.

Lev lashed out and kicked the cage. It crashed to the floor spreading straw, seeds and hamster droppings. The hamster looked dead but it had only frozen, its universe having turned upside down in an instant. Slowly it recovered and twitched, and, seeing freedom, made a dash for it. Lev watched it disappeared under the bed. A chase was on. There was fun to be had. He jumped up, intending to recapture his hamster. He kicked the bed aside a few inches and watched the hamster make another dash. He had never seen it run so fast, having always held it prisoner.

Suddenly it looked magnificent, sharp, full of the zest for life. Suddenly he found his respect for it. It was a wild animal like him. With a change of heart he opened his bedroom door, stood back, and invited it to run for its freedom - if only around the house. The hamster didn't get it and so Lev chased after it until it did. And then it was gone, for good. It might escape on to the street. It might get killed by a cat, or run over. Tough shit. That was the price of freedom.

◆

Lev met the Jew at the agreed time and place: at the east entrance to the Ghetto. The Jew handed back his boots, having repaired them for a fee, and some chocolate. Lev did not regard the Jew as a true friend - more a useful business acquaintance - but tonight he wanted to spend the evening in the company of the Jew. Like him the Jew was intelligent. Like him the Jew had spirit. Like him the Jew wanted better. He tugged on Isaak's sleeve and cajoled until Isaak was persuaded - on the clear understanding that Lev did not get into trouble and so, by implication, get him into dire trouble. Around these parts a Jew could not afford trouble.

After a short ride on Lev's scooter they ended up in a bar, at a table in a discreet corner. There Lev studied the same weary old world while

Section One: The Wild East

Isaak kept his head down, not wishing to draw attention to himself. Lev saw nothing but men old before their time, and heard nothing but the damp squib of constant repetition - polished so many times that all sharp edges had been removed. These men were deluded. They had nothing to say. Lev wanted to have something to say; experiences to boast about; something substantial to share with his children. Lev wanted a full life, one by which he could be measured. Isaak was less ambitious: he just wanted to survive, intact, whilst maintaining his dignity in a land where he and his kind were regarded as a necessary evil. Unlike Lev he could not complain - at least not on the outside. On the outside he could not risk getting angry. He dare not get drunk. He dare not use foul language. He dare not explode. And sometimes, on the inside, it was much the same. For him every waking hour of every day was an exercise in self-restraint, self-enforced humility, begging and buying time. For him and his kind the basic provisions of life - food, water, heat, shelter - were a privilege for which gratitude was always expected. Isaak was content to stare into his glass and recount his blessings, slowly. Lev on the other hand wanted to talk but struggled to get Isaak to engage. He grasped at straws.

"You happy here?"

Isaak looked up. "This bar?"

Lev waited for a proper answer.

"The ghetto or this country?"

"Both."

Isaak shrugged. "Of course not but it's all I know. It's all I have."

"You going to stay here the rest of your life?"

Isaak was bemused. "What else can I do?"

"Escape. Run away."

Isaak wanted to laugh. "Escape? Me? I'm a Jew, remember?"

"Only round here. Only in the ghetto. Out there who knows you're a Jew?"

Isaak closed his eyes and kept his cool. Lev was an idiot sometimes. He didn't have a clue. The silence was a big hint for Lev to shut up. He looked at his watch - a watch he had acquired cheap from another Jew.

"Shit. I promised to meet Franz."

Isaak opened his eyes: he was suddenly very alert. "A German?"

"A friend of mine. He's OK, still in school, harmless." Lev patted the Jew on the back. "Come on. Let's go. It'll be fun. You two should get to know each other - it'll be fun."

Fun? Isaak was not in the least bit convinced but he went along for the ride. He needed excitement in his life else he would go mad.

Section One: The Wild East

Secured on the back of Lev's scooter he assumed they were off to another drinking hole: perhaps one more upmarket, more expensive; one frequented by Germans. He did not expect to end up at a camp, a dump site. He sat on the scooter, unwilling to dismount.

"What are we doing here?"

"See the sun set."

Lev produced a bottle of schnapps from the saddlebag and patted his Jew on the back.

"Come on. Don't be a misery guts." He wanted them to be friends.

Lev climbed the ladder in a hurry. Isaak did so slowly. Franz was up there waiting. He had a six pack by his side and smiled when Lev flaunted the label on his bottle as he sat down. His smile fell away when a second head came into view. This was their private hideaway, not to be shared. Lev knew that. Lev should have known better.

"Who are you?" growled Franz.

Isaak felt his throat dry up. He was under interrogation, by a German. "Isaak."

There, he had said it.

"You're a Jew." Franz looked at Lev, as if condemning them both. "He's a Jew. And he's not wearing his star."

Lev tried to shake Franz by the shoulder. "He's a good mate. He does me favours."

Franz didn't want to know. The Jew was an intruder. The Jew was not his kind. The Jew was Jewish. Franz felt compromised. As a rule he did not frequent with Jews. To mix, socialize with them in any way could only confuse things. And when he was older he would do so only in the course of work, business. That was his mindset: one carefully crafted and encouraged by the establishment and his elders from the day he could look, listen and learn; read, write and report. Lev handed round the schnapps - again and again - to the extent that Franz eased up and recovered his composure. Against all the odds Franz found himself chatting with the Jew, and against all odds Isaak found himself not feeling insulted, but instead being insulting (but under his breath).

"You live in the ghetto?"

"Of course. All my life. I'll have my own place soon - with my own bathroom."

Where else would I live German?

"How old are you?"

"Nineteen."

"I'm nearly eighteen. What are the girls like in there?"

"Good. Just like out here."

Better than yours and not for you to touch.

Section One: The Wild East

"Good? You want good? You should meet my cousins." Lev had to have the last word when it came to the opposite sex, and sex.

"Lev says you're the magistrate's son."

"And?"

"No reason."

"He's off to see his fuehrer."

Isaak flashed Lev a look which spoke volumes - and Franz caught it.

"You a problem with that?"

"No. Why should I? Sounds like a great day out."

You sad bastard.

Franz was not convinced of the Jew's sincerity - or his opinion. Great day out? The thought of it dropped him back into gloomy introspection and Lev was left to carry on talking - much to himself. But as the sun slipped and the sky produced a glorious spectacle of colour so even he dried up, to be left feeling as he always did at such moments: remote, cut off; excluded from the thoughts of anyone important to him. Before he did though he was tempted by one last question for Franz. The schnapps gave him the strength to ask it.

"Your fuehrer. You really believe in that man and all his shit?"

Franz looked horrified. Would sort of question was that? Only a non-German, a peasant would ask such a thing.

"Of course!"

Enough said, thought Lev. Enough said. Now he was content to just watch the sun set and like the others sink beneath his own thoughts. He was the last to sink, the first to rise: suddenly he drained the bottle and flung it far away. The sound of it smashing below disturbed nobody. He jumped up and began to scramble down to the ground, imploring the others to follow.

"Where you going?" asked Franz. "Not home?"

"Not home."

"Well where then?" asked Isaak. "I have to get back. I shouldn't be out this late."

"Come on let's explore."

Franz and Isaak exchanged looks, but for completely different reasons: Isaak knew too much about the place; Franz knew too little (and wanted to keep it that way). But it was getting cold up there - and there was no choice except down.

It was dark below and lengthening shadows were consuming the decaying buildings. They left little to see and much to imagine. Lev kicked open the nearest door, as if on a mission or with unfinished business. He produced a packet of matches, lit one, and headed on in. His mind was made up: he was determined to see this place before he

Section One: The Wild East

left for he had no intention of coming back. Franz and Isaak hung back at the door: the German and the Jew were suddenly as one, on the same side.

Lev spotted a rag at his feet and transferred the flame from his match. Next he caught sight of a piece of cloth and placed it over the rag. (So frozen in time was it that it was stiff, solid, like a piece of shell.) Now he had a small fire burning. Satisfied by his efforts he walked around, in a daze; kicking aside empty tins and cartons, toothbrushes and combs, and all manner of things associated with the living. He saw a line of rusting metal bed frames, some still supporting rancid, collapsing mattresses. People had once been forced to live and sleep in this place. For Lev this did not come as a surprise. He saw a dirty old blanket - now near black - and snatched it up gingerly to throw on the fire. Now he had quite a blaze and enough light to reveal the place in all its glory. It was as expected: spooky, not nice. It spoke of hardship and suffering. It hinted at lives caged and condemned to slavery, else cut short. It hinted at crimes committed by evil men.

The flickering half light tempted Lev on, before the smoke drove him out. He saw a stack of empty suitcases, a broken child's toy, a snapped walking stick (it's ivory handle had been cut away); the odd shoe; more rags - rags but no riches - even a violin case. It was open and empty, and looked as if it had been stamped upon (perhaps in anger or jealousy). He saw fragments of newspaper - brown paper barely able to hold itself together - its news an insult to the truth. He saw scattered pages torn from a book. He trod on a hard lump of chewing gum. It felt like stone. He did not see the messages scrawled on the far wall - messages of hope, condolence and encouragement - nor the questions, the pleas, the insults, the idol graffiti, the final goodbyes. He did not see the rusty bucket which had once turned stomachs and which still contained the remains of human excrement.

The German and the Jew refused to step inside. Franz went further: he left in a hurry. It was left to Isaak to drag Lev away. Lev had questions but it did not occur to him to put them to Isaak. Had he, he might have got some answers. The camp - closed down and closed off - was an uncomfortable testament to a violent episode in recent history. Yet the German authorities had not thought to dismantle it and bury the pieces. Such was their arrogance. As far as they were concerned history was always on their side.

◆

The next morning it was Franz who received a letter from Berlin. He

Section One: The Wild East

recognised the handwriting and ran with it to his room. There he ripped open the envelope and devoured its contents. It was Bridget. She still fancies me, he concluded. And she wants to visit me - or me visit her. When he reached the end he started again from the top, without pausing. Second time round was just as exciting.

It was a clever letter. Bridget knew how to write a clever letter. Yes, Bridget was an intelligent girl: that he had established at summer camp. Franz began to fantasize. He could handle an intelligent girl. An intelligent girl was what he wanted. He had to have children some day – so best marry an intelligent girl and make them clever. Bridget was good-looking, and fit, and fit for purpose. And Bridget was not hard to handle: that he remembered from summer camp. Yes Bridget was definitely his perfect female. They would make a great pair he declared to an empty room. He had to see her again. She would save him.

Franz felt rejuvenated and, truth be told, well enough to attend school. But he also felt rebellious: so sod school. Let it wait. His head was too full, too difficult to keep up with; already expecting too much of him. Putting on an act he persuaded Mother to keep him off school. Strange thing was she was a pushover: she just accepted that he was still terribly, terribly sick. And he wasn't even expected to stay in bed. Franz watched as she walked away, searching for clues; wondering if she knew he was faking it; wondering if she, a mother, could really read the mind of her child. Girls at school had told him it was possible but he had dismissed their nonsense chatter. Now he wasn't so sure. Mother was very different from Father: now that was a fact.

He wandered the grounds – sometimes stalking Aneta, always avoiding Father – and formulated a proposal. The more he thought about it, the more he thought it was a brilliant idea. Come lunchtime he summoned up the guts to search out Father and put it to him. Herr Helmer was in the kitchen slumped in his usual seat: upsetting the younger staff and annoying the rest as he demanded a big lunch quickly. Mother was also there, floating around at the edges, sometimes on edge; not in charge on her own turf. Franz watched his father eat, like a horse, took a deep breath, clutched his grand idea, and stepped up to the mark. He stayed silent until Father stopped chewing and spoke.

"Feeling better today?"

"Not really."

"Well you're going back next week. School's important. Isn't that right dear?"

Herr Helmer looked to his wife for support as he cut into his next

Section One: The Wild East

sausage. He wasn't sure if he had it or not.

"That's right," replied Hilda, right on cue.

Satisfied, Herr Helmer began to chew again then stopped when he realised his son had something to say.

"Well?"

"Can I go early?"

"Go early? What go early?"

"To Berlin."

"What for?"

"To stay with Bridget."

"And who is Bridget?"

Franz turned to Mother for help who in turn gave Father a dirty look. He should have known by now who Bridget was.

"The girl I met last year at camp." Franz sounded hurt.

Herr Helmer wasn't having it. The request sounded complicated. It would make arrangements complicated. And anyway the travel was all arranged. And it was just one girl. A thousand others would come along. And his son was good-looking - like him. He could take his pick. Herr Helmer stabbed a piece of sausage and stuffed it into his mouth - from which fat dribbled. Franz kept trying until finally his father had had enough.

"No. No. No. Now that's the end of it."

The sausage fat tasted delicious. Let the belly pay the price.

Franz pursed his lips and breathed in deeply through his nostrils. He looked at Mother, furious, but she looked away. He felt the urge to fight on.

"Why not?"

"Because I say so."

"That's no answer."

Herr Helmer looked up from his mashed potato and glared: the outburst, small though it was, was highly disrespectful. Then he recalled his own youth, his own time spent standing in front of his father, and decided to give his boy the benefit of the doubt. His boy had much on his plate at the moment. Outbursts were inevitable. He lowered his voice and spoke slowly for added effect. He was in magistrate mode and handing out German justice to those who didn't know better.

"I think it is. End of matter. Now let me finish my lunch in peace and quiet."

Franz looked down at the mashed potato. He wanted to kick the door down but all he could manage was to turn and walk away. He did so, and carried on walking with nowhere to go. He was trapped. He

Section One: The Wild East

was tied to this giant sinking hole which one day he would have to manage, maintain, cope with. He had to get to Berlin. He didn't want to meet the Fuehrer but he wanted to be with Bridget: hold her again; kiss her again; perhaps get into bed with her.

In frustration he kicked a football against a wall, harder and harder. He kicked it into a large barn and followed it in, to kick it around some more. Then he ran out of kick and kicked the ball back outside, out of mind. He tried to visualize Fraulein Bridget in her uniform shorts and shirt; running around; jumping up and down, sometimes hysterically, sometimes to the beat of the drum in the heat of the moment. He remembered spying on her in the showers, through a gap in the wooden wall. He tried to replay the image of her pulling off her bra and knickers as if desperate for sex. It was most difficult: he could sense it, celebrate it, but not for the life of him actually see it. And now he wasn't allowed to go see her. He could join up, sleep rough, learn to kill untermensch, but he could not go see the girl of his dreams.

Housemaid Aneta walked past and killed the moment. Franz crept back outside to watch her tiptoe and sidestep about her business. His thoughts ricocheted. His common sense abandoned him. She's toying with me. She's playing games with me. She's playing hard to get. I'm a German. She doesn't think I'm good enough for her.

He smashed the football high up against a stone wall to announce his presence and proclaim his displeasure. She looked round sharp. As a rule Aneta preferred to look down - that was the way to keep out of harm - but she was forced to look straight at the trouble: one troubled Franz. He had her locked in his sights. It gave him great power. Then the ball smacked him in the face. A sting shot across his face. His hand went up and he cursed out loud. Then, seeing an opportunity, he tried to cry. Aneta was forced to come to his rescue. She almost ran. She could not ignore another living creature in pain. She closed her hand over his in an attempt to alleviate the pain she felt he must be suffering.

Franz, surprised, made no attempt to move it even though the peasant's hand was cold and dirty. Now she was his piece of dirt. Franz looked into her eyes – she was forced to look into his – and slipped his hand from his cheek, leaving hers in direct contact with his skin. The effect was electrifying. Aneta examined the side of his face and pronounced his eye undamaged, just a little red. She withdrew her hand to a place of safety.

"The skin is raw but fresh air will put it to rights. It will itch but don't touch it."

Unable to articulate his messed up thoughts Franz did not reply, nor

Section One: The Wild East

did he move. This girl spoke like Mother – different accent but she used the words Mother used. He was having an erection and was enjoying it. He placed his hand back on top of hers, and held it tight. He would not allow her to move away. Aneta delayed her protest, wishing to give him (and her) the benefit of the doubt.

"Please. I must go. I have work."

"No you don't."

Franz brushed her hair aside and pushed some behind her ears, and discovered that she liked having her hair touched like that. Aneta was caught in two traps: one of his making; one of hers. She liked them both. She hated them both. She was thrilled and terrified. She was engaged and exposed. Young Master Helmer looked good and dressed well. And Young Master Helmer smelt good up close. The young men in town came nowhere close.

Franz put his other hand around her waist and yanked her in close. She found it an enjoyable experience, and she was hating herself for it. She knew the German wanted to kiss her. She knew she wanted to be kissed by a handsome young man. In an instant she decided: let it be just the one kiss, then back to the status quo. A kiss can cause no harm. Master Helmer was nearly a man and to be kissed properly by a near perfect man would be a pleasurable experience. Let the German kiss me.

Franz kissed the fragile young thing. And again, with more force, as if determined to suck her dry of her sex. Second time round the girl was left exhausted. And again, this time squeezing her to near death; this time not ending the kiss but holding it in limbo. It lasted almost forty seconds. And in that time the girl recovered her will and began to struggle. But the fight back expired as it began: Aneta could not help but kiss the German boy again. He tasted too good. Local lads were not a patch on this.

Franz pulled her into the barn and down on to a large lump of hay the size of a bed. He went exploring: refusing to let go of her. Aneta didn't like that part of it but put up with it, for the kissing. Then she recognised that it was going wrong. They were too intimate now. They were pinned together. This was not right, not correct. But still it felt good – too good – and she struggled to struggle. She moaned but she did not sound miserable. She tried to ask him, politely, to desist but she had her mouth full - and anyway would Master Helmer allow her to speak her mind? She could not state her case so, in her absence, Franz found her guilty.

Rapidly the glorious event went downhill and became corrupted, and token love turned into cruel love. Affection was pushed aside by

Section One: The Wild East

violence. Franz wanted to bite her. Aneta wanted to punch him. Sweat and toil turned into sex and trouble. And there was nothing Aneta could do about it, except cry within. She could not scream as her nervous system was totally engaged in pleasure. Waves of sensual pleasure smashed against rocks of fear and outrage. The mix tormented her. She hated him. She loved him. She hated him. He was hurting her. He was loving her. She was caressing him. He was fucking her.

She could not push the boy off: this big German boy was too powerful. She could not tell him that it was wrong as part of her felt it was right. All she could do was strive to get through it in one piece, and pretend. And that she did, just. But it left her severely bruised and near broken. The boy left the girl depleted of strength, ashamed, her innocence torn to shreds. He had deconstructed her soul whilst trying, vainly, to repair his.

Afterwards, after the German stood up, adjusted his clothes and walked away, Aneta sat frozen, unable to rise to her feet. She had had her inside torn out and only the shell remained. And she had to get back to work. Her head began to spin. She was no longer a virgin: a fact she would not be able to hide on her wedding night. Aneta began to calculate. Would he keep it a secret? Surely yes? Why would a German boy admit to the world that he had had sex with a local peasant girl? She turned the question over and over inside her damaged head. The answer each time was yes. It was a hope she would cling to. Later the thought that she was nothing more than a piece of cheap meat would come to rot inside her.

Aneta stood up, and likewise straightened her clothes. She walked away from the scene of the crime, pretending nothing had change – except the loss of her virginity. No matter, she lied to herself. I had to lose it one day so why not to a healthy, clean living German boy. It was a massive lie. She scrambled around for positive attributes and threw them at him, hoping that they would make him a much better German. She returned to her duties, head down, assuming that young Master Helmer was now her close friend, her ally. But young Master Helmer would never speak to her again. Young Master Helmer would avoid her at all cost and at every turn. Now he had done it with her he didn't want to do it with her again. She was his wasted piece of dirt. She was Ukrainian. She was almost the enemy. She had to be German. She had to be Bridget, or failing that Paula.

Franz spent the rest of the day in a daze, else clinging to his motorbike, crazy with speed: either way preoccupied with his father's final judgement; mad at a world which up to now he had always regarded as a safe solid bet, dependable, true to its cause even if slightly

Section One: The Wild East

punctured in places by unpalatable truths which his generation was happy to ignore. Such truths, when they came within earshot, were pushed aside.

◆

Lev sat in his dad's chair clutching a beer bottle and sizing up the room, sensing its limits. It was still small, still cluttered, still full of useless crap; still void of anything remotely suggesting domestic warmth or affection. The light of the sun had no place in this room. The walls were smudged light green – they would never be painted again - and suggested the mark of a hospital ward, else a mental asylum. Yes that was it: he was living in a mental asylum, with a lunatic, his dad; and it was slowly driving him crazy. No wonder Luka had stormed out - dropped out?

Lev took a swig from the bottle, pulled the Reichsmark banknotes from his jacket pocket and began to examine them again: adding to the total as each one passed before his eyes. It felt like inspecting the troops before battle and it gave him a warm feeling; and it added up to a big wholesome number – big by his standards, and enough to get him started in a new life.

A new life.

Lev played the phrase over and over. He loved the sound of it, the feel of it; the meaning and the substance; and everything it promised would follow. He kicked off his shoes and rubbed between his toes. He scratched his head into submission, took another swig and settled back into memories of his big brother – some reinvented. He was being held up high to see the view. He was passing the ball and the ball was being passed back. He could see Luka licking his ice cream – then licking his ice cream! He could see Luka jumping into the river, clinging to a raft, climbing a tree, falling over drunk, sticking two fingers up at a German shitface – one his age and height but lacking the guts to fight. He could still hear Luka cursing dad, shouting into his face, refusing to back down. The two would argue long into the night, and if it was about something important they would continue into daybreak. Luka would shout louder and louder until dad could not shout back. Now the best bit: he could see Luka fighting with dad, and winning.

Luka was clever: he had waited until he was strong enough and big enough - and dangerous enough - to take dad on and win. And when he did, dad never dared to touch him again. And then, suddenly, without notice, Luka was gone. A quick hug and a kiss on the forehead was all

Section One: The Wild East

he handed to Lev on the way out. And now he was living his dream while Lev was beginning to live a nightmare. It wasn't fair. Life wasn't fair. Correction: life wasn't fair if you were Ukrainian.

Lev sucked the bottle dry and threw it at the bin in the corner of the room. He missed and it bounced across the tiled floor, threatening to disintegrate into a thousand fragments. It didn't. It rolled and slowed and settled down into a state of equilibrium as dictated by the laws of physics. Lev observed its progress, disappointed when it did not smash: that way dad would have trodden on it as he entered – fell into – the room, brainless through booze. Now that would have been hilarious. Lev heard a noise. Dad was rattling the door, trying to open it. The cursing started up. Lev looked up at the clock on the wall. Yes dad was drunk. He put his hands behind his head, leant back, stuck his feet out and waited for the game to begin.

Penkin stumbled in, grasping a bottle, and saw his son sitting in his chair - his chair! His son was looking cocky, clever, all knowing, and was in his chair.

"You. You're in my chair."

"I know."

Penkin didn't understand the point of the answer and closed in, accidentally kicking aside the bottle on the floor. It spun around and hit a wall, all the while making its second horrendous racket.

"Get out of my chair. Sit down. I want to sit down."

Lev didn't bother to answer.

"Hurry up. Out."

Lev began to move, but slowly.

"Hurry up. Stop pissing me around."

"I need to put my shoes on."

"Fuck your shoes."

Now in range Penkin leaned forward and grabbed his boy by the shoulder. He began to yank at his problem.

"Come on, out. Stop messing me about. I have to sit down."

"Alright alright grandpa."

Lev levered himself out slowly, enjoying every second of the moment he was skilfully maximising. Defiantly he removed his dad's hand, using his own strength to excess. His fingers, working like a pair of pliers, almost cut into the wrinkled aging skin of his dad. But his dad was too drunk to register the aggravated assault upon his person. Instead he collapsed into his chair, fleetingly happy: it felt snug and it supported his back correctly, like no other chair ever could; and it held the best position in the room. He was the king on his throne – without land or subjects, without wealth or legality, but still a king. He had

Section One: The Wild East

made it that way. He was king in his own house, a peasant upstart outside it.

Lev retrieved another beer from the fridge. It was German beer but he didn't care; and because it was German beer it was safe. Dad, the stupid arsehole, would not touch German beer. Even if he was dying of thirst, or sobriety, the stupid old git would not break his oath of allegiance. He would never be seen touching the stuff. And it was good stuff, better than the local shit. Yes dad would work for the Germans and take their money but he would not drink their beer. The whole thing was laughable if it wasn't so sad, so fucking sad.

He prised off the bottle cap, stood in the doorway and stared down at the man; openly hostile; in a superior manner designed to infuriate the old man. And it did. Penkin became uncomfortable when the boy would not stop staring.

"Stop staring! What are you staring at!"

"Nothing." It was the best answer possible.

Penkin looked around the room, as if searching for something which had gone missing – or appeared. Then he remembered something extremely important and lit up. He swallowed a large measure of beer and stuck a finger in the air.

"Lev I've got a bone to pick with you."

Lev laughed inside. Dad had called him Lev. That meant trouble. Except this time he knew exactly what was coming and would do nothing except enjoy the moment.

"What are you grinning at?"

"Nothing." Lev refused to stop grinning.

Penkin stuck his finger in the air again, forgetting that he had already done so.

"I've got a bone to pick with you I have."

"You've said that bit." Lev took another swig.

"I spoke to Kuts today."

"That must have been nice."

At the mention of that name Lev conjured up two old gits sitting side by side at a bar, drunk; trying to keep awake whilst replaying their exploits in the war for each other and anybody else who cared to listen in; else setting the world to rights with their insufferable moral indignation. Ukrainian independence? Lev just wanted to piss himself when he heard those two words joined together. Penkin suddenly roared, like a mangy old lion just before it was about to draw its final breath, or be shot.

"You threw in your job today! You threw in the fucking job I got you. My job!"

Section One: The Wild East

Lev was impressed. The old bastard could still roar when pushed. This time though it had no effect. He wasn't scared. He wouldn't run. He wouldn't bow down to beg forgiveness. In fact he wouldn't do anything except laugh. Yes laughter, that was a powerful weapon. Penkin, red, hot and tired, was roasting - like he had been left out in the sun all day.

"Why are you laughing! Stop laughing. It's not funny!"

"Yes it is."

Lev drank more beer. He was so calm and matter of fact about the commotion that Penkin was completely thrown. Confused, he began to subside. He could only fall back down to earth, be it a contaminated piece of waste ground where even the weeds protested.

"What was wrong with it. What was wrong with the job?"

"What was wrong with the job?" Lev couldn't believe he had to spell it out. "Are you serious?"

Penkin clenched his bottle with both hands, afraid to drop it. "What?"

"I was fucking assistant scum. Doing mindless shit all day – that's what was wrong with it!"

"We all have to start at the bottom."

For Penkin, that sounded deep, so he said it again.

"We all have to start at the bottom, doing something. We have to start with the shit."

"Oh fuck off."

This talk was tiring. Lev wanted to throw away his bottle and fall into bed.

"We've got to get you another job."

"Oh fuck off."

Penkin didn't like being told repeatedly to fuck off – especially not by his own boy. He tried to stand up and protest but failed.

"Here, pull me up. I have to get up."

"No. Fuck off."

"Stop saying that you little shit!"

Out of habit Lev stopped, but he was happy to start up again at the slightest provocation.

"Pull me up. We need to get you a job. Must get you a job."

"Get me a job. Get me a job."

Lev moved forward. He was in two minds. On the one hand he didn't want to do anything for his dad. On the other it would be fun yanking the old man up so hard it would hurt. Perhaps he could give the bastard a heart attack. He yanked as hard as he could and Penkin was up on his feet; swaying, head dizzy, heart pounding. He was still

Section One: The Wild East

alive. Lev was too close for comfort so Penkin pushed him away – or rather tried to. It was a misplaced poke in the chest, and it was painful.

"Ouch! That hurt you sod."

"Well get out of my way then. Don't fucking crowd me."

"I'm not in your way." Lev knew he was, which was why he said it.

"I'm hungry."

"Tough."

"I can get you a job I can."

"Doing what? Cleaning the streets?"

"No better. On the Helmer Estate."

Lev took time out. He was suddenly struck – and stuck - by a tempting offer. Then the temptation transformed itself into a lifetime's punishment, the ultimate family nightmare.

"I'd be working for you?"

"I guess so. I'm sure I can swing it with the man."

Lev shuddered to think how that would feel, day in, day out; never escaping from the presence of the most detested man inside his head. He thought of bright beautiful Prague. It was a wake up call.

"You've got to be fucking kidding me."

Penkin tried to touch his son, to reconnect. His breath stank. There was black between his remaining teeth. His clothes stank. His hair was becoming an infestation. Lev pushed him away, disgusted – disgusted that this man was his dad.

"Don't fucking touch me."

"I'm your father. I can touch I can."

"And I'm your son God help me."

"Wash your mouth out."

"What, with soap?"

Penkin hit his son on the shoulder. He had meant it to only be a tap. Lev hit back, smart, with twice the force but less than intended. Penkin snapped and slapped his son around the face. Lev, stunned, bit the bullet and reacted with all the ferocity and force he could fire up. He delivered a punch directly into his dad's swollen stomach. Penkin staggered back and fell into his chair – his comfy chair. He kicked out and caught Lev on the shin. Lev swore; threw his bottle at his dad; missed, and plunged in; determined to lay another punch. But Penkin got one in first. Lev staggered back, bent over in agony. To even the score Lev stamped on his enemy's foot. Penkin threw his bottle at his son.

"Bastard!"

"Fuck you." Lev left the room clutching his stomach.

"Come back here!"

Section One: The Wild East

No answer.

"You've got to get a job! You've got to earn money!"

"Do I. Do I really." Lev was speaking only to himself.

He began to climb the stairs: he was wasted; he wanted to see his brother; he wanted to be German.

Penkin massaged his foot and tried to ignore the madness which had erupted inside his own house. He hobbled into the kitchen and cut himself a thick slice of brown bread. He sat in his chair and chewed on it slowly; not wishing to consider; unable to reclaim his throne. He quickly fell asleep.

♦

It was an hour before midnight and Hilda Helmer trailed her husband up the stairs to bed. The stairs creaked. He creaked. She creaked. One maid – sometimes referred to as 'the old maid' despite not being old – remained in the kitchen: she was entrusted to shut up shop before turning in herself. Hilda restarted the dialogue her crusty husband had squashed earlier that evening, much to his annoyance but not to his surprise. He wanted to flee into the bathroom. His wife prodded him in the back. She would not be ignored.

"Our boy can look after himself."

"It's not that."

"Well what then?"

Herr Helmer tried to shake her off. "I don't know."

"You must know. Else why deny him?"

"Complications."

"Complications?"

Herr Helmer didn't want to spell it out as he wasn't sure he could.

"Plane tickets have been purchased. They're not cheap - in fact they're bloody expensive! And I have arranged transport to the airport. Everything's ready. There's the hotel."

Herr Helmer reached the top of the stairs and paused. He did not like the sound he was making: he was out of breath. His remedy was simple: he pretended he wasn't. His wife drew up alongside and took his arm to steady him. Together they carried on towards the bedroom. There was still a way to go.

"You can get a refund. They'll give you a refund. You're important - your son's important. Tell them he has to be there early, They won't dare cross you - that would mean crossing the Party."

Herr Helmer had no answer to that and was silenced. As he reached the bedroom and stepped inside Hilda started up again.

Section One: The Wild East

"I'm not happy with this."

"With what?"

"You giving him his own gun."

Now it was the gun again. On the subject of guns Herr Helmer was even more inflexible.

"Look woman he's used a gun before, many times - since he could walk."

"But he's never carried a gun around with him, never kept one in his room." She closed the bedroom door.

Cornered, Herr Helmer turned on his wife.

"Look our son is not stupid! He knows how to handle guns. He knows the rules. I trust him. You should trust him."

Silence from his wife. A good sign. A harsh look. A bad sign.

"He'll be signed up soon. That means pistols, rifles, machine guns."

"Well I'm not happy. And don't ignore me - Franz don't turn away."

"I'm not turning away. I'm sitting down to take my boots off." Herr Helmer sat down. "Look I'll tell him not to keep it in his room but locked up. OK?"

Silence. Then it started again.

"So what other reasons for saying no?"

Back to Berlin.

"For God's sake woman, give it a rest."

In the bedroom Hilda Helmer could be the equal of her husband. The years of marriage had made her stronger whereas they had worn him out. If her husband wanted sex then he had to earn it: as a start he had to stop sounding miserable or high and mighty. She removed her own boots and watched her husband undress. As he wandered the room discarding clothes, she followed, to pick them up. She created a bundle and pushed it into the laundry basket.

"I want a proper reason Franz. Give me a reason or I won't leave you alone."

Herr Helmer retreated into the bathroom, by now naked.

"We don't know who he might meet!" he shouted.

Hilda began to undo her buttons.

"Who he might meet?" Now she was confused. "He'll meet a decent German girl! She was at his youth camp. She's a signed up member of the BDM! She comes from a decent Berlin family. A good German family Franz!"

She heard her man start the shower and had to raise her voice.

"He doesn't want to marry her just stay with her a few days."

She heard her man take a long powerful piss.

Section One: The Wild East

"He'll get to see the sights. She may calm him down, relax him. That must be a good thing surely."

The sound of streaming piss began to diminish as his bladder approached empty.

"Franz?"

"What!"

"Well!"

Herr Helmer suddenly stuck his head round the door, looking not angry but very serious, very concerned. He spoke quietly. "I don't mean her. I mean Max."

"Oh him." Suddenly her husband was making sense.

"Why would he? He doesn't know where he lives - he'll rather be with her. Franz, she's a big girl and he's a big boy. Like us once. Remember!"

But her efforts came too late: her husband had gone under the shower. She gave up for the time being and carried on undressing. Still in her underwear she joined him in the bathroom and readied herself for bed while husband Franz scrubbed himself to death. Tonight her man was not singing in the shower. When he stepped back out on to dry land she had something else to say.

"Will we make a profit this year?"

"I expect so."

"Expect so? Yes or no?"

"Yes."

"Good. The subsidy runs out next year."

Herr Helmer stared into the mirror as he dried himself with a towel. The woman had done it again. She had pummelled him until he had run out of fight. Even being fully naked didn't excite her anymore. She didn't even notice – too busy talking. Hilda left the bathroom. She did not want to have to hear her man scrub his teeth, gurgle and spit.

When Herr Helmer finally rejoined his wife, rejuvenated by hot water, she had changed into her nightdress. And in her nightdress she was softer, more compliant, more pliable; sometimes more inviting. He tried to grasp her around the waist, intending to kiss her, but she was having none of it and pushed him away. He gave up and they divided: he took the left side of the bed; she the right. Years ago they had settled on left and right. Long before that they would rolled over each other and fought for position.

Hilda waded in again, taking her husband's hand as if to reassure him that she would not bite.

"I won't let this rest."

"I suspected as much."

Section One: The Wild East

Herr Helmer smiled: he had made his wife smile again.

"He needs his space. Give your boy some space, some freedom."

"Space? He's got space. Space is everywhere round here - as far as the eye can see. It's all we've got."

"Distance – distance between him and his parents."

Hilda began to shake her husband.

"Franz Helmer, your son is almost eighteen. He needs time away before we start driving him crazy and he starts resenting us."

"He'll be called up this year. What more 'distance' as you call it will he need?"

"That's exactly my point. That's not freedom. That's work, career, duty, rules. He needs to get away before all that comes down on him. He needs a bit of freedom – a proper holiday Franz! A holiday away from us, the estate, commitments."

Hilda pulled herself up close to her man. He could smell her breath - but he was used to it.

"Please Franz, let the boy have his holiday, with that nice girl in Berlin – Berlin the best of all places! The centre of the world! The experience will be good for him, set him up for the rest of his life – character build - that lovely phrase you always use!"

Herr Helmer stared at the ceiling, unable to look directly at his wife. Her argument had finally hit home and she knew it.

"I'll think about it."

"Say yes now."

Hilda grabbed on to her man, her husband. He didn't fight. She pointed at a photograph: a photograph of a small, sweet boy; a small boy less able to answer back (and without cause to). Herr Helmer could not understand why she was pointing.

"He's still got a lot of growing up to do."

"What?"

"Stuck out here, in the middle of nowhere. It's not good enough."

"Meaning?"

"He's missed out on a lot."

"Rubbish."

"No not rubbish! A big trip to the city is what he needs. And Berlin no less! We are talking about Berlin here."

It wasn't her words which were rapidly driving him out of existence now, it was her logic - cast-iron and impossible to counter. His wife could be faultless and infuriating at the same time.

"Is our child important to you?"

"What sort of question is that?"

"Answer the question."

Section One: The Wild East

Herr Helmer snarled.

"Yes."

"Well switch your brain on and show it."

"I said I'll think about it."

Hilda relaxed. She was there. She would start up again in the morning if she had to, right after they had raised the bloody flag. Heil Hitler.

Herr Helmer rolled over on to his side. "Switch off the light."

Frau Helmer moved to switch the light off.

Click.

In the darkness Herr Helmer suddenly had outstanding business which he had to put to sleep.

"We didn't raise the flag this morning."

"It's just one day."

"Why did you let me oversleep?"

"You needed it."

They changed sides.

"Did you book the car in?"

"Damn. Sorry."

"Do it tomorrow."

"I will. Goodnight," said Franz, once grumpy, now drowsy.

"Goodnight," replied Hilda, once impassive, again impassive.

◆

Franz withdrew and cut himself off. He wouldn't be touched or tinkered with. At home there was only one source of pain and that he managed to dodge most of the time. At school there were many and they were in danger of wounding him. He kept his head down, battled with his imagination, and snarled if baited. He wouldn't talk to anybody and gave only the minimum response necessary when Teacher questioned him. He avoided the Fuehrer's eye.

Paula tried to get close, over the fence and inside his head, which made him angry as she had not been invited. And the fact that he dare not direct his anger at her only twisted him up further. She was making him angry when she was trying to be friendly.

Headmaster was the biggest headache. That man - now detestable - could not leave him alone. He kept popping up out of the blue to check up on his favourite pupil; to enquire as to what Franz had planned to say on the big day; to reaffirm what he assumed Franz was feeling, that he was looking forward to the greatest day of his life. The man kept reminding him how important it was that he got it right: Franz was

Section One: The Wild East

representing the school. Worse still Headmaster had to keep stating the bleeding obvious: that the Fuehrer was the most important man in the territories of the Reich, in Europe, perhaps in the whole world; that a display of respect had to be total, faultless and worthy of the great man's attention. Franz could do nothing except hold on, not scream, not lash out; and say, with utmost politeness, whatever Headmaster wanted to hear. It was agony.

When he did lash out, poor Bruno was the unfortunate trigger and target. He accused Franz of discarding his friends and looking down his nose at them; and suggesting (though Franz never did) that he was better than the rest of them just because he was going to be an officer in the SS one day. Franz smacked him in the corridor, hard, which was a stupid thing to do as it was a very public place. Bruno stumbled, recovered, and hit back. Headmaster came flying through the air - as usual from nowhere - and pulled them apart – the limpet from the rock. He made it known that he was very disappointed, especially with Franz Helmer, his golden boy.

Headmaster lectured them both, until it hurt, and made each give the other a full apology and a firm handshake. It did not have to be warm, just firm. Both boys lied through their teeth and shook hands, as hard as they could to make the other hand hurt. Then Headmaster took Franz back into his office and made him stand. It was one of his long torturous lectures: partially corrective, partially sympathetic; definitely patronizing; extremely tiresome and tiring. And Headmaster reminded him to get a haircut. He even pushed a banknote into his hand to cover the cost. Franz felt insulted. The Helmers could pay for anything. But he took it anyway.

At school that week Franz discovered some new things: that boys could act like girls; that Headmaster could act stupid, like a boy; that Headmaster was a buffoon, an untermensch; that girls – Paula in particular – were more trouble than they were worth. At one point Paula grabbed his shirt, stared deep into his eyes – despite his massive displeasure - and refused to let go. He had to shake her off. He found it very confusing: the more he pushed her away, the more she wanted to give him her undivided attention; the more he turned to stone, the more she appreciated his finer qualities.

Franz became hungry for a return to sanity, obscurity: even long periods of classic boredom would be welcomed. Franz never thought that life could be this insufferable, this draining. It left him wasted, sores pasted across his face. After school he escaped on his motorbike - throttle wide open - ensuring no opportunity for his mind to wander where he didn't want it to go: in and out of complications which would

Section One: The Wild East

never resolve themselves. All his attention had to be focused on driving to the limit whilst staying alive. As was often the case he ended up at the disused landing strip where he drove around in one huge circle, body leaning at 45 degrees into the turn: no beginning, no end.

That felt good.

Midweek, he went on a motorbike rampage in the rain: he drove towards a distant thunderstorm, wishing to connect with its rage and energy, its cause and fatal attraction. It was the most fleeting whim and he soon gave up, knowing it was out of reach. Drenched and frozen to within an inch of what felt like death, Franz headed home, still feeling miserable.

Soaking he stumbled into the kitchen, demanding attention. He got it. And while seated, waiting for dry clothes and a hot drink, he received an instruction to join his mother in the main guest room. It was delivered by Aneta. He didn't look up. She didn't look down. He held his breath as she delivered the message in a whisper.

Upon entering the room Franz was in for a shock: there was Paula, being entertained by Mother like she was important or something. There was freshly squeezed orange juice and ham sandwiches. On seeing his wet clothes Paula simply smiled, as did Mother. Frau Helmer saw Paula as a perfect specimen. The girl had grown up and out since they had last met.

Franz felt trapped – the only man amongst women he declared to some higher authority inside his head. He was told that her brother had dropped her off and would be returning in one hour to take her home. Mother told him to join them when he had changed into 'something better'. He noted her exact words: she had used them from since he could remember and they always managed to sting. Not much later, in dry clothes and holding a hot mug of milk, Franz rejoined them, whereupon he was made to sit alongside Paula.

He sat with his hands stuck between his knees, wishing above all else for Mother to leave the room – just go away. Paula also sat with her hands between her knees, thinking much the same. Franz devoured the last of the sandwiches while Paula watched him. Mother continued to dote on her guest and Franz could not get a word in edgeways: a state of denial he valued. Not having to say anything suited him down to the ground. Finally though the poor girl was handed over into his keep and Frau Helmer left the room. Still connected to his motorbike, Franz asked the obvious question.

"Would you like to see my motorbike?"

"New?"

"Not that new."

Section One: The Wild East

"OK."

But Paula wanted to take the long route, through the gardens, to see the spring blossom. Franz kept alongside, constantly adjusting his speed. And then the stakes were raised: Paula took his arm. He tried to look composed, able to think. Paula tried to make him smile. She failed. Franz tried to loosen himself free. He failed. Frau Helmer tried to keep them in sight from a window. She failed. Then it got worse: Paula asked an awkward question, one which turned him back into a small child.

"Why are you being so miserable?"

Franz kept his silence.

"Why have you been so nasty."

Franz kept his silence. It was his only defence – or weapon - against this girl.

"Answer me Franz."

Paula tugged at his sleeve, and continued to tug until she received a minimum answer.

"Don't know."

"You must know."

"Dunno."

"You're going to meet him – you can't stay like this."

"Like what."

"All miserable. All nasty."

Franz saw a large pebble the shape of a new potato and kicked it way out of sight. It struck a large metal pot and produced a weird sound, almost musical. Meanwhile a penny dropped.

"Are you scared Franz?"

"No."

He sounded adamant. She assumed it was the truth. She tugged at her poor boy again.

"Kiss me."

"No."

"Why not!"

"Because I'm not in the mood."

She let go and walked on, in a huff. Franz panicked and felt required to act.

"Wait I'll show you my gun!"

Paula stopped in her tracks.

"What?"

"Wait here. Wait here."

Franz ran off, like that small boy, leaving Paula to stare at the barren scenery. Spring still had much work to do. She had had enough. She

Section One: The Wild East

wanted to go home. She looked at her wristwatch. Still another twenty minutes. Too long. She stamped her feet.

Franz reappeared slightly out of breath and brandishing a pistol in its shiny leather holster. He looked very pleased with himself, very proud, and suddenly Franz Helmer was what she had come looking for.

"Look. Watch."

He undid the holster clip and drew out his pistol. He pointed up towards the sky.

"It's a Luger, a Luger P08 semi-automatic. The best ever. It fires 8 rounds from its magazine – more with the drum attachment."

Paula was impressed, but not by the gun: Franz looked like a real soldier; a man who would protect her. She wanted him to salute her in his military uniform. She wanted him to grab her and kiss her - without warning.

"Can I hold it?"

Franz twitched. "Only if you're careful."

"Is it loaded?"

"Yes - safety catch is on."

Paula had never held a pistol before. It felt heavy, cold, exotic. It was typically a man's object, his object of desire. She began to wave it around, just like her father waved his gun around when he was boisterous or drunk.

"Don't do that!"

"Why not? It can't go off."

"No. But still, don't."

She threw him sideways. "I won't if you kiss me."

"No."

"Well let me shoot something then."

"Like what?"

"I don't know. Anything."

"A Bolshevik?"

Playfully she slapped him down. "Don't be silly."

Franz returned his Luger to its holster.

"I know. Come with me."

Franz led the way. Paula followed. Suddenly he was back in charge. He led her through a gate and out into the grounds beyond the formal gardens. Ahead of them was a small forgotten field. It supported a tough layer of grass and was used to exercise horses. Goats kept the grass short. A mangled looking tree occupied the centre of the field. Franz stopped when they were close enough to take pot-shots at it. He produced his pistol again, this time with the safety catch off. Now he felt ten years older.

Section One: The Wild East

"Careful now. It will fire."

"What do I do?" Paula wanted guidance, but with her dignity intact.

"Hold it like this."

He demonstrated then handed it over, like a newborn baby, and watched the girl. He was not pleased.

"No like this."

He took it back and repeated himself. This time the girl bothered to pay attention.

"That's better."

Paula smiled. Franz made a point of not smiling back. This was serious stuff.

"Aim down the barrel, along the line of the barrel, at the tree trunk."

"Like this."

"Sort of. But don't rock it. Keep it steady."

Paula did as instructed. "I've got it."

"You've got it."

"That's what I just said."

"Now squeeze the trigger slowly. Slowly. Slowly squeeze. Go on. Squeeze, but hard."

Finally she squeezed, hard. The pistol fired and the recoil shot up her arm. She nearly peed in her pants. She missed the tree completely.

Franz tried to sound sympathetic. "Never mind."

"Why didn't you warn me it would do that!"

"It's a gun? All guns do that." And anyway you didn't ask, another part of him quipped.

Paula elbowed him as she handed back the pistol. "I'm cold. I'm going inside."

"Go on then."

Back inside the two of them killed time through random motions and random talk as they waited for her brother to turn up. Franz guessed the girl was angry with him but wanted to make up and didn't know how. He lapsed back into his earlier state – a condition, ironically, he now felt comfortable in. Paula forgave him. She could only stay annoyed for so long. Tentatively she closed down the distance between them.

"Kiss me now."

Franz wavered. She had him. She knew she had him. She could feel it in her bones. He surrendered and stormed in, grabbing her around the waist, just like last time. They proceeded to snog, just like last time. This time he was allowed to rub his hands across her backside. Then the noise of her big brother's car destroyed the moment. Thinking as one they detached themselves and waited for his

Section One: The Wild East

appearance. They heard Frau Helmer welcome him into the house. They heard a servant offer to take his hat and coat. They heard him decline the offer. Horst had come to pick up his sister, not socialize.

Franz jumped up to look out of the window. Horst was still driving a Kdf-Wagen. Paula jumped up to adjust her clothing. Franz ducked as his mother strode down the hallway calling out his name.

"Franz where are you!"

"In here!"

Frau Helmer entered the room in a fuss. "Oh there you are. Paula your brother is here."

Horst entered the room behind her, holding his hat and wearing a short leather jacket.

"Paula."

"Hallo Horst." Her reply carried a trace of weight.

"Time to go."

"I know." And with that she left. As simple as that.

From the window Franz watched Paula get into the car. He was delighted to see Horst had painted a big black swastika on the bonnet. It looked rather neat. He made a promise: when he got his first car he would do the same. He raced outside. Paula wound down the window expecting him to say goodbye. He ignored her and spoke to her brother instead.

"Did you do that?"

"I had it done, yes."

"It's good."

"Thank you."

"Bye," said Paula, butting in.

"Bye," replied Franz.

"Bye," said Horst, completing the ritual; whereupon he drove off, satisfied that older brother and younger sister were locked together. He saw it as his job to protect his little sister.

Franz was left to wonder if Bridget could kiss like Paula. Then a cold sticky, electrifying shudder rippled down his back as he suddenly remembered the other girl he had recently kissed. He ran back inside, up the stairs, and into his bedroom. He jumped onto his bed and buried his head in the pillow: there he tried to plant other thoughts inside his head. It made no difference. He could not snuff it out.

◆

Penkin looked up. There was someone at the door. He opened it and did not like what he saw. It was a German. It was Helmer's boy

Section One: The Wild East

standing there like some bearer of bad news. This was too close to home. Franz, sensing conflict, took two steps back and blurted out his request.

"Is Lev there. I want to speak to him." He tried to sound casual but failed.

Penkin stepped forward and looked up and down the street, taking measurements. Some local kids were milling around, killing time by generating idle curiosity or idle speculation; else simply waiting for something gripping to happen. None of them were looking in his direction – or perhaps they already had and the fact was already noted.

Penkin barked at the German boy. "How long have you been standing there?"

"No time." Franz grabbed a number out of thin air. "Thirty seconds?"

That seemed to do the trick: Penkin eased off.

"Can I see him?"

Penkin was in two minds: enquire further or mind his own business. He decided to mind his own business.

"Lev! Helmer's boy wants to see you!"

There was a delay, during which Penkin guarded the Helmer boy closely, on the lookout for trouble, and Franz looked away, wishing to be anywhere else. They were miles apart, separated by race, country, class, culture and age. Their only link was Lev, and when he finally appeared he had a bruised eye and looked mean: like his dad he looked uncomfortable in the presence of Franz - now reduced to nothing more than just another German on the doorstep.

"What are you doing here?"

"Wanted to see you." Franz tried to sound upbeat and thought it best not to ask about the bruise.

"I'll get my coat."

Franz turned away and kicked dirt while he waited. Penkin followed his son back inside. Franz heard raised voices but could not make out the words. It didn't alarm him: he didn't like Penkin; Penkin didn't like him; Lev didn't like his dad; his dad probably knew that.

Lev reappeared in his sheepskin coat, all buttoned up, and Franz gestured towards his motorbike.

"Go somewhere?"

Lev looked around, suspicious. He meant nothing by it. It was a habit he had picked up from his dad. It was a habit he was comfortable with.

"Go where?"

"Does it matter?"

Section One: The Wild East

"No but I still want to know."
"Down to the river?"
"Fair enough."
Franz mounted his bike and Lev got on behind him. They drove off at a good speed and all the kids in the street turned their heads to catch the show. Lev stuck up two fingers. The gesture was reciprocated, many times over. When they reached the riverbank Lev jumped off before the bike came to a halt and scurried down to the water's edge; there to toss sticks, driftwood and small rocks into the river. Franz caught him up and did the same, but with less motivation or animosity. For a long time they didn't exchange words but just explored. When they did come back together it was by accident.

Franz sat down on a tree trunk then jumped up again, cursing: he had sat on some wet moss and was now sporting a wet patch. There was a silver lining: Lev loosened up and began to laugh. He upgraded the laugh to a whoop and descended upon Franz, intention being to pat him on his wet behind. But Franz was too quick and took up a defensive position. Lev closed in. Horseplay followed and after a few minutes they called it quits. They found dry grass on the riverbank and sat down, out of breath but all the more sane.

Franz forgot what he had wanted to say. He sank into gloom and Lev joined him. They sat, cheerless, with nothing to say and nothing to watch except flowing water. Any observer might have reasoned that they were locked in exactly the same thoughts, same mood, same heartache; each suffering the same injustice, the same sense of regret. They were inches close but a thousand miles apart.

Lev began to pick at a scab. Franz pulled in his legs and watched the ceremony unfold, arms embracing his knees. Then, despite being pretty sure what the answer was, he asked about the bruise.

"That bruise. What happened?"
Lev carried on picking. "Nothing."
Fair enough, thought Franz, that's not why I'm here. "Things have changed."
Lev stopped picking and started rubbing. "What d'you mean?"
"My trip to Berlin?"
Lev looked up, squinting. "You not going?"
Franz tightened his embrace. "No not that. I'm going but early, five days early."
"Can I come?"
"Of course not. You're not German."
Lev was pulling his leg. It was the follow-up which mattered.
"I'm going as far as Prague. We could go together to Prague?"

Section One: The Wild East

Franz didn't think twice about it.

"Don't see why not. But why you going there? You don't know Prague?"

"Luka's there."

Franz did a double take: Luka, the older brother, the curse of Penkin.

"What are you going to do there?"

"Do? Live of course. I'm going there for good."

"Have you told him?"

"He knows."

Franz left it there - and suddenly remembered he had a favour to ask.

"I need your help. I tried to write a letter. I need to write a letter but don't know what to say."

"You're the one who can write. Not me."

"But you always know what to say."

"What kind of letter?"

"To Bridget. A thank you, to take up an offer, and nice bits, to say I like her. She's the reason I'm off early."

Lev nudged Franz in the ribs.

"I'm serious. I've got to check it out with her. And I want to do it really nice"

"Why not phone?"

"I'd rather write a letter, say nice stuff about her. You know the sort of thing. You've written them before, just do me another. I'll pay you again."

"Like I want to fuck her?"

"Yes. Like I want to fuck her - but don't say that. Keep it sweet, dignified."

Lev leaned back and pushed his eyes up as far as they would go. In his book, from the earliest age, Germans were total hypocrites.

"Bridget darling you're beautiful. I want to shag you."

"Forget it. I'll phone."

The silence returned - this one born out of a need to recharge. Lev remembered the cigarettes in his coat pocket. He held out the packet with the offer of pleasure. Franz declined. Lev lit one up. Franz got up and ambled down to the water's edge: taking a route which snaked, which doubled back on itself, and which only seemed to get him there by chance. He had women inside his head and they were beating him up. One of them was there for all the wrong reasons. She had no right to be in there and was hitting the hardest. She made him feel cheap with Paula, unworthy. She avoided him – just as he avoided her. She didn't show him respect. He wanted to get angry with her. He wanted

Section One: The Wild East

to hit her. But that would mean confronting her. As a small consolation he kicked a large decomposing log, and for his sins hurt his big toe. He swore profusely.

"Calm down Franz. It's only a letter. Have a smoke."

Franz felt a large weight drop from his head.

"It's not Bridget. It's Aneta." There, he had said the word.

"Aneta? She causing you trouble?"

"Yes. No."

"Sit down. Have a smoke."

Franz sat down and this time took a cigarette. Lev lit it.

"You fancy her?"

"Yes."

"You want to sleep with her?"

"No!"

"You fancy her but you don't want to sleep with her?"

"No."

Now Lev was confused. "You fancy her but you do want to sleep with her?"

Franz took ages to answer. "Yes."

"That's more like it. I'd like to sleep with her too."

Franz clung to himself, arms locked. "But she's your cousin?"

"So?" Lev chuckled. "Just because she's my cousin doesn't mean I can't take her to bed, marry her."

Lev began to fantasize. "Even if they didn't let me marry her I'd like to be the first."

Franz had to stop him there, logic demanded it. "You can't be the first."

"What?" The humour evaporated, to be replaced by suspicion.

"You can't be the first."

"Why d'you say that?"

Franz looked away but failed to mask his rising anxiety.

"I said why do you say that?" Lev demanded an answer. His tone was threatening.

"Don't know."

"Have you slept with Aneta?"

Franz capitulated. He had to get at least one thing off his chest. And Lev was after all his mate through good times - and bad?

"Sorry."

"Who started it?"

"Her, I think."

"Was she drunk?"

"No."

Section One: The Wild East

"Were you drunk?"

"No. Don't know. Can't remember."

Lev looked out across the river to the far bank. He got up slowly, with a heavy heart and a strong sense of purpose.

"Come on." He beckoned Franz to follow.

"We going now?"

"Not yet."

"Not yet? So why we getting up?"

"Because of this."

Without warning Lev turned on Franz and punched him in the stomach. Franz fell off the bank into the sand below. He got up, bemused, and began to brush away the sand. The punch had not been all that severe.

"Why d'you do that?"

"Because I had to." And with that Lev jumped down to join him, and to punch him again, harder this time.

Franz staggered back clutching his stomach, barely able to remain standing.

"Stop it!"

"No!"

Lev tried to punch him again but this time Franz was ready. They exchanged blows. They exchanged foul language – some German, some Ukrainian. They traded all their frustrations and released their stress. Each grabbed the other, intention being to push him into the water. They were both successful. The freezing water was sufficient to douse their fire and stop the nonsense. They stumbled back on to dry land where, soaking wet from the waist down, they began to shiver violently. Franz, squatting and recovering his breath, looked across to Lev.

"Bastard."

"You should not have slept with my cousin." Lev carefully pronounced each word in between his chattering teeth.

"You didn't have to hit me."

"Yes I did. Family honour demands it."

"Family honour."

Franz wanted to laugh but his teeth were also chattering away. He had never heard of family honour amongst Ukrainians and certainly not in this family.

"But I forgive you now. We are friends again now."

Franz could not reply. He could not shut his teeth up. He felt his face. Something felt wrong, out of place. Something had swollen but nothing hurt.

Section One: The Wild East

"Is my eye bruised?"
"Yes."
"Brilliant. I want to go home."
"Can you drop me off?"
"Only if you promise not to hit me again."
"I promise."
They got back aboard the bike and Franz kick-started the engine, whereupon Lev tapped him on the back.
"What?"
"Did she entice you?"
"Yes."
"You sure?"
"Yes."
"Very well. I'll have words with her."
"No don't do that. It's gone. History."
"No. She cannot behave like that."
"Please, forget it. Let's go home."
"Very well."
During the ride back the wind dried them and froze them in equal measure. Back at Lev's house, with the old man out, Franz was invited indoors to warm himself by the fire. Franz had never seen inside before and was shocked by the squalid conditions in which his friend lived. It was one big ugly dump and it smelt bad. Franz got out fast and headed home at a speed reckless even by his standards. He felt light-headed, relieved of a burden.

When he arrived home he ran upstairs, did a quick change, and snatched up a special scrap of paper before running back down to the nearest telephone. There he was stopped in his tracks: the line was dead. Staff confirmed that the landline was down again. He didn't hang about. Pausing only to grab a hot bread roll, he rushed back out, kicked off the dogs, and drove back into town. He had to make that phone call. But by the time he reached the Postamt it had shut for the day, and it was dark and it had started to rain.

The Postamt was a miserable, run-down place. It was a place for miserable, run-down locals to loiter without intent. It was born out of a hurried, botched conversion: the building had been abandoned and left derelict during the war. There were three telephone booths lined up outside the Postamt. One of them was occupied. Leaning his motorbike against a wall Franz entered a vacant booth, only to find the phone not working. It had been vandalized. Same with the next one, except worse: there was vomit on the floor, and he stepped in it. Franz's earlier euphoria had faded away. His cause had transformed

Section One: The Wild East

into a chore.

He leapt out, now in a foul mood, and was forced to wait while some local youth hogged the only working phone. He was leaning against the side of the booth and smoking while talking - the booth was filling up with smoke. It didn't bother him but it did bother Franz. Franz closed in, to make it plain that he was in a hurry. His need was greater, and he had the authority. That was what he had been taught.

The youth paused and lowered his cigarette. Through the glass and the raindrops which ran down it he studied the German with open relish: I feel nothing for you except total contempt, total disregard, a solid hatred, and perhaps a little – just a little – pity. The youth continued to talk but the movement of his lips slowed, to the point when they ceased to move at all. Yet he continued to hold the handset to his mouth – a fact not missed by Franz. They stared each other down, separated by just five millimetres of glass. They were in a competition. The prize? That was probably superiority. The fuel was pure frustration on one side, pure contempt on the other – each supplemented with a sprinkling of racism, envy and social divide. The youth drew a swastika - badly - in the dirt on the glass. Franz could not rub it out.

Franz snapped: face screwed up and he kicked the phone booth. The opposition, seeing victory, beamed with delight. He was loving it while Franz was hating it. Franz yanked open the door and the youth dropped the handset. They were now in each other's face, with smoke in their eyes. Nothing was said. Nothing needed to be said: a declaration of disgust and the demand for satisfaction had already passed between them. It had been said a thousand times before: in every dismissive glance; in every snap reply; in every reprimand that had ever passed between Germans and Ukrainians. These two had never met before; never craved for what the other had; yet the animosity ran so deep it aggravated their senses to the point of torment.

Franz wasn't afraid. He just saw it beneath himself to get involved, to get dirty. (Lev was his golden exception to his golden rule – one born out of years spent growing up on the same ground while their parents worked the estate and cleaned up after the war.) So now he was stuck holding the door, getting soaked and looking stupid.

The youth was not moved to speak as he was enjoying the enemy's discomfort, and wished to prolong it. It was like prodding a blind man: the slightest touch inflicted mental torment – and all for minimum effort. Finally though all good things had to come to an end and he spoke to the German who looked like he was in danger of meltdown. It was the bruised eye which begged a question.

Section One: The Wild East

"Who smacked you then German?"

"None of your business. Get out. I need to use the phone."

The youth made a point of looking caught between a rock and a hard place. He pretended to be insulted by the harsh words as he pretended to still be making a call. Franz yanked the door back as far as it would go. Without realising it he held a fist.

"I said get out."

The youth stared back baffled: this was one angry young German. He could not believe someone – even a German – was losing it over such a trivial incident, a non-event. So much anger from a German, so little respect.

Franz grabbed the handset and pulled – with such force that he nearly broke it free. He had possession. Now he just had to occupy the booth.

"Steady there German."

"I'll say it again. Get out."

The youth looked at the handset. This had gone beyond silly: it had become an insult to his own standards of behaviour and his own clear conscience; a pathetic reminder of everything in life he wished to avoid. So he gave way – not graciously but without a fight. He raised his hands in mock surrender.

"You're the boss."

He stepped out of the booth and into the rain. Franz jumped inside. The door, spring-loaded, slammed shut behind him. Taking time out to catch his breath he watched with growing unease as the enemy walked over to his bike. But nothing happened: the youth bent over to check out its credentials; was impressed; and walked away. Franz watched and questioned his every move.

Not wishing to hang around in the smoke and cold Franz was intent on getting the job over and done with quick. Suddenly the thought of speaking to Bridget direct felt less daunting than writing her an intimate letter. He rubbed his sleeve across his nose, brow and chin before drawing forth his prized scrap of paper. On it was her telephone number. He dialled quickly, too quickly, and had to start again. On the third try he got it right. His earlier insecurity returned when a man answered. It was the father.

"Hello." Silence. "Hello?"

"Sorry. Herr Schrimer? Hello. This is Franz. Franz Helmer? Is Bridget there?"

There was an uncomfortable pause. "Hang on."

Left hanging, Franz began to wilt. When Bridget finally came on the line he was almost physically sick. He began to stumble over his

Section One: The Wild East

words. In contrast she sounded confident, at ease – no bad thing as in the course of the conversation this would rub off on him. Meanwhile he had a headache.

"Bridget. It's me, Franz." He spoke in a rush, like his father.

"I know."

Her voice still sounded sweet. She sounded warm, inviting. She was civilization but she made him feel like he wasn't. Franz tried to moderate his voice.

"I can see you – stay over – in Berlin – if that's still OK."

"Of course it is. That's excellent news."

Suddenly her voice dropped and sounded incoherent. Then it was gone.

"Bridget? Bridget?"

Then it returned and all was right in the world again.

"Sorry. I was just speaking to Papa – hang on. Papa?"

Her voice disappeared again, for longer this time, during which Franz came back down to earth.

"Sorry. Papa says he is looking forward to meeting you. Just need to know dates and times. How will you arrive? Train? Plane?"

"I need to check that out. I'll call you again when I know."

Franz suddenly lit up and bellowed down the phone. "And guess what, I'm meeting the Fuehrer!"

"The Fuehrer?" Silence followed. "Bridget are you there?"

"The Fuehrer?" She almost choked on her words.

"Yes the Fuehrer, honest, no kidding. On his birthday - on my birthday."

"Tell me all about it."

"There's not much to tell."

"When we meet."

"OK." Franz stalled then started up again. "Bridget, I –"

But a stone hit the glass behind his head, cracking but not shattering it. It killed the conversation dead. Franz dropped the handset and scrambled about to grab it back. In the dark and rain there was no obvious culprit, no obvious point of danger.

"Bridget, you still there?"

"Yes. What was that noise?"

"Nothing. I'll confirm the dates - "

Another stone hit the booth and Franz never got to finish his sentence. He had to start another.

"Have to go. Sorry. I'll call."

He slammed the phone down and stepped out into the rain to face the enemy. This time he was up against a gang of three locals: the

Section One: The Wild East

original lad plus two. Franz swallowed a lump and sucked in some cold clean air, intent on looking unshakable. His upbringing told him that he had nothing to fear, no reason to give ground: he was the superior race and this lowlife would not dare lay a finger on him. That was the theory - neatly expressed many times by his father and schoolteachers. But somehow he wasn't convinced and the only thing that made him stand his ground was pride and his precious BMW. The gang began to close in and hurl abuse, in Ukrainian. He was glad he didn't understand a word. One produced a knife. Another threw a large stone at him. It hit him in the chest and its impact was a wakeup call. This was three against one: get out!

Franz started to run – anywhere - in any direction which suggested the presence of people, preferably Germans. He ran towards the school and garrison. His luck was in: as he rounded a corner he nearly crashed into a German soldier out on patrol. The soldier hailed him down with strong language just before they collided. Franz tried to reinstate some sense of decorum. In front of another German he had to look like a proper German. The soldier grabbed Franz by the collar and pulled him in for a closer look. He immediately apologized when he realised his catch was German.

"Sorry son. You startled me." Then he remembered to let go.

Franz signalled that no harm had been done. Words would came later: he was still recovering his composure.

"Are you in trouble? Why are you out in the rain like this?"

Franz stuck a thumb out over his shoulder. "Three thugs, behind me, Ukrainians, down the street."

"Down where?"

"At the Postamt, by the square."

The soldier patted him lightly on the shoulder and walked on past, adjusting the leather strap of his submachine gun as he did so. All evening it had been rubbing his shoulder blade sore.

"Come on."

Franz did not need to be told: he wanted justice; he wanted to inflict humiliation. The soldier reached the square and looked around. Nothing. The telephone booths were empty.

"Well there's no one here now." The soldier saw a motorbike. It was German.

"Is that yours?"

Franz glared at his beautiful machine. It was lying on its side, like a dead dog, like it had been murdered.

"Yes."

Franz replied through clenched teeth. He picked it up and examined

Section One: The Wild East

it.

"The bastards kicked it over."

"Any damage done?"

"I don't think so. Just scratched in places - and a small dent."

"Can you get home?"

"Hang on."

Franz mounted his bike and started the engine. It roared when he opened the throttle. The soldier was impressed. It was a big brutal engine.

"Sounds good."

Franz didn't hear him.

"Do you want to file a report!" The soldier had to shout.

"No!"

"Would you recognise any of them again!"

"No! Perhaps one."

"OK lets leave it then!" The soldier was glad: no paperwork to fill in.

As Franz drove away the soldier looked around then pulled out his cigarette case. It contained Russian cigarettes, his main drug. He lit one and walked on, careful to protect it from the rain. He was back to being bored again. The only thing he had to look forward to was his next appointment with his favourite prostitute.

Franz flew home in a rage: angry that he had been threatened; angry that he had been victimised; angry that he had been made a fool of; angry that his word counted for nothing. When he arrived home he was ambushed by his mother and had to explain himself. Where had he been? Why so late? Had he been fighting? The incident with Lev was jettisoned while the one at the Postamt was amplified and extended to include assault and battery.

Frau Helmer wanted the assailants caught and punished: Herr Helmer too, on hearing the news. He wanted punishment to be a public event. Frau Helmer had to calm him down. He would file a report.

◆

The magistrates court was the centre of power in town, and its celebration; and as such was positioned at the head of the main square. There it was a constant reminder of who ran the place; of who held the reins of power; of who served and who was served, and who had the first and final word. The few Germans who came and went through the building came to administer the law or to enjoy the fruits of its outcome. The rest – predominantly Ukrainians – came to receive it and

Section One: The Wild East

often left empty-handed, else with a Pyrrhic victory.

Penkin spent an extended lunchtime sitting at a cafe on the edge of the square, there to watch its entrance and the human traffic. He was waiting for that particular moment; first sipping coffee; later sipping beer. He was on the look out for someone in particular yet just as interested in all who came and went. Today he needed to speak to Herr Helmer, urgently. So he waited and he spent his money in a trickle until he spotted the man leaving the building at 3 pm, having discharged his duties for the day.

Herr Helmer looked exhausted, mentally drained, and starving – just like a Ukrainian thought Penkin with a touch of malice. He marched off, military style, up a road and towards the best restaurant in town: a restaurant which, over the course of time, had come to serve Germans only. Only their better money and charm was good enough for its better food, welcome and reputation. Ukrainians were not barred. They were simply not welcome. In return Ukrainians had no love for the place, no desire to give it their custom: the place was full of Germans.

Before the war it was the place where anybody who aspired to be somebody had to be, to be seen. During the war its owner changed sides, and suddenly schweinsbraten and sauerkraut appeared on the menu, along with kartoffelsalat and German Riesling. Very quickly, in under a year, the make-up of the clientele changed from organic to inorganic; from local to foreign; from poor to rich; from patient to particular; from casual to choosy.

Penkin flicked away his cigarette and looked down at his boots. They were still clean. This simple fact increased his measure of self-worth, and they got him out of his chair and up on to his feet. He began to follow his boss, at all times keeping a discreet distance. When his boss enter the restaurant to take his usual seat Penkin stalled and hung around in the street, at a loose end; neither here, neither there; not part of the crowd outside, never part of the crowd inside.

Finally, just as Herr Helmer was tucking into a large cut of roasted beef, Penkin summoned up the courage to interrupt his employer's late lunch. He slipped in and approached the table - but not unnoticed: German eyes stared him down and tried to shrink him into oblivion. They are taking notes, he thought. They always take notes, he thought. They had marked him down as a no good peasant on the make and were waiting for the first sign of trouble. Herr Helmer had his head down and was so busy filling his stomach that he failed to notice Penkin standing a few feet in front of him, grim-faced, cap in hand, acting humble – and it was acting: it was his best performance to date. Penkin

Section One: The Wild East

watched him stuff his face and passed judgement, completely forgetting that he too had a habit of stuffing his face until his stomach was way past full. As for all the beer: Penkin didn't have a problem with that.

Penkin saw two Germans in front of him. One was the fat, overweight invader gorging on the spoils of war like a pig with his nose in the trough. The other was his employer who paid his wages and who sometimes treated him as almost - but never quite - his equal; and with whom he had once shared some quite incredible moments during the course of all-out conflict. Either way he wanted to spit on the food to catch the German's attention. Instead he coughed. Herr Helmer looked up abruptly. Penkin spoke first. He was determined to.

"Herr Helmer? May I trouble you?"

Herr Helmer was surprised to see Penkin in front of him but carried on chewing. Only after he had swallowed and followed through with another swig from his beer stein did he bother to reply. Always make the man wait, especially if he's not German.

"What are you doing here? Shouldn't you be at work?"

Penkin had already prepared his answer to that question.

"I had to come into town for supplies, and noticed you through the window." Penkin pointed for effect.

A harsh voice barked out from behind Penkin. "Helmer, give the man your loose change and tell him to fuck off!"

"He works for me. It's business."

"May I speak to you in private Herr Helmer?"

"This is private."

Penkin disagreed violently but said nothing. One hand released its grip on his cap. The other gripped it even tighter.

"And not until I've finished eating."

Penkin, stuck for something to say, continued to stand stupid. The truth of the situation did not bode well. Inside he began to devour himself with the indignity of his situation. He was surrounded on all sides by fat stupid lazy Germans – every insult he could summon up – and he had to work for one of them. Once, a long time ago, he had naively regarded himself as their equal – a fact he now kept suppressed lest it torment him to breaking point. Once Herr Helmer had not been overweight and overbearing and so stupid. Once he had commanded men in war. Once he had demonstrated courage, leadership, intelligence, virtue even; and above all a certain nobility in the way he exercised his duties as an officer in the great Waffen-SS. Ukrainians like Penkin had been impressed. But that was many years ago and time changed people. Herr Helmer interrupted his wandering thoughts with a stinging rebuke.

Section One: The Wild East

"Don't just stand there like a zombie, go wait outside."

"Wait outside, very good Herr Helmer."

Penkin turned and walked out, careful to avoid eye contact with other diners; afraid that were he to do so his mask of submissive deference might slip - then he would tell at least one of them to fuck off. There was nothing more likely to incite a rabble of restless Germans than an aggressive peasant upstart. Back outside he sucked in the fresh air and lit another cigarette. Inside Herr Helmer continued with his awesome task of clearing his plate and emptying his stein. It was as if Penkin had never interrupted him. Penkin had to remind himself that he was just in it for the money. It was all about money. When Herr Helmer finally did wipe his mouth, settle up and step outside – having kept Penkin waiting for nearly twenty minutes – Penkin restored his mask and removed his cap, as every German would expect him to. He was after all just another peasant. Boldly he stepped up to the mark.

"Herr Helmer may I have that word with you now?"

Herr Helmer looked right past Penkin. He was looking up and down the street, trying to decide the shortest route back to his car. When he spoke it was with a tired voice.

"If you must. But be quick about it. Then back to work. I don't pay you good money to hang about on street corners."

"No Herr Helmer."

No you don't, thought Penkin. But I do, so screw you.

"I just need to ask a favour."

"A favour?"

Herr Helmer did not like to hear that word coming from one of his employees. Handing out favours to other Germans was problematic enough: he was a magistrate and had to be seen to be above board, whiter than white at all times amongst the German community.

Penkin hastily corrected himself. "Pardon me. Wrong word. I meant to say I wish to make a request."

"A request? What kind of request?"

"I need an extra pair of hands on the farm, around the estate. Someone who could, over time, take on some of my responsibilities, become my deputy."

Herr Helmer belched, and looked around. He began to move. He wanted home.

"Is that all? Can't this wait until later?"

"The recent land acquisitions have increased the workload. And if you want me to spend more time at the factory."

"Yes yes but why now. This can wait."

Section One: The Wild East

Herr Helmer increased his speed, to escape his constant, long serving headache; and Penkin had to up his pace.

"Not exactly."

"Not exactly? What do you mean not exactly?"

"Well there's someone I have in mind for the job and I need to make him an offer now else he will be gone."

Herr Helmer walked on faster towards his car. He had a reserved parking place at the rear of the courts.

"So you find somebody else. I won't be pushed."

"I would like to give him the job. He would be very good. We would work very well together – which is good for you. In time he would be more than capable to take over when I retire."

"Retire?"

"Yes retire. He would take over and things would continue uninterrupted. Your son would find him totally reliable."

Herr Helmer was hooked. "Who is this person?"

"My son."

"Your son? You want me to give your son a job? What does he know about farming, land management - getting peasants out of bed?"

"I will teach him."

"No. I am not a charity for the Penkin family – nor anybody."

"But we need that extra worker."

"Not yet we don't."

Herr Helmer was saying no on a matter of principle: he did not want to be overrun by the Penkin clan. This one was more than enough. And he had never liked that brat who used to hang around the farm and house.

"How old is your boy now?"

"Eighteen Herr Helmer, same age as your boy."

You should know that you ignorant fool.

"Oh yes that's right. They were born months apart. I remember you falling over pissed."

Penkin saw his chance for a revival of fortunes and jumped in.

"I remember you falling over pissed."

That was a little too much.

"Penkin."

"Apologies Herr Helmer, no slight intended. But he really does need that job."

"No."

They reached the car and came to a stop, in all senses. The parking attendant saluted and rushed forward to open the driver's door. As the great man got in the attendant stood unsure of what to do next. Open

Section One: The Wild East

the passenger's door for one of the peasants? Penkin resolved the uncertainty by walking round to the driver's window. He had to try one last time. He owed it to himself.

"Please Herr Helmer. He will not cost much – I'll take a pay cut. And he will serve you well – I'll work him to the bone."

Herr Helmer started the engine. It sounded beautiful. "No."

"I have to give him a job. I promised him. He has nothing else."

Herr Helmer looked up. "You promised him?"

Penkin nodded, now reduced to the status of a beggar.

"Well don't make promises you can't keep. That's my advice. And don't expect favours from me. You've already done good by me. Don't forget that."

Penkin rushed out his next words. They were suddenly the most important.

"You said once I could always ask you a favour. You said that once."

"I said that? When?"

"August 1945."

Herr Helmer wanted to laugh but caught himself when he saw that his farm manager - undeniably his most useful, most indispensable worker - was totally serious.

"That was a long time ago Penkin. And anyway favours don't extend to inventing jobs for family members of my employees. As I said I'm not a charity."

"It's not an invented job. We need the extra man."

Herr Helmer gestured him away, in the way of an old soldier.

"Whatever."

And with that, sick to death of the other man's conversation, he drove off fast.

Penkin wanted to throw mud at the rear window but instead was forced to walk away, and pretend to be indifferent to the outcome. Like many things in his life it was a pretence which would collapse under the weight of alcohol. Boiling with frustration he wandered back to the main square to view the clock tower. There was little left of the working day: so may as well go and have a drink or two was his conclusion.

Angry with the contract life had tricked him into signing – it never paid dividends – Penkin did the only thing he could do to stay sane: he retreated into an alcoholic haze; slowly, measure by measure, alone; recalling those past events which now left him depleted, despised, and at times degenerate. He was resentful – but of what he did not know. He had possibly the best job in town; and lived in one of its better

Section One: The Wild East

houses; and other Ukrainians were forced to show him respect when he demanded it. He rarely demanded it. It created too much bitterness. And these days he lacked the guts.

It took only an hour to reach a state of satisfactory oblivion and then he staggered off home with high but ludicrous hopes that he could still persuade his remaining son to do exactly that, remain. And as he staggered he carried home the heavy burden of belief that his second son would be there, waiting for him; that his second son – the runt – would stand up and greet him, salute him even just like the Helmer boy saluted his father; that his second son – the clever one? – would listen to what he had to say, and accept, and conform; that his second son – the accident – would go back to his current employer, cap in hand and beg for his job back; that his second son would calm down and return to normal.

When Penkin arrived home, wasted, there was no son waiting for him, only the housecleaner. She gave him a dirty look and mumbled something incoherent – at least that's how it sounded to him. Then, getting no response, she raised her voice to a higher pitch. She was deafening. Penkin tried to walk round her but she blocked his way and stuck out her hand. She was making demands: this Penkin did not like. He pushed her aside and she was left screaming as he tore past. She had left a bucket of soapy water in the middle of the room. He felt required to kick it over. He had to re-establish his superiority. He kicked it over but it didn't make him feel the slightest bit better. In fact it only made things worse: he now had a wet floor. Somebody must mop that up he thought as, swollen, he slowly climbed the stairs towards bed and the state of oblivion it offered. He collapsed on his bed. His pillow smelt like a dead sheep. The sheets smelt worse. They were smells that no longer bothered him: they made no sense, even when he was sober.

His body had collapsed but his brain refused to stop functioning: memories resurfaced and produced heat, much like a severe rash. There was the Wehrmacht uniform, crisp and cool, which had once made him proud – of everything and nothing – and which had given him cause; and to which a German had pinned a medal. Helmer? There were the flags he had saluted: German then Ukrainian then German then black then white. There was the soldier's throat he had sliced through, from behind. There was the day Helmer's Tiger had broken down and he just had to laugh. It didn't happen like that in the newsreels. There was that day he had got blind drunk with Helmer - the day Stalin was declared dead and good riddance. There was the day the war was declared won; and the day independence was declared; and

Section One: The Wild East

he passed out blind drunk on both. There was that day he watched two Polish officers set fire to a synagogue, and thought himself a better man. There was that day he set fire to the red flag and raised the Ukrainian flag, and got drunk. There was that special day when he and Helmer took turns to buy the drinks. There was that day he shot a grey wolf dead with one round, impressing both Helmer Senior and Helmer Junior. There was that day he shot that Jew, before that Jew shot him (or so he had convinced himself). There was that day he was handed a screaming newborn child – his first son - and got blind drunk. There was that day he was handed a second, and got blind drunk, and slept for a whole day. There was the day his first son asked his first innocent question. And there was the last day. There was the day Helmer gave him a job, and they drank together to celebrate. There was the day he spoke back, drunk, wasted, and Helmer tore into him. It was the day he came close to losing his job, and the day he burnt the swastika and buried the traces like a coward. There was the day he threw away his medal - the same day he burnt his uniform. There was the day he showed his first son how to get drunk. There was the day he smacked his wife, stone sober, with both boys watching but saying nothing. There was the day his wife walked out and so to celebrate he got drunk, blind stinking drunk. There was the day he heard that she was dead and so he had to get blind stinking drunk. Finally his anguished, emaciated thoughts had nowhere left to turn and his collapse was total.

♦

Franz and Lev sat side by side on a makeshift bench: a weathered wooden beam resting on top of two wooden crates. An empty bottle at their feet was testament to the fact that they were a little drunk – but not so drunk as to be able to shift the shit life had recently dumped on them. Occasionally they scratched their backs and balls, bit into their fingernails, itched and twitched. They savoured the pages of a magazine which had passed through many hands and still both were agitated.

The best picture was the centrefold. It consisted of one man and two women: two interlocked, one disengaged; two simulating the act of love making, the other simulating the pleasure of watching it happen; two looking serious, serene, one looking contemplative; two totally naked, one still in underwear. It was a lot to take in. There was sex in the air: second hand, faked and frozen but in the air nonetheless. For Franz and Lev it was as real as real could be, and enough to make a grown man cry. When Lev began turning the pages Franz had pretended to be

Section One: The Wild East

offended. But that was soon cast off, leaving him equally enthralled. For both it was a great escape, a great relief. Sex permeated their brains, leaving no room for anything else – something the alcohol had failed to achieve.

They were sitting snug amidst the debris of an abandoned building site in the camp: a place intended for rejuvenation and removal of a shameful past. But the building works had been quickly abandoned. Lev kept licking his fingers and turning the pages, and unintentionally kept turning up the heat until Franz could take it no more. He needed relief, ultimate relief. He stood up, stretched, and went to great pains to keep his hard on out of sight. He approached a wall, his attention drawn to some crudely scratch letters. The letters made up two words: two names, two Russian names. Franz quickly distanced himself and sat back down. Hungry, he produced a bar of chocolate.

"Want some?"

"Ta."

In one smooth movement Lev looked up, snapped off a piece, and looked back down. The simple image of two naked women, holding each other up, enjoying the feel of their touching flesh, had fixated him. There was nothing dirty about these two.

"Your dad still giving you grief?"

"When he can. I just tell him to fuck off."

Franz was impressed: it was as simple as that. Just tell him to fuck off.

"And yours?"

"And mine?"

Franz was struck by a thought: up to now it hadn't occurred to him that his father was giving him personal grief. Father just was doing what fathers had to do.

"The same," he finally answered.

"That's fucking dads for you."

In his mind Lev had them sorted. In Franz' mind they were still a force to be reckoned with; still off limits; always in charge and above criticism. His attention was drawn to the picture.

"That's just two women. How can they do anything?"

"They improvise."

"They what?"

Franz was confused. Then he laughed, loudly. Suddenly the whole subject of sex was silly, almost insignificant. Then he remembered Bridget and just as suddenly it was all serious and important again.

"Aneta. I'm really sorry about that. Fucking sorry."

Lev waved the subject away.

Section One: The Wild East

"Give it a rest will you. If it wasn't you it would have been someone else. She was asking for it."

Grateful for that Franz moved on.

"Your dad. Do you hate him?"

Lev looked up into the distance, and the crumbling brick wall which blocked his view.

"Hate him?"

Lev genuinely did not know. When they clashed and hurled insults – yes he hated him then - couldn't stand to be in the same room. But other times? Like now? When the old man was far away and off his mind – and off his mind – it didn't occur to him to feel anything towards him, or against him, or about him. Lev gave the simple answer, the one Franz would understand.

"Yes. And you?"

"Me?"

"Yes you. Answer the question. You hate your dad?"

Franz looked very uncomfortable but Lev pushed on.

"You have to answer. I told you. You tell me."

Lev held his magazine to his chest, hiding its charms until he got an answer.

"No I don't hate him. I can't hate him. That would be unacceptable. I just hate having to respect him all the time."

Lev was impressed. It was a good answer, but a sad one. Franz stood up and advanced towards a large oil tank, like his life depended upon it.

"I need a wank."

Behind it he disappeared out of view. Lev, bored now, rolled up the magazine and stuffed it away. It was time to trade it in. He waited and grew restless. A pile of bricks drew his attention. He looked across to the oil tank and made a connection. He jumped up, walked over to the bricks, threw one at the tank, and missed. It drew no response from Franz. He swore and tried again, this time hitting his mark.

"Stop it!"

"You stop it!"

"Fuck off!"

Lev didn't stop. The bricks kept coming and Franz continued to curse but he would not be dislodged. Neither of them noticed the sound of an approaching vehicle. It's ancient diesel engine made a distinctive noise: it rattled and spluttered, and gasped for air as if drawing its last breath. It was a kübelwagen which had seen better days, and worse. It drew up at the main gate as if exhausted - like the three armed men who climbed out. Two carried rifles. The other carried a pistol.

Section One: The Wild East

On hearing the sound of many footsteps and a German barking orders Lev froze. He began to sweat. His natural instinct was to run, to hide, but that was displaced by the presence of Franz, another German. He stayed put. He had done nothing wrong, he told himself. He was just a kid, of no interest to them, he kept telling himself. Franz too had heard the soldiers. He kept telling himself that he was innocent, that he hadn't done anything wrong, that he was a good citizen. He fumbled as he did up his trousers. His effort had been wasted.

Three soldiers came into view: two privates led by a corporal. The privates saw Lev, a local, and went straight for him – like dogs on seeing the fox. They each grabbed an arm as if to snap him in half like a wishbone, or pull him apart like a Christmas cracker. They waited for the corporal to give instructions. Franz sat motionless, agonizing - apologizing - over his situation, while his friend was interrogated and assaulted. They shouted in his face: demanding to know what he was doing in a restricted area but too impatient to wait for the explanation. Franz saw this as not the German way. It was perverted, dishonourable, and Franz could not bear the thought that German soldiers were acting like common native thugs. He wanted to speak up for his friend but could not bring himself to reveal himself. When Lev protested a soldier hit him. When he stayed silent he was punched in the stomach. He fell to the ground in agony.

Franz jumped up, bristling with anger fuelled by the shame of the situation.

"Stop that! That's my friend!"

The soldiers spun round, caught off guard. The corporal pointed, furious that he had been caught out.

"Where the hell did you come from! What's your name!"

"Franz Helmer. My father is Franz Helmer Senior. Town magistrate."

On hearing the name Helmer the corporal froze, unsure how to respond. His men watched him, seeking guidance. He had none to give. Lev pulled himself back up on to his feet and shuffled towards Franz, instinctively seeking protection. One of the soldiers grabbed his arm and held him in check. Lev was no German. He was fair game. Finally the corporal recovered his composure and sense of authority. This was just a kid. Then he noticed bruising on the kid's face.

"Did he do that?" he asked hopefully.

"No! Someone else! Someone at school. He's my friend."

"Your friend?"

The corporal looked at Lev, as if his attention had been drawn to something unpleasant, unnatural. Unconvinced he turned back to face

Section One: The Wild East

his smarter catch.

"You're Helmer's boy?"

You're an idiot, thought Franz. He raised his voice. "I'm his son."

He objected to this man – an NCO of the lowest rank - using the word 'boy'.

"What are you doing here? This place is a restricted area, off limits."

Franz shrugged. He was recovering his composure quickly. This buffoon did not scare him and the sound of his voice suggested that he, Franz Helmer, was suddenly someone important, a force to be reckoned with. That thought began to intoxicate him and he came up with – in his view – a brilliant answer.

"Trying to get pissed."

The cheek of it snapped the corporal into action. He pointed at Lev.

"Throw that kid in the back of the jeep." He pointed at Franz. "You. You come with me."

Under duress both were led back to the army kübelwagen. It was standard issue metallic grey-green, scratched and dented. Lev was pushed onto the back seat – to be squeezed between the two privates – and Franz was directed to sit in the front. The corporal drove off at speed. He was in a hurry to rid himself of his human cargo. The easy life was all he asked for while he served out his term in the army. He had dreams of becoming a dentist, like his father. He just had to survive bloody national service and the sodding Ukraine.

During the ride Lev was not allowed to speak while Franz did not want to speak, which suited the corporal fine. On the way back to the Helmer estate, at a major road junction in what seemed like the middle of nowhere, the corporal suddenly slammed on the brakes – and almost sent Franz crashing into the windscreen. He looked sharply into the rear-view mirror. He still did not like what he saw.

"Get rid of him, now."

A soldier jumped out and pulled Lev out – not that Lev wanted any help - flooring him in the process. The soldier jumped back in and slammed the door shut while Lev stood up straight, defiant. He looked at Franz, as if to pass him a secret message, but Franz was not looking his way. The corporal shouted out of his window.

"You, piss off!"

With that he drove off and Lev stuck two fingers up, swearing until the jeep and the German scum it carried became just a dot in the distance. He hugged his stomach and set off towards home; plodding; in no rush to get there; in no rush to be anywhere. He felt his jacket pocket. He still had his magazine. He had not been beaten. Only his

Section One: The Wild East

stomach ached – but that would get better. For Franz it was the other way round: he was in a rush to get home; and things would get worse.

The closer to home the more Franz retreated into a simple fantasy, eyes shut: dressed in his Hitler Youth uniform he stood tall and proud as a medal was pinned to his chest; dressed in his Hitler Youth uniform he hugged Bridget and snatched a secret kiss; dressed in his Hitler Youth uniform he stood at the front of class and issued orders, even to the Direktor. The fantasy was cut short when the corporal drew up at the front of the house. The drive was littered with smart cars, all badly parked as if dumped. The house had guests: drinking, smoking, yapping; all comfortable in their bubble; some contesting for the moral high ground, others oblivious to it; all keen to be fed. The colonel was there, determined to get drunk and well on his way. As and when required his dutiful wife held him up, sometimes to the light.

With the engine left running, the corporal marched up to the front door, military style, and rang the bell. A nervous Franz watched as the corporal was received by a member of staff. Franz did not move a muscle. He had been told in no uncertain terms to wait in the car. His nervousness increased exponentially when his father appeared, looking angry, with the corporal in tow. Herr Helmer stormed towards the jeep. Now even the soldiers in the back were nervous. Instinctively they recognised the senior officer in the man.

Franz held his breath, expecting an explosion of words. But when his father drew up alongside none were forthcoming. Instead Herr Helmer clenched his jaw, released a deep exhausting breath, and looked his son over and over; as if taking notes; as if passing judgement; as if disassociating himself from his bag of trouble. The look of anger was replaced by one of deep disappointment and silent interrogation. Franz began to wilt. When his father finally did speak it was only to issue an instruction.

"I'll talk to you later. Follow me and behave yourself. We have dinner guests."

Herr Helmer headed back indoors. Right now he had nothing more to say. Franz swallowed the lump in his throat before it grew too large and followed him in. He had been saved – temporarily – by dinner guests. He felt an enormous gap opening up between him and his father. He felt beyond redemption. So why bother making amends?

An uncertain, possibly false smile returned to Herr Helmer's face as he rejoined his guests. In his short absence things had moved on: his guests were now crowded around the television screen. The evening news broadcast had commenced. The colonel stood arms folded tight, feet stuck out, legs strutting at an angle, swaying slightly; like he was

Section One: The Wild East

inspecting the troops. At this point Franz decided, for good, that the man was a complete buffoon. Today all military men were buffoons. But he still wanted to join their ranks, and be saluted. He leaned against the wall, by the door, wishing not to be noticed, and fell into a sour sore sulk.

Berlin beckoned. Berlin suggested. Berlin beguiled. Berlin beggared belief. Its broad boulevards, packed shopping malls, dense fast moving traffic, modern blocks and monuments to its nation's recent renewal filled the screen. Nothing was left to chance or the imagination. The image had been set as a commentator thrilled his audience with details of preparations for the big day. Its grand buildings, its modern architecture – big, boastful, ebullient - sucked in the audience even though they were standing far away on the outside looking in.

This was Berlin, for many so black and white. Everywhere flags lined the streets: so many flags; and red was their colour, their heat, even in black and white; and the swastika was the shape, the beat, the heartbeat. In black and white sunlight burst through the Brandenburg Gate. In Berlin the faces were always smiling; all 100% Aryan; all taken in by the illusion that this was the only place to be. Nothing could better it. Nothing compared. There was no other place to be, no other time worth living in. Berlin spoke volumes and hid its deceit. It enthused the masses. It lifted the soul. In Berlin you were not allowed to be disheartened. Berlin gave away its dreams for free. Nothing was out of place. Only the best buildings, the best architecture, the best human ingredients were given space. Everything sparkled. Everything was clean, smart, polished, up to scratch. Everything was rock solid. Berlin resonated. Berlin was perfect. But it was a hard place to be if you did not fit in.

Everything else was reduced to a sideshow. Just about everybody in the room felt a little reduced, stripped bare, even Franz - to the point that he began to resent it's magnificence, its superiority. He felt small. He felt he deserved better than a life in the middle of nowhere. There were the tallest soldiers smartly dressed in spotless black; standing to attention on street corners for the benefit of the tourists; steel-tipped by black helmets. They were the elite, the untouchables, and they knew it. Franz saw the crowd buzz around them as if desperate for handouts. He wanted a handout.

A woman, caught on camera, was straining to be unleashed and allowed to bite on the meat. Likewise her husband could not control his enthusiasm. His sense of nationalism had engulfed his sense of perspective. He wanted nothing more than to be in uniform, any

Section One: The Wild East

uniform. He wanted to march to the beat of the state. He wanted to carry the flag. He wanted to bear arms against the enemy - were there any enemy left with fight in them. Stuck in his 9 to 5 office job he wanted to go crazy - any excuse would do.

Out of the screen flowed calculated beauty and ambience: a hard uncompromising beauty carved out of stone; an ambience born of harsh measures. Nothing unplanned, uncensored, incompatible was allowed on camera. The system of the state left no room for improvisation. Public consumption was metered at all times. And the output from the television screens kept the nation glued to the spot. Right across Europe it was much the same glue, if not the same spot. In the age of television it was all about the immediate moment, and instant gratification. Franz tried not to join the party, but failed. The images were too powerful to deflect or resist. He peeled himself away from the wall and moved in. This was Big Berlin, in all its glory, with all its promise. He ended up standing alongside the colonel, arms also locked. The colonel slapped him on the back, and nearly toppled him over.

Franz saw the magic. Static pictures in magazines could not compete. It was a fantasy place full of fantasy people and it was where he wanted to be right now: in uniform, arm raised in salute, his future assured, his past packed away; not stuck out in the middle of nowhere surrounded by peasants - peasants who showed him no respect. He saw the black and white flags but he smelt the colour of red. Franz looked around. The adults were all glued to the screen. They had been hijacked by the visual feast. It was a drug. It gave a kick to those who were so far removed from the centre of gravity. They lapped up its vitality and celebration of everything that was German and was meant to be German. In their minds Berlin mattered the most - and they were at its edge, hanging on. Berlin belonged to them. They belonged to it. And belonging felt good.

Berlin. This was the place to be, to live, to start a career, to dump an old one. It spoke volumes – of what, nobody in the room knew or cared. Franz couldn't make sense of the expressions on their faces. He became afraid that he was missing out on something. Berlin had won. It had served its purpose. An image of the Fuehrer appeared and expanded until it filled the whole screen. It was an image of a young Adolf Hitler.

Then Goebbels appeared, in front of the Volkshalle. He was being interviewed. He spoke like a child brimming over with confidence - confident that the world around him was dancing to his tune. He smiled at the camera and spoke directly to the viewers. (His eyes could

Section One: The Wild East

scare small children.) He was in his element. He was being watched by millions of Germans, and in his mind he connected with them all. He had accomplished all he had set out to achieve, and more. Greater Germany was greater still, and the greatest power in Europe. And still he could not face retirement.

Goebbels was considered by many in the Party to be the strange one, the scary one, the one far too clever by half. When Goebbels spoke he grabbed his audience by the throat and held it firm: captivating and converting to his cause – the cause of his beloved Fuehrer. With his hook he reeled them in, like fish who had never learnt to swim. Even Franz was caught. He had been taught about - by - Goebbels at school. He had seen the old man before on TV but never like this: never so manic; never so animated. Franz looked around: nobody dared make a sound. It was just like school.

Goebbels fell silent. He had said so much. Like an aging, antiquated fashion model he brushed his long scrawny fingers through his grey straight hair and waited for the applause he knew was coming his way. He grabbed the microphone from the interviewer and stared into the camera at his viewers, at the Volk, at Europe, and at the rest of the world. He assumed the whole world was watching. Why would it not be? He wanted to shout 'We are invincible! We are the ultimate truth! We are the highest order of society! We are pure perfection! We are the Aryan nation! We are absolute!'

But he didn't. He was getting too old for that kind of thing. That was the job for the next generation. He remained calm, statesman like. He spoke of the coming celebrations, the city preparations, the logistical challenges. He thanked all those who had put all their time and effort into making it happen. He promised that the big day would be a day never to be forgotten. He thanked the Party and government departments, and praised the Sturmabteilung and Schutzstaffeln. To finish he thanked and praised the Fuehrer: for holding it all together; for maintaining the peace; for protecting their borders; for bringing peace to the minds of all Germans. When he ran out of propaganda he handed the microphone back to an interviewer now panicking over what to say next. How could he follow that? Off camera someone shouted Heil Hitler! Goebbels saluted and shouted likewise. The interviewer was compelled to do the same, as were those in the room. The colonel was the quickest and the loudest. Franz was not far behind him.

The broadcast moved on to foreign affairs and the latest images of central Warsaw replaced those of Berlin. An angry young crowd - mainly tanked up students with nothing to lose - was making its way towards the German embassy. They were chanting. Many had linked

Section One: The Wild East

arms in solidarity. They had secretly planned this action for weeks but it was no secret. A line of soldiers blocked their way – no police with water cannon this time. The protestors were ordered to stop, disband, go home. They didn't. They carried on undeterred. The protestors wanted their corridor back. It had been sold off cheaply - given away - by a previous, corrupt government. The present government, more in the pocket of the Third Reich than ever, wanted them to shut up, go home, and not piss off their true masters. They didn't, so the soldiers opened fired. Protestors fell to the ground where they were left to writhe in agony. The rest mostly scattered, some screaming, some shouting abuse at the soldiers - the Nazis thugs. The soldiers broke up the remains of the protest with violence and arrests, and short tempers.

The colonel clapped and began to remonstrate. A few others joined in. The colonel, twisting on the heels of his boots, slapped Franz on the shoulder then noticed the bruising on the face: not a good thing for a German to have. He had to give the boy his best advice. The colonel proceeded to bless him then impress upon him: teaching, preaching, boring him; finally scaring him. The colonel talked on and on, as if to stop talking would make his head fall off or his mouth seize up. The colonel instructed Franz in no uncertain terms that the bruise had to go before the big day. It could not be seen, to be remarked upon. It would not be allowed.

"By who?" asked Franz, now antagonistic.

"By the State!"

And how am I suppose to do that? thought Franz. Will it away? Make it heal quicker?

The colonel moved on to the subject of Franz in uniform. On the day his uniform had to be immaculate: washed and precisely ironed.

"Young man if you want to get on creases are important! And polish your medals. Look smart. Speak precisely if prompted to speak but do not speak first. Speak only if spoken to. Don't give opinions on anything, just agree. Opinions are dangerous – take it from me if you want to get on don't have opinions. They only cause trouble in the end. In the military you must be serious and attentive in front of senior officers. Don't smile even if they smile at you – it may be a trick."

Franz had no idea what the old fool was waffling on about.

"Show him you're worthy. Get the salute right! The salute must be perfect, without a hint of hesitation, a clean sweep. And when you salute really mean it. Put all your passion into it. Understood Franz?"

"Understood Herr colonel."

There was a late news item: Reichsmarschall Goering had been admitted to a private clinic, for 'tests' on the advice of his doctors.

Section One: The Wild East

(Privately they had serious concerns about his health.) The colonel sniggered and commented upon the amount of food and drink the old man could consume in one day, causing offence to those around him. Some only pretended to be offended.

"They say he's vowed to eat his way to a heart attack."

Franz was shocked by the lack of respect. This was not the German way. He was saved by the dinner bell.

"Good. Time to eat," said the colonel.

The guests peeled away, to regroup around the dining table, their sense of worth reinstated. They were living in the Ukraine and they were living in Germany – even though not once did Doktor Goebbels refer to it. Over the years he had the knack of saying everything and nothing at the same time. Only the Fuehrer did it better than him. The colonel rushed off to get the second best seat at the table.

Franz, exhausted, didn't want to eat: not with Father in the room; not with the colonel in the room. It was one of those times when he felt adults were alien inventions. He retreated to his bedroom and crashed out on his bed. Later he woke up and sat up, and looked around as if sensing arrest. It was dark, pitch black outside. Checking the coast was clear he crept back downstairs and into the kitchen. He needed food.

The lights were still on. Staff were still cleaning up and clearing away. The dogs did not greet him. They had been locked up for the night. Franz ordered a big beef and mustard sandwich and sat, stiff, as he awaited its arrival. Aneta floated around, busy, ignoring him as he tried to ignore her. They caught each other's eye just the once, and for a fleeting moment the connection threatened to bring the house down: she wanted to hit him; he wanted to grab her again. But it was gone, all over in less than a heartbeat. She didn't and couldn't without losing her job. He didn't and couldn't without losing his dignity. He grabbed his sandwich off the plate and headed back to his room, dignity intact. She buried herself in her duties: at the end of the day it was all she had, and that mattered.

While Franz sat and chewed, stony faced, Lev was walking home, walking away, walking out. He had been observing his dad with his cronies cemented in their usual place at the bar. Like them he had been drinking, but unlike them he had been engaged in silence - the superior kind. His dad had been boasting, inventing, avoiding the question; hanging on to his threadbare reality, afraid to lose it, afraid to share it. Penkin never knew he was being watched by his son, buried as he was in a corner behind a shield of animated, alcoholic bodies out for a good time. Lev had slipped away out when all the talk had become painful

Section One: The Wild East

noise, and the faces behind the noise had become contemptible, irrelevant; and the point of it all had become lost. On his way out he reached his final verdict: Penkin was a fake, and always had been.

Much later, while he was fast asleep, Frau Helmer stuck her head into her son's bedroom and watched, and wondered, and wished. She closed the door gently and crept away without making a sound, back to her own room and her snoring husband.

♦

Morning came around again and with it the raising of the flag, an action which demanded to be done. It was routine. The Helmers stood stiff in the cold as the swastika unfurled itself and invited praise. Franz stood to attention whilst doing his best to avoid bringing attention to himself. Synchronised, mechanical, the family of three looked up and saluted as one. No thoughts were generated. No words were spoken. It was pure show, for no one. To ensure peace the woman stood between the man and his son. Nobody moved except for the dogs: they ran around in circles, full of vitality until ordered to sit and be quiet. With that the morning gloom was total.

At the breakfast table Franz watched the food being served up, having convinced himself that he was safe. Father had said nothing, and he had his eye on the food coming his way. Franz slipped into a comfortable composure and began to contemplate Bridget – and then Herr Helmer growled like a dog to get his son's attention. The words were not pleasant: the talk descended into rant and there was no appeal. Judgement was final. Franz Helmer Senior was the magistrate and Franz Helmer Junior was in the dock.

"You do not enter that camp!" Herr Helmer thumped the table and nearly split his coffee. "That camp is off limits - to the whole world!"

Franz tried to pretend that someone else was in the room, someone less deserving. He wanted to tell his father to 'fuck off', but his upbringing would not permit him descend to such a level.

"You have let me down badly! Me, your father!" Herr Helmer paused. "And your mother!"

Franz gripped the edge of his chair. Frau Helmer stared down into the centre of her plate. She had no leg to stand on.

"You know that. Everybody knows that! So why did you go there? Why did you disobey me!"

Franz began to shake. His eyes filled with tears but he refused to cry. Two or three years earlier it would have been a different story.

"I don't know." He could barely be heard.

Section One: The Wild East

Frau Helmer offered her son a lifeline but he refused to take it.

"Did that Penkin boy lead you there? Was it his idea?"

"No."

Herr Helmer pushed Frau Helmer aside - right now they were barely man and wife.

"You don't know. Is that all you have to say for yourself young man!"

Franz didn't answer. He smelt a rhetorical question.

"You have embarrassed me and your mother."

Frau Helmer pursed her lips but said nothing.

Herr Helmer thumped the table again. "Strictly speaking you have broken German law and should be punished. I should punish you."

Franz nearly jumped out of his skin. He had never considered the law in all this. Wasn't the law there to keep the peasants in line?

"I am a magistrate."

Frau Helmer came to her son's rescue. "Franz he's not yet eighteen."

"True." Herr Helmer was forced to concede that point. "As for that Penkin kid, you are never to make contact with him again, never. Understand?"

Franz nodded but that was not sufficient.

"Tell me you understand."

"I understand," croaked Franz.

"You are never to see him, speak to him again. That kid will not step on my land again. Penkin will see to it."

For some reason the words 'on my land' rankled Franz. Somehow he expected it to be 'on our land'.

Business done, and buried out of sight, Herr Helmer waved his son away.

"Go away. Leave me alone. Let me eat."

Franz looked towards his mother, confused. He had barely touched his plate. She provided no support, the opposite in fact: she gestured that he leave immediately. He snatched up a sausage and his mug of coffee and did as instructed. He made for the kitchen. Frau Helmer looked across at her husband, her disenchantment unmistakable. She made no impact. Her husband was too busy eating, head down. Never had breakfast been such a damaging affair. And she did not like it.

In the kitchen, while he watched his order of fried bacon, egg and mushrooms being served up, a new predicament dawned on Franz: his motorbike was still at the camp. He stabbed his food repeatedly while he grabbled with the problem. There was no way out. He would have to go begging to his father. He needed him to collect it. He didn't want

Section One: The Wild East

to ask but neither did he want to be marooned on the island which was the Helmer House. And it was a BMW. The pain was reduced somewhat by the fact that he was able to ask his mother to ask his father. She had left him to finish eating alone. (She had lost her appetite.)

Franz sat waiting on the steps of the back entrance with the dogs. They had crowded in, expecting – demanding – to be taken somewhere exciting. As he hugged his dogs he dreaded the thought of a car drive with his father right now. It would be one long, torturous lecture. A sickening feeling engulfed his stomach. He stood up, hoping to shake it off. He didn't. It just made him feel dizzy. The dogs grew more excited and jumped around, sensing something was about to happen. The Mercedes was parked a few yards away. It had recently been washed and stood sparkling in the sunlight. Its headlights and bumper radiated a big smile. It was a beautiful machine of the highest quality and showed Germany in the best light.

When his father finally appeared, impatient and waving car keys, Franz backed away. Explaining the poor state of his stomach he excused himself. The dogs watched them both, confused while Herr Helmer dismissed his wayward son. Like a grumpy teenager he grudgingly promised to retrieve the motorbike sometime during the day. Franz thanked him, with a hint of remote capitulation as he watched his father drive away. Thereafter he wandered the grounds of the house, hoping to kick his sense of nausea. The dogs kept close by his side and planted in his mind the idea of going for a run. He needed to get away from the house. He needed liberation.

An hour later, whilst Franz was running through the countryside, being chased by - or chasing - his dogs, Herr Helmer was walking around the camp. He knew nobody could be watching him but still he was nervous of being seen. It was not on any map yet still it stuck out like a sore thumb. It deserved recognition: it had plenty of history. He felt this was both the place to be and the place to not be - all very confusing for a man driven by the simple philosophy of black and white, high and low. As a rule he could barely stomach shades of grey.

At particular places he paused, as if to catch his breath and take in the view, as if to reconsider. At one point he went quietly mad and threw a brick at an already broken window, then another, then another. Further on he remembered why he was there and began searching for his son's bike. He sat down and stared up at the sky. It was as it had always been and it did nothing for him. He sat for ten minutes or more before getting up. He found the bike propped up against a fence post, on the outside, close to the road. He had wandered nearly full circle –

Section One: The Wild East

but on purpose: he needed to see the place just one last time. He would never miss it for the world.

◆

It was the day before departure and Franz was lost, in his head and in the extensive grounds of the Helmer castle. He was dressed in his Hitler Youth uniform: he needed reassurance that it still felt good and looked good. It did, magnificently, and the cold breeze which hit his knees was ignored. He felt important, part of some greater good; part of something worth defending with honour and passion, and even precision of mind. In uniform he was forced to think straight and not let his mind wander. And the medals he had earned meant, in his eyes, that he was a cut above the rest. Bruno could go hang himself – or become a Jew.

Franz jumped up on to a stone wall, held himself in balance, and stared out across the land of the Helmers. It was vast. It was dull. But it was all his. It never changed bar for a few strokes of colour. It didn't inspire. But it was all his so he stuck with it. Riding through it at speed was one thing: to have it sat in his face was another. He struggled to digest it, to resolve the conflict it generated in his mind - such a boring place - and he gave up almost immediately. With his cold wet nose one of the dogs prodded the back of his leg. Franz fell from the wall and kicked out. The dog backed off to stand looking stupid. The other dog had yet to sniff them out, but he would. It was what dogs did, and did well.

Franz was angry. Today the Helmer empire did nothing except fuel his frustration and sense of isolation. He was being pulled in two directions – home and away – and the only thing he could do was kick out. (He dare not shout out.) He was in uniform and he was holding his pistol so attack! All he needed was an enemy to shoot at - and a proper enemy, not just a Jew. He was off to meet the Fuehrer, the greatest man alive; to stand before him; to shake his hand, perhaps even receive his wisdom; yet somehow the dream fell flat. He was off to see Berlin without parents: that at least was something to celebrate.

Franz moved on, pointing his pistol, aiming at nothing but wishing to shoot something – anything - just as long as it deserved to die – like in the films. He wanted to destroy, so he could rebuild. He wanted to set fire, to feel the heat. He wanted to splash, kick over, mess up, make a scene, so he could still be a boy. He caught sight of a large terracotta pot containing spring bulbs. It ranked as one of his mother's favourite things. Now it was a convenient victim. He took aim, then lowered his

Section One: The Wild East

pistol and kicked it over instead. That felt good. He looked around. Only a dog had seen him do the dirty deed. Seconds later he had concocted his line of defence: 'I meant to kick the dog – it was going to piss on the pot'.

Something moved. A rat? A mouse? A squirrel? A bird in the bush? A Russian? A communist?

Franz went hunting with his pistol. He settled on the base of a hedge, stared down the barrel and took aim. Then there was another noise, behind him: a creeping noise of stealth. The enemy! Franz turned and pointed his pistol. The look on his face suggested he was taking no prisoners. Mother! Paula! They were both staring at him. They were judging him. They were serving him up for dinner. He wanted to shout. He wanted to scream. He wanted to shoot them both in the head. The look in their eyes was something to savour. He was in charge. He was the master. He wore the uniform.

Frau Helmer became alarmed when her son continued to point his pistol, face locked in a scowl. She did not know that the safety catch was on. And Franz had forgotten. He waited for her to snap but it was Paula who spoke first.

"Franz what are you doing?"

Her words were enough for Frau Helmer to snap out of her moment of fright; her composure and authority re-established by an irrational fear of usurpation.

"Franz what on earth are you doing! Put that thing away!"

Franz, smacked in the face by reality, lowered his weapon. He was outnumbered, by two women of all things. Then the other dog appeared and, reunited, both were more excited. They circled around Franz: to protect him; to trap him; awaiting instructions – to attack! Feeling exposed Frau Helmer made the point of injecting normality back into the situation as fast as she could.

"Paula is here to see you. Her brother kindly put himself out to drive her all the way here. She wishes to wish you luck before you go."

Franz looked at Paula as if she was a long lost relative come to intrude on the family. She carried that look: that look all girls carried when they assumed they were in charge; when they assumed some boy needed their attention, a dose of their comfort and empathy; that look of ownership and censorship. Paula was doing it now. He swapped her face for that of Bridget and thought hard, until it began to hurt. No, Bridget had not done that to him as far as he could remember. He sucked in a big breath of air – just like Father would have done – and made it clear that he didn't need this kind of attention right now.

Paula spoke, intending to speak at length. But it was not going to

Section One: The Wild East

happen. Franz had other ideas.

"I just wanted to wish you luck Franz. I'm sure it will go well. You'll be great."

Franz looked down at his shirt. Disaster! A button was loose. It was hanging by a thread. That could not be allowed. He pointed at it with his pistol.

"That button needs fixing – before tomorrow. Sow it back on, or something." His words were delivered as a stark, no compromise, order.

Paula, startled, looked at Frau Helmer for guidance. She would never dare to address her parents like that. Frau Helmer looked extremely agitated, and hostile towards her own flesh and blood. Suddenly Paula wanted to be back home, back on her own farm, back in her own house – or at the very least back inside her brother's cosy car.

"You say please Franz. Have I not always taught you to say please?"

"Yes Mother you have Mother. But it still needs fixing, before tomorrow. I have to wear this on the big day - the big day everyone keeps going on about. You know that."

Frau Helmer pursed her lips. She wanted out, and got out, followed by Paula. Franz felt bad and good; detested and denied; in charge and in trouble. He chose to turn 180 degrees and walk away from the trouble. The dogs followed. He would carry on walking until he ran out of path. Then he would stop, look around one last time and sneak back indoors to his room. Sporadically he invented the enemy, engaged, raised his pistol and pulled the trigger without ever firing a shot. The safety-catch remained on. His pistol remained powerless, a piece of show; a piece of light but heavy metal. At one point he passed by the flagpole and the flag which fluttered on high. He barely registered it. He didn't stop and he didn't salute it. It was just another swastika, stuck up a pole and serving no purpose.

The backlash was not far behind. It hit Franz just before lunch. Herr Helmer was furious. He made his son stand to attention in the drawing room, eyes front. Franz held firm: he was still in uniform, still engaging the enemy; still defending his great big country and the nation who toiled to keep it clean and tidy, rich and righteous. Herr Helmer fought for control. He couldn't understand what was happening. His son had become a delinquent, a rebel. Such behaviour would not be tolerated. Herr Helmer paced up and down the room, stopping to look out of the windows; digesting the view as if searching for clues. Franz watched his father out of the corner of his eye, breathing in and out

Section One: The Wild East

slowly. He was waiting for the coming explosion.

It came: Herr Helmer turned on his son. He wanted to slam his fist down hard but there was no table top in reach. He slammed it against his thigh instead.

"You do not point guns at your mother! Never! You understand me?"

Franz tremble. "Understand."

He went further. "The safety-catch was on."

Herr Helmer's face flared up and his eyes nearly popped.

"What!"

He began to drill down into his son, as if searching for the source of the trouble.

"Let me make myself absolutely clear. You do not point guns at your mother! Never! Is that clear!"

"Yes clear."

"And you are never rude to your mother! You never answer back. You do not order her about! Understood?"

"Understood."

Herr Helmer rolled his eyes up and down his son. He had run out of steam. His son looked smart, presentable. He knew how to stand straight, stand out like every Helmer should.

"What's got into you?"

"I forgot I was holding my gun."

"Don't talk rubbish, you're a German! You can't forget holding a gun that's plain stupid!"

Franz felt a surge of defiance and broke rank. He looked down his shirt.

"This button here needs sowing back on – that's all I said."

Herr Helmer's mouth fell open.

"We have staff to do that. You know that. Don't bother your mother. Get it sorted."

Herr Helmer sat down to catch his breath. His son had worn him out. He pointed at another chair.

"Sit down. I want to talk to you."

Franz complied, thinking on the way down, if that wasn't talk what was it?

"I want to talk to you about our trip to Berlin. You're clear about the dates and the hotel?"

Franz nodded. "Yes. I have it all written down."

He didn't.

"I'll introduce you to some of my fellow officers. So I expect you to be on your best behaviour. Respect the uniform and remember your

Section One: The Wild East

place. Understood?"

"Understood."

As his father produced more of the same Franz began to close down. He replied 'yes' and 'understood' at the right places but otherwise was detached from the discourse. Instead he was drawn to the state of his father's clothes: there was dirt; there was mud on the boots. And Father smelt bad, of sweat. Franz felt clean and superior in his smart uniform. And then it hit him: he didn't want to take it off. No never! He didn't want to end up covered in dirt. He didn't want to end up a dirty farmer crawling across the land shouting orders at the peasants until blue in the face. He wanted to attack. Attack. Attack! He wanted Reichsfuehrer Himmler to pin medals on him! Could he fight the Poles? Were there any communists left to kill? How about the French? Why not attack the French?

Franz moved on to food. He was suddenly very hungry - no he was starving. Father was still going, around and around: what to see in Berlin; best behaviour; correct attitude; be at the hotel on time; don't miss train connections. Father was beginning to sound like Mother. Abruptly Franz stood up.

"I'm starving. Is lunch ready? I'm starving."

Herr Helmer, cut short, threw his hands up and likewise stood up. Like his son he was impatient and fed up.

"Yes. Probably. Off you go."

Franz flounced off towards the dining room. Herr Helmer followed behind. He put the incident down to stress: meeting the Fuehrer was no small thing. He had to admit it but even he could go weak at the knees on the day.

♦

In the afternoon Franz dutifully attended a meeting of his local Hitler Youth cell. They were a small outfit, with no official number to put on their official flag, but boys were boys and they proudly protected their collection of flags. They had their own meeting hut: not big, but big enough for these boys stuck defending the outer edge of the empire. The rule was when you entered the hut disharmony and disorder was to be left outside. Boys being boys, the rule was often broken.

There they congregated, mainly once a week, to listen to their cell leader. He was a middle-aged man who took it far more seriously than most of his boys. Boys being boys, they didn't always listen to what he so much wanted to say. The boys tried to act as equals, but failed. The boys tried to act mature, but failed. Boys being boys, the big boys

Section One: The Wild East

bullied the smaller boys - sometimes with good military reason. Boys being boys, some loved to fight as some men loved to fight. They craved the excitement, the emotional chaos, the thrill of victory versus defeat. Boys being boys, they loved to beat their drums and keep the place awake, or wake it up. And boys being boys when they were told to march they really marched.

Their wooden hut, painted crisp green by boys years earlier, stood next to their football pitch. Sometimes they played each other. Sometimes - rarely - they played a visiting cell. Sometimes they played a junior team of locals - but only under supervision, lest it turned nasty. They took pride in the fact that they had won the majority of their fixtures (just). They scorned the opposition when they won: bad losers versus sporting winners. They scorned the opposition when they lost: bad winners versus sporting losers.

The Fuehrer was there as he was always there, from another time and place. His glorious picture hung in the prime spot. His perfected image was still ruthless, still cunning, still feigning innocence. His blue eyes were still able to lock the viewer in. His hair was still shiny, near black, still gloss. His gaze still consumed the crowd, no matter what the size. Like the picture his intelligence was still stuck in one place.

Today the standard, run-of-the-mill meeting felt different for Franz. His trip to Berlin was now old news but still he was the centre of attention - more so as he was leaving the next day. His presence almost supplanted that of his leader and it reduced Bruno to the role of a forgotten player. He played it for all its worth. Secretly each boy objected to him getting all the attention but was outnumbered by the rest. Some, the younger ones, asked to go with him. He ignored them. They were stupid. In uniform, surrounded by the same uniforms, Franz felt re-energized. He soaked up the attention, and when their leader praised him and raised a salute - Heil Hitler! - Franz convinced himself that all were saluting him. It was a jolt of electricity: his self-confidence was back, perhaps with a vengeance.

As always the meeting ended with the call to march, to beat the drum, to celebrate the cause. The flags were handed out to grabbing hands. Some lost out. Drums were retrieved from cupboard space. Boot laces, braces and straps were rechecked before the boys stepped out into the sunshine - sunshine was always on cue for the Hitler Youth - and arranged themselves into standard formation. It was all done by the book.

All the boys loved to march. Each wanted to hold a flag, to be at the front. Each tried to sing the loudest. Few could out perform the cell leader. He had the biggest pair of lungs and no other use for them

Section One: The Wild East

except to shout at the world. They marched into the centre of town, and out again, now bigger than boys and bigger than their boots. The boys marched down the hill, then back up it. Always the same hill. Always the same beat. Like a repeating record, one stuck in a groove, they drew little attention but generated much irritation. They never stopped for the traffic.

◆

That evening Franz reread all his letters from Bridget; this time with total seriousness, like heavy homework. He was now regretting that he had allowed Lev to write his, and feared that she would find out. Later, while he sat staring at his kitbag, stuffed, Lev was out roaming the town. Lev was almost at peace with himself and it felt good. There were small kids out and about: fooling around; wishing for trouble. There were big kids out and about: getting drunk; looking for trouble. Once he had cared – craved even – to join in and wreak havoc. Now he was content to walk on. He found letting go easy.

He stopped at the entrance to a dark alleyway and peered into the gloom. It smelt of mud and shit and rotting vegetation, with a hint of tobacco smoke thrown in for good measure. He could make out the shape of a tall man in the shadows. He was leaning against a wall, smoking. Lev clenched his jaw and stepped forward. The man - tough, mean, well-built - wore a long army trench coat. He was a German soldier. The soldier, startled, suddenly moved forward and Lev froze. Perhaps, by a fluke, this was not his soldier.

"Penkin?" whispered the soldier.

Lev relaxed a little but kept his guard up. This was his soldier: a corrupt German who wanted to get rich quick and go home; back to Germany proper, back to Hamburg, back to a sanity of his own making.

"That's me."

"Closer. Let me see your face."

Lev approached as requested, determined not to be intimidated.

"You got the money?"

"Yes."

"Show me."

"Let's talk about price."

"No. Show me."

Lev did as instructed.

"Count it out. I want to see it counted."

Lev produced his wad and began to lift each note held in the palm of his hand, adding to the count as it was transferred into his other hand.

Section One: The Wild East

The soldier watched with eagle eyes each note being exposed, his face locked intensely on the moment. Lev had hoped to barter and bring the price down, do a part exchange even, but now he accepted that this was not to be. It was a fixed price deal, non-negotiable. Take it or leave it. Lev took it.

When he finished the soldier – a sergeant – pulled a gun from his pocket and pointed it at Lev.

"Bang."

Lev tried to get the joke but without success. Force of habit meant he was now detesting this stupid German monkey; this illegal alien who had invaded his land and who presumed to be better than him.

"It is a Mauser?"

"Of course."

Of course, thought Lev. You're so fucking perfect.

He held out the money. It was snatched up and replaced by the Mauser. It was a pocket pistol but still it felt heavy. And it felt good. It felt like quality. Lev held it up and took aim at a streetlamp. The handle felt ice cold and smooth.

"And bullets? I need bullets."

"Here." The soldier produced two small, identical boxes and handed them over. "Don't use them all at once."

It was like giving candy to a baby.

"Business done," said Lev, and without a pause he walked away, wishing to create distance as quickly as possible.

Fuck you, he thought.

The soldier headed off in the opposite direction, business forgotten.

Fuck you, he thought.

Lev, now feeling superior, consumed the darkness while at the same time fending it off. He rounded a corner and caught up two young men ahead of him. A bottle was passing between them. They turned sharply on their heels and nearly dropped the bottle. When they realised it was Lev Penkin they grinned. Lev smiled back. It was Sava and Burian. They were back in town: pissed and out of control. Lev greeted them with the passion and relief of a native engaging with his own kind. They both slapped him on the back. It was their standard, formulated greeting for their own kind.

"You're both back. Work done?"

"For now, 'til we get called back. They're still constructing."

"Good rates?"

Sava sniffed and sank more vodka. "Good enough."

Burian spoke. "You look like shit Lev."

"Thanks."

Section One: The Wild East

"But then so do we," added Sava. He passed the bottle over to Lev. "Take some."

"Of course." Graciously Lev helped himself and watched as Sava resumed his task in hand. It had been ongoing for years now.

Sava began to strip a poster from a wall. It had been recently pasted up. With big red capital letters it spoke out loudly in both German and Ukrainian. It was a recruitment poster for the German Civil Service, Foreign Zone. It was temptation. With dirty broken fingernails Sava picked away at its edges and ripped away the top layer of paper in long thin lengths. It was like the start of a wallpapering job – one of many jobs he and Burian did to earn a living. They built houses, of any size and value, for anyone regardless of nationality, colour or faith; then decorated them. They fitted things. They fixed things. They cleaned up. They pulled things down. They dumped things. They stood in the rain and mixed cement. They took money from anybody. They mostly spent it. They saved little: reason being that as they had little to look forward to why bother saving?

Lev and Burian monitored his progress, sharing the bottle and the passing thrill.

"What you been up to Lev?"

"Same old shit."

"Nothing new?"

"No – sorry yes, I'm off to Prague."

"Prague? Why Prague?"

"My brother's in Prague."

Sava paused.

"I remember, he buggered off to Prague." He kicked away the paper which had accumulated at his feet.

"Holiday?" asked Burian.

"No. Hopefully to stay."

"Stay? How long?"

"To stay. Stay for good."

Sava stopped stripping paper and took possession of the bottle, satisfied by the damage he had done.

"Shit so you're out of here? Good for you. You'll come back and see us yes?"

Lev shrugged. "Don't know. Don't want to come back."

He watched the bottle being drained. It was almost empty. Sava handed him the bottle.

"Come on Lev let's go get really pissed. We have to do our heads in."

"No. Sorry, can't."

Section One: The Wild East

"What?"

"Got to be up early tomorrow."

Lev passed the bottle back. Now it was empty. And yes it was cheap nasty crap vodka. He was learning to hate the stuff.

Burian threw the bottle aside. It smashed across the pavement, sending glass everywhere. Burian was confused.

"Early? What's to get up early for round here?"

"Train. I'm leaving tomorrow. Got to get my train."

"Fuck. That was quick."

"No it wasn't."

"Well whatever. You can still get pissed."

"No I can't."

Lev suddenly felt deflated. He looked at Burian, and Sava, and the remains of the poster – as if that act of sabotage made any difference to the way the world worked. He remembered all the shit they had done together: all the bitching; all the pointless talk; all the worn out jokes; all the fighting; all the time wasted. It was shit he didn't want to see, touch or smell again. He didn't want it to get up his nose. He turned and began to walk away from it all. Burian swung round and tried to grab him by the shoulder. All he got was a fleeting touch. Lev shook him off and continued, undisturbed and unashamed.

"Lev where you going – it's us!"

"Hang on Penkin! One drink Penkin that's all!"

Lev didn't look back. Suddenly he felt very good about himself again. It was a state of mind he was coming to experience at an ever increasing frequency.

"You can't just dump us. We're your mates. Don't walk away I'm talking!"

Lev stopped, turned and stared, almost into the abyss. He held firm his outward appearance of solid, sweet indifference.

"You owe us a few drinks!" shouted Burian.

"A goodbye drink!" added Sava.

Burian laughed. "And then another goodbye drink!"

"And another!"

"And we end up pissed!"

"How about it Lev?"

Lev was not taken in by it. He had broken the connection, snapped it for good. It could not be put back together by any means.

"Sorry but no."

"We're your mates damn you!"

Lev gave them his 'I give up' look and walked on, not giving a shit about what was happening behind him. Burian rushed forward and

Section One: The Wild East

grabbed him by the arm, forcing a confrontation.

"Don't just walk away and fucking insult us!"

"Penkin's turning into a bloody German!" shouted Sava.

"Burian let go." Lev sounded tired, which only added to the insult.

"No."

"Very well." And with that Lev kicked him squarely in the balls.

Burian collapsed in agony, clutching both his balls. Sava was caught between two halves: one half wanted to laugh, hysterically; the other wanted to punch Lev Penkin. He decided to stay neutral: Penkin was looking fucking evil now.

Lev looked down at the buffoon writhing on the ground. It was a sorry sight.

"Sorry Burian but you were asking for that."

Again he turned away and walked on: pleased that he had tied up another loose end; pleased that he had a good gun in his pocket; proud of the fact that he could fight his friends as well as his enemies. He felt sure now that, if he had to, he could fight family. (Time to take on the world perhaps.)

◆

Lev paced up and down at the main gate of the Ghetto, trying not to watch the guard who was watching him from the safety of his booth, perched on a stool and chewing gum. The guard was fat and loathsome. He was an Ukrainian guard, part time. He was on the late shift and hated it.

When Isaak appeared, looking suspicious, Lev lit up and walked forward until he was almost on top of the barrier. The guard stood up but said nothing. Just watching was easier on the brain. He didn't notice the Jew, just the Ukrainian - trying to get in?

"Why did you call me?" asked Isaak, hands in pockets. It was not cold but he felt cold.

"To go out. It's my last night."

"I can't go out. It's too late to get a night pass."

"No problem about that." (The guard knew exactly what Lev meant.) "I have a car."

Isaak approached the barrier - but not too close.

"A car? Since when did you get a car?"

"Since today. Fancy a ride through town? No drinking, I promise."

Isaak was not that stupid. "But have you been drinking?"

Lev held his hands up in mock surrender. "Only a little I guess. Only a little, promise."

Section One: The Wild East

It was true and Isaak believed him. He had learnt the signs for when Lev was telling him a lie.

"Can I drive?"

"Yes, as much as you like."

Isaak was sold. The chance to drive a car again was just too much. He still remembered the first time with much pleasure.

"OK. If you can get me out of here."

Lev approached the guard who held out his hand even before the offer was made. Lev pushed a note into his hand, and a packet of quality cigarettes as a tip.

"Got any cigarettes?" he asked Isaak.

"Some."

"Give them to me."

Isaak stretched and handed over his half empty packet. It crossed the barrier. He watched it go. His cigarettes had left the Ghetto without him. Lev handed them on to the guard who didn't particularly want them: they were the cheap, nasty kind. But he took them anyway. He could hand them round and hold back the better ones for his own private use. The barrier was raised and Isaak was permitted to cross the line, slip out. As he did so another, older Jew slipped back in, possibly legally, possibly illegally. Either way he frowned at Isaak. He did not like Jews breaking the rules. It would only end in tears and trouble.

As if to welcome him to the party Lev handed Isaak all his current lottery tickets.

"Here, you have them."

Isaak accepted graciously but with blank expression.

"What if I win? I can't cash them."

"Pay someone to do it for you."

That made sense and carefully Isaak tucked them away.

Lev's car was parked well down the street, and off the street, and he led the way almost with ceremony. Isaak trail behind, breathing in the fresh air of his temporary freedom. It was an old car, nothing special; not German but Czech and Lev seemed to treat it tentatively, with kid gloves; still checking out all the controls and levers. Isaak sat in the front and waited for lift off. And when it came it was fast. Isaak decided to attach his seat belt.

Lev didn't speak. He had nothing to say. His intention was to motor along all the streets he had walked or run down year on year. He had to get past all the places and buildings which inhabited his youth for the last time. He did not intend to see any of it again. No going back. Only going forward. Isaak was loving it: so much to take in at such speed. He consumed it all. He felt alive. This was a good night out.

Section One: The Wild East

They had both cut loose. Both were on the run. Both suddenly felt like they had somewhere to go, and fast. Where to was not the concern, only the speed at which it happened.

Lev drove past his old school. It now looked like a feeble attempt at education for the masses. The gates were locked by a big padlock and chain - as if anybody would want to break in. As they flew past the library Lev slowed, as if to show respect. He wished now he had spent serious time in the place, if only to see what was on offer. He speeded up again once it was behind them. As he replayed the memories, and stripped them bare, and threw them out like old newspaper, Isaak became forgotten. Isaak grew impatient for his turn at the wheel. He kept looking across but Lev was always looking ahead in deep concentration. He was determined to cover every part of town, leave no stone unturned, discard everything which was useless.

Isaak was jealous. He wanted to wrestle the wheel away from Lev. He would never own a car even if he could afford it. There were cars in the Ghetto - his parents had one, an old rust bucket which didn't work - but cars were not allowed to be imported into the Ghetto. The Germans were very strict on that. Only spare parts were allowed, for which Jews paid a fortune, and they were rarely new. It was economic injustice on one side, economic advantage on the other.

They reached a set of traffic lights - one of the few in town - and waited while they were red. It was very late now and the street was deserted. They had the whole world to themselves but neither of them could make use of it. Another car drew up alongside. It was bigger, faster, cleaner. There were four fit young men in it. They could have been brothers. They stared across, as if on the warpath, as if at the zoo and wanting to see the caged animals close up. They were clearly Germans.

Lev looked ahead and held his breath while he waited for the lights to turn green. In this land there was no amber. Isaak did likewise, except he also gripped his thighs tightly. When the lights flipped Lev held back and the other car was gone in a flash, with the sounding of its loud horn and some waving. Nothing was said: instead the encounter was instantly forgotten. It was an anticlimax. Worse things had happened before and worse things would happen again. You could not avoid bumping into Germans. They did after all own the place. Finally, when he had had his fill, Lev offered to swap seats.

"You can drive?"

"Of course." Isaak felt insulted.

Isaak drove, slowly at first, then faster and faster as his confidence grew. Lev stared out of his window, miles away in his heart never

Section One: The Wild East

miles away in his head, doing his best to let go. Isaak took a roundabout at high speed and the car tilted at a perilous angle. Lev protested. For the first time the Jew was pulling all the ropes. As they came off the roundabout and screeched round the next bend Isaak suddenly had to slam on the brakes. Lev was thrown forwards and nearly bashed his head in against the windscreen. Rubber burnt and both broke out in a heavy sweat. A police car was blocking their side of the road.

"Shit."

"Bugger."

It was all they could say.

Beyond the police car a van had crashed into a tree. A man was slumped over his wheel; probably drunk; possibly dead; possibly passed out. A policeman peered in through the window, looking barely concerned, bored almost. He had run out of sympathy for such behaviour. The other policeman flagged down Isaak, ordering him to stop, even though Isaak had already done precisely that. He ordered them out of the car. Isaak complied quickly and stood to attention. Lev did so slowly, under protest.

The policeman looked at his catch, first one face then the other, then back again.

"Who's car is this?" He demanded to know.

Lev shot his hand up. "Mine."

He quickly whipped out his fake ID card and the policeman flashed a perfunctory look at it before setting all his attention on Isaak. Isaak was doing his best to not shit in his pants. The policeman waved a finger.

"Show me."

Isaak produced his own ID card and waited for the backlash. The policeman screwed up his face and looked across at his mate who was now banging on the window and trying to force open the door. The door was stuck, jammed by the distorted body frame of the crumpled van.

"Where's your star!"

"It fell off. I wanted to go back for it but my friend didn't have the time. He was in too much of a rush."

Lev looked across at Isaak, undecided as to whether to back him or not.

"Raise your arms!"

Isaak raised his arms in a flash whereupon the policeman rammed his spare hand into all the pockets he could find and produced a yellow star badge.

Section One: The Wild East

"What's this Jew!"

Isaak wanted to faint. It was his easiest way out. The policeman dropped the star - as if it was too poisonous to hold - and slapped Isaak across the face. He loved slapping Jews across the face: he had no one else to slap.

"Show me your night pass!"

"I haven't got one."

Isaak felt the ground opening up beneath him. He was a lost soul, a lost cause. He was in for a battering. It would be hell. He was as good as dead.

"Get in the back of the car!" He spoke to Lev without turning his head. "You, clear off out of here."

He wrote down the registration number and watched the young Ukrainian - one of his own - clear off. Lev did not look back at Isaak. Isaak did not look at Lev. They were separate again, each alone again. Were they still friends? Impossible to tell. Lev sped away as Isaak was thrown into the back of the police car. The other policeman kicked the van door in frustration and rejoined his partner. Let the drunken sod sleep it off, or die. Someone would come and collect him in the morning - like rubbish which had to be taken to the civic dump.

At the first chance he got, Lev, far away, dumped the car he had stolen earlier and headed off to one of his usual haunts. He really needed a drink, a stiff drink, or two. This was one more thing he had to let go of and he needed a strong shot of alcohol to achieve it. (His brother had once warned him never to party with the Jews.)

Isaak ended up in a cell for the night at the local police station. He was told that if his parents or 'a load of Jews' coughed up the right amount he could be out by tomorrow. He was given one phone call.

Section Two: Going Underground

Going Underground

On the morning of his departure there was no time and little light for the raising of the flag, so duty was set aside. Franz dressed to travel, and rechecked his kitbag and his uniform contained within. It would be a heavy day and from the moment he awoke, pre-dawn, Franz felt it bearing down. It kept him subdued, unresponsive. He avoided all thoughts about the day ahead. It was no day for celebration. He just did what he had to do to take one step forward. But he did it on knife-edge. He wanted to go as much as he wanted to stay. He wanted to try the new but did not want to let go of the old, the familiar. He was soon to be regarded as a man but right now he was happy to remain the boy he had grown up with.

Franz did not know why but he was driven to take his BMW for a spin. Barely awake, it stretched him like an elastic band. He wanted to snap back to normality. Throttle open, he screamed past two labourers from a local village. They shuffled along, moving more like prisoners than free men. They recognised him and were surprised to see him up so early. One passed comment. The other laughed. Restrained by deadlines he soon stopped and sat with the engine running. This was his land and he wanted to snatch up a piece to take with him. But he couldn't. He could only look on - until he ran out of time and had to get home.

The early rise, before dawn, had crushed the senses. The hot breakfast was no tonic and the Helmer family remained lethargic. With heavy introspection Franz ate his breakfast, with nothing new to say to his parents. They in turn watched his every move and likewise had nothing new to say to him. Herr Helmer hid behind small, inconsequential comments, conscious that someone had to say something; and as head of the household that duty fell upon him. Frau Helmer on the other hand had nothing to say but plenty to give. She imagined him on the day: looking perfect; the image of every German mother's perfect boy on the edge of manhood. He was her perfect poster boy. Unlike her husband Frau Helmer desired perfection but did not demand it.

Frau Helmer checked her son over thoroughly, making sure he was ready to be released into the big wide world. She made sure his packed lunch was up to scratch and gave him all her spare cash. Franz thanked his mother and added it to his existing pile. He now felt cash rich. She checked he had his tickets on him along with the list of telephone numbers and addresses she had carefully copied out. She hugged him

Section Two: Going Underground

close until he was straining to break free, and protesting. She kept demanding assurances that he would be alright and Franz kept giving them. (In comparison Herr Helmer demanded only once an assurance that his son act 'fit and proper'. And Franz gave that too.) When it was time to depart for the station Frau Helmer finally let go. The break was clean and quick. Despite the protest she would not come to see her son off at the station. So he took the dogs instead.

Father and son, Franz Senior and Franz Junior, drove to the station along empty roads, in poor morning light and with nothing to say. The cold was held back by the car heater and the silence was only broken by the odd outburst of barking as the dogs spotted something of interest or danger. During the drive Franz entered a sleepy, dreamlike state such that only his body maintained the connection with reality. It was only broken when they hit town.

◆

That morning Lev awoke slow to think, slow to respond, slow to take charge of his life. But when he did something felt wrong, terribly wrong. Then he was shot right through with a bolt of realisation: the alarm had already gone off and he had knocked it to the floor to shut the damn thing up. He sat up, felt his head, leaned out of the bed and picked it up. Time said he was really late. Cursing, Lev dragged himself from his warm bed and hurried to make up for lost time. He threw cold water over his face and dressed, not bothering to brush teeth or comb hair. He grabbed his bag and left the room. He had packed it the day before with all that mattered. It did not amount to much. Most of his worth was wrapped up inside his old leather wallet.

Downstairs he shot into the toilet and took his final, symbolic piss. Then he was forced to shit. He did so, under duress, and made a point of not flushing the toilet. Let it be a leaving present for that man Penkin. Next he rushed into the kitchen to steal food – if it was still edible he wanted it. Yes now it felt like stealing, stealing from his own house, stealing from Penkin. Stealing felt good.

He took yesterday's bread, cheese and some decent cuts of ham. He wrapped it up and stuffed it into his bag. He drank up the last of the milk then was off: out and off; out and off and on his way; out and off and on his way and looking forward to a bright new future alongside the only person who truly mattered to him in this brave new world of first class versus second class, us versus them, German versus Ukrainian, Ukrainian versus Russian, Jew versus non-Jew. It didn't feel right, or even productive, but it was all he had going for him. It

Section Two: Going Underground

was the system, so he had to play it.

Lev was stopped in his tracks by the sight of Penkin fast asleep in his chair: snoring as usual; dead to the world as usual; indifferent to what his son was doing, as usual. He corrected himself and walked on as normal past the living room and towards the front door. He was determined to leave without a single word being spoken; without anger, without pity, without regret, without a care. He almost made it.

Just before he reached out for the door handle he stopped and turned to take one last look at Penkin. That sad man who sat snoring was no longer his dad but just Penkin, and any old Penkin. It was a common name. Lev wished for Penkin to be awake: to see him walk out for the last time; to feel regret for the past; to feel the pain of his present predicament; to feel afraid for the future; to beg for a second chance; to fall to his knees, helpless like a child. But the drunken sod was soundly asleep and snoring as if to keep at bay all the sounds of the world which conspired to drown him out; as if the act of snoring was a noble activity. Lev wanted the man to open his eyes, if only a little, for a second or two; to share the pain; to be stuck with the final, lasting image of his second son walking out on him. But no, Penkin remained fast asleep, exhausted by what life continued to throw at him; snoring as if it was his only way of taking in oxygen.

Lev produced his now precious German Mauser and pointed it squarely at the man's head. Then he pointed it at the heart. Despite time pressing Lev savoured the moment. It felt delicious on the tongue, a little daunting perhaps, deranged even, but so what. Yes this was what guns were made for: to rid their owners of unwanted, undiluted pain; to set the record straight; to wipe the slate clean by wiping out. Yes guns were a great invention. But he had a train to catch, so he pulled the trigger.

Click.

"Bang," said Lev in a calm quiet voice.

But nothing changed: that man Penkin was still snoring. Yet still Lev left the house feeling satisfied, free and superior. After making the point of slamming the door behind him – to wake the bastard up – Lev immediately hid his gun away. That man Penkin would never know that he had been killed in cold blood by his own son. That would make it twice in a row now. Third time he might not be so lucky.

Conscious of the time, Lev tried to break into a run, but for all his efforts he was reduced to a pathetic plod. The railway station was not that far but there was so little time, so little time. As he lumbered along, bag slung over his shoulder, looking for all the world like a zombie, Lev began to feel bitter and twisted – twisted up again when he

Section Two: Going Underground

had so successfully untwisted himself. He always had plenty of time but it was never in the right place at the right time. On the other hand he rarely had enough money but he always had it at the right time, and always managed to use it to make a little more. A feeling of dread began to rise up inside him: he wasn't going to make it. He was going to miss his train. He was going to be stuck here, here in this shit hole some called home while others made themselves a life fit for living.

Suddenly everything changed in an instant and Lev was saved: he heard an approaching truck. He knew that truck and it was going his way. He waved it down, furiously, as if his life depended on it – which perhaps it did – and begged the driver to give him a lift to the station. Payment of an outstanding favour meant he got his way. And he was on his way.

♦

The mainline station was busy. The train going north was due to arrive sometime in the next twenty minutes or so and many would be joining it. Few would be disembarking. Most of the time the station was a stale, empty place: doing nothing despite being something so important it was on every map. And then twice or three times a day it would burst into life, bristle, then quickly close back down, having expelled its human seed or captured its remains.

Herr Helmer parked the Mercedes in the German zone and Franz attached the leads to the dogs. The dogs were excited, looking forward to a good walk. They would be disappointed. Franz stroked each one, hard. Had he been able to hug them he would have done that too. He needed a hug right now. Franz found it difficult to say goodbye. He didn't know it but he loved them. Likewise they didn't know it but they loved him.

Herr Helmer led the way in and quickly through the ticket office come waiting room, not intending to stop until he reached the platform area reserved exclusively for use by Germans. That changed when he spotted Penkin spying from a window and trying not to be seen. The man was red in the face and looked positively unwell. Penkin was being the perfect Penkin.

"Penkin what are you up to?"

The words blasted across the room and everybody looked around at the German. He looked dangerous. Franz flinched, feeling very uncomfortable despite his superior status in this part of the world.

Penkin, caught off guard, nearly fell from the slippery wooden bench which spanned the length of one wall. He had the look of

Section Two: Going Underground

someone caught doing something terribly wrong. It was Herr Helmer and Herr Helmer had him in his sights. Franz held on to the dogs. They were straining at the leash. They wanted to attack.

"Seeing my son off."

Penkin waited for the next question but it never came. Herr Helmer had no more interest in him and was moving on. Penkin watched the young Franz falling in behind his father. Franz Helmer was nothing like his own son - he never had been. It was the same thought Penkin had entertained many times before, and one he could never take forward, evolve or deconstruct. Its existence inside his head continued to stump him.

The German zone of the platform was empty save for two soldiers taking leave and looking all the more tired for it. They were totally switched off. The addition of the two Helmers doubled the population but still the Germans were heavily outnumbered, not that they noticed: they were cut off in their own zone. The numbers did not matter. Franz passed the leads across to his father and said a final goodbye to his dogs. They had no clue. They were more interested in what was happening further down the platform. It was full of life: foreign workers returning home; long distance commuters setting off to work; locals awaiting the return of family members. It gave off a lot of noise and a lot of unfamiliar smells. An extended family of peasants loaded up with shabby suitcases looked miserable as they said goodbye to other, equally miserable peasants. Amongst it all stood Lev, impassive, stoic, bag wedged firmly between his feet, arms folded.

Franz saw him and the sight calmed him. Everything was going to plan. He would not travel alone. Herr Helmer saw him but made no connection with his son. How could that boy and his son be connected? The Penkin boy was in the non-German zone. When he boarded the train he would be confined in the non-German section, unable by law to cross into German First Class. The two could never meet. No, it was chance. The two were not in league, and anyway for one German to be seen berating another in public was simply not on. Germans must never fall out in front of the natives.

Franz, dreading the arrival of the train, made a quick dash to the toilets. A sign on the door - in German and exclusively for Germans - said 'temporarily not in use'. Franz ignored it and rushed in. The cleaner inside, a discreet Jew, thought it best to leave and apologized on the way out. He would come back later.

Back with his father Franz waited in silence, unaware that his father was busting a gut to think of something right to say. The task was beyond him so in frustration he slapped his thigh and pulled the dogs in

Section Two: Going Underground

close to his side. They were straining at the leash to be set free. They wanted to run, chase, mingle with the crowd. And in some ways so did Herr Helmer. Franz just wanted to get on the train with minimum fuss and sit in his own carriage, and wait for Lev to join him.

Finally the train arrived and as it pulled up the crowd, disturbed, began to move and fight for position. At that point father and son found things to say to each other, and it was the obvious: farewell and 'Heil Hitler!'. The accompanying handshake was short and firm, nothing more than business like. A station porter picked up the kitbag and held open a carriage door for the Germans. As his son stepped onboard Herr Helmer said his last.

"I'll see you at the hotel then. Have fun but be good."
"I will."
"You are a Helmer. Remember that."
"I'll remember."

And that was that. Simple. The door was slammed shut and the porter tipped his hat. Franz opened the window and waited for the train to move so he could wave. Lev meanwhile had jumped onboard third class and grabbed a seat immediately by the door. He did not look out, only around, and then only to check out the scenery and the faces. He was happy to close in and close down. Penkin, face against the window, wished he could still see his son. Seeing he could handle: talking he could not.

The train blew its siren and pulled out of the station. It began to shake and rattle as it increased its speed. It wanted to be gone, away from this place. Those left on the platform began to scatter: back to town, back to the country; back to their special lives in a very special part of the Reich. Franz waved – and remembered to smile - for as long as was necessary then sat down. He had the whole carriage to himself, which felt good, but still he felt vulnerable - which was stupid for a German. Lev glanced out only once, to check that the station, and everything it was connected to, was slipping away out of sight. Open countryside was what he wanted to see. He wanted emptiness.

Meanwhile Isaak awoke in his cell, having barely slept on the hard bed. Only total exhaustion of the mind and body had overcome its discomfort. He had only managed to get about three hours sleep and every bone in his body was aching. He was in a dreadful state, in a dreadful state. In time he was given the standard breakfast ration and allowed to make his one phone call. Watched by the duty officer behind the desk and held by another Isaak rang the number of the communal telephone inside the Ghetto. When the message reached his father the man was furious - furious at his son's stupid conduct - furious

Section Two: Going Underground

at the fine he would have to pay to recover his son. On hearing the news his mother became worried, and would remain worried until her son was safely back in her arms back inside the family house back inside the Ghetto. All three were expecting a quick release.

◆

As the train sped on Lev sat surrounded by bodies: some broken, burnt out; some buried in - or by - their thoughts; some keen to make conversation and break the boredom; some alert, on guard; some shut down, switched off, not wishing to waste energy. For Lev they were an annoyance, a reminder that he had not left it all behind. So he sat tight and, as time began to weigh heavy, he forced himself to stare out of the window, pretending to be interested in the nothingness of the passing scenery. He could only brood.

Franz on the other hand sat alone in German class, desperate for company. It was too much space and time to fill by himself. He wanted to put his feet up but the sign said no. Rules were not there to be broken. He could only brood.

The next stop seemed to be in the middle of nowhere but actually it somewhere important: it was the Polish-Ukrainian border - a place of irritation for the German government. There Lev jumped out and, with Franz holding open his door, jumped back in. Franz had stuck his neck out, in both senses. Together, as predicted by the laws of mathematics, the two negatives combined to form a positive. Lev, bowled over by the step change in the quality of the fixtures and fittings, kicked off his shoes and stretched out across one line of seats, as if to sunbathe. Franz, not to be outdone, followed suit. Sod the sign. If peasants were breaking the rules why not him?

With six hours or more to kill the carriage became their private space, a shared bedroom with a 'keep out' sign on the door. No one else was allowed in. No one else could get in. No one could see them, hear them, judge them or dictate to them. Despite being cooped up in a small space they had all the freedom in the world to think and say whatever came into their heads - like the camp rooftop but with better seating. And it would remain so until they reached Lvov.

They talked. They pooled their resources: Franz had the food; Lev had the booze. They played cards. They nodded off. They prodded each other awake. They played cards again. They talked some more. And so it went on, round and round, up and down. They speculated about the future but with little success. It was too far away. They revisited the past: turning it over, pulling it apart for closer

Section Two: Going Underground

examination; editing, discarding and disowning. They compared notes. They compared guns: proudly Lev produced his new Mauser pocket pistol and, not to be outdone, Franz produced his Luger P08. They swapped weapons and pointed them at the windows, and pretended to shoot the enemy. Then they swapped again and put them away. For now they were nothing more than toy pistols being fired by toy soldiers.

They compared mothers, both talking about them in the past, even though only one of them had good reason to: one had been mostly strict but always fair and reliable; one had been mostly lazy, unreliable, inconsistent and impossible to understand at times. They compared fathers: one was always too strict, too powerful, too sure of himself; one would always be an arsehole; both were remote, beyond reach - on top of a hill or down in a hole.

Lev talked about his brother and Franz was jealous. He had no brother - and why not? Was it not the duty of all good Germans to have at least two children? Lev replayed the day Luka had stood up to their dad, fought back and defeated him. That was the day the balance of power had shifted and Penkin was proved to be weak, undeserving of respect from his children. From that moment on Lev had merely bided his time until he too had the muscle to stand his ground, fight back and win. Such talk was all wasted on Franz: he could not conceive of a world in which you crossed your father. When respect was due respect was given. (On the few occasions he had failed to do so he had later disowned himself for such behaviour.) It was a rule which, when older and married with children, Franz intended to exercise. (He did not like having his life planned out, yet he had planned it out.)

They talked about growing up 'together' but apart: many times Herr Helmer had pulled them apart; many times Frau Helmer had let them play. Penkin had merely looked on, calculating, as if watching how his investment was growing, performing. For both of them the friendship they had made had been the first substantial act of rebellion. For Lev more had followed, for Franz none. Their friendship had started off in all innocence, driven by natural circumstance and the desire of all small boys to find allies against a world full of bigger boys. Over time, as it was frowned upon and became apparent that it was the wrong thing to do, so they enforced it; refusing to let it go while more and more concealing its importance. The more it was the 'wrong thing to do' the more they protected it; the more bloody-minded they became. It became the one big secret.

The mothers had never been the problem: if anything they had encouraged it with the odd wink here, the odd suggestion there and the occasional wise statement like 'once you've made a friend you don't let

Section Two: Going Underground

him go' or 'it's good to mix it up a little'. No, it had just been the fathers. And so now they had their secret bond and in the privacy of the German class carriage they could exercise it to the full.

They laughed about the time when Franz, aged ten, had joined the junior branch of the Hitler Youth and Lev, afraid he was missing out on something, had asked Herr Helmer if he could join too. The look of complete bewilderment on the man's face still stuck in their minds like a treasured possession. A few years later when Lev first saw Franz dressed to impress in his new 'proper' Hitler Youth uniform he had simply laughed and pointed at the toy soldier. He had said Franz looked stupid so Franz had kicked him, so Lev had kicked him back: neither very hard, just enough to preserve dignity on both sides. The next time Lev did such a thing Franz had not been alone: he had to step in to prevent Lev being attacked by another member of the Hitler Youth. After that Lev learnt to take the boys in brown seriously - or at least give that impression - and likewise their Fuehrer, their greatest German alive. You did not ridicule that man's manner of speech, nor his moustache, nor his ramblings on the radio, nor his twisted vicious vision. In fact, German or not, you quickly learnt not to go anywhere near him. Keep him distant and he did not shock or cause you harm. Yet funnily enough Lev, like many others - including Germans - had discovered that he could openly laugh at Reichsmarschall Goering, poke fun at his great size, and get away with it.

Now Lev said that whenever he saw the Hitler Youth on the march he saw only a group of stuck up, brainless morons - Franz excluded of course - who had nothing better to do than to make a racket. Franz conceded that he was probably right. Most of the others - Bruno especially - were not the brightest bunch and were easily led. And yes, over the years it had turned into a tiresome routine: the same town marches; the same stuffy roll calls; the same boring speeches - but he loved the uniform and the summer camps where you got to meet real good-looking girls. That bit he defended with zeal.

They recalled all the stupid things they had done, and the clever ones: like the time they came across an unexploded bomb and nearly blew themselves up, but then made money out of it. Franz should have reported it immediately to his father but instead left it to Lev, who in turn told Luka, who in turn claimed the reward which he later split with Lev. Lev in turned shared his half with Franz.

They veered between talking serious and talking nonsense; between attack and defence; between guarded words and outright confession. Lev found it easy to wind his German friend up. He simply had to talk about girls: German girls versus Ukrainian girls. He only had to say

Section Two: Going Underground

something rude about German girls and their - preferably naked - bodies and Franz would come storming to their defence. Lev could have dirty thoughts about Ukrainian girls, non-Germans, but not German girls. On the subject of the opposite sex Franz was a total hypocrite. If Franz tried the same, in reverse, Lev would simply laugh it off. He knew Ukrainian girls like Franz never would.

And when they ran out of talk they were happy to sink into the silence and contemplate what they had left behind and what lay ahead. Lev had left it all behind and had little, possibly nothing, to look forward to. Franz by contrast had left nothing behind. He carried it all with him and he had it all to look forward to. Like it or not his life had a big plan. Lev had no such thing. He did not even have a roadmap, just total freedom to roam - and the risk which came with it.

Meanwhile while Franz and Lev tossed and turned, rolled and stretched, Isaak sat huddled up in a ball of self-conscious restlessness, wondering why time was moving so slowly and leaving him stuck, to die. His eyes scanned the wall in front of him, up and down, from left to right; down and up, from right to left. It was a blank white wall and he wanted to write all over it. He wanted to turn it into a piece of paper. But he had no pen, no pencil. He had asked the guard for such but had been refused. What did a Jew need with pen and paper? Make notes? Spy and take notes? No way that was going to happen. But it was not about taking notes, Isaak simply wanted to maintain his daily diary. Instead he would have to remember his thoughts for later recording - and with so much time to spare many came his way.

♦

Their overnight stop in Lvov was uneventful save for a couple of annoying Polish youths and the sex. The Poles came free. They could not resist the temptation to wind up a German with airs of superiority: he referred to their sweet home as Lemberg. Lvov - or Lemberg - was an ancient town; a town well worn by its inhabitants, and worn down by wars – wars between Poles, Austrians, Prussians and Russians, always with Ukrainians, White Russians and Cossacks providing the cannon fodder. The town had been built in part by Jews, but now there were no Jews, and the vacuum of commerce had barely been filled. Their houses had been reassigned to those in the know and their shops sold to those with a record of incompetence. It was a dull place for most of the year, except in high summer when it died in the heat and choked on the dust. On the surface it was a place bereft of vitality, emotion. Beneath it was a hornets nest of denial, anger, bitter

Section Two: Going Underground

resentment and guarded ambitions. Through sheer necessity a warm welcome for strangers had been discarded: best they move on was the general consensus.

Lvov - or Lemberg - was a town always far away from the mainstream; yet strongly dynamic as ethnic group rubbed shoulders with ethnic group, and traded. Regardless of political outlook and personal temperament trade mattered, and trade went on, though it rarely soared. Respectability was nailed to doors and windows, but no more. Vice and prostitution maintained their presence. Criminals, businessmen and law enforcement officers drank side by side in the same bars. The new department store, still outnumbered, fought against the small shops.

In the back streets children skipped in and out of the gutters, or sat on walls and swung their legs to the beat of a nursery rhyme. Some leaned against buildings and chewed on time as if begrudging its passing. The degree of boredom which afflicted all varied from the short-lived to the serious. They had not been taught to smile so they did not smile. They were not well-educated so they had no expectations, only blunt motivation and frequent frustrations to manage. They had been denied emotional freedom by their parents - also emotionally crippled - so they baulked at any friendly gesture, any warm expression, any touching sensitivity. In time they would discover sex – and plenty of it – but never that True Love. They would remain a cold lot, and slowly freeze over. Lev recognised the place. Franz did not.

Franz was beaten, best of three, in an alcohol induced arm wrestle with the Poles while Lev looked on, faintly amused. The sex had to be paid for at the local brothel - cash in advance. The two were in and out in under thirty minutes and back in the room reserved for Franz all the worse for wear. Franz had to smuggle Lev in under the eyes of a sleepy hotel desk attendant as strictly speaking it was a service provided only for Germans passing through. There they drank more beer and counted the cost, and wondered about the next day whilst arguing over the past hour. Franz now regarded himself as a ladies' man, an old hand. He had it in his head that sex was something he handed out as a favour, much like a doctor handed out pills to the unfortunate. They fell asleep only through boredom - boredom with the place, boredom with each other. Travelling was supposed to be exciting: they were finding it tiresome as so much free time had to be digested.

◆

Section Two: Going Underground

They arrived in Prague the next day, late afternoon, by which time Lev had persuaded Franz to stay one night. It had been hard work. Lev was asking Franz to lie, go back on his word, and Franz agreed for one reason only; the best reason, to delay separation from his best friend. Letting go of Lev was proving difficult.

Prague was different from their home town: Prague was busy; Prague was moving; Prague carried an air of history and sophistication. They felt it the moment they stepped off the train. This was a new kind of land and it immediately woke them up, stood them to attention. They were in an alien world: the world of the crowded, fast moving city. No empty spaces here. No wasted breath. No wasted time. Or so it appeared.

Franz was a little confused. Wasn't Berlin suppose to be the busiest, most spectacular place on the planet? Dazzled by its grand architecture he had to keep reading the signs to remind himself that this was only Prague central station. If this was just their station then what was the rest of Prague like? For Lev it was a case of 'dream come true'. He sensed this was a place where he could live an invisible life and make money. This was a place where he could die quite content. No looking back for Lev.

They headed up the stairs away from the platform towards the world waiting for them outside. The magnificence of the building planted the feeling that they had left somewhere inconsequential, wasted, wanting even, and arrived somewhere special, somewhere with glamour and dignity. And it was not even Germany proper yet. Franz took that as a good sign. They sat down near the station entrance by a tobacconist and watched the world fly by, content to soak it all up. With a change of plan Franz had to make that important phone call but delayed until he was sure he had got his line right, and had found the courage. His luck was in: Bridget took the call and he found it easy to lie to her. He took control of the conversation, said what he had to say, quickly, and before the girl could ask questions said he was desperate to see her. Before it got too theatrical - it was never emotional - he cut short the call by declaring he had to go help his friend who was in a spot of trouble. After he put the phone down and collected his change he felt quite proud of his achievement.

A growing commotion outside drew them outside. Something ugly was brewing in the shape of an ugly crowd. There were the ugly faces of students holding up provocative placards and faceless policemen who had no intention of letting them protest. On any other day the students would not be ugly but pleasant, even accommodating. But not today. Today was a good day at this special time in this special year to

Section Two: Going Underground

make a protest. It was a time to stick up two fingers and ensure it made international news. On a point of principle some Czech students had a beef with their sad, sold out government - a government which had no intention of standing up for the true interests of its people. In return the government had a beef with those students to whom it had given a first class education only to see resentment thrown back in its face, not gratitude.

The students who were protesting this day had the least to lose, the most to gain. They had been reading too much, watching too much, learning too much, and ignoring the advice of their parents who had grown up in harder, less forgiving times. This was their first protest, and as such their innocence was magnified beyond sweetness to suit the moment. They failed to see what the big deal was: thinking and shouting it out loud was an ancient part of human nature. The protest looked more personal than political. The students took the arrival of the police as an insult. All they wanted to do was protest politely, express themselves with intelligence and vigour, then go home or go and get drunk. Some played upbeat music loudly from portable radios, but the sweet sound was soon swamped.

Franz and Lev took opposite sides, whilst at the same time declaring total neutrality. Lev wanted to be in there with them as one of them: angry, making trouble; standing up for the underdog; setting the world to rights; having fun. Franz thought the whole thing was undignified, outrageous, a scandal. Though a bit of him did find it exciting to watch.

With his head in the clouds Lev started to shout and stamp his feet. Having just arrived, an outsider, a Ukrainian, he felt protected, beyond reach. He had no idea what the protest was about but felt sure it had right on its side. In his world there was no other possibility. When he started moving towards the front line Franz tried to pull him back, but without success. Despite that he refused to let go: just as he could not let go spiritually he could not let go physically. The time was not right yet. They were best friends and best friends had to stick together.

The voice of a Ukrainian attracted the attention of the police and two turned on him. His shouting became louder and more heated, and he spat at his new enemies whilst Franz pleaded with him to stop. Lev wanted to hit a policeman, just one of them, just for the pleasure of it, and he kicked out. That was enough: Lev was thrown into the back of a van and Franz followed him in. They joined a couple of despondent looking students clutching hands for strength. Detached from their group they were now lacking it.

A now hysterical Lev began to laugh. He was lapping it all up. He

Section Two: Going Underground

had arrived in style. He had made his entrance. In reality it was a catastrophe but he did not see it that way yet. He felt invincible, else he had a death wish. Franz on the other hand was petrified: his universe had just collapsed. The policeman on the door looked them both up and down before settling on Franz.

"He's a Slav. You're not. You German?"

"Yes." The reply had to crawl out of Franz's throat.

Franz gulped and then remembered that, yes, he was German; and not just any German but a special German, a special German with a special mission. He was just about to say something, bounce back, when the policeman swore and kicked the door wide open.

"Fucking hell! You. Get out of here." He pointed the way out with his thumb - not that it was necessary.

"Not without my friend."

Franz spoke as he had been taught to speak: calmly, with authority, with the knowledge that he was in the right.

"No."

"Then I don't go."

Franz was feeling power rising up within him, and it was real in every sense. He pulled out his letter from his jacket pocket and unfolded it. The letterhead with the bold red swastika begged attention. Franz smiled, appreciating its impact. Yes a swastika could still scare. He held it out, up to the man's face with all the ceremony and weight of a civil right's lawyer.

"Look who sent me this. Look what it says. See where I have to be. See who I have to meet."

Franz did not swear. He kept his cool. Like all good Helmers he took command of the situation and turned it around. Father would have been proud.

The address at the top of the letter grabbed the policeman by the throat and forced him to read on. He did not get through it all but jumped to the signature at the bottom. That was enough: he got the point and backed down. There was nothing in his rule book about how to deal this. Best be rid of it. He gave Lev one last dirty look of wishful thinking before telling him to also get lost. Lev gave back as good as he got before following Franz back out onto dry land. They both landed on their feet - each now smug for different reasons - and returned to the station to reclaim their bags. They purchased cigarettes and chocolate, and settled back down in their chosen spot. They had just had a dangerous little adventure and even Franz was loathed to admit that it had felt good. And still Luka had yet to show. He was very late.

Section Two: Going Underground

And then he appeared, as promised, cutting a path through the crowd, knowing he was late. Lev could not take his eyes off him. That was his brother. He stood up, shouted, and waved his hands high in the air to attract his brother's attention. Luka drew up out of breath, and with space to spare. He had been running, possibly to make up time, possibly from something. Their faces lit up and they became tongue-tied as each locked on to the other; each looking for change, and finding it.

Luka looked Lev up and down as if to make sure it really was him. Lev looked back as if to reassure him that it was, and nothing less. Lev wanted to reach out and touch his brother - his brother who had put on weight - but held back, sensing now was not the time. They were in a bubble - with Franz clinging to the outside. There were no mothers or fathers to get in their way; no Ukrainians, no Germans, no Jews; just two brothers alone, possibly two broken brothers in need of repair. Neither was sure what to do next. Neither was sure of what the other was expecting. Reunions were something neither of them had experience of.

Instinctively each took a step forward and closed the gap: there were no tears; there were no hugs; but smiles did break out. Each had tonnes to say but no way of engaging. Questions demanding release were held back. There was dialogue but it was emotional not vocal. Speaking was too difficult to attempt. They would talk lots later: now was not the time, and Franz was in the way. Luka turned on him.

"Do I know you?" he asked in his native tongue.

The question was delivered with his standard overtone of threat, even though this time he meant it as a slight provocation. He was confused by the presence of an extra body.

Franz refused to be intimidated and folded his arms. "You'll have to speak German."

Franz struggled to place the face and link it to his vague memories of Luka when he and Lev had been small and Luka had loomed over them all powerful.

Luka switched back to his brother. "He's a German?"

"Franz. That's Franz Helmer."

Luka's eyes lit up. "Ah yes. Little Franz Helmer. Now I remember."

And still they stuck to Ukrainian, which Franz didn't like.

"Follow me," said Luka.

It was an order: Lev picked up his bag and followed his brother. Franz picked up his kitbag and followed Lev. He had no other option except to follow. Luka walked away fast, avoiding the disturbance

Section Two: Going Underground

outside, and more importantly the police. He kept looking back over his shoulder. There were too many policemen out today, a situation he did not like. He moved fast. He was nervous, on edge. He always had to get somewhere fast, or get away fast. Then suddenly he stopped, having realized that the German kid was still with them.

"What's he doing?"

"He's coming with us," explained Lev. "He's staying just one night then going on to Berlin. I said he could. I asked him."

Luka looked at Franz as if he, like all Germans, had stolen something from him. But he said nothing and instead walked on; and on; and on, never once pausing. Lev kept close to his brother: ten years had been stripped off him. He could see his brother was not happy about the situation, as could Franz; but whereas Franz didn't care, Lev did.

Franz was impressed by the city, if not its inhabitants. The city looked set for celebration, a glorious Nazi celebration, but none of its citizens appeared to be in a festive mood. Each and every one hurried on his or her way as if to avoid the thunderous call of the red banners, bunting and flags. There were only so many swastikas and party lines a man could digest.

In time the splendour of central Prague was left behind, to be replaced by the mundane of any modern city. They passed through narrow streets littered with muck and rubbish bins stuffed high; and grey, soulless tenement buildings - buildings devoid of colour but filled to capacity with those unable to get out and move on up. In the poorer places they passed by people who had the poor faces to match. They passed by a gang of bored, dangerous looking kids but one look from Luka and they were no trouble.

Franz became miserable. The place was depressing and he was regretting his decision to break his journey. He missed the colour of green - green grass, green fields, green hills - and all the space it filled. And all around him were glum, unhappy people on the move; all with somewhere to go but no positive wish or reason to arrive. He looked at Lev. Lev seemed happy enough. Perhaps it was just him: after all he was a German in a foreign city in a land ruled by the Germans. He tried to shrug off his mood but to no avail. Lev meanwhile was taking measurements. He saw locals who were better dressed, better behaved, even better fed, but not smarter. He saw poor people, broken, without fight. Yes he felt sure he could outsmart all these people.

Finally they stopped walking and entered a building, to begin a long climb up its stairs. It was a block of flats, the kind which always had a reputation. Franz refused to climb, demanding a break first. He had to

Section Two: Going Underground

rest his legs. Lev was glad. Luka was not and told them to get a move on. When they did reach Luka's flat, on the fourth floor, he opened his front door slowly, in the manner of someone expecting trouble on the other side.

The flat gave off a bad smell: a mix of decaying food on dirty dishes, dirty clothes and dirty bodies. And it didn't look appetising. Visitors had to tread carefully along a hall piled high with all manner of goods. The living room was no better. You had to find a space, make space, or squeeze in. The place was a warehouse by any other name. Human beings came second. Luka was proud of it and lived comfortably in its skin. Lev accepted it. Franz was appalled. Neither said anything. They dumped their bags as instructed and sat, starving, while Luka turned over his thoughts.

"Have you two eaten today?" he asked.

"We had breakfast," said Lev.

"Why doesn't he speak German. I know he can speak German," said Franz to Lev.

Lev had to shrug him off. He couldn't take sides.

Luka looked at his watch - an expensive watch which caught Lev by surprise. "I can eat now."

He led them back outside and on to a nearby cafe, his regular: a cheap, shabby place where food was hastily prepared whilst minds were on other matters; a place where the menu on the wall had nothing to hide and little to say for itself; a place where hygiene was a bonus. Regular customers looked up and registered Luka as he entered. They looked at Lev, curious, and at Franz, baffled. The owner knew Luka and tolerated him. He was not welcoming and delivered their order expecting no thanks and receiving none. They tucked into their cheap food and beer and said little more than was necessary - though this place was a much a place for talking as for eating: talking of the kind best not overheard. Franz cut into his sausage with hunger but a lack of relish. This was not home cooking.

Soon after they began dining a smart, well-dressed man entered the cafe. He wore a matching suit and tie. He power dressed. He splashed on the best aftershave. He wore the best jewellery. He never allowed his hair to grow out of shape - it had to be controlled. He always carried a silk handkerchief in his left trouser pocket. His expression was razor sharp, his intentions closely guarded. He carried an air of authority which made many look up and take note. Some felt their food had been spoilt.

The man had a swagger, a way of moving through air without getting touched and around obstacles without giving way; a way of

Section Two: Going Underground

recognising or ignoring those around him without doing either; a way of dropping neatly into the nearest chair or conversation as if it had been specially prepared for him; a way of taking charge of other people's lives as if it was his duty. He could have been an actor in a film but he was nothing of the sort. He was the real thing: a nasty man with too much power, too much time, plenty to spend; but no emotional commitments, no belief system. He was a man with no way out and as such a man who resented anybody else enjoying what life had to offer. He was a man who exercised power without compassion. When duty called (the law was always on his side) he was more than happy to shoot a man dead.

Without pausing he called out for a coffee and pastry as he made straight for Luka; smiling on the way, both to himself and at those around him. It was when he started to speak that it was revealed to Franz and Lev that he was a German. He asked Luka how he was today and slapped him on the back; and before he could answer he asked Luka to introduce his 'new friends', as he put it. Luka did so, under protest, and with a whisper. The German's eyes lit up when Luka introduced his brother - a complete surprise.

"Luka you didn't tell me you had a brother!"

And as for Franz, that seemed to register concern in his eyes, or a deeper fascination. Furiously Lev tried to work it out: his brother and the German did not act like enemies but neither did they sit comfortably like friends. It was more a standoff, a polite gesture, perhaps an ceasefire. Franz was simply relieved to be joined by another German. It broke the isolation.

Next the German introduced himself - Inspector Kleine, of the Gestapo - before imposing his conversation and forcing those he spoke to to respond. In this case that meant Franz. It was in his nature - and his job - to learn more, know more, and store it away for later use. The table became his and there was nothing Luka could do to stop him. He sat, uncomfortable, ignoring his food. He watched his little brother eat instead, as if keeping watch, and he ignored Franz, as if blaming him for the bad day he was having.

Lev looked lost, wishing to hide, whilst Franz soldiered on. Inspector Kleine kept smiling, and sometimes licked his lips between words. He was intrigued as to why the young German was here in all places with Luka of all people. There had to be a story here. In Franz he saw again what he had seen so many times before: a thoroughbred German youth, one ripe for picking. The challenge was too much to ignore. He had to knock them down, screw them up. He remembered his own youth, his glory days, and the slow fall from grace; and he

Section Two: Going Underground

wanted others to suffer for it. And as was his nature, he also saw the funny side of it.

"So you are one Franz Helmer, from the Ukraine sector. Where exactly?"

"Sumy, on the border."

"You were born there?"

"Yes."

"Your father settled there after the war?"

"Yes."

Each time Franz answered 'yes' he felt its strength diminish: given time it would begin to sound like 'no'.

Then Inspector Kleine remembered the other two seated and could not resist a dig.

"You must have lots of Ukrainian friends out there. No friendly Germans?"

Franz did not answer this time, unsure as to whether he was being insulted or not, or made to look a fool. Meanwhile Inspector Kleine picked up where he had left off.

"And why did he do that?"

"Don't know what you mean."

"Was he given free land?"

"Yes. When he left the service."

"Army?"

"SS. Waffen-SS." Franz felt his standing rise when he said that.

"Officer was he?"

"Hauptsturmführer. He still is."

"I'm impressed."

Inspector Kleine was lying. He folded his arms and slipped down his chair, only to pull himself back up when his coffee and pastry arrived. "Tell me what did he do in the war?"

Franz didn't like the constant stream of questions. It was an interrogation. He looked at Lev but Lev looked away. He looked at Luka but Luka simply got up and walked out front to have a smoke. He had no inclination to intervene. Lev wanted to join him but felt required to stay at his friend's side.

"He commanded tanks. Fought the Bolsheviks."

Franz chose his words carefully, somehow feeling it was important to give precise answers.

"Did he now. He must have been one of the best, a real hero. And what unit did he serve in?"

"2nd SS Panzer Division Das Reich," replied Franz proudly. The words rolled off his tongue, each one precisely pronounced for

Section Two: Going Underground

maximum impact.

"Really?" Now Inspector Kleine was impressed. "Wish I had been there."

Franz sensed something disingenuous.

"How many battles did he fight in? Did he kill lots of Russians your father, blow up lots of tanks?"

"I suppose so - he had the best - he commanded a Tiger."

"He hasn't told you everything then?"

"I don't know. He's told me some."

Franz folded his arms. He was growing angry. He did not like giving this man information but the man was a policeman, the special kind, and he could not refuse. He turned to Lev again but Lev was watching his brother outside and wishing he could be free of Germans for good.

"So your father has a big house in the country?"

"Yes."

"And lots of land to go with it?"

"Yes, and he runs a factory. My father works very hard."

"I'm sure your father has a very strong work ethic. After all this man served in the SS and they take only the best. He's done well out of the war. A hero and king of the castle."

"He's a magistrate if that's what you mean."

That wasn't what Inspector Kleine meant but he let it pass.

"And does our supreme leader inspire you?"

"Of course!"

"And you want to serve him, fight for your country?"

"Yes, of course! I'll do my National Service with the SS then apply for their officer training. That's the plan."

"You wish to serve the SS?"

"Yes."

You have a problem with that? thought Franz.

"Your father must be very proud of you."

"He is."

"And tell me are you looking forward to the celebrations, the great event?"

"Of course," croaked Franz, not wishing to give anymore away.

"And why's that?"

"What do you mean?"

"Simple question. You must know what it all means."

"Of course I do!"

"So why are you looking forward to it?"

"That's a stupid question."

Section Two: Going Underground

Abruptly Franz stood up, almost knocking over his chair. He had taken enough. Lev looked up in alarm.

"A stupid question which never gets an answer," noted Inspector Kleine.

And with that he gave up and looked away, attention drawn to what was happening outside. A man had stopped to talk to Luka. They were sharing a cigarette, in haste. He got up and left without explanation. He had to be outside where the action was, where business was being done.

Together Lev and Franz watched him confront the third man while Luka stood back, as if to avoid the fallout. They could hear nothing but saw the man become distressed under the verbal assault of Inspector Kleine. Luka seemed to remain unaffected. For maximum effect Inspector Kleine clenched the poor man's collar and pulled his face close in towards his; at which point the man tried to push off the wicked German. Like boxers in a ring they were separated by Luka whereupon the man stormed off disgusted. Inspector Kleine gave his regards and walked off in the opposite direction, a totally calm man. That left Luka, less than calm. He looked back into the cafe, as if checking if the incident had been witnessed. Lev and Franz stared back at him, as if begging for an explanation. They looked like two lost souls, like all they had was each other. Luka re-entered the cafe, saying nothing except 'time to go'. He led them back to his flat in dead silence.

Back home Luka retreated to his bedroom, followed by Lev, leaving Franz to his own devices. He heard the two brothers talk in Ukrainian. It was talk which grew louder and more excited. It was talk which included laughter. He wondered if they were talking about him. He wanted to go in and break it up. He sat on the sofa, surrounded by second hand, stolen or illegally imported goods of all shapes and sizes - right down to the smallest packets of pills. He thought back to his big warm bedroom in his big warm house and he missed it, badly. He wanted to be there, or Berlin, but not in this dump. No, correction, he wanted to be in Berlin. He wanted to be with his Bridget.

And then without warning Franz was left marooned when the two brothers left the flat to go for a stroll - a private walk, not for Germans, declared Luka defiantly. Franz felt insulted, left for dead. He had been locked up, locked in, locked out. He had no experience of being treated like this and it hurt. What should have been a cause for a good time had instead produced a flat, awkward, gut wrenching, drag of precious time. His only salvation was a small television tucked away in the corner of the room. He turned it on. A war film was playing: the same war; the same heroes, the same enemy; the same outcome. Franz had

Section Two: Going Underground

enjoyed viewing the like of it many times before but this time he found it terribly dull. He left it on to simply break the silence and clung to his one clear thought: that he would leave first thing in the morning, at first light, no hanging about.

A stack of LPs caught his eye. He picked up the one on top. It was in English, from America. And to make matters worse the man on the cover was a black man, one of those Negroes he had seen in books. The Negro wore a shiny suit and was holding a trumpet. Franz didn't know how to react to his image. He threw it back on the pile before it could contaminate him. Yes, America, that made sense. America: the land of corrupt minds, ostentatious wealth, gluttony and vice; a moral wasteland. Luckily America was far away from Europe. Luckily so were Americans.

Franz was bursting to explode with anger, and inflict it. He wanted to get angry with Inspector Kleine but Kleine was a German officer and that was not acceptable behaviour. He wanted to get angry with Lev too, but no. Lev was his only friend in these foreign parts. So he fumed until the pressure became too much and demanded release. He took it out on the Negro who was smiling up at him, happy, having fun. He brought his fist down hard on the face and shattered the vinyl inside. Terrified of being found out he hid the damaged article deep within the stack and pretended that all was right in the world. He reminded himself, repeatedly, that he was on his way to Berlin, to meet the Fuehrer, the greatest man on earth and inside his head. His Fuehrer would make him feel better.

♦

It was now Isaak's third night in jail and things had moved on. It was no longer a crime of late night joyriding but one of car theft. Isaak was not the serious suspect in this but to walk free a fine (code for bribe) still had to be paid - a heavy fine as befitting a Jew. His father was even more furious and made this very plain when he turned up to see him. Isaak received a severe verbal whipping while his anxious mother looked on and stored away mental notes. Fear for their child had almost been pushed aside by fear of financial meltdown. A slightly amused guard looked on.

Isaak promised his father that, given time, lots of time, he would repay the money, with interest, but this did nothing to reduce the man's fury. Life was hard enough, his father declared, without it costing a fortune. Isaak was spared more fury when the guard chopped the interview and led him away. Isaak looked back at his mother on the

Section Two: Going Underground

way out but she avoided all eye contact. She had sat in stony silence throughout, saying nothing; never once interrupting her husband; never once contradicting him. Father was, after all, head of the family, and money matters were always his sole preserve and anguish.

It would take time to find the money, so until then Isaak would remain locked up. On the plus side his father had paid a 'deposit' on the understanding that his son would be well-treated. And he would be, most of the time. Isaak's status was upgraded from 'Jew prisoner' to something closer to 'prisoner-guest' - a situation reinforced by the fact that he now had some personal belongings with him: spare underwear; toothbrush, toothpaste and hairbrush; even his book. All care of his mother. Isaak had everything required for a stay away from home - everything except his liberty.

Boredom was now his biggest problem but Isaak coped well. He had his book to finish. He was teaching a guard to play chess. He had even offered to paint his cell but this was refused on the grounds it might not get finished before they had to let him go. Now, just as he had settled in and come to terms with his lot, there was a new shock and his world was turned upside down. Isaak was given a cellmate, one who could not be regarded as sane and safe.

The man, not actually much older than Isaak but looking far older - far more worn out by life - was barely a man: more part animal, part petrified child. He retreated to the corner of the cell and sat, huddled up on the floor, trembling; afraid to look up and out at the world around him; unwilling or unable to engage in talk. He had been arrested for disturbing the peace; for refusing to give his name and address; for refusing to cooperate with the police. He had not been arrested because he was barely human, because he was a wild, untamed animal. He had not been taken into care, and would not be, for nobody cared about him.

From the opposite end of the cell Isaak watched his new cellmate, both fascinated and alarmed; afraid the creature might attack; aggrieved that he had to share his cell. He passed the man a plate of food and watched him eat it with his fingers, ignoring the knife and fork provided. The man did not drink water from the cup, he sucked it up. His hair was a clotted lump of grease and dirt. His clothes were old and torn, and barely fitted. His shoes barely held together. He carried a rotten stench; a strange brew which normally only inhabited woodland, muddy fields, riverbanks and bogs, and which never seeped indoors. This was a wild man; a wild animal, ensnared, caged, and now surprisingly timid. It was as if he had been left to die but refused to die; wishing instead to be an inconvenience for all. Isaak tried to talk to him but the man did not respond with talk: he mumbled, incoherently,

Section Two: Going Underground

wishing to express himself but unable to. The frustration was clearly visible on his face. In that regard he was fully human. Isaak would take pity on him, but not yet. He was dreading their first night together.

Section Three: Capital Sin

Capital Sin

An uncomfortable, restless night spent sprawled across a hard sofa meant an early rise for Franz was no problem. He had barely slept a wink. His morning mood was uncompromising: he had to get away, fast; he had to put space between himself and the bad, dangerous brother of Lev. But his problem now was how to get back to the train station. That he solved by knocking on Luka's bedroom door - loudly - to wake Lev. Grudgingly Lev promised to get up straight away and see him off. Furious, Luka told him to fuck off and tried to get back to sleep. (Later Lev would apologize for his brother's outburst but the apology would not be accepted.)

Armed with a street map - one donated under protest by a semi-conscious Luka - the two friends found their way back to Prague Central station, along near empty streets in freezing cold morning air. Those who noticed them only really noticed Franz - storming ahead with attitude like all good and bad Germans. The two did not make proper talk: famished, Franz sulked while Lev brooded over the possible cause of his friend's morning sulk. He put it down to the nasty Inspector Kleine - a nasty piece of Germany. He wished to be gone quick.

Back at the station they sat and ate breakfast in a cafe, and watched the growing flow of travellers - mainly commuters; some still half asleep, on automatic, relying on routine to guide them to their destination. Whilst eating they engaged in limited small talk only, unable to broach the big subjects; preferring to hide behind trivialities. Things which should have been let out to breathe remained bottled up. Remaining on best terms was best achieved by saying nothing during bad times. Lev gave Franz Luka's telephone number, and that was that.

There was a big elephant in the room: the chance that they would never meet again. The head said there was no reason why not but the heart suggested that it would never happen. Each would go his own way, a long way away. Neither would admit that ending to their story and the fear hung around their necks and over their heads; ready to crash down or strangle them at any moment. It hurt. It weighed them down as they made their way on to the platform. It choked the final farewell. It sucked the life out of it when Franz boarded the Berlin express. It reduced final contact to brief eye contact and a perfunctory modest wave. 'Goodbye' was all they could say to each other. One word: it should have been so much more. A great opportunity had been missed. As the train pulled away each was left gasping for air and

Section Three: Capital Sin

Franz, exhausted, crashed out in the comfort of a first class compartment. Had he managed to stay awake he might have shed a tear for his parting from Lev, or for his fear that Lev was heading in the wrong direction.

The sound of an announcer cut into Franz's dream and pulled him out of sleep. He was awake, in his great city of Berlin! He had arrived, in Berlin! Berlin! Berlin where Bridget lived! Berlin where he and the Fuehrer would meet! Berlin, the centre of all power, of all he believed in! And as he stepped off the train and began the long walk down the platform so there was the Fuehrer staring down; always looking at him, as if looking for signs of weakness, as if tempting him on. Yes Berlin was stuck in a state of grand celebration for its greatest hero.

Franz made his all important phone call to Bridget then waited. The coming reunion made him slightly nervous, very proud, and extremely eager. He sat around. He walked around - no demonstrations or bad feeling here. The sight of the grand station, Lehrter Bahnhof, raised his energy level and swept away the sludge of his early morning fatigue. He had arrived, in the greatest city in Europe, possibly in the world, in true Germany; not some half forgotten border outpost on the edge of empire. Lev could keep his Prague. He had his Berlin. And suddenly, like Lev, he had no wish to go home. He was home from home.

Franz stared up in amazement at the grand entrance. Lehrter Bahnhof was a truly magnificent place, and he expected nothing less in the capital city of the Third Reich. He noted the human traffic which swarmed around him, sometimes into him. A member of the Hitler Youth bumped into him and Franz smiled, but he received only the opposite back: the glare of someone who had just been insulted or approached with intimacy. Reminded of his duties in the Hitler Youth Franz looked around to try and spot any Jews, any yellow stars in the crowd. Then he remembered that Jews were banned from German cities. Still, it made for a good game and best watch out: just in case one of them had sneaked in to spoil things.

There were all the usual party uniforms he had grown up with - though worn here as much by fat old men as the young and virile. And yes the Hitler Youth was out in force, in gangs; marching here, marching there; as if on manoeuvres; as if staking prey. Surprisingly he had no wish to join them. He felt no urge to get into uniform. And then there were the foreigners, everywhere: Italians, Spaniards; a few French; a few English; even the odd American. He spotted three BUF and five PNF party uniforms. All had come to celebrate Germany he boasted to himself. All were here to join in, be part of the German experience, he thought proudly. And the Fuehrer was here with a

Section Three: Capital Sin

vengeance: everywhere one looked he was to be seen, and obeyed. You could not walk away. You could not keep up. You had to give in. You had to celebrate.

And then Fräulein Bridget broke through the crowd. Franz straightened up, straightened his clothes, and corrected his hair. In Berlin he felt it was required to look his best and act his part. He began to walk towards her, slowly, still unsure. When he was sure he moved up a gear. Her face had not changed but her body definitely had. Memories of their previous physical encounter at that summer camp came flooding back, and it stirred up feelings both innocent and intimate. Two years fell off him and the drive towards manhood and maturity was temporarily put on hold. But it was a brief interlude and as Bridget walked towards him - not yet seeing him - in a body bursting with femininity and begging to be taken seriously, so the sexually charged, sex starved Franz returned to take control. Franz had locked on to her chest. Those breasts hiding beneath: they were definitely bigger. They were lovely now, simply gorgeous. He had to get his hands on them. She was more seductive, hopefully less tiresome, definitely less a girl, hopefully more a woman. More memories came tumbling to the forefront of his mind, such as the one where he had glimpsed a fragment of her stripping off for a shower through a crack in the wooden planks which made for a wall. Later he had regretted running off like a coward, afraid to be caught red-handed, afraid to bring dishonour to the Hitler Youth. Right there and now he simply wanted to have sex with her. It was what he had been designed to do.

Suddenly Bridget saw him. She walked faster. She almost ran across the concourse as Franz moved towards her. She stopped in her tracks with room to spare. He did the same. The gap between them had been reduced to just two metres but it still felt a long way. Franz had no wish for words: he just wanted to grab her and squeeze the juice out of her. Then he noticed a man was tailing her closely. He had stopped as she had stopped. When Franz saw his face close up it dawned on him that this was her father. Great. Herr Schrimer was checking up on them. Had she brought her father along or had she not been able to leave him behind? Either way it was bad news. All thoughts of sexual engagement went out of the window - pushed aside by something more suited, more polite, more civilized. Boring words of introduction had to be said.

Herr Schrimer stood like both protective father and security guard or nightclub bouncer; coiled up, ready for trouble, face set in stone. He was wearing an expensive, tailored suit, with gold cufflinks and bow tie to match. His shirt with stiff collar was a faint shade of blue.

Section Three: Capital Sin

Everything about him was precisely placed, perfect. He looked the perfect German and his intelligence was evident even before he spoke. Bridget too had put on her best; to appear her best; to be best; to look keen. The Schrimers had style. The Schrimers had money. And they were both so immaculately turned out that Franz was made to feel like a tramp, a peasant from the estate. He tried to shrug it off but the feeling of inadequacy struck, and stuck, like a dirty stain which refused to be washed away.

The Schrimers stood there, so confidant, expecting the same of him. Franz could not match them and instead came across as glum-looking, lost, abandoned even. Life on the farm had taught him that you didn't act happy without good reason. 'Nothing should be faked' he had once been told. Luckily it lasted no more than a handful of seconds - the kind which seemed to stretch out - for suddenly Bridget produced a big broad smile and all was right in the world. Franz beamed back, just as broadly. He was back on firm ground. Now he just had to figure out what to do next. He was stumped. A polite calm peck her on the check? All he could do was stare into Bridget's eyes - eyes he knew well from photographs. She solved his problem by thrusting out her hand and uttering a simple 'hello' below her breath, still smiling. Her voice sounded sweet, inviting. It was the voice of a child who had no problem making friends. Franz responded likewise, except that his voice sounded unusually deep and hoarse. It was the voice of a man unsure but standing his ground. For an extended moment in time Herr Schrimer was entirely forgotten.

Bridget enticed him to talk, and he did, and the two began to warm up; and as they did Franz sensed that Herr Schrimer was monitoring him, measuring him, perhaps taking notes. They threw random recollections at each other, reliving the highlights of their summer together until, tired, Herr Schrimer forced his way in under the pretext of introducing himself. He took command of a conversation which, in his view, had lost control. He pushed forward, forcing his daughter aside, but in a nice way.

"Franz Helmer. Welcome to Berlin."

His manner was business like but his eyes were all over the young man from the Ukraine.

"Thank you Herr Schrimer."

The reply was as flat as it could be and Franz stood to attention, as if in class, awaiting instructions.

They shook hands. It was perfunctory. It was a very German handshake.

"Follow me," said Herr Schrimer, trying to sound upbeat and failing.

And without looking to see if the children were keeping up he led

Section Three: Capital Sin

the way skilfully through the crowd, towards the exit, and on towards his parked car. Herr Schrimer was a fast, no nonsense, walker and it was a struggle to keep up. Without warning Bridget joyfully hooked her arm around that of Franz - the act sent a shock wave up his arm and into his head. He nearly fainted, but managed to hold on, to enjoy it. (But watch it, he told himself. Herr Schrimer was a parent and Bridget was his daughter. He would be watching.) The sensation diminished when she began to skip alongside his big strides. Franz had a small girl on his arm, not a woman.

On stepping out of the station into the vast capital light of day Franz was immediately overwhelmed. He felt out of place. He felt like a foreigner. Then he reminded himself that this was what it was all about: the Party, the Fuehrer, the heart of the Third Reich. And this was it, not to be missed. The car Herr Schrimer led them to was a big black Mercedes saloon. It spoke power. It spoke money. It spoke government. Immediately Franz compared it with the family estate. Yes this machine was younger, more expensive, brighter and better looking. It won hands down. While Herr Schrimer put his kitbag in the boot Franz took the front seat, not thinking to ask. Bridget got in the back without complaining and examined the back of his neck, for no reason other than it was there. She wanted to talk. Franz did not.

When they drove off Franz did nothing except look out of the window, at the faces and the places, and the flags. The red, the black and the white were all begging for a fight. Here he saw affluence and self-belief as the norm. He saw the aspiration for perfection. He saw everything was neat. He had seen it in the eyes of Herr Schrimer; even in the eyes of Bridget though he did not remember seeing it there before. The Schrimers were totally sure of themselves and he felt required to live up to the same, no matter how difficult. Back home feeling and acting superior had rarely been a problem: there were few Germans surrounding him to force comparisons; and plenty of second class, second rate citizens to make it easy. Here he was just one of an average in a vast crowd of mainly superiors.

Now he was in Berlin everything previously experienced and held as sacred felt second rate, poorly executed. For Berlin it appeared no expense had been spared. Nothing was too good for the capital city of the glorious Thousand Year Reich. Here Franz knew he had to be on his best behaviour, always, and live the values which defined all good Germans. Here there was no place for poor performance. And with the advantage and drive of youth he assumed he was up to the challenge.

Traffic flowed easily, almost to plan. All cars, mostly gleaming clean, were mostly brand new. There was no speeding. Speeding was

Section Three: Capital Sin

not tolerated unless on party or government business. There was little sign of rust or rampage. The Beetle Mark 2 and the bigger Beetle roamed supreme. Beetles were almost king. Citizens looked clean, well scrubbed, well turned out, secure and secured. Almost every German looked content; else distracted; else busy, as if rushed off their feet by some unseen force driving them along, forcing them to reach out for new heights. Each German was expected to meet the standard and never complain. Uniforms, party and military, government and associated, littered the landscape and spiced it up. They stuck out, as intended. You had to look at them, and admire. (How could you not do so? Grey suits were so boring. Armbands were so cool.) Where dense they could swallow you up, even spit you out, until you felt worthless. When it came to looks civilians were overwhelmed by soldiers.

Herr Schrimer sat composed, in charge, during the journey. Only once did his control collapse due to emotional eruption: an official convoy of big black cars flew through a red light; loud horns forcefully blowing all out of its way. Herr Schrimer had to slam on the brakes hard, else crash. He swore, then apologized, unreservedly, as if he had committed some great sin. Bridget crashed into the back of the front seat and laughed while Franz nearly smacked himself senseless on the windscreen. They both thought it hilarious. Herr Schrimer did not. He worked for the government and hated being kicked around by it.

By the time the car reached home Bridget had calmed back down and had stopped looking at Franz. She had longed stopped asking him questions. The car drew up outside a grand house. Its impact was not wasted on Franz. Compared with others he had passed on route this one was big, in a big street, surrounded by other big houses. This street was where big people lived big lives. Franz suddenly felt his was smaller - house and life - even though his house was big and on a big piece of land, and his father had lived a big life. It didn't add up. Bridget was the first to jump out. Franz was the last.

The young slim woman who opened the door as Herr Schrimer parked the car was not Bridget's mother, Franz knew that; and she could not be her sister, Franz guessed that; and when she opened her mouth to greet Herr Schrimer he discovered that she was not German - probably Polish he decided, definitely not Ukrainian. Ukrainian or not she reminded him of Aneta, badly.

When Frau Schrimer did appeared to greet them Bridget was subdued, back on best behaviour.

"So you are the Franz Helmer? Welcome to our home. I hope your stay will be pleasant?"

Section Three: Capital Sin

"Thank you Frau Schrimer. Thank you for having me." Franz thought her German sounded funny, unGerman.

Satisfied with that Frau Schrimer turned to her husband and continued to speak, but in French. Franz was impressed, as he was when he walked on into the house. It was dripping with money and charm, decorations and history. Everything inside impressed and looked expensive. Those who lived in this place boasted breeding, taste, and a strong sense of tradition and family history. Framed photographs of previous generations worked their way up the stairs, spaced out with mathematical precision like in any art gallery. Franz was near timid when he stepped off the welcome mat. Home now felt extremely austere - austere beyond that which was necessary to live the correct, virtuous life. The contents of his house appeared cheap now, second hand. He found himself apologizing for it in his thoughts despite a battle not to.

Frau Schrimer had prepared a special lunch for their new house guest and it was ready, right now. She made that clear so they went straight into lunch. She had the full support of a hungry Franz. He was like a dog seeing the bone and let off its lead. Bridget ran on ahead to ensure possession of her usual seat. Franz sat down as directed and was immediately puzzled by all the cutlery laid out. He had never seen so many knives and forks in one place for one person. Unnecessary extravagance. But he pretended not to care. Next he had a strange feeling that his parents were about to join him, then another that Lev was on the doorstep, shut out but still knocking on the door.

Some weird watered-down soup arrived, dished up by the Polish girl. Though it had few bits in it and not much going for it Franz tucked in with care and his best attempt at decorum. (Shrewdly he waited for others to begin each course to be sure of the way of the knives and forks.) But after that, despite the strange, unfamiliar course - wine in the chicken? - he got stuck in and began to devour at speed. The Schrimer family slowed and took turns in watching him. In time Franz glanced up to see Frau Schrimer with her eyes firmly fixed on him. How long had she been watching him? Then he realised Herr Schrimer was watching him on and off, but less so. Bridget pretended she hadn't and returned to looking into her food.

Franz returned to keeping his head down and forced himself to slow. He did not enjoy the rest of his meal, not even the desert which was scrumptious and addictive. The occasion had been spoilt. This Schrimer family was treating him like a peasant. They spoke over his head in French. Had he understood he would have learnt that his hosts regarded his accent as poor, colonial. In their book Franz Helmer was

Section Three: Capital Sin

not even East German but Eastern German. And during the entire sitting he avoided looking at Bridget, not wishing to be seen gawping or treating her as his object - mainly an object of lust. Likewise he avoided the Polish girl when she served food or removed plates. He did look at her just once, to confirm his fears. She carried the air of someone stuck in a job. Just like Aneta.

Over lunch Franz was politely but firmly questioned about his life back home. Never once was he asked about his coming appointment with the Fuehrer. He didn't notice this, too busy as he was justifying his existence whilst remembering to edit out that which he thought best to keep secret. He had reached the age where he no longer felt required to tell all, explain all, share all. He wanted independency and privacy at his core. He was asked to describe 'life on the farm'.

"It's the Helmer estate," he declared.

It had two villages, he boasted, each with a river; and it had a factory, and a railway line running through it all. Once started he couldn't be stopped. He had been stung. It stretched as far as the eye could see and his father ran it all, like clockwork. He got no response; only nods, only silent acceptance from the Schrimers; but a big smile from Bridget, possibly to demonstrate that she was on his side. She knew her parents could be polite bullies at times. Franz was drawn to recycled memories and images of the bumptious, bigheaded colonel and his sad, annoying wife. He tried to link them to the Schrimers, but couldn't. It was too soon to judge them negatively yet. He had only just arrived in their territory.

"It's tough out there," he announced with a flourish. "But worth it. You live life raw. You're in touch with the elements. You see death."

After that poetic outburst Franz was standing rather proud - even if stuck in a seat. He didn't know what he meant by that last remark, or why he had said it, but it sounded grand and luckily no one picked it apart. He had never constructed such a stream of words before - words he began to believe as he spoke them - but then he had never been put under pressure quite like this before.

"What are other Germans of your age like out there?" asked Frau Schrimer.

"Tough. Like me. We are all tough. We have to be."

It was exactly what Bridget wanted to hear.

"Why?" asked Herr Schrimer. It was almost a double act.

"Why?" Franz thought the question a stupid one. "We're in the middle of nowhere, surrounded by the enemy that's why."

Frau Schrimer looked at Herr Schrimer and raised her eyebrows. She did it almost with contempt, and definitely for show. She passed

Section Three: Capital Sin

another comment to her husband in French and this time Franz really wanted to know what she had just said. Franz felt the deadly Inspector Kleine was here spreading his muck.

"How do Germans treat the local population?"

"Fairly. Always fairly. The colonel is strict but fair," lied Franz. He had nothing more to say on that peculiar subject.

"The colonel?"

"Garrison commander. He runs the place."

"I see."

She obviously didn't but Franz didn't care. Next he was probed about his hobbies. Franz shrugged. It was an easy question for which he had a simple answer.

"I ride my motorbike and attend Hitler Youth. And hang around - and go on patrol. That's about it really."

That was good enough for Bridget.

"How fast do you go?"

"As fast as our roads allow - which is fast."

"Tell us about your parents Franz."

Frau Schrimer continued to speak as someone who always expected a complete answer, and got it, and who backed it up with the threat of more.

"My parents?"

Franz didn't know what to say. His parents were his parents. They always had been. Father was the war hero, a landowner, a magistrate, an important person. Mother was a war hero's wife.

"He fought in the war. He runs the estate."

"Wehrmacht?"

"Waffen-SS, 2nd SS Panzer Division Das Reich." As usual Franz pronounced each word carefully. These were words which usually impressed.

"I served with the Wehrmacht," said Herr Schrimer, unimpressed. "Can't say I enjoyed the experience. Did Herr Helmer enjoy it?"

"I don't know. I think so. I assume so."

"He's never told you?"

"No, not exactly." Franz felt a sense of deja-vu, or even conspiracy in the questioning he was suffering lately.

"Our Bridget says you enjoy the Hitler Youth?" Frau Schrimer again.

"Of course. Why wouldn't I?"

He had answered back clearly defiant for the first time and had to swallow a lump in his throat. Herr Schrimer didn't notice the burst of attitude but his wife did, as did Bridget.

Section Three: Capital Sin

"And you find it a worthwhile activity, absorbing?"

"Yes." Franz corrected himself. "I suppose so. I mean there's not much else to do out there - except hunt down Russians." The joke fell flat. "You have to join up or you miss out on everything - and others will talk."

Franz was surprised that he had been so open - and with strangers, strangers he was struggling to like. He told himself to be more careful next time.

Released from the formality of the big lunch Franz was shown his room. It was a girl's room: Bridget's older sister he guessed. There he was finally left alone - Frau Schrimer having pulled off her daughter - to unpack, recover, recharge. He let loose the contents of his kitbag, except the gun, and tried to stamp his authority on the room. It didn't work. It was a girl's room through and through. This was not right he told himself, but he dare not complain. Best get used to it. The gun sat heavy on his mind, loaded, even though it wasn't. Leave it where it was, or find a hiding place? Out of the blue Bridget ran in and jumped on to the bed.

"Is this your sister's room?" asked Franz.

"Yes, she's in France studying."

France? What was wrong with Germany? Franz hid his dirty look.

"Why didn't you say your mother spoke French?"

"Didn't think it was important - it's not - anyway why do we want to write about boring parents?"

Fair point, thought Franz.

Bridget waited patiently until it looked like he was prepared to give her his full, undivided attention, never ceasing to smile for one moment. Her smile never wavered or changed much in the way of shape. Franz found it tiresome - it was literally tiring him out - but one look at the rest of her body swept such negativity aside. And she was throwing herself around on his bed. She was accidentally seducing him: luckily he still knew the rules, more so in someone else's house. And then her dam broke and it all came flooding out: all her plans to keep him entertained, not bored, happy while he was here in Berlin with her. They would visit the zoo, the park, the museums, the cinema, go shopping at the best shops. Would he like to buy his parents some nice presents? No, said Franz. They would be here soon: they could buy their own presents. They had all the money.

That didn't put Bridget off: the next 'to do' on her list was to show Franz her own room. She wanted to show it off, whist showing off. She dragged him off towards it, and he was happy to be dragged. She might be acting like a big little girl right now but she looked and

Section Three: Capital Sin

charmed like a feisty young woman. Luckily she didn't spot his unplanned erection and he managed to keep it out of sight until it had subsided. 'Bridget's Room Keep Out' said the sign on her door. She was proud of it. He thought it was stupid but said the opposite.

Upon entering Franz was disappointed. This was a girl's room and it stank like a girl's room always did. (It was mainly cheap perfume.) He saw dolls piled up in a corner. Discarded? To be dumped? Some did look ragged. Or still precious possessions? There was lots of pink, and flowers, and flowery patterns; and unfinished doodles on paper; and vague attempts at painting; and there was mess everywhere. There was a big diary on her desk - pink of course - and books everywhere, stuffed on to shelves else piled up. This girl had many more books than him. And there was a flute, and a violin case. Now he remembered: yes she was learning the violin. Had she dumped the flute? The good news was that there was a record player in the corner, and records alongside. Thank God for small mercies. Franz went straight for the vinyl, like a hunting dog who had sighted prey. He picked up a couple to inspect. It was more of that American stuff. But no black people this time.

"What's this?"

"Rock and roll."

"How did you get it?"

"Father bought it for me, on his travels." Bridget opened a drawer. "Look I've kept all your letters."

Franz was forced to look in. Yes she had kept them all. They alarmed him, like unused hand grenades. What had he written? What had Lev written? Lev: he wanted to think about Lev but she was in the way.

"Would you like to read some?"

"Not now. Perhaps later. I'm really whacked." And then he remembered. "I must register my arrival."

"Register?"

"With the Party, at their office. I promised my parents I would do it on my first day here. I should go right now."

"Do you have to?"

"Yes I must go now."

But despite the sudden urgency Franz didn't move. He had no idea what to do next: like how to get there; whether to ask for help, a lift, a taxi? But Bridget was well ahead of him.

"I'll take you there!"

"You sure?"

"Of course I am." Bridget was very sure. "Do you hope to shake his hand?"

Section Three: Capital Sin

"Haven't thought about it." He had of course.

Bridget grabbed him by the hand and pulled him along as she headed out of the room.

"I'll go tell Mum and Dad."

And she did, and Franz waited for something to happen. Bridget had to work hard to convince her parents that it was safe for her to go but her determination overcame them.

"He needs me to show him the way. I promised," said Bridget defiantly.

And then they were off, by bus and tram, into town and its powerful heartbeat. On their way Bridget pointed out everything worth pointing at. Franz didn't have to say anything, which he was pleased about. At one point he did make the effort and asked if she had spotted any Jews. She looked confused and didn't answer. He had meant it only as a joke. In exasperation he pulled out a smoke and offered her one. She declined, shaking her head: 'an evil thing' her parents had said.

◆

Isaak's cellmate did not smell now, only his clothes, for today was bath day: a 'once a week' luxury, just like in the Ghetto. After taking his, like a duck to water, Isaak had run a second, and after much passionate persuasion his cellmate had stripped and got in. Once in he learnt to relax again, and splash, if only a little. Now dry, he sat waiting to be told what to do next. Next was lunch.

A guard handed Isaak a tray of food and gave him a message from his father: 'money still a problem but not to worry it would sort itself out'. Today the tray catered for two. This guard had no wish to deal with the crazy prisoner. Isaak invited his cellmate to eat as he placed one plate of food on his lap and grabbed a slice of bread. His cellmate duplicated his movements. The morning bath had freshened up his mind and spirit as well as his body. It had been a long time since he had engaged in warm conversation as an equal and now the long repressed desire to engage exerted itself again, using a rusty but deep-rooted skill which refused to die. Human beings could not help but talk, especially to someone prepared to listen to every word. Life demanded to function, not freeze.

Isaak found himself comforting the mind of a child. His father would be proud of him. The cellmate asked who he was, and why he was here, and if he really was a Jew. Isaak confirmed that he was indeed one of those Jews. The Yellow Star never lied. Who else would want to wear one? And yes, he was from the local ghetto. He had lived

Section Three: Capital Sin

there all his life.
"I just want to be left alone. Is that too much to ask?"
Isaak wished he had said that.

◆

Lev and Luka ate lunch at the same cafe. They were in sync and Lev was half way home towards settling in. Yes he knew his brother had his fingers in many pies - some unsavoury - but was more than willing to lend a hand. They were brothers, bound: that had to make for good business. Lev knew it. Luka knew it. But first the past had to be dealt with, kicked out, so they talked about Penkin; in particular his annoying habits and state of mind. There was the same old chair; the same old talk of independence; the same old complaints against the Germans; the same old morning cough; and the socks which got changed only every fourth day as a rule.

A man with attitude wandered in, sat down behind Luka and ordered his favourite steak. He was Czech. While he waited he twisted round and gently tapped Luka on the shoulder.

"We meeting later?" He spoke in a near whisper.

Luka did not need to turn round.

"Yes," he replied quietly, in Czech.

Satisfied, the man's interest gravitated towards Lev and his eyes flickered as they counted. He was unsure what to make of this fresh face, though he saw the clues. He said nothing and returned to his normal seating position.

◆

When they finally arrived at Party Central Office Franz had to pause, draw breath, and remind himself of the person he was expected to be. He had seen this building on television as something almost mythical and now here it was: a very real place set in stone and marble, steel and glass. And it was a busy place, a hive of activity. On the steps leading up to the grand entrance, beneath the classic flags, impressive - robotic - SA storm troopers stood guard for the tourists. The taxis which arrived to drop off visitors were outnumbered by chauffeur driven cars doing likewise. Its energy and power leaked out of a building built for no other purpose than to clearly announce its importance and place in the city, and in the country. It maintained the myth of the Party, and administered its first and last rights without interference from anyone except the chosen few at the top of the hierarchy. You entered

Section Three: Capital Sin

unprotected and hoped for a friendly, positive encounter. You always left not quite the person you were before. Such was its spell, efficiency and brutality.

The Party set the thinking, the moral framework, the direction life was expected to take for the greater good; and it set it from here, in this one vast modern building designed to impress and impose. Here party officialdom resided, entrenched: organising, administering; executing the rare but absolute orders of its leader or, more often, the orders of its leader's leaders. Once the party had been a violent monster, a weapon for change, a trumpet for revolution. Now it was a career path, a route to the top, a place which gave you a safe job and a very good pension. And if you got to the top all you could do was look back down, perhaps enjoy the view and wonder what to do next.

It had its old guard rubbing up against the new guard, sometimes smoothly, sometimes with sparks flying. The old believed the slogans and songs. The new simply sung as and when required. Without wars of national salvation there was little to do except keep order amongst the rank and file by promoting a few here and demoting a few there; by handing out awards; by organising grand celebrations.

"Come on," commanded an anxious Franz.

Bridget fell into line, wishing to take his hand; trying, and failing. She was the less self-conscious one.

Franz marched towards the main entrance and its revolving door. He was still Hitler's youth in spirit and routine. He was on the march again and it felt good. Bridget was temporarily forgotten. As he pushed on the door and entered he had to steady himself, afraid the place might swallow him up. Despite the bright lights he had entered the heart of darkness.

Eyes straight ahead he marched right on up to the reception desk and stood, silent, until a man bothered to raise his eyes and pay him attention. If the desk clerk wasn't impressed by his entrance, Bridget was. Franz gave his full name and reason for being there. He showed the man his letter but got no reaction other than 'business as usual'. Eyes back down the clerk wrote on a ticket in a book, ripped it out and handed it to Franz without looking up.

"Take this to room 2B down that corridor." He pointed at some double doors. "Third on the left."

He took no notice of Bridget, or if he did he didn't object.

And here, like everywhere else, the Fuehrer was watching: this time in the form and substance of a full size bronze statue depicting a knight. It stood in a ceiling high alcove designed into the building for that specific purpose. He ruled over every aspect of this place - though he

Section Three: Capital Sin

did leave all the paperwork to others.

As Franz reached the double doors there was a noise behind him and the commotion of a sudden crowd. He turned, sensing trouble or fun. There was both. A small army came storming in from outside. It was a protection unit: humourless, poised and well dressed. Within it, travelling not so fast, came a huge fat man in a stupendous light blue uniform (blue with a hint of lavender). He was aided by an impressive gold topped walking stick. Today the uniform was not medal-soaked. It was Reichsmarschall Herman Goering in full flow.

Despite his slow speed the Reichsmarschall was in a rush: in a rush to arrive; in a rush to get business done; in a rush to leave. He was always in a rush. The protection squad fanned out and took up positions. Everything was done by the book. Franz watched, fascinated. He could not take his eyes off the grand man. Nor could Bridget. They knew who it was: it was just that he didn't match the smooth statesmanlike image portrayed on screen or in the papers. The portraits and photographs did not report the folds of fat which accompanied this most important person, not even those under his chin. Hidden from the entire world, the fat which enveloped Reichsmarschall Herman Goering also held him together. And his hair was suspiciously too black. Was the Reichsmarschall really that fat, that bulky, that slow - that frustrated? He was.

On some days his chest was flooded with medals, and insignia to match. Even Reichsfuehrer Heinrich Himmler had ceased to compete with him. Goering was a force unto his own. He was not mad. He had just taken his favourite pieces of the past and fixed them, and polished them such that they now served up his rolling present. He lived in it, relating all his present needs and expectations to this dislocated reality in a way which made perfect sense to him but no one else. In his mind as he had grown larger so the world had grown smaller, less deserving of his time, patience and energy. His acolytes serviced his dignity and his competitors kept him on his toes, just.

The Reichsmarschall still loved his airplanes and rockets. He could not get enough of them. Every year they seemed to get bigger, faster and louder. The jet fighters of the Luftwaffe were his pride and joy. He wanted them to reach the moon before he died, and plant a swastika which could be seen from Earth - especially America.

Over time the Fuehrer and his immediate associates had grown used to it all and put up with him - after all he had earned the right to be a pain in the Aryan arse. In private they regarded him as a joke - except of course the Fuehrer who was above party politics, and all other personalities in his empire. He did not engage in such behaviour,

Section Three: Capital Sin

despite his belief that dog should eat dog when that dog is the better dog.

Staff watched the big man whilst trying not to be seen watching; many trying to determine if he was in a foul mood. These days it was impossible to tell. The face was that of a mad old man who was fuelled only by his past; who could only communicate by shouting; who could only look down at others - with the one exception. His arrival meant trouble: trouble for some poor official up the food chain; trouble for some official senior enough to have to deal with him but junior enough to collapse under his weight and pressure, and irrelevant enough to receive no first aid. Today he had a bee in his bonnet and it wanted to sting.

The Reichsmarschall stalled, as if in pain, before moving again, sometimes short of breath but never short of determination. He should have been in hospital but had discharged himself early: he was the Reichsmarschall; he could do whatever he wanted; only the Fuehrer could tell him what to do, and these days even he didn't think it worth the bother. The Reichsmarschall didn't give a damn that he was beyond fat and obese. Before he was dead he intended to eat and drink all that was worth doing so. Exercise was a forgotten thought, along with running the country. (That task he had delegated almost 100% to others, leaving his official position pointless, almost meaningless.) Reichsmarschall Herman Goering was a free spirit, but contaminated.

Franz held on to a door handle, unable to move. Had he seen a wizard, a warlord or a dragon? Suddenly all his heroes were springing to life. Who next? A member of the protection squad fixed his sights on him and moved in, and then another. Franz gawped as they came straight for him. He didn't know it but he was under attack from the state. Bridget gripped his jacket and tugged, suggesting he should move away, fast. He didn't take a blind bit of notice. He had frozen on the spot. The two security guards pushed him out of the way with such force that he slipped and fell. As if tied to him Bridget knelt down by his side to help him up, to protect him. Instinctively she wanted to stand him up on his own two feet.

As Franz lifted himself up - fighting off Bridget all the way - the Reichsmarschall came lumbering past with a full head of steam. He looked down at the overgrown boy on the floor and laughed. The doors were pulled open for him and he passed on through without pause. And he was gone, just like that. In another part of the building, high up on the fourth floor, some poor unsuspecting soul was about to have his day spoilt by uncompromising demands and an extended period of near hysterical haranguing.

Section Three: Capital Sin

Once back on his feet - dignity having taken a fall - Franz pretended that nothing had happened. Bridget tried to smooth his ruffled feathers with the best words she could muster but he brushed her off. He wanted to dump the incident in seconds, not drag it out minute after laborious minute.

"Wait here," he said, almost snaring, and picked up where he had left off, which was to enter the next powerful part of this most powerful building.

Room 2B was clearly indicated and Franz walked up to its thick wooden door. Its top half consisted of rippled glass through which one could just about make out big wooden desks, wall high shelving and slowly moving figures. Franz knocked tentatively, holding up his ticket like a nervous pupil on his first day at school. A slim stiff body changed direction and answered the call. A young woman with a friendly smile took his ticket and read it with precision. (She recognised the bad handwriting.) She invited Franz in.

If was an office full of paperwork, lists, charts, directives and deadlines. It was an office which had to make it all happen, all come together on the day despite the confusion, despite the mistakes. Franz produced his letter and apologized for being early. She ignored him, concentrating on the letter instead. When she did speak though it felt welcoming despite the fact she used the minimum number of words possible and had played out this scene many times before. (Repetition and routine did not bore her. It was better than chaos and change.) Franz was given confirmation of his hotel booking and reminded that he was three days early. That irked as he had just told her he was early.

"It's sorted," he said.

Next she issued him with a special ID card and wrote down his number in a book. (Cross-referencing was everything in a state which preferred to know who you were, and where, and why.) Finally Franz, chest now puffed out, was told that an escort had been assigned to him for the duration of his stay. His escort was the leader of a Hitler Youth cell specially assembled for the duration of the event. Franz would march with it on Parade Day. Franz was asked for his current address and informed that the young man would contact him.

Business done, Franz was politely and firmly ushered out. He now felt like a very important person. Take note Bridget. On his way out he was struck by a sudden thought.

"Do you have my uncle's address somewhere in this place?"

The woman looked at him, for the first time fiercely, like a headmistress who had been asked a pointless or peculiar question by one of her pupils, or teachers.

Section Three: Capital Sin

"Why would we?"

"He's a member of the Sturmabteilung."

She relaxed: suddenly the question made perfect sense. "Name and rank?"

"Sturmhauptführer Max Helmer."

She pointed. "Go to that room opposite. They maintain all central registers."

Franz thanked her again and did as instructed, flashing his new ID card at another official. This one was a scrawny little man, forced by middle-age to wear thick lenses if he wanted to see detail. Franz was pleasantly surprised to find his enquiry was quickly dealt with, and assumed it was down to his new elevated status - not realising that it was just a matter of a busy man wishing to be free of interruption. With his uncle's address folded away Franz left, head held higher than normal.

On his way out he found Bridget waiting like the dutiful wife and still looking keen. He swept her up on his way and outside, before moving on, he took in the building one last time. The storm troopers continued to stare ahead; their brains frozen by ideology; their wild instincts domesticated, contained for release only to order. It was as if they had not moved an inch - they had of course but then had simply moved back the same inch. Somewhere deep within the building the Reichsmarschall was bringing the house down whilst some official undergoing a nervous breakdown tried in vain to placate him. Outside the official's office two members of the protection squad shared smiles while the rest stood grimfaced. They regarded smiling on duty as unprofessional.

On their way back home Franz was forced to shared his experience with Bridget. (They did not talk about Reichsmarschall Herman Goering: he was too much of a shock right now.) Bridget in return was forced to share a cigarette. It made her cough but she kept at it; wishing to impress him with her sense of adventure.

"Don't tell my parents will you. They mustn't know."

"Of course I won't." Franz felt aggrieved. Why would he do such a thing?

He persuaded her not to take the direct route home but instead 'show me something', as he put it. She thought of a stroll in the park - a perfect end to a perfect day in her mind. There they walked past two men in uniform slumped on a bench, the worse for wear. They were BUF and out on the town. Franz thought they were drunk. Bridget thought it was outrageous. Franz thought it was funny. Franz thought the two men looked second rate, miserable; a poor substitute for the real

Section Three: Capital Sin

thing.

> A walk in the Park before it gets dark
> Is often the way to let emotions sway.
> They wanted to walk. They wanted to talk.
> They wanted to hold hands, like lovers do.
> They had time to spend. Time to cement.
> They walked for a mile to lengthen the smile.
> They were driven to perspire by the speed of intent.
> They wanted to sweat glands, like lovers do.
> One wanted his. One wanted Bliss.
> They both wanted a kiss, like lovers do.

They approached a large monument and stopped; then circled around, to check they were alone; then reached out; then began to snog, madly. Franz had taken the lead and Bridget had followed. But she did not lose her head and firmly set the limits of what Franz could do, and where. Franz did not complain. It was early days. There would be more to come. After they had exhausted themselves they did not hang around. It was getting cold and the light was beginning to fade. Moving on Franz spotted a beer cellar and had to have a beer - his first in Berlin so it would be special. Bridget was not happy with this but right now her opinion did not count. She gave in and decided to treat herself to a small glass of house red. They crept inside, guard up.

"House red? What's that?" asked Franz.

Bridget looked up as if caught in the glare of headlights. "Wine? A glass of red wine?"

Franz nodded, refusing to look stupid. "Oh that."

And with that he put on his best 'over eighteen' disguise and approached the counter while she settled down at a table. He returned quickly with their order, looking clever. He had the big glass. She had the small one. He threw his beer back. She sipped slowly and watched him - when not looking around to see if anybody was watching her. She remained unsettled. She wanted to be off home.

She watched him slow and overtook him. She began to push him on, urge him to drink up quick. Franz laughed her off and Bridget became irritated. Then he became irritated by her irritation. He reminded himself that she was sexy but right now he couldn't sense it let alone react to it. She tugged at his sleeve and reminded him of the time, twice. He pulled away, refusing to work to her timetable. (Where was Lev when he needed him?) But finally he ran out of beer and had to give ground - at which point Bridget was up and out of her chair and

Section Three: Capital Sin

back outside. Franz had no choice except to follow. They said little on their way home: they had run out of talk, steam and harmony. They were just a boy and girl again, under a cloud, and each in a different mood.

Back home they were greeted by the Pole. When she answered the door Franz looked away, down the fancy street full of fancy cars which had not been there earlier. The Pole gave Bridget the look she reserved especially for such lapses then fell back as Bridget brushed past in her hurry to get in. But her way was blocked by Frau Schrimer who made it quite clear, in no uncertain terms and in French, that dinner was 'desperately waiting to be served'. Head down Franz crawled his way back indoors, avoiding the looks of the dangerous Frau Schrimer. Meanwhile Bridget had locked herself in the nearest bathroom and was checking her breath for signs of cigarette smoke or alcohol.

At the dinner table Frau Schrimer sat annoyed while her husband sat impassive. The subject for discussion over dinner was, of course, the trip to Party Central Office. Only then did Bridget mention Reichsmarschall Herman Goering and how incredibly fat he was. The Schrimers smiled. With the genie out of the bottle Franz added that the man was really really fat - so fat that he looked terrible. How was he able to move himself? Franz laughed, and Bridget laughed, and the Schrimer continued to smile. For a long time now they had been in on the joke. After that talk dried up and there was the return to observation and calculation, and more consideration - mainly by Frau Schrimer.

After dinner it was back to Bridget's room, and that small step back in time. The big little sweet, sometimes bittersweet, Bridget returned. Booze and fags and sexual attraction were forgotten as letters were produced to be read out. Franz had to sit through it all, arms folded, face stoic, smile forced as Bridget read out his words of wisdom, exuberance, adventure and near passion. As his mind ticked over in neutral so he began a game: spot his words; spot Lev's words. And try to keep count? No. He soon began to see the difference: Lev was blunt, direct and more flirty; and almost, but not quite, sexually explicit. His own contributions were more formal, by the book, repetitive: friendly definitely, and even wholesome (or 'sweet' as his mother would say); and always respectful. After he had sat through enough of that he persuaded her to 'give it a rest' and go switch on the television instead.

Having escaped to another room Franz threw himself down on a sofa in front of a big wide television screen, bigger than what he had back home. Bridget switched it on and joined him on the sofa. On purpose or by accident she left a gap between them. He noticed and

Section Three: Capital Sin

closed it. Bridget did not seem to mind. She did not move. Franz wanted to grab her there and then but feared the Schrimers would be lurking, spying on him. It was only his first night: wait, he told himself. Plan the battle like every good general. Waiting around for something to happen was something he had practised a lot back home.

They joined the middle of a science fiction film: a black and white renegade from the early 50's. Earth was under attack and out near the rings of Saturn the best of the German military was repulsing the alien invaders with relish. The aliens were filthy hairy beasts who could only scream weird sounds. The Germans who stopped them were an elite force: the best space warriors of the SS were risking everything to save Earth. The German Moon and Mars fleet had intercepted the alien attack force at Saturn. Captured aliens had been put under observation by the German High Command. They watched the aliens throw themselves again and again at the bars of their cage, their shark like teeth extended as they tried to chew their way to freedom. They watched the aliens turn on each other. These were mad monsters, and stupid, the Grand Admiral of the Space Fleet concluded: stupid that these alien barbarians thought they could defeat the defenders of Earth. The aliens looked suspiciously like tall actors in padded costumes made of painted pre-cast rubber.

The odds were heavily stacked against the fleet. Most of its fighter pilots would never see their homes, wives and children again. But none were afraid and none regretted the decision to fight for their country and their planet. It was a fight to the death. Earth had to be saved. The alien barbarians had to be destroyed. That was the script, all neat and tidy. The dialogue was rubbish. The acting was poor. And the special effects were crude. But Bridget loved it. Franz had seen it before, and second time round he didn't. He slouched, sometimes watching the daft film, sometimes watching Bridget getting all excited. After awhile, mainly out of boredom, he began to spoil it for her. Bridget flew into a minor rage and protested as only an angry child would.

"Franz shut up! I haven't seen it! You're spoiling it!"

With that he grinded to a halt and stayed silent. Sod her. He switched off and began to fidget and scratch himself. He wanted to run with his dogs. He wanted to be out on his bike, in the middle of nowhere. He wanted to get drunk with Lev. He wanted to pick a fight.

Captain Von Damme, having destroyed four alien craft, was singled out for attack by three more. Like a plague of locust there was no end to their numbers. They isolated him from his squadron and gave chase. He flew around the moon of Rhea out of sight, did a u-turn, and came at them head on, guns blazing. He took two of them out. Spinning out of

Section Three: Capital Sin

control one disappeared into outer space while the other smashed into the moon and exploded. The remaining opponent managed to land a hit and Captain Von Damme was forced to land on the moon.

On fire, he steered his space fighter down into a large crater and managed to come to rest on a flat plain. Meanwhile the alien craft was still on his tail, firing but always missing. Drowning in smoke Captain Von Damme escaped from his cockpit and ran for his life. He took up defensive position behind a large fake rock and checked his plastic weapon. There he waited, calm, determined. The captain knew what he had to do: he had to save the earth; he had to destroy these evil monsters. The rock was made of fibre glass. The landscape behind him was painted scenery.

The alien craft landed with a bump and the noise of sirens. Three aliens appeared. They were large blubbery, hairy beasts with ugly faces and just the one large eye. They growled and advanced towards the burning craft. The large swastika stamped on its side seemed to infuriate them and they began firing their weapons at it until the whole thing blew up. The German space fighter blew up with all the spectacle of a small exploding truck. Captain Von Damme, or 'Wolf' as he was known, aimed carefully and took one of them out. The alien dissolved into a thick soup of green yuk and slime. The other two turned and began firing. Wolf took up a new position and fired back. A second alien was hit. Now it was one on one: a fair fight in an unfair battle.

The remaining alien screamed abuse and waved its weapon around in the air. But Wolf was not afraid. Wolf was a veteran fighter, one of the fleet's best. He was more than a match for this piece of dirt which dared to invade his solar system. He took his time. He chose his moment then reappeared to shoot again. But no! Nothing happened! His gun was out of charge. As the alien headed towards him, weapon blazing, Wolf scrambled to find a spare cartridge somewhere on his suit and, thank God, he did. He ripped out the old and slammed in the new. He crossed himself as he thought of his wife, his children, his home, his country, his planet. He drew breath and jumped out from behind the rock. He aimed and fired, almost point-blank. The alien was instantly vaporized.

Wolf sat down, exhausted. He crossed himself again and thanked God. This particular battle was over. Now the war just had to be won, and he felt sure it would. Good would always triumph over evil. And the German space fleet would always be there, at battle stations, to make sure that happened. Wolf put out a SOS signal from the radio built into his helmet and in time another fighter picked up his signal. A rescue craft was dispatched to bring him home. When the war was won

Section Three: Capital Sin

Captain Von Damme would receive another commendation and another medal, and big long hugs from his wife and children.

The film played out its obvious ending: the alien invasion force was smashed; the alien scum fled; the survivors of the fleet returned to Earth as heroes. Germany had saved the day and the entire world. Against the odds the Third Reich had triumphed again. The Swastika was now planted on the many rocky moons of Saturn - Rhea, Dione, Iapetus and Hyperion to name just a few - as testament to its crowning achievement. And when the credits began to roll Bridget jumped up and said goodnight. She offered out her hand but Franz delayed, hoping for more. When he did shake it his was limp. Satisfied and sweating, Bridget retired to her bedroom, tired but not yet ready for bed. She was restless. She had much on her mind and it would not easily be shifted.

Franz watched her go, twitching slightly, afraid he had upset her somehow. And then the national news came on, which surprised him: here television didn't shut down at 9 pm. And next he received a greater shock: it was in colour. Colour television! It blew his mind. Why hadn't anybody warned him! He could see the blue sky, the brown earth, the green trees; the red of barbarian blood; the colour in the faces. The black and white he did see was submerged and sidelined. He soaked up the colour: it was a beautiful sight even though the images being broadcast were not. Colour transmission was being rolled out across the country and Berlin was getting it first. Franz didn't want to go home now. He didn't want to go back to black and white. He pushed off his shoes and rubbed his feet together as if trying to light a fire. Like Bridget he was tired but unlike her he was driven to stay up late and watch TV.

He watched Sir Oswald Ernald Mosley of the BUF step out of a jet airliner at Templehof airport and wave before stepping down for the official welcome. The leader of the British Union of Fascists looked pleased with himself. He was amongst friends. They took him seriously here. They had laid out the red carpet. Senior figures in the party had turned out to greet him. (But not the Fuehrer, or Reichsmarschall Herman Goering, or Doktor Goebbels, or Reichsfuehrer Heinrich Himmler.) He saluted some old Nazis in his own distinctive way and they saluted him back in theirs. It looked more comical than serious, more competitive than friendly. Business done the English fascist and his henchmen was driven away in a convoy of black limousines to a smart hotel. There they would smoke cigars, drink gin, and hang around.

After that Franz lost interest for it was more of the same: more on

Section Three: Capital Sin

the mess in Russia; more on the Polish problem; more on the international response to the celebrations and those countries who would be sending representatives. All the usual names would be there - Franco, Mussolini, Piasecki, Szalasi and Sima. Only when news switched to the Jewish problem in British Palestine did Franz sit up and take note. At which point Herr Schrimer walked in and sat down.

The news reported a terrorist bombing in a place called Ramallah. It blamed Jewish terrorists and showed dead and wounded being placed in the back of ambulances whilst the British military police looked on, tired, as they tried to maintain order. Franz felt required to express outrage - partially manufactured to impress Herr Schrimer.

"See they're not like us. They don't fight fair. They hide."

Herr Schrimer could not let that pass unchallenged. "You think we fight fair? You're from the Ukraine, is what we did there fair?"

Franz ran for cover. "I don't know anything about that, you'll have to ask my father. He fought in the war. He won medals."

Franz almost spat the words out as if to poison the strange Herr Schrimer.

"Perhaps I will."

To Franz that sounded like a threat.

"Those British are weak. They let their Jews run riot. They don't deserve an empire."

When it was further reported that some of the terrorists had been killed Franz clapped and punched the air with a fist. Herr Schrimer looked at him with blank expression, as if to remark 'I was never like that.'

Franz tried to sound statesmanlike. "Why do they do such things?"

Herr Schrimer gave no reaction, at least not on the outside. He was thinking of his daughter, and what would become of her. His response when it came was scathing and sarcastic, and wasted on Franz.

"You could argue they are fighting for living space like we fought for ours."

"Who makes them fight like that?"

"We do."

That last comment drew a total blank and Herr Schrimer decided to change the subject.

"So tell me Franz how do you find my daughter?"

Franz took his time before answering, knowing he had to get it right, like on exam day. When he did answer it was good.

"She's as I remember her Herr Schrimer."

"Which is?"

"Remarkable. Very German."

Section Three: Capital Sin

Herr Schrimer had to smile. "Good answer."

And with that he left the room. Franz felt he had been let off the hook. He waited a little, until the path was clear then, like Bridget, retired to his room tired but restless, and conscious that Bridget was just on the other side of the wall, possibly naked. He wished Lev had been there to witness his day. He was missing him, and their private chats; and though he didn't recognise it, their shared insecurities.

Bridget was not naked, not even half undressed. She was sprawled across her bed, searching for comfort from her personal possessions which surrounded her on all sides. Franz loomed large. He was now more important to her than her parents. She felt it in her bones: Franz made her body go weird inside. But he was an odd mix: he could set her on fire or brush her aside; he could be sweet or sour. She replayed their snog in the park. She wanted more of the same. He should be with her now not stuck in front of the television! She rolled over and back again, unable to find a comfortable resting place. She cradled the image of his first appearance at the station. He had looked fantastic. She rolled over again. She wanted him by her side right now. And alongside all that her plans for his stay kept nagging her, demanding realization.

There was a sharp tap at the door. That would be Mother. And it was: the door opened and her mother walked in before Bridget had a chance to object. Frau Schrimer sat herself down on the end of the bed and examined her daughter as if for defects. She could not see anything amiss but recognised change was in the air. Having a boy on the edge of manhood in the house was not a good idea - that had always been her position, but not her husband's. Bridget turned away, objecting to the scrutiny and demanding to be left alone. She refused to answer any questions. She refused to engage. She wanted her privacy back. Finally Frau Schrimer got the message and left the room, afraid she had a rebellion on her hands.

♦

As the brothers settled in for the evening and Luka surveyed his stock there was a sharp bang on the door, followed by two more in quick succession. Lev followed Luka to the door. Both were on alert. It was Inspector Kleine.

"I want a word with you. Outside now." He looked at Lev. "Not you."

"Wait here," said Luka. "It's just business."

"That's right. Just business." Kleine mimicked Luka in a mocking

Section Three: Capital Sin

tone which left Lev angry, but not Luka.

Lev watched the German escort his brother down the corridor and on down the stairs. By now he had classified Inspector Kleine as the enemy, regardless of his dealings with his brother. He rushed back indoors to get a window view. Below he saw the inspector push a young woman - no a girl still - into the arms of Luka who in turn spun her around, inspecting her like a piece of meat. He checked her hair by running his fingers through it. The scene looked creepy. Kleine was creepy. And Lev didn't like it. But he was old enough to know he wasn't expected to like it. The girl - never a woman - looked broken and dejected. Inspector Kleine on the other hand positively cheered up when Luka led her away, by the hand, like a caring father. He looked almost as sad as her. Kleine set off in the opposite direction and Lev stepped away from the window, disturbed.

He was examining the labels on the bottles of French cognac and English gin when there was the same bang on the door. He opened it, not scared but poised for trouble. It was Inspector Kleine again, in a mood more foul than last time. He barged his way in. Now Lev was scared. Did the German want to see his travel documents? Was he about to be arrested?

"Why are you here? Why don't you go home?"

The questions were unexpected and they made Kleine appear weak.

"This is my home now. I'm here to stay."

"You expecting your big brother to feed you, look after you?"

"No." Lev replied firmly, and with relish, feeling he was in an equal fight.

"The poor bastard can barely look after himself."

Lev was not drawn to comment, sensing that silence was the best thing now. He watched Kleine look around the room at all the varied items which littered it.

"This will draw attention," he said under his breath.

He turned on Lev one last time before leaving. "Don't you go getting ideas. I want you out, gone."

Lev was tempted to slam the door in his face. He didn't. He just shut it, hard. Did his brother really have to do business with this German scum who thought he owned him? Blood up, Lev needed a cigarette to calm himself down, and in desperation he ripped open one of the cartons. He would promise to pay for it later.

◆

Overnight, in a strange bed, Franz suffered a strange dream. He saw

Section Three: Capital Sin

his father, in his tank; fighting aliens, Russians, Ukrainians and all the peasants who worked his land. He saw his father fight himself to death. He saw himself flying a space fighter, and fighting the same enemies. He saw the big fat Reichsmarschall ahead, but dead; blown up in outer space; face still grinning. He had Goebbels screaming 'attack, attack, attack!' in his face. He saw the Reichsfuehrer standing at the rear, present but in the barest sense. He saw the Fuehrer staring down from a vast screen, in full glorious colour; as always never pleased, never displeased, never giving much away. With the Fuehrer nothing came free. It all had to be paid for, including delivery. He had to fight on and on.

He snapped awake in a strange room with a strange smell - it came from the sheets. It was the smell of scented detergent. He heard noise coming from other parts of the house. It should have been familiar but it sounded strange. He tumbled his way into his pants and trousers and crept to the bathroom, hoping not to meet any Schrimers on his way.

Business done, he crept back.

Fully dressed he carried on creeping: down the stairs and into the dining room where he found Bridget waiting - probably for him he guessed. (He wasn't sure if he liked that or not - a female banging on his head first thing in the morning was a headache.) She had eaten her fill. She was smiling - excessively for that time of day. She welcomed him to the table and asked what he wanted for breakfast.

"The usual stuff."

It was all Franz could say but it was enough for the Pole: she served him the standard fare. He could take it or leave it. Franz wolfed it down trying not to watch Bridget watching him eat; trying not to swap the Pole for Aneta; trying to remember Lev. (At this time of the day ignoring sharp reminders, remembering the vaguely distant, thinking anything complicated proved difficult, near impossible for him.) And while he ate Bridget talked on and on about what they could do today, before finally settled on a trip to the zoo. He accepted, not giving a damn. He tried to concentrate on just one thing: how to keep on the right side of Bridget and how to avoid her parents. And just as he thought of those two Frau Schrimer popped her head around the door. Checking up on him again, Franz reasoned. He needed to get out - yes let it be the zoo, he could do with a dose of wild animals. Meanwhile he kept on eating, forced to admit that the food was better here than at home.

The door bell sounded which the Pole answered. There was talk at the door then she called out for Bridget. More talk followed and Bridget in turn called out for Franz who in turn dragged himself away

Section Three: Capital Sin

from the table, brain now furious with the thought that someone out there had found him. Right now he wanted to be left alone. It was a boy: a boy on the edge of manhood, perhaps just two years behind Franz but a boy nevertheless in Franz's eyes, and not worth the recognition. But recognition was demanded as he was dressed in the uniform of the Hitler Youth, impeccably so. It suddenly hit Franz that his lot back home were a scruffy bunch.

The boy stood stiff, with stern expression. But before he could announce himself Franz jumped in first, having guessed who he was and why he was here. In his mind the rule was this kid would talk up to him, as he would talk down. He was the older, that made him senior, the wiser one.

"You're my escort?"

"That's correct." The boy did not salute. "Gebhard Strasser."

"Right."

"Hallo," said Bridget. She sounded sweet, and hence out of place.

"Hallo." The boy replied as if under duress, as if the smiling girl in front of him was a danger to be avoided; or perhaps just beyond his reach.

Bridget invited him in but he declined the offer, preferring to remain outside. Franz was happy with that. A true toy soldier, he thought, with a metal rod stuck up his arse. Just as he turned away Gebhard, the toy soldier, pulled something out from a breast pocket.

"Hang on there I was told to give you this!"

With an air of authority he thrust forward a sealed envelope, just like he had seen the military do in the war films. Guard up, Franz took possession. It carried the Party stamp. It weighed heavy. Slowly he opened the envelope and took out the letter then held back.

Bridget nudged him to complete the action. "Go on then read it."

He read it, and as he did so his mouth fell open and his head began to buzz. Time slowed but his pace quickened - with nowhere to go accept round and round in circles. It was an invitation, stating a specific time and place, and it was non-negotiable. It could not be refused. It was a black hole slowly sucking Franz in.

"Well? Tell me."

"It's an invitation to meet the Reichsfuehrer." His voice trembled. As his mother was not there he turned on Bridget. "Do I have to?"

Right now she was the last person to turn to for advice as she too was overwhelmed. She was in danger of wetting herself.

Gebhard cut in. "Of course you do. You don't refuse an invitation to meet Reichsfuehrer Heinrich Himmler - and it's not an invitation stupid it's an order."

Section Three: Capital Sin

Franz could not argue with that. He sat down on the doorstep: his legs were to weak to take his weight. Bridget sat down beside him - she had to. She put her hands between her knees, tightening her skirt around her legs as she did so, and in doing so gave hints as to her sexuality. Gebhard noticed. Franz didn't. He was elsewhere, clinging on for life. The toy soldier looked down at them both wondering what all the fuss was about. He turned the screw.

"I've had mine. It's no big deal. We've all had them."

He was lying: it had been a big deal.

"We?"

"My cell. We're a special cell - special for the big day. And I'm it's leader."

His announcement boomed out proudly. He was back on the higher ground. He had regained authority over this country bumpkin from out east.

Franz looked up the Hitler Youth trooper standing over him, immaculately turned out and so full of himself - so full he might burst like a balloon at any moment.

"What's so special about you?"

"My birthday - our birthdays. We share the same birthday as our Fuehrer. Don't you? Isn't that why you're assigned to my cell?"

"Yes," croaked Franz. He broke the spell. "Let's go to the zoo."

"Great!" exclaimed Bridget and up she jumped, like a coiled spring released.

She pulled Franz up on to his feet. And he loved every moment of it. The other kid might be a cell leader but he had a woman in his life: that won hands down every time. Gebhard watched her smile - too much - and thought it a sign of weakness, or corruption. (He didn't know which.) The girl was weak at the knees, throwing herself at a second class East German. She was an insult to the Bund Deutscher Madel.

Heading ringing with the latest smack Franz disappeared back inside: there to waste time before conceding to Bridget's master plan. He had some more coffee and more bacon and thought of the poker faced brat standing outside - better that than think of the Reichsfuehrer. Bridget was patient and waited, and watched. She reminded herself that he was her guest and therefore could do whatever he wanted. She just wanted to show him her zoo: a simple need that she now had to get off her chest, now it was stuck there.

Outside Gebhard Strasser fought the boredom by reminding himself that duty came first, that orders were orders and he always followed orders. Always razor sharp - and so prone to cut himself - Gebhard had

Section Three: Capital Sin

already picked up on the country accent and added it to his list of grievances. He didn't want to be here, forced to 'escort' some twit from the backwoods of a German colony. He had a cell to lead, and a war to fight: the war of crime on the streets; the war of back street subversion; the war of immorality. Gebhard stood stiff, as if glued to the spot, arms nailed to his side. Like his body his mind stood stiff, locked on to the simple task of waiting for the next instruction to appear; sometimes in a mood, sometimes vacant; sometimes with loathing, sometimes with hate; rarely with forgiveness, rarely conceding defeat; never with comedy, never with charm. Long ago the grand, guarded sulk he had acquired since he had first been forced to chew on nasty sour food had become the essence of his soul; and later he had dressed it in a bright brown uniform. Now he was perfection. Others may disagree.

His uniform was his pride and joy. He never allowed mud to remain on his boots for longer than necessary - mud never made it through the night on his boots. At the end of each day, no matter how tired, he would clean them, scrupulously, and make them presentable for the next day. He had to stay clean, a cut above the rest. He had to set an example for others to follow - else they might not follow. In his mind of limited means but great aspirations the nation had to be supervised, watched and watched over, and most of all kept in check. Gebhard did not regard people as good, only compliant, dutiful, above criticism. He regarded it as his sworn duty to hunt down and expose the thieves, the liars, the troublemakers, and the misfits. They had to be exposed and reported to the authorities. For him the ban on Jews in his city was a shame: it would have been fun to chase them down and round them up. At the moment Gebhard was only a danger to himself. When older he would be a danger to others.

The simple act of 'going to the zoo' became a battle of wills between Bridget and Gebhard Strasser: each wished to lead the way; each regarded Berlin as their own backyard. Franz thought it funny as they argued over the best route to the zoo. At times he saw himself as a man surrounded by children. The zoo was the pride and joy of Berlin. Everybody went there, and not just to see the animals. It was a good place to hang out, relax and talk without fear of being overheard, and possibly reported. Inside was unlike the world outside. Outside the wild ran free. Inside it had been tamed, caged. Inside you didn't have to fight and kill for your food.

On the way Franz invented another game: spot when Gebhard was smiling. The odds were against him. Gebhard never seemed to smile. It was as if he hated the very thought of doing so. And when it came to talking about the Jews, Gebhard refused to be drawn, as Franz

Section Three: Capital Sin

discovered when he joked about his 'spot the Jew' game.

"Have you ever spotted a Jew here in Berlin?"

"Of course not."

Too serious by half, thought Franz. Where are you Lev.

And when they arrived Bridget was shocked to discover that it had been taken over by the Party, just like the rest of the city. Everywhere there were huge, snarling swastikas; blood red and crying out the same old message. Bridget kept her thoughts to herself, not trusting Gebhard Strasser, and as they entered she took Franz's hand. She wanted him to trust her, feel safe. He allowed it, but only because he trusted himself.

On the inside Bridget was the child again, scampering here and there; sometimes pulling Franz along with her zeal; sometimes leaving him behind. And when she let go of him he found himself missing the pleasure, for pleasure was what it was now: the pleasure of being held by a woman. Yet in his mind he was holding her - never her holding him. She was holding on as he was the stronger one, the one in control. Gebhard Strasser became neatly forgotten, but he still tagged along, determined not to enjoy himself.

At Bridget's insistence they treated themselves to ice-creams, and licked, hard; like time for such things was running out fast. Franz saw an opportunity to act the superior gentleman and paid for Bridget's. Gebhard refused his offer, preferring to pay his own way and be beholding to no one. Franz and Bridget licked theirs together, in unison, and with wild abandon as it became a race. The ice-cream temporarily dragged Franz screaming and giggling back into childhood. Gebhard remained cautious and on alert, afraid he might stain his uniform.

At the monkey house a gorilla sat and scratched; and gazed out, impassive; giving nothing away, possibly taking nothing in; perhaps contemplating life outside the cage, in the land of the free; that place where humans were allowed to run wild and do mad, bad things in the name of intellect and breeding. He could not remember now if he had been born free. He only knew for certain that he would die in prison, whilst being stared at, like dying was something unnatural. He wasn't even that sure exactly what freedom was, or meant. But there was always food, and always on time, so he tried not to think too hard about such things. And the humans always scooped up his shit, which was good. They were good for something, his long lost cousins.

The gorilla's sad eyes wandered between Franz, the bigger human beast, and the other slightly smaller, weaker looking human standing stiff and strong in bright clothes. It was no contest. He had already decided that Franz was the threat, the competition. The other one was

Section Three: Capital Sin

just an eyesore; crazy looking; all bark and no bite.

Most of the animals passed Franz by as he passed them by. His mind was barely set on animals behind bars, more on Uncle Max. One caged animal was much like another, and in his mind no match for those out in the wild. A bear in this place looked pathetic, an easy victory. Back home a bear presented a real threat. It took courage and daring to hunt one down and kill it. He looked around, feeling supreme: these soft city kids didn't have a clue.

The more he thought about his uncle the more he wanted to see him; to see what had happened to him; to check him out; to make comparisons and award points. He had a sudden urge to compare his father with someone and Uncle Max was that natural someone. Uncle Max had popped up in his childhood, in that time when his framework for life was so simple it didn't need thinking about, explaining, or justifying. It was simply done. And on and off Uncle Max had been part of that. He had to go see Uncle Max.

He had to go see Uncle Max.

He had to go see Uncle Max. Surprise him. Would Uncle Max recognise him? The last time he had met Uncle Max he had barely reached his chest. Now he might well be the one looking down. Yes surprise him. The Helmers loved surprises - or so he had been taught.

◆

Lev was stuck in the back of a white van, heading somewhere fast, or fleeing fast. Sometimes he wasn't sure which. It was a bumpy ride and Lev was rattled. Luka was up front with the man who had approached him over lunch. Grudgingly, as if under oath, Luka had introduced him as his 'mate', and jokingly as his 'boss'. The man had grinned at Luka on being called 'the boss'.

Their destination was a long way out of town. They left behind the neat assembly of inner town planning and continuity, and made for the border strip between city and open country; between industry and farming; between the serious money and the struggling beat of country life. Luka and his mate, 'the boss', the leader of a criminal gang fell into talking Czech and stayed there - though Luka spoke little and listened a lot. Lev became temporarily forgotten, which was fine by him. His stomach was playing up and he was feeling sick and very soft. Lev saw his big brother as a small man alongside the boss. Perhaps the reference had been no joke. Luka held on to him, stood in his light, even when seated. Lev stared out of the back window and pushed such controversial thoughts away. He did not want to

Section Three: Capital Sin

downgrade his brother.

In time they reached a deserted industrial estate - a grey dull derelict island of decay and disenchantment surrounded by the green land of the living and breathing - and drove in at speed. The gates had long since been whipped away. Lev felt queasy. He had to get out and stand on his feet but when the door opened he was told to stay put by the boss. Luka did not question the command. There was business to be done here - not Lev's business the boss had decided on the way. He and Luka were here to meet a particular kind of man: a man who did not welcome unknown faces unless forewarned and forearmed.

The buildings were in a state of collapse and Mother Nature was slowly reclaiming the land with force and determination, and a complete lack of fanfare. Weeds were in the ascent. They blossomed. Windows were mainly missing, else smashed. Doors were falling off their hinges. Concrete was cracked. Paint had peeled to the point of total disintegration. It had never been a nice place. Now it was a non-place, an ulcer on the landscape, an open wound. Everything had been smashed or grabbed. Once it had hummed and hassled, and haggled with the market place. Now it collected flies and entertained colonies of ants with its dead meat and decaying matter. It was a scrap yard of shift patterns and overtime sheets. The work had been wasted and the daydreaming dumped. The goods and services had gone elsewhere. The rush hour had been brushed aside. Only wicked wild dogs scraped a living.

Here the masonry suppressed you and made you suffer. You were forced to chew on stone, or if really stuck, get stoned. The remaining tough tissue of the buildings was red brick. Here the bricks saw safety in numbers. Those that were broken and strewn around lacked all measure, all purpose. They were being reduced to rubble. A few skeletons of defunct machinery remained; stained, sticky, and rusty. All the useful cuts of metal had been stripped off, like meat off the bone. And there was the stuff which had slipped in unnoticed, as if this was their natural retirement home come graveyard: rusty baths, rancid fridges and crumbling gas cookers. They could easily and suddenly disappear just as they had arrived.

This place was not for the living, nor the dying, but simply those stuck in a state of decay, without rights or ambition; the kind that could be worked until wasted. This rock hard place, constructed from a set of templates, was not a place to continue life but a place to waste away, wanting. Here soft creature comforts could not take root, only weeds and sour grass, thorny bushes and the occasional limp tree. In this place you were hard. Your skin was hardened. Hurt was a luxury.

Section Three: Capital Sin

Gracious intent was abandoned outside else snapped in two across the back of another man's neck. Stay here too long and you might forget to engage in wishful thinking - worse still forget the art of thinking your way out into a brighter future.

The wild dogs, alerted by the sound of a diesel engine, stood guard with gritted teeth and watched from a safe distance. This was their home, their territory, through which they sneaked by day and ran by night. They had staked out their claim and now stuck with it, until death. For them humans were a dangerous mix: both a familiar and unfamiliar substance; both warm and cold; both precious and provocative; lame and tame. Humans were not superior flesh, just dangerous meat. Unfortunately they were rarely a source of food. That had to be snatched from elsewhere - anywhere at any time. Once, as domesticated dogs, some of them had always had the appetite for human engagement. Now, wild, they did not take kindly to human intrusion. They monitored the situation carefully, growling their concerns. Come too close and they were prepared to strike. Keep your distance and they remained interested. Look scared and they could be deadly. Fire a gun and they would scatter, only to reform.

The three wise men muttered as they talked and passed around a cigarette. It was not the talk of equals. Lev tried to catch proceedings through the windscreen; wanting to take it in, even in the absence of good sound. He could smell money in the air. The three argued, briefly, as if protocol demanded it; before settling down into constructive talk. Luka talked the least and fidgeted the most, else shuffled around as if on lookout. The other two stood loud. He stood uneasy and Lev saw it. When the three men disappeared inside a buggered building - a nasty, forlorn construction even when it had been brand new - Lev felt he had to get out of the van and rediscover the sunlight. He was suffocating.

Lev fell out and looked around. He was reminded of another place much closer to home. His mind played a trick and he decided now that that place had more dignity, more purpose, more authority; perhaps even more charm. He almost tiptoed across the concrete patches, the puddles of green weed, and the dark crumbling remains of tarmac. He wanted to reach the doorway unnoticed for a better view of what was going down. There were other men inside, all heavily tanned. Three he counted, crouched over a small struggling fire; rubbing hands, keeping warm; sheltering their egos; staying alive.

They uncurled themselves and stood up slowly, wanting and waiting to be counted. There was business in the air. The boss walked around, stranger by his side. Luka held back, arms crossed, looking mean for

Section Three: Capital Sin

no reason. Lev could tell his brother was putting on the family 'hard man' act. He saw a power grab being played out. He saw the weak and possibly useless attempting equality and equilibrium with the strong and the strict. He didn't feel sorry for these miserable men: once, he suspected, they had probably had it good, had it better than him or his brother.

Another argument erupted. The three men under examination looked at each other like there was a spy amongst them, like they were being sold down the river. The boss told two of them to come forward smart. They did so only after first looking to the stranger for permission. He gave it. Satisfied, the boss told them to get in the back of his van. The one rejected protested at the insult, his sudden anger sweeping aside his earlier submission. The other two hesitated. They stuck by him and vented similar anger: as three they were stronger than two. Economics made no sense here.

A nasty row broke out. There was pushing and shoving. Luka stormed into the fray. He went for the third man who was excess to requirements and grabbed his wrist tightly, forcing his hand aloft. The poor man was caught off guard. He cried out in pain but Luka held him tight. It was a deformed, withered hand. It did not shake. As the lone spectator Lev watched it play out and it sent a shiver down his back. He had to shout - to save his own soul if no one else's.

"Luka!"

Luka turned and nearly exploded. "Get back in the van!"

Lev was nearly thrown off his feet by the blast. He didn't hang around but before tearing himself away Lev threw his big brother a foul dirty look. It had last been used when Luka stole his petty cash. It had not been petty. It had been very important: Lev had only been nine at the time. He scrambled back into the van, almost throwing himself back inside like a piece of lost luggage. In no time the two men who had been selected joined him. They sat, sold short, and said nothing. Each had a lot on his mind but not a lot to say. Each had little control over his destiny but little determination to increase it. Each had a hungry stomach but not a hungry head. Lev felt vulnerable.

Even as the van drove away the men had dumped their friend from their minds: he was a liability, a cripple; a waste of space. There was no future in knowing him. (When the three had been children growing up together these two had ridiculed him yes, but equally they had protected him. Now he was somebody else's problem, or his own problem.) After a long drive back into town the two men were dumped at an address where they would work and not complain. And Lev ended up feeling sick again.

Section Three: Capital Sin

◆

Bridget and Gebhard argued over the location and the best way to get there; and after two tram rides; and forced hilarity; and a forced march led by Gebhard they found the address. Flat 5 Steinstrasse. It was an apartment block in a fashionable street, which pleased Franz. It matched the Schrimers for class and posturing.

A young man, wearing the uniform of the Sturmabteilung was just entering the building. He removed his cap, to reveal looks which could crack the ladies wide open, if he so wished it. Like many young men in uniform he was in a hurry, with a mission, and without second thoughts. He bounded up the stairs as if towards some feast or party, or some great reward. Franz followed him in, and up to the first floor where he saw the storm trooper knock on a door and enter swiftly. It felt strange to be on his trail, as if spying on him. Franz wanted to shout out to the world that he was not spying on anybody, and as he drew close he realised it was his uncle's flat. His uncle had a visitor but no matter, Uncle Max would be pleased to see his nephew. Franz straightened himself, checked his hair, forced his best smile and knocked.

No answer. He knocked again. Nothing. Stumped he knocked one last time, apologized then, bewildered, wandered back down the stairs with a look which alerted Bridget immediately.

"There's no answer."

Franz spoke in a whisper, as if announcing a sudden death in the family.

Bridget didn't understand. "Well he's not in then?"

"But I just saw that other man, that storm trooper enter?"

Gebhard Strasser saw the chance and took the initiative. "This isn't right. This is not right."

Gebhard often made a point of repeating himself: it sounded good; it sounded like he was in command. He stormed into the building and like a heat seeking missile shot up the stairs towards flat number 5. Franz followed, running to catch up. Bridget in turn chased after him, not wishing to lose him. They all arrived out of breath and in a little adventure of their own making. Gebhard banged on the door, and again and again; refusing to go away; refusing to take no for an answer. Franz backed away, wanted to hide, wanting no part of it. Bridget watched Gebhard Strasser like a hawk, sensing danger. Finally the door was suddenly flung open and a man stood holding on to it as if ready for a fight. It was Uncle Max and he was in a bad mood.

Section Three: Capital Sin

He stood welded to the door. His face was pale - turned pale by the uniform of the Hitler Youth. He looked around for others but there was just this one - possibly dangerous, possibly not - and two other kids. Perhaps they were lost. Perhaps they had the wrong address. He listened out for whispers in the crowd, but heard none. It was just these three kids, standing in a silence of his own making. He did not dare turn around to check if his 'best friend' was safe. He wanted to keep his 'best friend' completely out of the thick of it. He wanted to protect and spare his 'best friend' from all and any danger. He looked like a schoolboy on whom a big joke was being played out by all the others. He looked totally lost for words. He looked for the trick but there was no trick, just these three kids; one of whom was a blushing girl; one of whom was the Hitler Youth; one of whom was . . . but before he could make the connection Gebhard Strasser spoke.

"Herr Helmer?"

"Yes?" Right now Sturmhauptführer Max Helmer was happy to not broadcast his rank.

"You have a visitor."

Uncle Max stared back at the little shit in the smart uniform and saw a big shit in the making.

"Do I. And who the fuck are you?"

The eyes of Gebhard Strasser turned nasty and he said nothing. Franz moved in quickly.

"It's me, Franz."

Uncle Max looked at the second face and something hit him - familiarity, family. Franz? He looked the face over and over: yes it was his nephew - big boy now - and he was stuck. He could not shut the door on family, nor could he let him in. He was begging for a way out. Franz was begging for a way in. Bridget wanted to go home.

Uncle Max preferred to say nothing as in his world talk became gossip which in turn became poison. But he had to say something, and quick.

"Franz?"

"Hello uncle."

"What are you doing here?"

"The celebrations? I'm here for the parade."

By 'here' Uncle Max had meant his front door.

The explanation evaporated into thin air and he looked at his nephew as if the boy had been transported there by magic; else a scam, a plot to catch him out. And suddenly much came flooding back. And then he realised he was in his dressing gown.

"Excuse me I've just got up."

Section Three: Capital Sin

Uncle Max kept telling himself that it was just coincidence - this little shit in the uniform staring at him, threatening. Meanwhile all three strained to look over his shoulder but he moved forward and blocked their view. Then the head of the storm trooper popped up above his shoulder. He had stood up. He looked startled, scared even. A storm trooper scared of a few faces? Franz didn't get it, nor did Bridget. Gebhard Strasser did. He saw a dirty boy doing dirty tricks to please his master. He saw the devil, the despicable; eyes down, looking to conceal himself in his own shame. He had a question for the sick man.

"What's his name," he said, pointing at the man in the room.

"None of your sodding business."

Gebhard walked away disgusted. This was a disgrace, and at such a time. He would be found outside kicking stones.

Uncle Max had a fatter, rounder version of his father's face. Or perhaps he didn't. Franz could not decide. The eyes made it all different. The dressing gown did not impress, nor the untidy hair. Franz wanted to apologize on behalf of the family. Uncle Max did not invite him in. He seemed to take no interest in why Franz was here. He just wanted the whole lot of them to go away, immediately.

"Look it's not convenient right now. Give me your number and I'll call you. We'll go out somewhere. Dinner, you fancy dinner?"

His uncle sounded desperate and Franz nodded, as if to reassure him. He took it badly but said nothing, deciding that it was his fault for turning up unannounced. He turned to Bridget for help. She gave the man her telephone number, but wished she hadn't. They headed home, tails between their legs.

When they arrived home and she discovered her parents were out, Bridget was determined to play, play music, play music loud: her music, the music her father had brought back from abroad. But there was still the serious Gebhard Strasser: she felt required to invite him in, so as to get him to leave. The Pole made them tea, and gave them cake, and watched the boys consume in private disgust. Gebhard Strasser was in no hurry to leave. He wanted to outstay his welcome for as long as possible so as to annoy the high and mighty Franz. Franz on the other hand didn't give a damn. He charged his way through chocolate cake brooding, reliving the moment at his uncle's door, examining it for clues or innocent explanations.

Bridget asked Gebhard if he wanted to come upstairs and listen to the new rock and roll music, the stuff from America. He said no, definitely not: that rock and roll was foul black music. Bridget looked lost for words so Franz stepped in, just for the fight.

Section Three: Capital Sin

"It's not foul. It's rock and roll. White people like us play it. It's all the rage in Britain and France."

Gebhard shook him off with new thoughts.

"My cell is meeting at noon tomorrow at Oranien Platz on Oranienburger Strasse. You can find it?"

"I can find it."

"We are going on patrol."

"Patrol?"

"Yes patrol. Patrolling the streets is one of our duties. You are not familiar with this?"

"Yes I am. We do the same back home." It was a necessary lie.

"Are you joining us, seeing as you have been assigned to my cell?"

Franz was caught. He had to say yes. But then again, why not? It might be fun. And it would break the boredom. Bridget had got pushed out the way.

"Yes I'll be there."

"On time?"

"On time."

Heil Hitler, thought Franz. Bridget asked if she could come and both boys looked at her as if she was mad. She bit her lip, realising she had asked a stupid thing.

Satisfied that he was still in charge Gebhard allowed her to show him to the door. Franz watched him go, satisfied that he could beat him. But Gebhard Strasser had the last word and the timing was so perfect he could had been saving it for this moment.

"By the way I might report him."

"Who?"

"Your uncle."

Gebhard smiled and walked on. Franz was stuck on the spot and trembling slightly. He wanted to shout 'fuck off!' as loud as possible but was trapped by the truth of the allegation. Then he remembered he had a gun. He wanted to hold it. He wanted to load it. He wanted to use it.

Bridget stood at the front door and watched the boy in uniform walk - almost march - away, as if to the worse kind of civil war. She saw a religious, puritanical maniac with a hint of soldier. She saw a type of person she instinctively knew she must avoid in later life if she was to prosper. She hoped Franz would not go the same way, into mental oblivion. She remembered the summer camp and thought 'no, no way'. No way?

Chocolate cake gone, Franz was led away by Bridget, up the stairs to her bedroom. There he was told to sit and listen. Franz made it clear

Section Three: Capital Sin

he wanted to kiss. Bridget made it clear she wanted to dance: kissing came after dancing. She loaded a stack of singles on to her record player and set the arm in motion. Something switched her on inside and she began to move to the music. Franz watched her, fascinated but far away. No way was he into this strange routine of the natives. Bridget laughed and begged him to dance. She demanded that he dance. She needed him to get up and join in; to prove that he was fun to be around; not glum, not serious, not a plain Nazi. She demanded they danced face to face, his face in hers. There could be no distance between them. She seized his hands. They were sweating. The poor boy had to dance if he was to survive. Franz was in her bedroom and music was playing. He had to dance. That was the rule round here.

Franz just didn't get it. It looked like a stupid thing to do. It would expose him, leave him vulnerable to accusations of inferiority. He resisted but she wouldn't have it. She kept trying to pull him up. Only when he realised it would allow him to grab her round the waist did he cave in and, like the caveman, step out into the light. He did not want to be cut off, left out, marked down as a killjoy. He did not want to end up like his dad.

It wasn't so bad he discovered and slowly, gradually, he fell into the moment. It sucked him in. His mind closed down and his body opened up. But still Franz could not dance, not to save his life. He just moved around. It was painful to watch. Bridget helped him, steered him. Like a mother teaching her baby to walk she moved him to the beat. Bridget was no child but also she was no woman. She was just a teenager, dancing to rock and roll music like her life depended on it - and in this time and place perhaps it did. American music was fun, invigorating. Nazi music was deadly dull, as dull as dishwater. It closed you down. It left you with a headache. It left you old before your time.

Franz began to move as Bridget moved. The sound was less important to him than her moving body. She was hot and sweaty. And she was hot. He lost himself in her heat, in her wild abandon. He saw more energy in her than he had seen at the zoo. And he found the beat and latched on, and held on. And he felt great, and forgot why he was in Berlin, and who he had seen, and who he had to see, and how he had to be seen. They locked hands. He pulled her in. She pushed back and let go. She wanted to dance, not be hooked. She allowed their fingers to entwine but that was it. He tried to kiss her but she was a moving target. She kept on rocking, kept on baiting him with her body to do likewise. But it was the body he wanted, not the beat of some strange foreign music. America was a strange place if they danced to this.

Section Three: Capital Sin

And then the telephone rang downstairs. The sound cut like a knife on the ear. The Pole answered it and was soon knocking on the door. It was for Franz: it was his uncle on the line. He gave her the dirtiest look possible - one he had previously used on Aneta to great effect. The Pole brushed it aside and returned to her house duties. She had no time for this little shit from out east, and dropped every hint possible; this time to great effect.

Franz took the call in a trance and agreed to meet his uncle for dinner, in approximately half an hour. 'Take it or leave it' his uncle had said. He gave his address and said goodbye, exhausted by simple conversation. After he put the phone down, nothing felt right. He had been swept away by an unknown force. He rejoined Bridget but sat as if broken. The thought of meeting his uncle now filled him with great unease. It wasn't supposed to be like this. Uncle Max was in the Sturmabteilung. Uncle Max was a true blue Nazi party official. He didn't notice when the music faded and Bridget sat down beside him, concerned by his silence.

"What's wrong?"

"Nothing's wrong."

She took his hand - or rather it slipped into hers.

"Does your uncle scare you?"

Franz swallowed his next word. "No." He tried to grab her. "Let's kiss."

Bridget pushed away. "No. Not now."

So they sat in silence until the doorbell rang to tear them apart. Bridget rushed to answer it, and called out to Franz that his uncle was here. Franz stood at the top of the stairs, out of sight. He could not make a decision about taking the next step. He could chase Jews, and bears; and shoot at Russians; and screw the servants; but he could not make this decision. He felt the Helmer name slipping from his grasp, along with the officer uniform of the glorious Schutzstaffeln. And then in his mind he saw Gebhard Strasser watching him for defects. He decided to make a move.

"Fuck you," he said as he went down the stairs.

His uncle had not stepped inside. He was not even on the doorstep. Bridget pointed out, across the street, and there was Uncle Max, standing by a fast fancy sports car. He stood remote, unable to step forward and engage. He was smoking fast. He looked wasted, even slightly worried; definitely in a hurry; definitely unsettled by the appointment which he had made. He did not look like a Helmer - a fact not lost on Franz.

Franz eased out into the open, beyond Bridget. Strangely now he

Section Three: Capital Sin

did not want to leave her behind. His heart was pounding as he made to cross the street. But try as he might he could not go through with it. And as he tried, his uncle's half weary, half worn smile fell away; to leave a void which right now could not be filled. Here was a German without family, without Party, without country, without belief in anything except himself. And when that failed it was total failure, total meltdown. But like before Max Helmer would pick himself up and carry on as before. He still had to be caught.

Franz gave up and retreated back indoors, where it was safe, where Bridget was. He looked out through the hall window and traced his uncle's movements, which were few: he moved round the car; open the driver's door; and got in, in a hurry. Uncle Max had got the message and that made Franz feel a bit better. Everything was neat and tidy for now. He watched his misfit uncle speed away then sat down on the bottom of the stairs, watching - by accident - the Pole retrieve a vacuum cleaner from a cupboard. Meanwhile Bridget was getting ready for a bath.

When Franz heard the bath filling up and Bridget entering the bathroom he sat himself down at the top of the stairs, better to listen in on her. Then he moved in closer still and sat down directly outside, like a tramp hoping for a throwaway coin. He wanted to know exactly what she was doing, and how. He could hear her on the other side of the door, moving around, testing the water. He heard the water slap the sides of the bath as she slipped in. On the other side of the door Bridget was in her element: she was having a hot bath; her parents were out; and she had a boy around the house who had the hots for her. She just didn't know how to play it. She had an ally, an accomplice: her yellow rubber duck. It joined her in the bath like an old friend for whom discretion was taken as read.

Franz played it out inside his head for maximum pleasure: he saw Bridget, ripe for picking, strip off and slip naked into the bath; feeling herself, touching her breasts. He could barely contain himself. She was just on the other side of the door. He backed down, afraid of his own fantasy, but could not lie in peace. He had to make way for the Pole who was heading straight for him, hoovering like hell. The Pole made no comment but her face said it all, and Franz read it all. She was just a Pole and he felt it within his rights to tell her to fuck off. He didn't and instead gave her the benefit of the doubt. She was bored, he told himself. Just like Aneta, he told himself. In his mind they had to talk. But what to talk about? She stalled when she realised she was the centre of his attention.

"What?"

Section Three: Capital Sin

"Nothing. Just watching."
"Why?"
"Don't know. Bored?"
"Well don't." She carried on, the German threat dealt with.

Behind her back Franz stuck up two fingers. He wished she was Aneta, so he could fuck her second time round without regret. He carried on waiting then, as his patience became exhausted, he knocked on the door.

"When you coming out?"

There was the splash of water and a long pause before Bridget replied.

"I thought you were out?"

"I changed my mind. Wanted to stay here." It was the perfect lie, just one centimetre to the right of the truth.

A long silence followed until Bridget had more to say.

"I'll be out soon, hang on."

"Don't worry I'm not going anywhere."

He heard her giggle, and took pride in the fact he could make her giggle. Bridget appeared in her bathrobe and headed straight for her room. Franz followed behind, like a lapdog, tongue hanging out. He swore he could see her through her robe. The outline was clear, and there were pressure points: her nipples; her hip bones; her thighs; her bum. It was all there to be read, and was, avidly.

He called after her. "You said we could kiss after we danced. We've danced, let's kiss."

No reply at first: then Bridget made a sudden dash for her door, jumped inside and closed it before Franz could touch her. She was laughing while Franz stood on the other side and conducted an experiment: would Bridget let him in without him having to do anything? Yes she would. In time the door was slowly opened and Bridget sat down on one end of her bed. Franz sat down on the other. He watched her calm down.

She sat there, still wet inside her bathrobe, hair wet at the ends. She was a glorious sight. At the very least Franz had to touch her robe. He leant forward and she let him touch it. He pulled it back to reveal one delicate, perfectly formed, man-sized monster of a breast. It was not big but it was a monster to him. He had to touch it, claim it. He reached out slowly, trembling with pleasure, and she allowed him to touch. He went further: he rubbed it. He moved in closer. He positively massaged it, almost out of existence. Almost in heaven Bridget had her eyes closed but still she had her eye on him. He snapped and lounged forward, his hand travelling up her leg. It was

Section Three: Capital Sin

erratic, like his brain. She snapped and stopped him. She pushed him away.

There was a noise at the door: the parents were back - back from the dead as far as Franz was concerned. Bridget wrapped herself up. She gave Franz a frosty look, expecting him to leave the room quickly. But he didn't. He had been insulted so was determined to make her pay by embarrassing her out of existence. He was tempted to sing out loud a Ukrainian folk song; one Lev had sung to him many times whilst drunk many times. But he didn't. He lacked the nerve to take on such people. He did however have the nerve to sit and wait for one of the Schrimers to poke their head round the door. He was determined to spook them. It was Frau Schrimer. She looked at her daughter, and saw the signs; and looked at Franz, and knew the signs. Politely but firmly she asked him to leave the room. Franz got up and left without saying a word. Bridget wanted to cry. Back in his room he thought he could hear comments being passed in French. It didn't sound good. It didn't sound German.

Later Franz, his wounds licked, stole some time on the phone and rang his friend. He needed someone safe - someone who knew him - to talk to. He needed a direct line to Lev. But Lev did not answer: Luka did, in a rush. He did not want to hang around. No, his brother was out. No, he didn't know when he would be back. He was not his brother's keeper. Yes, he would say he called. Of course he would take a message. Why wouldn't he? Franz put the phone down less than convinced. Luka neatly slammed down his. The sound of a German voice was always something useful to hate.

A winter wasteland, a frozen thought.
A hollow indifference, a sad resort.
Swollen landscape dug from ditches.
Cows catch cold. Dogs court bitches.
Footsteps in other people's mud but still defiant.
Thoughts become congested as ideas are compliant.
Bright blue-eyed boys caught in a squeeze.
Lonely Hearts Club Band never to be conceived.
The rhythm of the rock yet to discover its race.
No lipstick with which to paint his face.
Imagination ceases to pump the blood.
Hard rain falls to create a flood.
No direction home, just solitude beyond.
Forced to walk on by. Damage done.

◆

Section Three: Capital Sin

The Hitler Youth cell, a small tribe of managed misfits, stood waiting for Franz at the Oranien Platz, on the freshly cut grass lawn - an area once occupied by the New Synagogue. With the exception of Gebhard Strasser the faces were old before their time: each weighed down with a philosophy which allowed no room for questioning, or judgement, or deviation from the official norm. Truth had been pre-designated so why bother? In their trademark uniforms they were expected to perform; and perform their actions to perfection. Simultaneously they had been lifted up with great Party talk from the earliest age and dumbed down by it in equal measure. It had left them unable or unwilling (yet) to think outside the box, beyond the herd: for out there, alone, it might be dangerous; and the truth - the real, uncontained truth - might have a sting in its tail. So the vast majority of them stayed inside where it was warm, safe, and the rules were understood; and the rewards were reasonable. Only Gebhard wore a smile: he was in charge, giving orders. He wore the rank. He was in heaven.

Then Franz arrived on the scene, in uniform and with a gun in a holster on the hip; and with a girl. A girl! Bridget had refused to be left behind, demoted to second class status when Franz went off to war. Franz was happy for her to come along because it would upset Gebhard and, strangely, because he actually felt he would miss her company all day long. He wanted her by his side. She was his trophy.

Feathers were ruffled and Gebhard was silently outraged. But the rule of politeness embedded deep within him at an early age left him unable to complain, or explode, or demand she leave. The boys was stuck with a girl in their midst. Some expected trouble to follow. In time a few would relax and reach out a little while the rest ignored her. Franz saw the signs and with a piercing look dared anybody - especially that twat Gebhard - to complain. He would stand by her. She was his girl. And she had made the effort: she was in uniform, the uniform of the BDM, which was perfectly acceptable. And this was Berlin, and they were the elite. So why the miserable faces? He didn't get it. He didn't bother to introduce her: they didn't deserve her. Likewise Gebhard didn't bother to introduce them: he didn't deserve it. And as for Bridget: she was left in limbo, like a stranger in town - even though she had been born and bred in the capital city.

Bridget also saw the signs. No matter, she thought. They are just a bunch of typical boys. Franz stood tall over all of them. The sensation she was causing fired her up and she began to enjoy her isolation and notoriety. Bar Gebhard she knew she could have fun at their expense. She had Franz by her side. She looked at him and smiled, wishing to

Section Three: Capital Sin

laugh out loud at the gang of boy soldiers. He shared the joke and the same gesture: though dressed in identical uniform Franz did not feel part of this little tribe of tin soldiers. He wanted to keep his distance and declare his superiority. Instinctively he knew all great leaders remained outside the crowd, beyond their reach, so to rise above it.

In time the drive and passion to take stamp his authority would grow but for now Franz was happy to let Gebhard Strasser play leader and issue orders. He thought back to the border patrol, and Father: that was serious stuff, with live rounds and deadly targets. This was kids stuff: time filling for toy soldiers. So what was he doing here? He asked himself that question more than once. To have a laugh, he answered each time.

Gebhard issued the order and they moved off, alert; almost synchronized; intense with expectation, as if going off to war; but reassured by the knowledge that it was, in the end, just a game. Berlin was busy and needed watching, that was their directive. Berlin was becoming hectic as its people began to wind themselves up for the big day and the influx of visitors grew: some German; some foreign; some from the distant, outer edges of the Reich. Trade was good. The owners of hotels, B&B's, bars and restaurants were licking their lips as people and money flowed in. Business was booming. But there were lunatics in town and they had to be watched. They were disruptive and setting bad examples of behaviour. On the other hand they were guests, fascists, and had to be put up with for the duration.

Franz and Bridget trailed behind, still sharing their private joke. Bridget even hooked her arm around that of her man Franz. It was the most natural thing to do and he accepted it completely, without a second thought. It was a boost to his ego. He bet the tin soldier Gebhard didn't have a girl. He bet Gebhard had never had a girl.

For them boredom did not set in: Franz was a tourist, seeing Berlin; and Bridget was seeing Franz, happy, sparkling, just as she had hoped he would. In her mind all was well. All was fitting together beautifully.

There was a pair of twins and Franz was fascinated. He had never met twins before and wanted to talk to them both, at the same time; as if expecting them to answer as one. They looked identical in their identical clothes and they walked abreast most of the time, as if to protect each other's flank. They knew much the same; had experienced much the same; but did not always think or react the same. Franz and Bridget discovered this straight away: one smiled at them both; the other turned away from the uninvited girl and the boy from far out east.

The cell walked with intensity, at times almost breaking into a

Section Three: Capital Sin

march and having to force themselves not to. They did not wish to draw attention. They observed everything which was moving - bodies and transport - as if taking notes; and on one level they took it all in; and on another they maintained closed minds. (Too much unsolicited variety caused a headache.) They were deadly serious about their responsibilities and commitment to the state: unlike Franz who was only slightly serious (when he felt like it); and Bridget who had been raised to secretly question such a position. He had grown beyond it. She had never grown into it, for which she had her parents to thank. In later years it might be a cause of trouble for her, a cause of disenchantment for him.

At one point Franz was stopped by a policeman. He took it as a compliment: it made him important; it made him the centre of attention. The others watched him; perhaps looking up to him as he looked down on the pompous policeman with the fat face and protruding stomach. Berlin policeman were soft, he concluded. They would not last five minutes back home. The scorn was etched across his face but the policeman was used to it: this was the Hitler Youth; this was trouble. His own son, a typical Hitler Youth fanatic, bored him to death with endless preaching. He always answered back, to the point now that they were barely on speaking terms. When they did converse it was more to satisfy the emotional needs of the wife and mother.

Franz could see Gebhard was hurting over all the attention he was getting. If only Lev was here to see the commotion. He would be pissing in his pants with laughter else threatening to 'do the policeman over', or something equally manic. Franz could see him bubbling at the indignity and stupidity of his best friend, a German, in uniform, being hassled by another bloated and balding twit of a German, in uniform. It would have made his day. A harsh attack on his gun broke the daydream. Franz made it clear that his gun was empty and produced his permit, which he had had the foresight to bring with him. The policeman, stumped, let go and moved him on. He had seen the address under the stamp: just another peasant boy who would soon be gone back to the back of beyond.

Gebhard saw his chance and mocked Franz for carrying an empty weapon. Franz refused to let the kid get to him and returned a friendly smile to prove that he didn't give a damn as to what the tin soldier had to say. Bridget gave Gebhard the same, to make it clear where she stood: she stood by her man. 'He's a man Gebhard', she wanted to say. 'You're just an annoying boy in uniform.' And as they moved on she held on tighter to her Franz, to the point that it made walking difficult and he had to push her off; which he did gently. And she loved him all

Section Three: Capital Sin

the more for it. Today Franz was strong. Today Franz could do no wrong.

The cell encountered the Waffen-SS: three officers seated at a table, drinking while watching the world go by; distant, uninterested, yet still strangely magnetic, especially for a bunch of boys in uniform. In the sun their deadly black widow uniforms sparkled with the glitter of polished metal. The ribbons added a light touch of colour, and artistry, and even poetry; but it was always the black which stood out. It shone in some weird reversal of the rule of light and dark, sunlight and shade. In the Waffen-SS black put all other colours in the shade.

The soldiers saw that they were having an effect and reeled them in. Franz was the first to be captured, the first to talk. He didn't stop. Facts tumbled out until he was stopped and offered a beer and a place at the table by a Hauptsturmführer. He accepted without hesitation and waited for the questioning to take place. After Gebhard declined - saying he was on duty - the rest felt compelled to do likewise. They were left standing; to shuffle and scratch, and exaggerate their state of boredom as bored boys did whilst Gebhard tried, in vain, to stop Franz from grabbing all the attention. In contrast Bridget's attention was grabbed with a wolf whistle by the youngest officer. He winked at her. It sent a charge of electricity up her spine and back down again. Despite all the hints her father had dropped Bridget was drawn to these good looking men in black. She was also offered a place at the table.

The senior officer asked Franz if he was in charge. Gebhard cut in before Franz could humiliate him.

"I am. I command this cell."

The Hauptsturmführer clapped. "Good for you!"

Gebhard thought he was taking the piss, and he was right.

With his glass held secure like a shield Franz tried to play the part of an equal. He failed: he wanted them to adopt him. His intentions were naked: he wanted to talk to them; he wanted them to talk to him. He wanted to leave the Hitler Youth behind, if only for ten minutes.

The officers of the Waffen-SS were dressed in power. They consumed it. They stored it away until it was needed: for those occasions when they had to fight and kill, trap and terrify, or simply impress and indoctrinate. Today they were not out to do any of those things. They were just here for the celebrations and the chance to drink lots, and perhaps end up fighting each other over women, wine and song. The soldiers had plenty of stories to tell - or make up - and loved nothing better than to tell them to the next generation: especially if they were the Hitler Youth; especially if they wanted to be soldiers. It all was so natural: one generation of fighting men passing on the baton -

Section Three: Capital Sin

and the buck - of the war to the next - a war which dragged on and on despite the lack of a worthwhile enemy. (Without a formal surrender or negotiated peace this war could never stop. It would go on and on, creating employment for many and career opportunities for a selected few.) These boys of the Hitler Youth thought they had heard it all before: on TV and at the cinema; whilst not appreciating that reality was in the detail, and the devil in the detail did not take sides, only victims. When it came to detail, the soldiers had an abundance.

Franz took a large bite. He wanted to hear their tales of daring. He wanted to talk. He had something to say. It was as if he had something to give back. He left the others behind, even Gebhard, when the soldiers learnt he was from the Ukraine, on the border: that place where life was lived on the edge and the enemy was only a stone's throw away. They had latched on to him, spotting a forceful, intelligent head above the shoulders. In no time they had learnt his name; that he was nearly eighteen; that he shared his birthday with the Fuehrer; that he intended to join the Waffen-SS after National Service; that he wanted to enrol as a cadet officer. With their heads rolling with so much information one of them asked if he planned to invade the leftovers of Russia. The other two laughed. Franz didn't get it. Confused he struggled on, desperate to be taken seriously. He had fought the Russians, he declared, at the border, on patrol. He had nearly killed one. Bridget blanched. She did not want to hear this, not from him, for it came from the heart.

"And what do you want to do once you've joined us"

"Kill Russians?"

The three smiled, in a way which left Franz wondering which side of the line he was on. Were they with him or not? What did he have to do to prove himself? Surely killing the enemy was enough?

One of the men, impressed by the outburst of inspired heroics offered to buy him another drink before he had finished his first. Without hesitation Franz accepted and began to drink at speed. Bridget was secretly alarmed. A furious Gebhard could barely contain himself. The rest meanwhile had become strangely intoxicated by the sight of 'one of theirs' fusing with 'one of them'. One of the twins also wanted to join the Waffen-SS. It was the best show in town. The other didn't have a clue what he wanted to do: he just watched what his brother did and took notes.

The junior officer concentrated on chatting up Bridget. He tried to persuade her that he was not dangerous, simply wild. She loved the attention but blushed at the bits she did not enjoy. Franz didn't, but had to put up with it. It was a small price to pay - any anyway wasn't that

Section Three: Capital Sin

how all good soldiers acted? Chat up the women at every opportunity. Sensible rule he thought: the best chance of getting to have sex with a woman. The man ceased fire when his senior officer gave him a dirty look.

The rest of the cell were attracted to the black light but had nothing to say, not even Gebhard. And all but Gebhard were content to listen as the soldiers dug their way into Franz - and out the other side. Franz was happy to let them in, completely forgetting the wider audience. In return they shared their wild stories and cigarettes with him. Bridget repeatedly declined the offer of a smoke. She could not be seduced so easily. Gebhard managed to force his way in and get one.

The three men played it for laughs: hiding truth in a game of lies; fighting battles they said when in fact it had been boredom; battling against the odds when the odds were heavily stacked in their favour. They said the current enemy was a rough, tough, bloodthirsty militia led by a rogue, suicidal Russian general when in fact he was a broken old man; still clinging to his soviet dream; still able to raise troops and smash them against the solid wall of German defences until he went blind. (But it was the thought that counted, and the audience which mattered.)

Franz told them about life back home; about his dogs, his motorbike, the army colonel and his wife, and some of the bits in between. He boasted about his father, the war hero, and repeated some of his father's own boasts; and all three soldiers fell silent as he spoke. Something which was not lost on Franz or the others. And he boasted of his father's capacity for drink, which made the men laugh.

"You and him get on OK?" asked the senior officer, possibly quite sincerely.

"He can talk too much."

"He's an ex-soldier, and one of the best - he's bound to."

The men roared with laughter.

Franz, frowning, looked at Bridget and smiled, for she was smiling. He looked at Gebhard, and took delight in his suffering.

The senior officer put another question. "Do all your family live out there?"

Gebhard jumped in. "His uncle lives here."

Franz glared back. He turned back to the senior officer who, by some unseen force of Nature, was always the focal point of conversation.

"My uncle lives here in Berlin. Sturmhauptführer Max Helmer."

He suddenly stopped talking and seized up. His engine went cold. He had stepped on a landmine which might explode if he moved his

Section Three: Capital Sin

foot. Luckily the announcement did not stir further interest: in fact it fell on deaf ears. These three men turned their noses up at the Sturmabteilung and covered their ears. They didn't like the smell or the sound. Men in the Sturmabteilung never fought wars they just shouted at those others who didn't and stamped their shiny boots like nasty little brats.

But it did start to go wrong when an officer picked on his gun. No it was not loaded, Franz was forced to admit. That drew amusement. No, he was not carrying live ammunition. That drew more which made Franz furious, until he was handed a live round: one of the officers produced an identical Luger pistol and unloaded a single bullet from its chamber. He placed it neatly in Franz's hand, closing it slowly, saying with all seriousness 'treat it well'. The bullet felt icy cold, hard and smooth like an elongated pebble. Franz squeezed on it and promised to follow the advice, despite having absolutely no idea what to make of it - the bullet or the pronouncement.

Gebhard tried to ridicule the exchange with the fact that Franz now had one bullet, which was one more than nothing. He failed miserably and had to lick his wounds when he received a stern rebuke from the soldier and silence from his own troops. They watched Franz as he carefully loaded the bullet and checked that the safety catch was on. Franz, the new kid on the block, the kid from out east, was now armed and dangerous. With his gun put away Franz resumed boasting of life on his father's grand estate on the border, on the edge. His recovery did not last: he blew it when he mentioned Lev. They're not all bad, he exclaimed as he described the local peasants. One of them's my best friend, he stated proudly. Mixing black and white was not a good idea. These serving officers did not like shades of grey. It led to indecisiveness, moral ambiguity, guilt. It led to decline. Their sudden, uncomfortable silence revealed his crime and sealed his fate. In a flash he shut up. Gebhard looked like he was recording every word for future use.

The senior officer slapped his thigh, then the table in a grand gesture: a signal that it was time to leave, to escape the band of boys. They had become tiresome. They were clinging. With that signal Gebhard barked his own orders and in near copycat style clapped his hands.

"We go now. No more wasting time. We have a lot to do."

Despite the exchanges of scepticism his cell followed orders and began to move, as one; bar Franz who drained his glass as slowly as possible and made a point of dragging himself to his feet; likewise Bridget who circled around, waiting for Franz to lead on.

Section Three: Capital Sin

The cell walked on, without good reason, with everything around them looking much the same as ever. When one of them wanted to stop to pee Gebhard reluctantly gave his permission. Franz laughed. The boy disappeared down a side alley alongside a large office block, to reappear animated, with no look of relief on his face.
"There's Englishmen, but!" He stopped short, out of breath.
"But what?" snapped Gebhard.
"They're doing graffiti! On the wall! It's disgusting!"
"Graffiti artist!" shouted one of the twins, accidentally tripping from outrage into joy.
Led by Gebhard the mob rushed in. Graffiti was unacceptable, a cardinal sin in the capital - a city where perfection was the norm. Such behaviour was scandalous. Franz followed, fighting his way to the front. Half-heartedly Bridget tried to keep up. She did not want to lose him to the mob.
They piled into the small enclosed space; some pushing on others; some almost tripping over in their haste to catch the villains - or at least catch sight of them. Two members of the BUF turned to face them, scowling. One waved his spray can of chrome yellow paint. He had painted a large star of David. Its dimensions were near perfect and it stood out bright as an act of wickedness in a country where bad had been made good. It could not be ignored. His accomplice had painted two slogans, one under the other: 'Jews are still here' and 'Jews are here to stay'. He was on his way to completing a third: 'Jews still in town'. Neither looked intimidated but neither was looking for a fight.
"Hand over those canisters!" blared Gebhard.
The two men, both in their mid-twenties, looked at each other for reassurance and laughed: here was a bunch of stupid kids dressed up like stupid Nazis with stupid ideas in their heads. It was all so stupid.
"No." replied one calmly. His accent was French.
His eyes locked on to those of the nasty little ringleader and the eyes of his accomplice locked on to Franz with equal intensity. Franz took it as a compliment. He was a serious threat and he didn't even have to scream and shout like Gebhard the tin soldier. There was pure hatred brewing: pure hatred on both sides in equal measure; caused simply by the word 'Jews' scrawled on an otherwise spotless wall of a bank. (Had Doktor Goebbels been present he would turned it into a good piece of insidious propaganda.) Face red with rage Gebhard pointed at the words.
"Why did you write that despicable nonsense! Those are insults! You should know better of all people!"
The two men exchanged more looks and laughed again, and

Section Three: Capital Sin

proceeded to speak in French. Instantly the penny dropped with Bridget and Franz, and most of the others. The slow ones would catch up later. It angered Franz that they were not speaking his German in his Germany. They were cowards. They were hiding. Just like Russians. Bridget meanwhile listened intently but decided not to share their words - better the insults were kept to herself.

Gebhard spat, walked forward and grabbed one by the collar.

"Scum. You're French scum."

The Frenchman spat in his face and pushed him off. Gebhard nearly toppled over and the Frenchmen laughed again. Hatred. Pure hatred. It had set both bodies alight. Each mind had purpose but no control, no means of measure. It was all or nothing.

"Get your gun out Franz! They're under arrest."

The Frenchmen were bemused, wishing to laugh off the new threat but unable to.

"Are you Jews?" snarled Franz.

Bridget felt faint and had to steady herself. Franz was turning into a monster before her eyes. A monster. She had fallen for a monster from way out east. No, she would not have it. It was that Gebhard Strasser. He was a bad influence. He had corrupted her Franz. And that Hitler Youth uniform: that was a bad influence; a dangerous commodity. These two Frenchmen: they were trouble from out of town; out of pure spite they were bringing out the worst in Franz.

"Yes," replied the one who had not yet spoken. "We are Jews from Paris - Paris, the greatest city in the most civilised country in Europe no matter what your crazy dictator says - and you can't touch us, scum."

"Stupid scum," chanted the other.

"Stupid scum brats," they chanted together.

Pure Hatred. It overflowed in all directions. It ran along the ground, into the cracks between the paving stones; between sanity and madness; between war and peace. It dissolved into the air. It worked its way into the hair, the skin; onto tongues; even into eyeballs - such that they had to be rubbed repeatedly for relief. Pure Hatred. You could eat it, chew it over, swallow it whole. But you could not spit it out. Like the strongest acid it dissolved vague half-truths, complete lies, unwelcomed uncertainties and insecurities. It crushed intelligence in favour of satisfaction. It hijacked emotion. Pure Hatred: producing it, milking it, manufacturing it, was a full time business and one best left to the experts. And the Nazis had done it well, perhaps too well. They knew their stuff (but little else).

Franz drew his pistol and Bridget's eyes lit up. One of the twins began to tremble. He wanted to hold her hand. She was so close: he

Section Three: Capital Sin

only had to reach out and take it. But he didn't have the nerve. Franz pointed his prized Luger. The French were not laughing now. He had them in his sights. But neither did they back off. They threatened him to do his worst. Somewhere in a dream Franz had already pulled the trigger. Somewhere in a dream Franz had killed his first peasant. Stand off. Pure Hatred on both sides.

While everyone else stood frozen, hypnotized, Bridget swept forward through the ranks. She wanted to make peace. She placed her trembling hand over the one pointing the pistol. It was also trembling, like the rest of Franz. The pistol was wobbling slightly, like the rest of Franz. Franz wanted to shoot a Jew. He wanted to shoot both Jews. Pure Hatred. But his sanity, still operating alongside the growing madness, said 'this is going too far'. Luckily he had not released the safety catch.

"He's only got one bullet," she explained.

Gebhard wanted to strangle the bitch. Pure Hatred. Franz looked at her, angry, but, realising his mistake, lowered his weapon and stuck it away. Gebhard swore at him.

"Coward!" he screamed. "Give it to me! I'll take them prisoner!"

"Fuck off clown," snapped Franz.

Pure Hatred: pure hatred for a tin soldier beyond his means.

The Frenchmen laughed again, but with a touch of nervousness. One sprayed the wall a little more yellow.

"You were going to shoot me Nazi boy?"

Franz clenched his fists as his arms began to shake and fail. The Pure Hatred flowing through his body had nowhere to go.

"Jewish scum. I could have killed you."

"Don't be stupid, of course not. I'm a French citizen. They'd hang you soldier boy for premeditated murder."

'Soldier boy'. The words stung Franz on the face. Gebhard tried to grab the lethal canister. He was kicked off and the two men ran. Gebhard chased after them. Franz joined the chase. And the rest joined in, like animals released into the wild. Their blood was up. They could sense fear. They all hated the Jews. From their earliest days each wanted to chase a Jew, to his death. Pure Hatred: part of the school curriculum. Bridget was left standing but she had to follow. She had to see what would happen to her lovely, not so lovely Franz. Summer camp had not prepared her for this.

The chase took them into a car park at the rear of the building. Twisting to avoid the bumper of a parked car, one of the Jews tripped and fell. Gebhard Strasser was on to him and over him in seconds.

"Jew!"

Section Three: Capital Sin

He began to kick. The sensation of physical contact felt great. Pure Hatred: it enabled total physical contact of the most violent kind without cause to reflect upon the damage being caused. Pure Hatred did not allow for touch or feel; or smooth smile; or kind caress; or simple hug; only hit, harm, scratch, smash, bite, bruise and bugger. And like sex it was its most infectious when it was its most physical. It was Pure Hatred which brought them together and Pure Hatred which kept them apart.

Unable to contain himself Franz joined in. "Jew!"

Next in turn a twin took up the challenge. "Jew!"

Then another. "Jew!"

Pure Hatred: it gave this little tribe a temporary identity above and beyond dress ware; it tied them up in knots and made it difficult to break out, walk away, say 'sorry', say 'I made a mistake'.

Bridget caught up, and her breath was taken away. The other twin was holding her hand, holding on to the nearest thing to a mother he could find. The rest stood in an arc, enjoying the spectacle. They could not bring themselves to kick, or bite. They could shout, yes, but right now they were not shouting. A few looked at Bridget. She was the only sane face amongst them. The twin held on tight. Was this foreign Jew about to die? Pure Hatred: it didn't allow for weakness, for guilt, for reasoning; it demanded furious, speedy results. Pure Hatred did not allow you time to think, only time to kill. By now Bridget was terrified while Franz and Gebhard were indestructible. The Jew on the ground yelling resulted in his mate running back to help.

Bridget threw herself at Franz. "No Franz no! Stop it!"

She pulled him away. He staggered back, suddenly exhausted. The Jew was out of reach: he could not kick. The Jew, back on his feet, spat at Gebhard and crept away, backwards, always facing the Hitler Youth. The other also spat and they swore endlessly in their native tongue. Bridget tried to not take it in. Despite Pure Hatred persisting, Gebhard also began to calm down. A motor could not run at high speed forever. It would burn itself out. Like Franz Gebhard had to recover his breath and recharge his battery. He failed when he looked at Bridget.

"Fucking women!"

"Fuck you," replied Franz.

"Stop it both of you!" implored Bridget. She held Franz's hand tight. He barely noticed. For some strange reason he now wanted to kick Gebhard Strasser to the ground and shout 'Jew!' in his face for all to hear.

The two Jews kicked a car as they left the car park and reminded themselves that they were dressed in the uniform of the BUF, so the

Section Three: Capital Sin

joke could continue. They headed off to find the nearest bar, there to practice their English and down a stiff drink or two. They had dropped their spray cans. No matter, they would buy some more. Before leaving Paris they had vowed to make this now infamous city stink; and while they were here that's all they would do - that and avoid the face, the sound, and the thoughts of that crazy old man.

Franz fixed himself on Gebhard and began to shake again. He spoke, slowly, accidentally mimicking his father at his worst and best.

"Insult her again and I swear I'll break your fucking neck."

Gebhard's face twisted up. He did not reply. The tribe studied him, as if he had been exposed, or was simply fading from view. He avoided their looks - and so struggled to find somewhere to rest his eyes. They wandered around the scenery looking for a home. He was five years old again and struggling to stay afloat. Pure Hatred: it was the only thing which kept him going when all else was failing him. Pure Hatred: Gebhard Strasser would make a career out of it, given half the chance. Perhaps he would, for his father knew the right people.

Franz needed to sit down to stop the shaking and to preserve his image. Bridget needed to sit down: she too was shaking. Likewise Gebhard. But only Franz and Bridget did so: they found a bench and sat together, making it their own. They were mentally exhausted and mentally scrambled in different ways for different reasons: Pure Hatred had corrupted his emotions; something not far off simple love had corrupted hers. They both were inches apart and miles apart. Franz was still high. He had never felt so good and so bad at the same time. It was a unique sensation, one he had never experienced before. He hoped to experience it again. But it didn't tear him apart. It joined him up. He felt complete. And Bridget was his witness. He turned and looked at her: she was still there, looking after him. He smiled. She didn't. No matter. In time she would smile again.

Like before the rest had to stand around and wait. Bridget glared up at the awful Gebhard Strasser, wishing him bad luck; loathing written across her face. Gebhard wanted to smack her in the face, and Franz knew it.

"You fucking keep away from her - away from us you stupid tin soldier!"

For Gebhard, still angry, still high on Pure Hatred, this was too much. To be insulted, bullied, by some cretin from out East was unacceptable. He finally exploded. Pure Hatred. Pure Hatred: it could not be sold; it could only be handed out, absorbed, inherited. It came in all sizes as it could not be rationed out. It was too volatile. It could not be chewed, cut up, dissected for analysis. It had to be swallowed, raw,

Section Three: Capital Sin

in one lump; and quickly, lest you threw it back up. Pure Hatred: it was an alien substance but it lived comfortably inside the human host. (Some humans took it into their hearts, and died young because of it.)

But Gebhard didn't quite have the balls. Instead he found an excuse to walk back through the car park, back to the disgraced wall. He spoke before turning away, expecting his troops to follow. Some did. Some did not.

"I'll talk to her anyway I like. She shouldn't be here."

He spat, accidentally at her feet, and walked on, quickly.

Franz jumped up, looking dangerous. Bridget tried to hold him down, saying words which were just words, but he flicked her off. He followed behind Gebhard, step for step. Gebhard knew he was there but kept on going. He needed to show his mettle. He got as far as the car park before Franz pushed him in the back.

"City boy, you're shit. You don't deserve to wear our uniform."

Gebhard stalled and Franz pushed him again. The rest kept their distance, sensing a danger zone opening up. That included Bridget: she was afraid to get too close to Franz. He was transforming into a wild animal - the kind her father had warned her about years ago. Gebhard turned and pushed back. Franz laughed. That changed things: somebody clapped; another whistled; some took sides and cheered. Franz moved in and quick as a flash thumped Gebhard in the chest. Gebhard nearly fell over. Recovering his balance, he chose different tactics.

"Go on Herr Helmer, use your gun! On me! Look I'm defenceless!"

Franz returned an icy stare, the look of someone full of Pure Hatred. He wanted to do as asked but knew he couldn't. He wanted to kill him, wound him, just scare the tin soldier shitless but knew such an act was impossible, unforgivable. It would destroy him. He was stuck. And the fact that he was stuck like that, knee deep in glue, fuelled his Pure Hatred. And that in turn produced more of the same in Gebhard Strasser: Pure Hatred that this peasant from out east was intent on stripping him of all his dignity, his well-earned authority, for no reason except that he didn't like him. Gebhard wanted to kill him, with his own gun. Yes everything they had preached to him in the Hitler Youth made perfect sense. At the end of the day everything boiled down to the fight. You had to fight to win. You might have to kill to be sure of winning outright.

Franz lost it and punched the enemy opposite again and again, in quick succession. Thoughts of Lev swirled around at the back of his mind: but those punch-ups had been friendly affairs, over and forgotten in hours if not minutes. This was a drag which would drag on and on.

Section Three: Capital Sin

Deep down he knew that. Gebhard returned fire, but with less accuracy. They grabbed each other by their brown shirts. They pushed and shoved and the other boys cheered and clapped. It was a party. And there was a war of words: 'arsehole'; 'shit face'; 'eastern prick'; 'tin soldier'; and more, with each delivering less and less. There were lost battles to be refought; unfinished business to be finished; previous humiliations to be righted and released.

There was the telling off, for no reason.
There were the sharp words which still stung.
There was the face which took the mickey.
There was the face which threatened without relief.
There was the teacher who spoke too much like he knew too much.
There was the father who didn't listen at the right time.
There was the mother who listened too much.
There was the kid in the playground who stole the show.
There was the kid up the tree, beyond reach.
There was the early to bed.
There was the girl on the bike.
There was the stolen cash - a few coins in the pocket.
There was the resentment, the taunts.
There was the relentless message of how to run his life.
There was the isolation which struck out of the blue.
There was the continuous threat of the Jews, the Russians, the West, the East.
There was the wish to break out; the wish to escape, to start again.
There was the noise of the crowd: too many salutes; too many speeches; too many demands; too much take, too little give.
There was the heat of the moment.
There was the fight in the middle of the night, with no end in sight.
There was the sharp rebuke at the dinner table, followed by the silence at breakfast.

Only Bridget, disgusted and disappointed by what she saw, and one twin, lost, stood well back, beyond the tight little crowd of wound up belligerent boys. She expected better than this: that was what she had been brought up to believe. They had all been raised to be better than this, better than a savage. They were the country's future. They would be the next set of parents raising family. And as for Franz: she didn't know what to think, what to say, how to feel; she didn't know who he was, who he had been, who he had pretended to be. Certainty had flown, crippled.

Gebhard pushed Franz against a wall and Franz grazed the side of

Section Three: Capital Sin

his forehead, just below the hairline. It was not much. It did not feel like much when he touched the wounded area. But when he found blood on his fingers it fired him up to the next level. He slammed back into Gebhard, pushing and pushing and pushing him backwards, until Gebhard tripped over a bollard and went sprawling to the ground. There was great applause from the audience, along with a higher level of excitement, and fear. Then it all crumbled away when a policeman stormed in. He had been watching the spectacle from a distance, arms folded; enjoying every moment of the frenzy until now, when he felt duty-bound to step in and play the part for which he was getting paid. (It was a small price to pay.)

Gebhard picked himself up, bruised, still trying to look strong and in command. Franz cradled his minor wound with pride, advertising it as if it excused his own behaviour. The two were back in the classroom, heading for detention. The policeman grabbed each by the shoulder and pulled them together until they were standing side by side. They looked at him like he had appeared out of thin air.

"Stop this now. Say sorry."

Nothing. Silence. Pure Hatred was still cooking even though the heat had been switched off. It would take a long time to cool and it would never completely vanish. It might even recover, resume, and fix itself on to another suitable target.

"Apologize now!"

Still nothing. Still silence. Bridget stepped forward.

"Just say sorry to him Franz! Please!"

He heard her voice: a strange, dislocated voice, the voice of that child again. He could not ignore, or refuse it. It was too tender, too fragile. It was having a strange effect on him.

"Sorry," he growled.

"And you," ordered the policeman.

One of the boys booed and Gebhard looked around, angry. And then the crushing truth dawned on him: some or all of them - his cell - were not taking him seriously! And it was all down to that Franz Helmer, that bad boy from the back of beyond. And there was absolutely nothing he could do about it, except possibly pretend it wasn't happening. That Franz had won - but then he suddenly remembered. He would go down fighting.

"I'll tell them all about your uncle Max, your queer uncle Max."

Franz's face went white as a sheet. He found it difficult to stay standing. The strength fled his legs and they could not hold his weight. The policeman looked at him, both bemused and intrigued, then switched his attention to Gebhard, more in disgust. But he had had

Section Three: Capital Sin

enough.

"Both of you, get out of here, out of my sight. Go!"

Gebhard shrugged and began to walk away, to nowhere in particular. Franz did likewise, followed by Bridget. Everybody else hesitated, unwilling to choose, then slowly drifted after Gebhard; some wishing they didn't have to; some wishing they could stay with Franz. He was far more exciting, and he carried a loaded gun. The twins were split down the middle. Such moments would always be their curse. What one did, or thought, or said, or felt would always be of interest to the other, and so rebound, in an endless cycle of extreme harmony or disharmony.

The policeman watched the incident dismantle before his eyes and raised his eyebrows. Finally he began to walk away - but not before Gebhard turned, raced towards him and grabbed him by the sleeve.

The policeman shook him off. "What now?"

"Two graffiti artists - they trashed a wall down there. Two Jews in British uniform, spreading Jewish lies. Jews!"

"English?"

"No French - at least that's what they said."

The policeman was tired. He didn't want to know. It had been a long long day, and they were French - or English. It wasn't worth the aggravation.

"Forget it. It will get cleaned up."

Gebhard stood his ground, seeing a chance to impress. "You going to report it? File a report?"

"No - yes. Yes I'll file a report. Someone will come and clean it up. Now go home."

As the policeman walked away Gebhard deflated. He had been discounted. He wanted to take the policeman's number and report him but the policeman was gone, long gone, glad to be rid of the mad tearaways who inhabited the Hitler Youth.

Franz whistled and walked on. He had Bridget clinging to him again; wishing to have him back; happy she had him back; hoping to find him again; wishing to change him. She would wish for another summer camp, with him, as he was. Just the two of them, running and jumping into the lake, or river; flat out on the grass, gasping for air; kissing, touching, feeling. Her head was spinning while his had settled down into some strange new calculated state of calm. He had to see his uncle again. Otherwise he might go mad.

◆

Section Three: Capital Sin

The two Penkin brothers were arriving back at the flat, arms knackered from carrying between them a large heavy suitcase. They had not been away to somewhere sunny and special. They had not had a good time. It was a suitcase stuffed full of valuable items gained through honest dealings with dishonest people who in turn had gained possession through unscrupulous means. The true owners were still angry, or sad, or confused. A few were dead, some killed illegally by the state for refusing to fit in. During negotiations Luka had never asked any questions; had never asked for any names; and had not asked for a receipt. He had just argued the price during inspection. Lev was not happy: earning a living from thieves, scum and pickpockets had not been his intention - if it had, he had moved on. It was not a new start, just more of the old; except worse, and in a worse place. During their journey home they had both been conscious of the tell-tale rattling the suitcase made; and each had tried to minimise it, like controlling a noisy dog. A case full of swag was exactly what it sounded like when it shook.

They climbed the stairs, relieved that they had reached home without being stopped, only to discover a girl standing outside their door. She was smoking a cigarette, quickly, as if a train was about to leave and she needed to be on it, smoke free. Lev immediately recognised her: it was that girl; the one that devil Kleine had 'delivered' to Luka just two days ago. Those two days had aged her: she looked older but none the wiser. Upon seeing Luka she backed away a little. She looked apprehensive, cornered: she might not be welcomed but she could not leave. Lev turned to his brother for guidance, but nothing: Luka simply ignored her. He didn't ask her why she was there as he already knew. He looked nervous, which confounded Lev. Did this little slip of a girl scare him?

"Well?"

Luka put the suitcase down gently to avoid the rattling of old bones. "Well what?"

"Well aren't you going to ask her what she wants?"

The girl skipped back and forth between the two faces, trying to work out who was in charge, who was trouble. As in a sulk Luka went and stood by the nearest window.

"I don't need to." He looked and up down the street.

Lev stared his brother down, confusing him with their father. He had hit a wall. His brother was keeping secrets from him: something he thought would never happen. He gave up and turned his fire back on to the girl. She looked pale, tired, withdrawn. She avoided eye contact.

"Well?"

Section Three: Capital Sin

"What do you mean?"

She spoke softly, with an accent which suggested her roots were the far western tip of the Ukraine. Her reply was timid, but honest. She was not trying to be difficult. It was a child speaking, a child wishing.

"I mean what do you want with us?"

"Nothing. Just waiting."

Lev folded and locked his arms in annoyance. No one was talking to him. Something was going on and he was the one left outside.

"Waiting for what? A bus? Not us - we're here - so you can't be waiting."

He just managed to avoid shouting at her.

Tongue-tied the girl looked to Luka for support but he had none to give. He wanted nothing to do with it. Lev did likewise and received the same remote look into the distance: the kind which abdicated all responsibility; the kind which tried to pretend innocence whilst failing miserably; the kind which lost friends.

"You know what's going on - tell me."

Lev spoke to his brother as an equal, possibly more so: the difference in years had been ejected from the equation. But Luka did not want to spell it out. He did not want to hear the sound of his own voice. He preferred to let his little brother work it out. There were more than enough clues. The boy was not stupid. His brother had never been stupid - unlike their father who had taken stupidity to new heights. (Luka always thought of Penkin in the past tense, and by implication felt he was dead. Only logic repeatedly fed by facts kept Penkin alive in Luka's mind.) Luka stuck instead to watching the street below. He was expecting someone, someone bad.

When Lev pressured her to divulge her name, her age, and even where she lived, Luka became agitated.

"Leave it Lev, stop bothering her."

"Leave what? I'm just trying to be friendly."

And he was: he just wanted to make friends in a place where he had none. Franz was gone, off to mix with the gods. All he had was an older brother - one he was now struggling to fit into the natural order of things. His older brother was not living up to the ideal of what he expected an older brother should be. His brother was losing respect.

Luka became more agitated when he saw a certain car - recently washed and waxed - draw up outside, braking sharply. It was Inspector Kleine's car.

"Come on, we have to go. We can't stay, can't hang around here."

Next he saw Inspector Kleine charging towards the entrance, in a big big hurry.

Section Three: Capital Sin

"Can't stay? We fucking live here! What's got into you?"

Inspector Kleine was late. He hated being late. He was a clock watcher, a time keeper. He was well organised, usually: too much office paperwork had delayed him but the paperwork had to be done - paperwork went with the job. (He hated watching over the Czechs. They were too clever by half and created too much paperwork.) He bounded up the stairs and shuddered to a halt when he saw the crowd. He took in Luka; and the girl; and the large suitcase; and finally, reluctantly, Lev - with whom he exchanged a look of pure hatred. He finally settled on the girl, like a wolf settles on a lamb, or a banker on a bonus. She tossed aside her cigarette and looked at the floor, and locked herself in. She did not want to come out. She did not want to play. She wanted a mummy - any mummy would do.

Lev tore himself away from Kleine and glared at his brother in open disgust: he had finally made the connection, and Luka was part of it. Kleine also rounded on Luka, preferring to pretend that the brat of a younger brother was gone, a good riddance.

"Why are you still here. You know you shouldn't be here. That's the rule."

"I forgot. Been busy. Sorry."

Lev wanted to punch the German, as he wanted to punch his brother. And as for girl, well he simply wanted to hold her hand and lead her away; and tell her that everything would be alright, that things would get better, that he would be her friend. But he couldn't, reason being he didn't believe any of it himself.

"Come on Lev, we go."

Luka picked up the suitcase as he spoke. It suddenly felt a lot heavier. He could have been going away; setting off on a road trip; perhaps a package tour for sea, sun and sex. But in reality he had no idea where he was headed: he only knew he had to be gone for an hour. One hour: that was the agreement - the arrangement - with Inspector Kleine, one which Inspector Kleine had always stuck to. In some things Inspector Kleine was meticulously scrupulous and easy to do business with. But Lev was determined to have the last word, to make it clear to the whole world (which wasn't listening) that this Inspector Kleine did not scare him; that this devil Kleine could not intimidate him; that this German, Kleine, was a corrupt, despicable German sex fiend.

"You going to sleep with him? A dirty old German? I hope he pays good money."

Lost for words, throat tied up in knots, the poor girl's mouth fell open and her eyes wanted to pop. Luka panicked and dropped his

Section Three: Capital Sin

suitcase. It fell onto its side and made one hell of a racket, and for a few seconds was the centre of attention. Everybody looked at it, as if it had just fallen over dead. Luka stepped forward, hoping to intervene and make peace before war broke out. But it was too late for that: Kleine had grabbed Lev by the throat and had him pinned up against the wall. He was on fire. He was ready to explode; ready to pull his gun, stick it in the stupid kid's big mouth, and pull the trigger. It was only the grain of truth which held him back - the first straw rather than the last.

And still Lev did not show fear. He was not intimidated. He did not wilt. He glared back with a fixed expression of rebellion. If he was going to die young, in this dump, then he couldn't think of a better way to go than to piss off a high ranking German monster on the way. Lev was not yet afraid of death: he had not lived long enough to have lots to lose. The act of dying itself he only feared if a) he had time to fear and b) it was clearly going to be slow and painful. After all just how much hurt was out there, and just how much of it could time deliver?

"I could kill you right now and nobody would give a damn."

The threat from Kleine came as a whisper, right up close to his ear. It was not meant for general circulation. On someone older such a threat would have struck deep but on Lev it had nowhere to go so it bounced off and fell to the ground. But that aside, it was still true, and Lev recognised the truth. It was a truth he had lived with all his life: he had become insensitive to it. He merely stared back with a tired look on his face: it was the look of an old man waiting to die, preferably without pain or fuss or nonsense.

There the two remained stuck, both quickly coming off the boil as they ran out of steam: Kleine breathing heavily into Lev's face, wondering how to play it; Lev staring back, trying not to breathe in, trying not to think of anything - least of all the danger and stupidity of his outburst. It took a gentle but firm intervention from Luka to break the deadlock.

"It's OK Inspector Kleine. We're going, right now. Come back in an hour - no two hours. You have the place for two hours, no problem."

Kleine relaxed and let go, wishing to push the irritating little brat from his mind. He watched Lev slide out of his grasp and away, as if guided by nothing more than the pull of gravity. It was like watching a snake. Lev ended up at his brother's side - the safest place to be right now - still ready and willing (if not able) to fight on. He felt he had little to lose, little to live for, but plenty to die for; and if he could take one German bastard with him then so much the better. He remembered

Section Three: Capital Sin

he had a gun. Unfortunately it was on the other side of the door. He vowed from now on to always keep it on him. He looked at the girl, as if to prove himself right: yes this poor girl was worth the fight.

Kleine looked down at the suitcase. He was interested.

"No one hour is fine."

He pointed with an index finger, like it was loaded, like it was a gun. "What's in there?"

"Usual stuff."

The reply came from a timid, nervous, subservient Luka now on a par with the girl - unlike his younger brother who objected to every word being spoken and who was rebuilding his strength as Luka's was declining rapidly.

"Stolen?"

"No I bought it, legal like."

We, thought Lev.

"We bought it," he said out loud, demanding recognition.

Kleine smiled and released the smallest chuckle of delight. Sheepishly Luka grinned. It was a desperate act, one intended to lighten things up, but it merely made him look like a fool. Lev saw it, and saw through it; as did Kleine; as did the girl. (For her, so used to being on the bottom, grounded down, it was a moment of light relief, of fresh air.)

"Open it, now." It was Kleine the policeman speaking.

Beaten into a corner, Luka did as he was told. Crouching, and with everybody watching, he removed the leather strap, unlocked it, and undid the clips. He opened the suitcase and stood back to reveal its contents - a random collection of stolen goods: some good stuff buried amongst mainly second rate crap. It had been a bulk buy.

Kleine peered in and rummaged around, stirring the pot. He picked out a gold-plated pocket watch, a silver ashtray, and a stainless steel pen before waving Luka in, satisfied he had taken his cut.

"You can keep the rest."

"Thank you."

Thank you so much, thought Lev.

Disgusted, Lev could not look on as his boneless brother shut the suitcase and stood up, to attention. They had just been robbed and brother Luka was happy to take it - happy to even thank the robber for not taking it all! His brother was a coward. His brother was a true Penkin through and through. And he was a Penkin - so where did that leave him? He didn't care to know. He looked back at the girl. He just wanted to be her friend, her angel. He just wanted her to be his friend, his comfort. He didn't want her to sleep with Germans. Let that

Section Three: Capital Sin

German bastard go fuck himself.

Lev watched in horror as Kleine produced a key and unlocked the door - their front door! That bastard had a key! Luka had given him a key! He watched with growing dread and sense of outrage as the devil Kleine snatched up the girl roughly by the hand. He was taking her inside and out of sight: inside to have his way with her; inside to run his dirty hands all over her young tender body; inside to violate her body; inside to rape her. Lev couldn't bear to think about what would happen to the poor girl once she disappeared inside. Inside. He could not allow this to happen. He rushed forward, reached out and grabbed her other hand. For the first time she wanted to scream.

Without formal declaration a hostile tug of war began, with the girl caught up in between. She was the prize and the sacrifice, the be all and the end all. Pulled hard in opposite directions she began to squeal. Kleine found it funny at first and laughed at the new game. But when Lev wouldn't let go, and pulled harder, always harder than him, so pulling him backwards. Kleine got angry, really angry. There was no funny side to this. He began to shout and swear; and the girl began to scream; and Lev began to curse the all-powerful Germans, the all-powerful Nazis, the all-powerful all powerful - anyone in fact who wielded too much power. Lev would not let go. His life depended on it.

It took Luka, the neutral, to break the deadlock. He jumped in and prised Lev and the girl apart. It took some force to overcome his mad brother's grip. Next he apologized, profusely; and the girl was dragged indoors; and the door was slammed shut; and all before Lev could protest or take further action. He had been stabbed in the back by his brother. Lev turned on him - his weak little brother.

"You going to let him do that! Let that happen! She's just a girl! He's probably breaking his own fucking laws!"

"We have to! We have an agreement."

The explanation sounded worse than the most feeble excuse. It was a total sellout.

"Tell him to go fuck his agreement. We don't do agreements with the fucking Germans! And get him out of our fucking house!"

"Yes we fucking do! If you want to survive in this place - make something out of nothing - you make fucking agreements! And it's my fucking house - not yours!"

The two brothers glared back at each other, with a fury not exercised since they were toddlers in the hay. Then, with nothing left to say to each other over the incident, they walked away, to go get a stiff drink or two or three; Luka clutching his suitcase - it was always his suitcase -

Section Three: Capital Sin

and Lev grasping for a cause he could win, or a way out. Going home with his tail between his legs was not an option.

And inside, away from prying eyes, Inspector Kleine slowly disrobed the poor little girl whom he had picked up off the streets with an offer of some place better. He started with free alcohol then proceeded with his slimy dirty hands. For him it was all in a day's work - a fringe benefit which came with being an inspector in the Gestapo, far away from his homeland and all the moral baggage which came with it. For Inspector Kleine life was disgustingly sweet in the conquered lands.

Much later, when Lev and Luka returned to the flat, slightly intoxicated, Lev would sit with his feet up and drink some more. (With so much now said and rediscovered, silence had returned in force, for longer periods of time. It was much like the old days.) He would watch his brother drink some more while he dug into his bulk buy; and he would listen while his brother mumbled out loud about how he could move it and at what price. Later Lev would watch his brother wander around the flat, checking and counting his stock, and still mumbling; and Lev would wonder what he was doing there.

♦

Isaak stared out of the window, as an alternative to the four walls, floor and ceiling he had come to know intimately, despite his resistance. The number of stacked steel drums had multiplied, like lice. Identical, they made an useless pile of once useful items. Yet with their precise, circular features and repeating imagery, they stood out with a certain charm amongst the mud, the mess and the surrounding debris. He had a flashback to his childhood: he was sitting in an inner tube, floating on water; its protruding air valve scratching his back. He was splashing and screaming, and going nowhere loudly; and he was totally ignorant of his status in the world. Back then he assumed he had somewhere to go. Wasn't that the point of it all? He was too tired to tell. Grown up, he was now too tired to yell.

As quietly as possible, not wishing to disturb, Isaak dragged his bed up close to the window. He needed to be close to the outside. The wholesale movement of metal freaked out his cellmate such that he had to reassure him, repeatedly, that all was fine, that it would all turn out for the good. His cellmate jumped up and at the window. He had to see what was out there. Seeing nothing he settled back down, but with an eye fixed on Isaak and in a pitiful state of questioning. A guard walked past the window. He stooped. He looked miserable: perhaps

Section Three: Capital Sin

because his shift was starting; perhaps because it was ending and he had to go home to the wife. Isaak wished upon him more of the same. He swore loudly, sending shockwaves around the cell, and again he had to calm his cellmate. There was fear on his face: fear that he was being left behind on this new journey of the mind. Where Isaak went he wanted to follow - it was always a better place to be.

Later two guards, bored, ordered their two prisoners outside, beyond the backyard and on to a small strip of scrubland. Again, like clockwork, Isaak had to calm his cellmate whilst at the same time convince himself, with the power of logic, that there was nothing to fear. He was worth good money. Why shoot him? He told himself he knew these people: they were not inherently bad, just brutal in their ways. The guards produced a battered old leather football. They wanted to play football, but not against each other. Their prisoners had no choice: play or be beaten and thrown back inside. Isaak chose to play. He had forgotten how sweet was the smell of fresh air and the tingle of strong sunlight on the skin. A couple of makeshift goalposts were marked out.

The guards had muscle and mean determination. They had to win: losing was not an option. The opposition had nothing except exhaustion and stiff limbs. But they were forced to put everything into it. A lack of interest was not permitted. They played to win with the promise of double rations. They played to win like their lives depended on it. The guards ran back and forth, like crazy, like it mattered. Isaak and his cellmate could not keep up. They were shattered after a few minutes. If they got the football they lost it in seconds. But the guards didn't have it all their own way: they had to stretch and strain as their level of unfitness became apparent and unravelled their bodies.

The guards scored and scored, and scored again. They took it very seriously and even tackled each other when the opposition would not. Isaak managed to score twice, his team-mate once - but only because a guard knelt down to tie up a bootlace. By the end of the match - which only lasted twenty minutes but felt much longer - Isaak was close to physical collapse while his cellmate was close to mental collapse. His brain was in danger of being swept away by too much excess energy. They lost 16-3. The guards went wild. They pranced around like idiots. They grabbed each other in celebration and declared their supremacy. They had scored a great victory. Now they wanted to beat the Germans.

◆

Section Three: Capital Sin

Franz made Bridget take him to Steinstrasse. She became invisible along the way. He heard nothing when she spoke. He saw nothing when she moved. When they reached his uncle's address he stood impassive, in stony silence outside the apartment block. On the outside he looked as solid as a rock. He was managing to keep it all concealed, all locked up. Bridget wanted to say something, something preferably sweet, but bottled out: the look on his face said danger, keep out. He looked up, straining his neck. 'Guilty until proven innocent' was the thought that tormented him; but then he was a Helmer so surely 'innocent until proven guilty' should be his tune? Was he not expected to take the moral high ground? Was that not what the Helmers had fought for? Inside his uncle Max was looking through his old photographs. His head was thumping but he held on.

An elderly lady pottered along, heading slowly towards them. She was walking her dog, a Dachshund, her third. He kept trying to race ahead and she kept tugging on his lead in response. He was more than happy. She was just about content. She saw two uniforms ahead but refused to be intimidated - yet still she stopped to catch her breath, using it as an excuse to soak up the sight of the army milling around. 'Don't ask for trouble' an ancient voice of youth inside her head told her. She pushed on: she was proud and would not be intimidated. Then as she drew nearer and her eyes properly engaged with the danger ahead, she realized they were just kids; just kids standing around: one looking stern, rough, rebellious; the other looking very forlorn and trying to conceal the misery of her broken heart. On top of that both looked like they were made for each other. She knew the signs - as she knew the uniforms.

Finally she had to stop. She pulled her pet in close as she waited for the big boy to let her pass. He didn't. He just stood in her way, staring up, glaring up. She looked up, wondering what all the fuss was about. Finally she caught the eye of the big girl and held on to it tight. The girl got the message and nudged the boy.

No response.

She gripped his arm and squeezed. That did the trick. Franz returned to earth and stepped aside. Dissatisfied by the act of impoliteness the old woman moved on. She did not smile or say thank you - but then again nor did Franz. She was old and strangely dressed, and she shuffled along like one of the peasants on the estate. Franz wanted her gone, out of his head. He looked away from her and her stupid dog, and back up at his uncle's window. Still there was nothing to see but plenty hidden.

Finally Franz snapped, broke off, and walked away from the scene

Section Three: Capital Sin

of the crime - a crime which had not been clearly classified, nor had necessarily taken place. He had to have more beer. He told Bridget if she really cared about him she would not complain, but come along, and join in. So Bridget followed, pulled along by an invisible rope tied around her neck. It was choking her. But she had to watch over him. He might get lost. He might get into trouble. He might cause trouble. (She thought she was the only one who could keep him out of trouble. Perhaps she was.) The look on her face sent out a complicated message: realisation tinged with sadness; refusal blocked by circumstance; disappointment alleviated by denial. He spoke to her only once along the way, demanding she say nothing - not to her best friends, not to her parents - about the incident with the gun or the bust up with Gebhard. Bridget responded with a slight nod which said 'sure' and a heavy look which asked 'why would I?'.

They found a busy bar but did not enter. At first the problem of being in uniform stumped him with the lack of a solution then it drove him mad. Franz was saved by a stranger who offered to buy him his drink 'for a fee'. The man was only five years older than Franz but the generation gap had already crept in and set up shop. Franz agreed and a fee was paid in the form of a drink. The man tried to chat up Bridget, the sexy girl in uniform, but soon gave up. He drifted off in open disgust at her aloofness and lack of charm.

To prove that she was not weak Bridget treated herself to a glass of wine, hoping it would revive her, give her confidence to strike back. According to his current routine Franz drank at frenetic speed before slowing to a gentler pace, having made his point (of what, he did not know) to his audience (which did not exist). They stood miles apart, up close. He did not engage. He did not look at her. He wanted her there but did not want her to see him like this. Best look away. If she got too close he would have to scare her off. He would do it, he promised himself: no regrets. She was hard work sometimes. He was supposed to be on holiday - holiday meant no hard work.

She in turn felt he did not want her to look at him so she turned away and pretended to take an interest in those around them; at the same time concentrating on the time she saw on a clock inside, and Time itself, and its calculated passing, which at the time was slow and laborious. She felt a gloom descend and despondency gained a foothold. She could not shake it off. She could not escape it.

Franz felt nothing - not even her obvious hurt - nothing except the large lump of hurt which had occupied his head again. Along with too much 'heavy stuff' it had fallen from the sky and was now banging against his brain from all sides. There was no relief. It would not go

Section Three: Capital Sin

away. The fighting, the Jews, the tin soldiers, the shame of uncle Max, the pain of Reichsfuehrer Heinrich Himmler: they had all made their contribution in one way or another. The beer proved useless as medicine, but he carried on drinking it anyway. Beer was all he had right now.

Bridget made it her duty to maintain the space: the physical was easy; the emotional was tough. Franz was not like a parent: in her world you could approach your parents any time you liked, regardless of how they felt or your reason. They might object but they would never turned you away, never refused you. Right now Franz was off limits and beyond reach. He had retreated into inner space, that private place where no one else could go. She sipped her wine slowly, trying to enjoy it but failing. She could have been drinking tepid water.

There was a television set on in the bar, mounted high up on a wall for all to see. Its volume was set high, to match that of the regulars. A great cheer went up which turned Franz's neck. He stepped up to the window and stared in. Bridget did likewise, as if to demonstrate that she was still with him, still on his side. On the screen a column of army trucks moved slowly along a crowded street. People were cheering, gesticulating, clapping, whistling and without knowing it inciting exactly the same inside the bar. Their blood was up. There was a bearded man in the back of one truck, standing up, handcuffed. Some in the crowd were throwing things at him: stones, sticks of wood, vegetable matter; the occasional egg. They wanted him dead and alive: dead because he deserved to die; alive because he was sport, a living soul to hate. Armed soldiers sat behind him; watching him, not watching the crowd. According to custom they passed a cigarette around. He was a valuable prize and to lose him would drop them in deep, deep shit.

The prisoner ducked to miss an egg but still it caught him and shattered. Its yoke ended up mainly on the trousers of a soldier, which really pissed him off. A great cheer went up: in the street and in the bar. There was no difference, no disconnect between those in the bar having an early evening drink and those hundreds of miles away in Minsk, now part of the Polish Eastern Territory. They all hated the handcuffed prisoner: he was famous; he was Russian; he was a warlord, a drug baron, a terrorist. But they had misjudged him: he was not beaten. He gave as good as he got. He swore and spat back at the crowd. Had he not been handcuffed he would have jumped down and attacked. He would have slaughtered them all for what they had done to his country: Germans first, Poles second; then Ukrainians, Latvians and Lithuanians. Like clockwork he had conducted raids across the

Section Three: Capital Sin

border to kill as many as he could before disappearing back into the chaos which was the remains of the Soviet Union. And still he had not got satisfaction. He refused to be broken, even if his country was. He had carved out his own little empire but now he had been captured it would dissolve back into the earth, to vanish like a sandcastle on the incoming tide. (Some might suggest that the date of his capture was suspicious: close as it was to the Fuehrer's birthday.)

Franz and Bridget remained detached from it all. They did not join in. They did not raise their voices or their fists; or bare their teeth in hatred of the man who had been reinvented as a monster. They just stared in through a pane of glass at the altered universe on the other side. They were watching reality TV whilst those inside were watching another version on a smaller but louder screen. Somebody threw the dog a bone. The prisoner barked. Others in the crowd laughed but the laughter quickly transformed into fury: he was not taking them seriously; and he was beyond reach. They could not lay a finger on him.

And as Bridget watched the drama run its course, the pounding in her head intensified. She had to escape the violence. She had to get home. She wanted to be home, safe; in her room; tucked up in bed. Her eyes began to fill. She gulped. The drinkers inside were calming back down as the truck moved out of vision, but their hate was still obvious, still fully exposed. She didn't want to be in this place any longer. She couldn't handle it. She had to get out. Finally, on the verge of break up, she turned to Franz and demanded his attention. He knew she was looking at him with intensity and tried, pathetically, to pretend he hadn't noticed. Miserable, he gave up ten seconds later and faced his accuser.

"What?"

"I want to go home. Now."

The sound of her creaking voice said it all. Nothing else needed to be said. There were tears in her eyes. This was their secret weapon and he knew that resistance was pointless. Franz capitulated. He couldn't handle a flood right now. He had enough on his mind to cope with.

"Come on then."

Rope cut, she pulled away and started for home. Franz was left for dead. He followed on behind, not wishing to catch her up; conscious that he was returning to a place where all he could do was park himself and stare at the walls, stranded. He was far from home; far from his family, his dogs, his motor bike; far from the land where he could wield power, where he was known.

The pair arrived home both still burdened, still separated; one

Section Three: Capital Sin

clearly upset, the other impassive but secretly downcast. Once the door opened Bridget pushed in and ran up the stairs - a child in distress, a child running away from a bad, mad once sweet now sour experience. Her folk in the photographs had seen it all before but, being deceased, were unable to impart the wisdom - or the impatience - of their years. The Pole stood back at arm's length and waited for Franz to step inside. She held the look of a teacher holding a special grudge against one of her pupils: the one who was always late, always causing trouble, always answering back. Franz threw her off and waded in, under protest, into a house full of strangers. He was intending to follow Bridget up the stairs but his path was suddenly blocked by the Schrimers. They closed ranks. Stumped, he stood as if looking for a fight while swaying slightly under the influence of alcohol. He would not be beaten. He would not submit.

Frau Schrimer looked up the stairs then back at Franz. Her look said it all and Franz expected her to start laying into him - probably in French - or start preaching; like she really knew what he was going through; like she was an expert on his life. He was ready for a fight but he was to be disappointed. She just said one thing before chasing after her daughter up the stairs.

"You are leaving tomorrow I hope?"

On anybody else, or at any other time, the words would have cut like a knife but today, on Franz, they just hit tough rubber and bounced off.

Herr Schrimer, arms folded, took a deep breath before speaking.

"I suggest you have some dinner. It's been waiting for you."

"I'm not hungry yet," declared Franz stubbornly, despite his hunger.

"Well go and eat and then go to your room. Natalia will serve you something."

The force behind the words made it a command and Franz retreated to the dining room where he sat at the table and waited; now hating every second he was spending here in this house. He hoped Lev was having an equally bad time of it. He looked around the room at its display of wealth and thought it excessive, corrupt; and he just didn't get it. Why have lots of knives, forks and spoons lying around, cluttering the place up? This was not his mother's way.

He didn't know it but Herr Schrimer was just outside, loitering with intent, trying to understand what was going on. From a window he and his wife had caught sight of their daughter returning with the new boy in her life, and straight away had seen that something had gone seriously wrong. Their daughter's balance and well-being was in jeopardy. Herr Schrimer did not like problems such as Franz inside his house. He did his best to keep them outside, in the cruel world where

Section Three: Capital Sin

they belonged. The graze on the side of the boy's head merely reinforced his position.

On the edge of his seat - and the edge of his pants - Franz watched the Pole's every move. He held his knife and fork pointing up as a challenge and sulked - as she sulked, as she produced a plate of food. She planted it almost beyond reach and Franz had to stretch out and pull it in. She did not leave the room but watched him eat; arms folded like her employer; like a prison guard watching the prisoner eat his last meal. It did not take long for Franz to object to her game of torment. He banged the butt of his knife against the table.

"What's your problem!"

The Pole shrugged, applying understated reaction with a little theatrical zest to wind up the nasty little German even further.

"Get me a drink. Water - no beer."

"No. You've had too much I suspect."

Franz stood up. "I order you to get me a beer!"

Accidentally he had just performed a very good impersonation of his father while drunk and battering a restaurant manager who knew better than to give him another drink. The Pole laughed and in retaliation Franz grabbed the pepper pot in front of him. He threw it at her but missed by miles. It landed on the carpet, scattering its contents. She looked down at the mess, horrified, then back at him, the nasty little brat, astonished.

"You can clear that mess up."

"You do it. You're the servant stupid!"

At that point Herr Schrimer reappeared.

"I suggest you go to your room now." He spoke as if to a child.

Franz heard the sound of his father, a million miles away in the heart of the country, and began to sink.

"But I haven't finished eating," he mumbled.

"I'll bring you up some sandwiches."

Franz crept out of the room, refusing to admit that he had done anything wrong. Herr Schrimer watched him go with almost scientific curiosity and apologized to his housekeeper. She waved the incident away and went to get a dustpan and brush. Such a mess would not be tolerated by Frau Schrimer.

Halfway up the stairs Franz stopped suddenly. He would not back off so easily. He would not be told when to go to his room - not by that man anyway. He swore at the Schrimers, confusing them with the French Jews; and at the day, and how it had gone bad; then doubled back to go hunt down the television set. He wanted to watch something, preferably in colour. There was a film on, the only

Section Three: Capital Sin

interesting thing on. Unfortunately it was in black and white. No matter. Colour was for the corrupt, he lied to himself.

He tried to lose himself in the sofa, spread out and relax in front of the screen. But he failed and instead sat stiff, waiting for the next fight, while on screen a knight in shining armour, on horseback, blond hair blowing in the wind, was doing exactly the same thing. A medieval maiden - an iron maiden - was fleeing an angry mob. She was German, healthy and with good looks - but not sexy as that was not permitted. Likewise her hero the knight was tall, well built and always on the side of good. His moral compass never wavered. His sense of right and wrong were never in conflict. They never confused him. The angry mob were dirty, vicious, out for blood; and definitely did not look like good honest German folk. Franz suspected they were probably Jewish, or French.

Again Herr Schrimer suddenly appeared as if out of nowhere. Franz could not shake him off. Herr Schrimer switched off the set.

"We don't watch that rubbish in this house. Now please go to your room."

Franz held his eyes tight shut and tried to think of what he would do or say if he was back home. He found no answer. Like a cornered cat he slipped past Herr Schrimer and skulked away. His manhood had been reduced by fifty percent, perhaps more. Time had taken a turn for the worst - about five years backwards - and left his dignity in tatters. As he passed by Bridget's room he heard mother and child speaking in French. He paused to listen, wanting to know what was being said, then moved on, contemptuous of their intimacy. Entering his room he made a point of kicking the door shut, hoping to leave his mark.

Later that evening, cuddled and calmed and brought to her senses by her mother, Bridget would take a rational approach towards dealing with her problem. She would sit, shifting from side to side, and sift patiently through her collection of letters from Franz, scanning them for highlights. Some she would immediately throw into the bin. Some she would hesitate over, brood over, and try to relive the moment when she had first read them. Some she would decide to keep, to treasure, to hide. Sometimes in his letters Franz deserved to be heard. Other times he deserved to be ignored. Like an analytical machine Bridget would identify the best bits. Her mother had told her often, from the earliest age, to preserve the best of the past and use it in the pursuit of the future, to lessen the pain of the present. And she would do all this whilst clutching her favourite doll.

And during all this Franz would be hunched up close to the wall which divided them; wishing to be gone, but stuck; afraid of tomorrow,

Section Three: Capital Sin

afraid of meeting the Reichsfuehrer, afraid of meeting his parents; afraid that a great lie, a great sin was about to explode in his family and bring shame down upon the Helmer name. He would bang the wall in frustration, then again, despite the pain. To add to the misery he was stuck in a girl's room - a room he didn't understand. If it were possible he would jump on to his motorbike and drive at manic speed through the streets of the city, and scream, and pretend to be back in the Ukraine, where he, an outsider, felt at home.

Bridget would hear him thumping and pause, and think about hitting back before finally deciding no, that would be a childish thing to do. But she would take pity on him and would still have positive - passionate - feelings for him. And she would still want him to hold her and let her kiss him. And she would go to bed that night wanting him by her side so she could hold on to his body, and pretend.

♦

It was the middle of the night, in a cold cell which looked like it had been carved out of concrete from the inside out. Isaak stared up at the ceiling, wishing to see the stars; brain slumped, dumped even; body almost as cold as the air which circulated around it. Time was slowly beating him down, reducing him and dragging him towards mental oblivion - a process augmented by the sounds coming from the opposite side of the cell. In a cruel parody of deep sleep - one which tormented its victim - his cellmate tossed and turned and cried out; like a wild animal caught in a trap, or being slaughtered. He was a prisoner of another world: one in which he was all at sea, being tossed around by stormy weather, being smashed against rocks; one in which he was breaking up, suffering meltdown. He was miles from shore but he was not allowed to drown. He was forced to keep on thrashing and thrashing and thrashing around to stop himself sinking. He was going nowhere. He was simply spinning around in a whirlpool of his own madness and suffering. He was forever sinking fast.

Isaak wanted to throw something at him to shut him the hell up. But he had nothing to throw except complaints, and they would not be heard. He turned on to his side and looked at the pain being played out across the concrete floor. There was no escaping it, no hiding from it, no disguising it. It could not be dampened down. It could not be drown out by a louder harmony. Isaak could not guess what was inside the poor man's head but he knew that, whatever it was, it was no worse than what was lurking outside. Like the cries of a baby it was just louder, more fragile, more demanding of attention. And to make things

Section Three: Capital Sin

worse Isaak could relate to most of what he heard, and much of what he suspected was going on inside the poor man's head. He had been there - perhaps not as badly or as madly - as had other members of his family. Over time the Ghetto took a heavy toll on those forced to scratch a living within its walls.

Isaak did not like nightmares, especially his own, of which he had had many: perhaps the worse being that in which his parents were suddenly arrested, without warning or reason; then tortured, never to be seen again. Finally Isaak could take it no more. He shook his cellmate awake. Like God or the Devil he entered his cellmate's mind and blew away everything that was happening there.

"What's wrong! Tell me what's fucking wrong or fucking shut the fuck up and let me get some fucking sleep!"

Startled but still sleepy eyes greeted him, along with a blank, blameless expression which had only questions - no answers - to give. It was the look which was normally the preserve of babies, or the very old on the edge of death: both wondering what was happening, and why, and what was about to happen next; and would it hurt? Isaak had a wounded, possibly broken, soul on his hands: where he came from life was important, valued, and the total count mattered - the more meant the merrier. It demanded that Isaak be strong, take charge and recover the situation. The challenge was accepted and Isaak pulled his cellmate in close to his chest; there to hold him and hug him; there to show the world that he was not beaten, that he was even stronger than before. Übermensch? They wanted Übermensch? He would give them something better than that.

"Are you my friend?"

"Yes I'm your friend. I will always be your friend."

And it was true: Isaak was his true friend.

They had found common cause: beating back the nightmares; refusing to collapse under the weight of all the oppression; remaining human, intact, with a sense of humanity attached for completeness, and dignity.

◆

It was late, dark, cold and it had begun to rain. It was a vicious night and Penkin was staggering home first through mud - which he cursed - then across slippery paving stones, which he cursed. He was drunk and he had lost his way - without admitting it. He staggered on; cursing the wind and the world around which it blew; cursing those who had harmed him and those who had helped him; cursing the past which

Section Three: Capital Sin

would not let him be; cursing the present in which he was stuck. He did not curse the future: that had become forgotten. He staggered on, fuelled by his rage. There was no going back, only forwards, towards his death.

Time was pushing him on. He had encountered death from afar, and up close. He had seen it happen right in front of his eyes and he had never blinked. He had made it happen without having to draw breath. He had held back when he could have intervened. He had joined in when he could have walked away, back to the moral high ground. Time stopped pushing and for Penkin time suddenly stopped short. He slipped and fell from a bridge. The bridge, forgotten, crumbling, spanned a disused railway line. Penkin broke his neck and died instantly. He never knew what hit him. That had been the story of his life: he never knew what hit him, not even long after the event. He would be buried without family, friends or enemies to see him off.

Section Four: Passing Out Parade

Passing Out Parade

Franz awoke from a troubled sleep, one in which he suffered constant harassment from all sides and for all reasons. He shot up, still tired, kicked out, and got up, under duress. After a trip to the bathroom he packed in a rush and almost ran from the room, glad to be rid of it; entertaining the belief that he would be moving on to some place better. Outside Bridget's room he paused and read the stupid sign for the last time. She might be in there. She might not. Either way she was a waste of time. Either way girls were a waste of time. Either way he had to go downstairs if he was to escape this house. On the way down he felt the generations of family dead bearing down on him, making judgements and drawing conclusions.

The price he paid for breakfast was to share the table with Frau Schrimer, now a volcano ready to explode. She could not bring herself to speak to him, which was fine by Franz. He kept his eyes down while she kept hers on him. The heat she emitted was oppressive, as was her coldness. She watched his every move as Franz slipped into a chair and was served a plate of hot food by an equally restrained Natalia. Finally, as he began to cut his way through layers of bacon, Frau Schrimer began to mumble in her native tongue - first to herself, then to him. When the diatribe in French became too much Franz banged the table with the butt of his knife.

"I'm German! I only speak German!"

Taken aback Frau Schrimer switched to German and began to berate him for his behaviour. She had put him on trial. The graze on his forehead reinforced her opinion of him, and backed up everything her daughter had told her.

Forced to listen to a twisted account of the previous day had the undesired effect of making Franz close down, look down, and concentrate on demolishing the food on his plate in double quick time. He simple had to get out of this stuck up place and breathe fresh air again. Only the odd - truly odd - accusation pricked his ear, such as 'you lot, you think you're so special' and 'you think you're the future'. Special? What was the French bitch blabbing on about? His refusal to take the bait wound her up even more and Frau Schrimer lost all composure. She slapped the table in frustration. Startled, Franz nearly dropped his fork, but he held on. He would not cave in.

"Look at me when I'm talking to you!"

Franz looked up, world weary, completely lacking any serious intent.

Section Four: Passing Out Parade

"Why? What's the point?"

The strange lack of outburst stopped Frau Schrimer in her tracks. His cryptic, measured response had derailed her. She looked up at her husband for a way out: he had just entered the room to give Franz some information.

"Your taxi will be here in about twenty minutes. Are you ready and packed?"

"Ready and packed," replied Franz with a heavy dose of sarcasm. It had not been intentional. It had just spilled out.

As Frau Schrimer left the room Franz watched her go, satisfied that he had won. Herr Schrimer meanwhile continued to exercise his duty as host.

"I'll leave you to it then. Have a safe journey."

Herr Schrimer was making every effort to be nice. Franz was not.

"Hope it all goes well tomorrow."

"Thank you." Franz found that hard to say.

With that Herr Schrimer helped himself to coffee and said nothing more. They both sat in a comfortable silence.

When the taxi arrived Herr Schrimer escorted Franz to the door, said farewell, and watched him get into the back of the taxi, as if to make sure that he was gone. Frau Schrimer watched proceedings from a window. Franz did not look back. He wanted to move on at all speed. Speed was what the taxi ride gave him. The changing view from the car window offered him escape then snatched it away: he had one particular place to go; he had to be there on time, for a time; he had to play a part. There was no alternative.

The grand hotel immediately gained the upper hand when Franz arrived at its door. After paying the taxi driver he looked up, drew breath, and tried to imagine himself as one of those kind of people who frequented such places: rich people; privileged people; powerful people; cultured people. Foreigners? Would he have to mix with foreigners? No poor people here, he guessed. No one like him, a peasant from out east. He wanted to turn away but duty called, as it always did, and this time with greater insistence and magnificence to match.

Upon entering the building he was hit by the thick flow of human traffic. The place was busy and he had to queue for the reception desk. There were the usual uniforms on display, though unusually some were being worn by old men - men older than his father. Some were being trailed by expensive looking women, or had them hanging off their arms: the kind of women who were expensive to maintain; the kind who took comfort in the fact that their man would stand by them no

Section Four: Passing Out Parade

matter what their indiscretions or bad behaviour; the kind who thought they were above criticism; the kind who thought they had something worth saying. Franz thought he had escaped the vanity of the Schrimer house, but no, it was rife here in Berlin. He remembered the colonel's wife. He looked up at a picture of the Fuehrer but the Fuehrer had nothing to say, no advice to give. Franz dug deep when it was his turn at reception, wishing to be seen as important as those around him. Such effort was wasted as he was swept aside in double quick time, barely acknowledged with barely a kind word. He was handed the key to his room and told to be ready 'for the call'.

"For the call?" asked Franz brusquely, in retaliation. "What call?"

The receptionist sounded tired when he spoke. "The call for your appointment."

"Appointment?"

"You got the letter?"

"Oh that. Yes."

Franz tried to sound upbeat. Inside he was quaking inside his standard issue Hitler Youth boots.

"Well you are to meet the Reichsfuehrer and then later it's a visit to the stadium for rehearsals, familiarisation. You do know all this don't you?"

"Yes," snapped Franz.

Swept along by the anticipation of what was to come, he took a lift to his room. The lift was an indication of the pure luxury ahead: carpeted; furnished with polished brass; its mirrors squeaky clean. It glided up with a smoothness which almost disconnected it from the physical world. Franz could have been flying. His room was situated at the end of a long corridor and as he walked towards it he checked the number on each door he passed by, as if to reassure himself that he was on the right track and making progress. He looked back down the corridor to check he wasn't being followed before turning the key in the lock and stepping inside. He wanted to be impressed, made to feel important, and he was: it was a grand room, as befitting a grand hotel in a grand city. But the positive feeling didn't last: it was a grand room for grand people, not for the likes of peasants like him. Stuck on his spot he searched around for cover, trying to size up the lay of the land, trying to take it all in - though in reality there was not that much to take in.

Finally he continued on in, threw aside his kitbag and sat down on the end of the bed; afraid to touch anything, move anything, use anything; afraid to reveal himself even to an empty room. It was a double bed. He had never slept in a double bed before. He felt like a

Section Four: Passing Out Parade

fish plucked out of water and left to dangle while it drowned in fresh air. In time he stood up again, stretched, and approached the window to check the view. It was as he had now come to expect: everything out there was big, beautiful; designed to impress and overwhelm the visitor.

And then it hit him: he was alone, in the greatest city on earth, without a friend, without family, without a girlfriend; about to meet one of the most powerful, secretive men on the planet - the man whom he wanted to serve but was terrified to meet face to face. Franz stared at the telephone. It was big. It looked heavy. He could make a phone call: a call out to the big wide world, to the back of beyond if he wanted to. He wanted to call Lev. All he had to do was cross the carpet and pick it up. He scrambled about inside his bag and found the scrap of paper with the number. He told himself to do it, make the call. He picked up the phone - yes it was heavy - and was about to start dialling when a voice cut in, asking what service he required.

Franz froze. He had no answer, only insecurity. He replaced - almost dropped - the handset and stepped back, feeling stupid, and then miserable instead of stupid. He collapsed on the bed with a massive headache, feeling trapped again. The knowledge that his parents would arrive later that day did nothing to relieve him. If anything they were crushing him. Until they were there, they didn't exist - possibly a blessing, possibly a curse. They were just unreliable memories. He tried to think of Bridget - Bridget at her best - but she was too much - or too little. He tried not to think of the Reichsfuehrer but he was too much.

Suddenly the loud ringing of the telephone shook Franz awake. He had fallen asleep. He looked at the clock by the bed. He had just lost twenty minutes of his life. Suspicious, he picked it up and slowly drew the earpiece to his ear. A voice - a different voice - announced that 'a young lady by the name of Bridget Schrimer' wished to see him. The bolt from the blue went straight through his head and out the other side, leaving him simultaneously disorientated and charged up. She had to be kidding right?

"It's OK. Send her up." He tried to sound masterful, in control of events.

He lingered by the door, going nowhere; torn between opening it and looking out or waiting for the knock. He decided on waiting. He did not want to look too keen. He heard approaching footsteps, then nothing. That 'nothing' seemed to last an age. Finally there was the knock at the door. Franz held himself in check, barely breathing, not wishing to be rushed. Make her wait. Make her wonder. Make her worry. Only when a second knock followed did he answered the door.

Section Four: Passing Out Parade

It was Bridget and she looked nervous, and a little wide-eyed.

"Hallo."

"Hallo."

"Can I come in?"

"Sure."

The exchange - minimal and unemotional - fell flat. Franz stood back to allow Bridget to enter his room. She looked around; trying to take it all in; trying to act with confidence and maturity. But it was so big, so impressive that she crumbled and became a child again: a child to be thrown into another adventure without warning. Like a child lost she circled the room, with Franz watching her all the way. (He grew bigger at her expense.) Suddenly this big alien space was his ally not his enemy.

"This is all for you?"

"Yes, all for me."

He kept his distance as she moved around, touching surfaces, opening drawers and sliding back the wardrobe doors. She looked inside the wardrobe: so much space for just one person. She examined the trouser press, finding it funny.

"You going to use this?"

"Probably not."

Bridget locked on to the big mighty handset.

"You have room service?"

"I suppose so," replied Franz, not knowing what he was meant to do with 'room service'.

"Let's try."

"Try? Try what?" Franz moved in, unsure where she was leading him.

"Let's order something. This is all paid for isn't it?"

"I suppose so."

Bridget didn't care that Franz sounded unsure.

"Well let's do it then."

He watched, impassive, as she made the call, and without hesitation or deviation went straight to the point: she ordered a bottle of champagne. Franz wished he had thought of that, and had made the call. Satisfied, Bridget sat down on the bed and bounced up and down, as if to test the springs. She was really testing herself. Franz stood feeling awkward; not knowing whether to join her; not knowing if this was Bridget the little girl or Bridget the wannabe, would-be girlfriend.

Bridget had cheered up. The glum expression worn at the door was gone. For her reconciliation was proving easier than feared, and without having to say a serious word to him - without having to say

Section Four: Passing Out Parade

anything in fact. Just take it as read. Boys could be hard and they could be easy. Even the toughest, best looking boys could be easy, especially if they were not particularly bright.

"You looking forward to it all?"

"Yes," lied Franz.

"You going to stop fighting?"

"Yes." Another lie.

Bridget smiled and patted the bed. "Come and sit down then."

Franz sat down as instructed - again trying not to look keen - on the lookout for something to happen. Inches apart, their body chemistries began to react. Seeing a quick payback Franz made a quick apology to clear any remaining bad air.

"Sorry about yesterday."

There, done.

"That's OK."

And that was that. Simple.

Bridget took his hand, as a gesture, desperate to reengage. She gently touched his head to probe the wound. He ignored it. He just wanted to kiss. A knock at the door ruined any chance of that. It was the champagne. Bridget nudged him into action.

"Go on you get it. It's your room - and you look eighteen."

It was sound advice and Franz let a waiter - a young man much his age - into the room. The waiter greeted them with warm but mechanical words and placed a bucket on the table. The waiter stalled then, realising that no tip was forthcoming, turned sharply and left the room with a passing sour shot of 'enjoy'. The champagne sat in ice in the bucket, waiting, while Franz and Bridget basked in their sweet little victory.

"I'll open it," said Franz finally, boldly.

(He was the only man in the room: that had to count for something.)

"Don't shake it!"

"Why not?"

"It will go everywhere! We don't want to waste any, or make a mess."

After giving his girl a look designed to demolish Franz carefully popped open the bottle and filled the glasses. And in a wink of an eye they were side by side on the bed, sipping champagne, feeling smart, feeling superior; each feeling good about themselves and about the other. Then Bridget spoilt it by asking about the Reichsfuehrer.

"You seeing him today?"

"Who?"

"The Reichsfuehrer silly."

Section Four: Passing Out Parade

Franz felt himself sink. "Probably. Don't know for sure."
"Looking forward to meeting him?"
Franz gritted his teeth. "No."
"But he's your hero?"
"So?"
Stumped, Bridget relaunched the chat.
"They say he's a hermit - lives all alone in a big castle, spying on everyone. He keeps a file on everyone - everyone except the Fuehrer."
"Well they're stupid."
Bridget kicked the bed with the back of her shoe in protest. "That's what my father says and he's not stupid!"
Child, thought Franz. She's that child again.
"What are you going to say to him?"
"Say to him? Don't know. Hallo?"
Bridget giggled, thinking Franz was being funny. He wasn't. He was being deadly serious. With no more questions she returned to the task of sipping champagne and trying to relive the better moments they had spent together; and she waited for his mood to pass whilst forgiving him for it, deciding that on such a day his behaviour was entirely natural. She had forgiven him for the previous day using the same excuse, the same technique. Forgiving was easier than fighting: that's what Father had taught her many times, and it made sense. Less blood was spilt. Bad blood did not ferment.
Into his first refill Franz suddenly burst into speech. He spoke of the Schutzstaffeln and boasted that he would be one of its best officers; and serve with distinction; and go down fighting (whatever that meant). Bridget sipped her champagne slowly, enjoying the bubbles, and listened (as if to an older brother), and relaxed. She took none of it seriously. Franz sank his and, wound up by his declaration, suddenly put a blunt question.
"Are you proud of me?"
Bridget was caught on the hop. She had never been asked such a thing before. Recovering quickly she told him what he wanted to hear.
"Proud? Of course I'm proud." She stopped drinking, waiting for more.
"Show me." Franz considered it her duty to make him feel better.
Bridget put down her glass and showed him. Franz put down his and responded in kind. They kissed, no holds barred, all burdens temporarily removed by alcohol. But for all his blustering Franz was the fragile one, and Bridget felt it; and she led him to her breasts where he undid her shirt buttons and pushed on into the one true place of security and comfort. She was happy for him. And as he kissed her

Section Four: Passing Out Parade

breasts she told herself that things were good, beautiful. But no more she told herself. It stops here. But it didn't. Franz carried on, seemingly with her approval for she made no protest. Moreover she adjusted her position to accommodate him.

Then she lost the plot. The boy was between her legs - her legs had opened. Still OK Bridget tried to tell herself as she drowned in the pleasure and the thrill of the risk. And then she was completely lost and Franz took full control. He had control over her body. He had electrified it. He began to pull aside her underwear. The child had fled and the woman had still to take control. When he crossed the last hurdle, underpants pushed down, her knickers pulled down and in a twist, that was when she pushed back. The physicality of it was too much to bear. She did not want to lose her virginity here, in a hotel room; or now, without protection; or to someone who might only be after her body. She wanted romance, and commitment. She wanted the real thing. She pushed back with force and Franz responded in kind. The desperate need for sex had driven out rational thought. He was on autopilot, dive bombing. He had to have sex. His body demanded it and his brain conspired to make it happen, and make it legal.

Bridget twisted and turned, and thrashed about but she did not cry out. She did not want to draw attention from the crowd - in her mind there was always a crowd. Franz held her down with sheer body weight and a constant stream of kisses, and tried to force his way in. Time was of the essence: he was about to explode. But he found it impossible to proceed. Finally he lost his temper and shook her violently.

"Bitch."

Terrified, Bridget began to punch. Seeing the moment gone Franz let go and she rolled away, to slip to the floor; crying her heart out and trying to pull her knickers back up. She was shaking. He was shaking. Their world was shaking. Shamed, Franz retreated from the bed and sat on the carpet, face turned away, not wishing to be seen. This was not how it was suppose to end. He was about to become a soldier. He deserved better than this. She owed him one.

Bridget struggled to her feet, rubbing that accursed part of her body which provoked both pain and pleasure in equal measure. She crept away, unable to speak. She was a torn rag doll. Now Franz was absolutely sure he would never see her again. There would be no more letters.

"You're still a child."

It was his last remark, and his most cruel, and it was possibly true.

Weeping, Bridget fled the room, taking the stairs to avoid meeting

Section Four: Passing Out Parade

people in the lift. By the time she reached the main lobby she had managed to dry her eyes and recover enough composure to walk out without attracting attention. Attention was the last thing she wanted right now. She wanted to be invisible and slip away unseen. Crying was for babies, she told herself as she headed home - to face some hard questioning from worried parents.

> Boy meets girl. Girl falls in love.
> Boy beats girl. Nothing is enough. Girl feels crushed.
> Boy retreat, still raging with lust.
> Girl recovers, only just, unable to fake
> the injustice of her mistake.
> Boy marches on, battles to be won.
> Girl retires, washing to be done.
> Boy is late, out with his mates.
> Girl stands waiting at the gate.
> Dinner is ready. Table is set.
> Boy is drunk, wants more beer. Breaks open a bottle.
> Makes a toast.
> Girl plays along. She has to make the most, but deep inside she is now a ghost.

Franz had no time to reflect upon his behaviour or situation for the phone rang. It was reception again. He was wanted - expected - to be in the lobby in ten minutes, in uniform. The order was barely disguised as a firm request. The voice, female, did not say please. Franz did not say thank you. He wanted to tell her to fuck off but Duty called. He sank another glass of champagne at breakneck speed whilst changing into his Hitler Youth gear and slipping into his Hitler Youth persona. He felt better for it: somehow the uniform and all the baggage which went with it shook off the tension and turmoil. It gave him somewhere to hide. Time to impress my leader, he told his reflection in the mirror. His reflection did not respond. Tie pulled up tight, he went downstairs to face the music; dreading the thought that Bridget might still be hanging around, lingering with a bleeding heart. But she was nowhere in sight, which strangely disappointed him. Somehow he still felt he commanded her attention. Somehow -

His drifting thoughts were chopped by a sharp, curt voice.

"You Franz Helmer?"

Franz looked around. A junior officer of the Schutzstaffeln was pointing at him. He was a young man, good looking but stiff and stern; driven as he was by his passion to execute all orders handed down to

Section Four: Passing Out Parade

him with efficiency and to the letter. Franz walked towards him, feeling an immediate rapport, but he was mistaken. Ignoring him completely, the officer man ticked his name off a list.

"Come with me, all of you."

Two other boys, also in uniform, scuttled forward and together the three of them were led outside to a black car which carried the distinctive markings of the SS. It was an official escort. The three stood looking at each other, each waiting for another to take the lead. But here, at this moment in time, the Hitler Youth was leaderless. The officer had to push them on into the car. It was like dealing with cattle. Sitting in the back Franz looked back one last time, but no sign of Bridget. She had abandoned him.

The three boys wore solemn expressions and did not speak during the journey. They could have been on their way to a funeral, or prison. As the car sped through the busy, buzzing streets of the capital, Franz could not help but think that everybody out there was having a better time than him. Somehow that didn't add up. Their escort did nothing to relax or reassure them: he was too pre-occupied with keeping to his schedule and was not in the habit of making small talk.

The car drew to a halt in the forecourt of a large spectacular building: designed with the attributes and look of a medieval castle it drew both praise and derision - the former loudly, the latter in secret (sometimes from the same audience). Both famous and infamous, it was the main headquarters of the Schutzstaffeln. 'Beware all who enter' was the message on the faces of the guards who stood at the main entrance.

The officer ushered his catch up the steps and on inside - careful to salute all officers coming the other way. He was in his element, back on hallowed ground; back where the real action was. Without giving them any information or clues as to what was about to happen he led the boys up a flight of stairs - stairs as befitting a ballroom - and down a long wide corridor; and on into a plush, lush anteroom. Teutonic Knights watched them all the way and propaganda teased them along and portraits of mighty men now dead reminded them that it was all about Duty, Duty, Duty. There the officer told them to sit and wait and do nothing. Job done he left the room, to nip outside for a quick smoke. (Yes, he was now just as nervous as they were and he had to have a smoke.) The anteroom was not empty: two other boys sat, in uniform, adrift and looking exhausted. They barely acknowledged the faces of the fresh batch, the fresh kill. Franz had a deep uneasy feeling, like he was about to meet the devil - or the devil's sidekick. Sensing the occasion was about to engulf him he began to dread the moment. Only

Section Four: Passing Out Parade

the large intake of alcohol kept him together, above and beyond the substance of all that was happening - or about to happen - to him.

The door of the inner office - the inner sanctum - opened and the new batch collectively drew breath. But it was just another boy, in uniform. He looked tired and weak at the knees. Behind him came another officer. He waved the broken boy on out of the way. The new batch exchanged glances, wondering who would be first. It was Franz. His name was next on the list. His surname had beaten the others in the war of letters. The officer quietly read out his name and beckoned him on in. Franz stood up, arms and legs stiff, and struggled to respond. It could have been the day of his sentencing for crimes committed, or the firing squad. Such was the reputation of Reichsfuehrer Heinrich Himmler (one he mischievously cultivated). Franz followed the officer into a large expanse of office space where the rules of time and space suddenly shifted; leaving Franz to count every microsecond which passed and every faltering step he took. Suddenly he was sober, and in dire need of his mother.

◆

And there he was, seated behind a large desk at the far end of his large office; imposing his will upon his empire with the lightest touch of a pen as he signed documents, or the faintest trace of interest as he listened to a verbal report. He did not occupy much space. He did not make grand gestures. He sat on his dreams. He did not make emotional contact. He had not done so in a very long time: he was divorced; his children did not speak to him for he kept his ex-wife under virtual house arrest. He had become isolated from true human intimacy and the emotional traffic which went with it. Instead he played games with his staff: playing on their fears, ambitions and willingness to please. Never once did he give the game away. Only with Reinhard Heydrich did he let his hair down - something he would never do with the Fuehrer. And as for the other two - that club-footed rat Goebbels and the fat bumbling fool Goering - well they could go to hell. (It never occurred to him that he might meet up with them there - there, that place where they would be forced to drink from the same cup into which each of them had just spat.)

Were it not for the fact that he was in the uniform of the Reichsfuehrer, Heinrich Himmler could have been mistaken for a portly, aging bank manager; one nearing retirement but unwilling to leave office and hand over the keys to his successor; or a headmaster, in a similar vein of self-imprisonment; or a chief constable who never

Section Four: Passing Out Parade

compromised and who never took prisoners, and who never thought 'Right' could work against him. But he was none of these people: he was the Reichsfuehrer; the only one who had ever been and perhaps the only one who would ever be. The job was not a guaranteed position: the future sometimes had the knack of suddenly turning on the present and biting its head off.

Himmler wore glasses with thick lenses: the price paid for taking on too much paperwork during his lengthy rule. The Nazi movement was turning him blind. His grey hair was thinning fast now. Time was not on his side - just as it had never been for his victims. His cheeks were fat. In any other existence, in any other universe, he could have looked cheeky: with an added smile he could have passed himself off as a clown. But in this world he was seriously serious all of the time. And if he did smile it was only to conform to the mood of the party or the social gathering. His Fuehrer smiled - sometimes - so he had to smile too. It was a smile which grabbed you by the neck and held you down; and dared you to talk back - let alone criticize.

From his office he set the rules, watched, considered, discarded, made adjustments, and became bored. He had accomplished everything. He had been instrumental in stop-starting the history of his nation. He had no more enemies to destroy, only time consuming sycophants to deal with. Like goldfish in a pond or dogs in a cage he would throw them food and watch them tear each other apart for a bite of the action. But even that could prove to be boring. When the paperwork overwhelmed him he might break a pencil in protest. Smiling: he had to keep smiling. Every other day he had to remind himself to smile at least once. And saluting: he had to keep saluting. Excited: he had to be excited - for his Fuehrer, for his organisation, and for the masses.

His brain rattled along to a rhythm, like an old engine. These days it was a blunt instrument: hating complexity, it simplified more and more, until the meaning was lost and only the measurement was left. He slammed it down here. He slammed it down there, as if swatting flies. It struggled to entertain - whether it be colleagues, social acquaintances or ideas. Himmler got a thrill from watching his reputation precede him. He ensured it was well fed by the publicity machine. His image was far removed. He had never got his hands dirty in public. He had never been caught on camera in the wrong place or at the wrong time. He still smelt of roses while many of those around him smelt foul.

His cruel mind was neatly contained; set aside from his conscience so unable to compromise him, contaminate him. And his acts of cruelty were carried out by others. He remained above it all, clean, alongside

Section Four: Passing Out Parade

his whiter than white Fuehrer. There was no mud on their shoes, only polish. Occasionally the dirt seeped out and threatened to drive him mad - or sane depending upon your viewpoint - but each time he managed to squeeze it back into its box. Sentimentality was a human condition he detested. He had turned vindictiveness into a science. He had made brutality a test of loyalty, a measure of manhood, the food to feed ambition. He had neutralised his enemies with clinical precision and patience worthy of Bismarck at his best. He had turned them into political eunuchs. And by accident he had also neutralized his small circle of friends. He scared them. They bored him. They pretended. He pretended.

Himmler did not look up as Franz approached his desk and the officer fell back to stand discreetly to one side; hands folded behind his back; stiff and straight as per the rulebook. Himmler had no need to look up. He had his list in front of him and the next name on that list was Franz Helmer, son of retired officer Hauptsturmführer Franz Helmer who had served in the 2nd SS Panzer Division - with distinction it said in his notes.

"Franz Helmer?" Though he spoke softly the Reichsfuehrer did not sound inviting.

Franz took one more step closer to answer yes but never got the chance. The Reichsfuehrer finally looked up and strained his eyes as he spoke again, a curious look on his face.

"It says here you intend to apply for officer training in my organisation after completing national service?"

Franz wanted to answer with a simple 'yes' but nothing would come out. His voice had dried up. To help matters along the Reichsfuehrer tried his best to smile, but like the accountant who could never balance the books he failed and was left with a frown on his face.

"Yes?"

Franz nodded profusely, trying to maintain a presence and not look like an idiot in front of the second most powerful man on the continent. Feeling himself being examined, he drew himself to attention: shoulders back, arms straight down; looking only ahead. Franz hoped he was not causing offence by avoiding eye contact, not knowing that the Reichsfuehrer did not give a damn. He was used to such backward behaviour. Let them all fear him. Let them all follow him. Let them all do his bidding without question. That was how he operated his empire.

"Are you strong enough? Do you have the discipline? That is the question I must ask myself time and time again of today's youth."

Franz was confused. The question did not seem to be directed at

Section Four: Passing Out Parade

him. The next question was.

"You like living out east?"

"Yes Reichsfuehrer." Franz clicked his heels as his words punched the air.

"There's no need to do that."

"No Reichsfuehrer."

"And is it a good place?"

"Yes Reichsfuehrer I think so."

With conversation beginning to flow, just like between two normal human beings, Franz now found it possible to breathe and broaden the scope of his answers. But it was not to be: the Reichsfuehrer looked back down at his list, contemplating the fact that no one had ever given him a different answer to that particular question. He had a dislike of small talk and the wasted word - his words were cut and dry. His next question sounded tired.

"It states here that your father served with distinction, a war hero. You must be proud of him."

"Yes Reichsfuehrer."

Finally the Reichsfuehrer moved matters on: he pointed at Franz with his favourite fountain pen. It was a gold fountain pen and engraved upon it were the double runes and death's-head of his organisation. There was no other pen like it: when it was made copies were strictly forbidden.

"Turn around."

Franz turned to go.

"No. Turn around, 360 degrees, slowly."

Franz corrected himself and the examination proceeded. The Reichsfuehrer noted the colour of the eyes. Perfect. The eyes were perfect. As was the hair. The boy could become a perfect Nazi. Then he saw something amiss.

"What's that on the side of your head? Have you been fighting? Have you been fighting?"

The tone of his voice changed considerably and the atmosphere went colder still. Franz went red, red with fear.

"Just a minor mishap, a misunderstanding. I hit a wall."

"Well don't let it happen again. That is not the sort of behaviour I expect from those who presume to be the best. You understand me?"

Franz swallowed hard to get the right words out. "I understand Reichsfuehrer."

'Those who presume to be the best.' The words ran around inside his head: were they a compliment or a taunt?

Business done the Reichsfuehrer returned to his list and placed a tick

Section Four: Passing Out Parade

against the entry for Franz Helmer.

"You know what I expect of you tomorrow?"

"Yes Reichsfuehrer."

"Good. Make him proud. You only exist for him, and me. You can go now. Send in the next one."

And that was it: short but not sweet. Franz was led away and out, and the next body was led in.

Back outside Franz sat traumatized, bewildered. It had been interrogation versus rapture, heartfelt truth versus necessary lies. Franz had shaken Bridget off but let the Reichsfuehrer in. The big moment in his life had lasted a few bare, brittle minutes. It had come and gone like a high speed train, leaving him flattered by the shock wave - his fault for standing too close to the line. Franz had suffered worse moments in front of his headmaster, or his father, but nothing had ever prepared him for this. He felt he had been stripped naked for examination; disassembled then put back together again. He felt the spirit had been drained from his body and placed in a bottle marked 'for future use'. The Reichsfuehrer had neutralized him with nothing more than the sound of his voice and the reputation which preceded him.

For such a short passage of time it had been a strange experience, one which would stick in his mind and never diminish. Franz told himself that it had been a rare privilege, the highest honour, to meet the Reichsfuehrer; even if he could not bring himself to cherish it. He really wanted to go home now, not back to the hotel and all its stuffed creatures.

After the next two were roasted to the same degree the same young officer drove them back to the hotel. Again they sat through silence, each exhausted or deep in thought. Jumping out of the car when it stopped, Franz felt a sense of relief, like he had survived a dangerous mission. But his next mission was about to start. He barely had time to draw breath before he was bundled with others into a waiting minibus. He was off to the stadium for rehearsals. The twins were sitting on the back seat looking apprehensive but Franz did not acknowledge them. They looked weak. He craved strength, and wanted solitude. He sat alone.

◆

In the Ghetto Isaak's mother, Diza, returned from the vegetable garden exhausted, joints protesting, but satisfied, buoyant even: food was growing up fast. Everything was coming up roses. Only her jailed son was spoiling her day. For completeness she desperately needed him

Section Four: Passing Out Parade

back. Her tired mind received no support from her tired body and she had not been sleeping well since they took him from her. She was beginning to fail and fall apart. She stepped back indoors, out of the light, scrubbed her hands then sat down in her usual place at the kitchen table; there to dry them with a mean old towel. The pieces on the chessboard had not moved. It was still his turn. She would wait for however long it took. She did not hurry time and she did not let time hurry her - most of the time.

Diza sat still, conserving energy. Yosef had been gone well over an hour which was a long time in the Ghetto. The weekly meeting with other elders was set like clockwork to last exactly one hour: that way it remained focused and idle talk died a death. She knew how long it took him to walk there and back. It was ritual. The elders discussed all the issues and concerns; the outstanding repairs; the dangers and current mood on the outside versus that on the inside. The elders made decisions to which all stuck, religiously. It stopped the community falling apart. It stopped its people falling apart.

The electric light flickered - a reminder that the midday blackout was fast approaching. She tried to reignite some old memory, pre-Ghetto; make it stronger, more persistent; wishing to reconsume it. She failed miserably. She was stuck, knee deep, in the present; and it depressed her. She decided to boil the kettle and prepare a pot of tea for her husband. He would to appear any moment soon, any moment soon.

And he would.

Yosef was only a few streets away, walking home fast; avoiding the mud; clutching an envelope; afraid to drop it; unwilling to pocket it. He had to hold on to it for his sanity depended upon it.

They did not like to be apart, Diza and Yosef. They needed each other close to stay strong, to survive intact. They were living in a shit hole but they were not covered in the stuff. They kept clean religiously. They refused to let it stick. On bad days they huddled up together, around their precious family photographs for warmth. On good days, in the sun, they reminisced: about their youth; about life pre-Ghetto; about how they met and fell in love; about when they started a family; about decent Christians. Holding hands they held on, each refusing to die unless the other died first.

The streets were not so much streets as empty, unexploited spaces residing between the random, rambling constructions of human habitation and activity: buildings in a desperate state of disrepair; some remarkably well-preserved. There was no squalor. Squalor was not permitted. (Standards had to be maintained.) There were no

Section Four: Passing Out Parade

streetlamps and few pavements. You travelled along dirt tracks or through mud in your horse and cart or, if you were really lucky, in your clapped out old car. When you passed by others you rarely bothered to greet them as, with the community being so small, so confined, you saw most people nearly all the time. There were only so many times you could say hello in one day. There was only so much small talk in such a small place. In that sense the isolation was your protection, sanity and shield. The fact that the Ghetto was off limits to Ukrainians, and of no interest to local Germans was a bonus. It was a bubble floating in a sea of sewage.

Everybody knew everybody, almost inside out. You could not be a stranger. Gossip was rife, a ritual amplified. It kept you in touch. It relieved the boredom. The immediate past was buried deep, or locked away at the back of a cupboard: but the photographs were not torn up; the evidence was not destroyed; the crimes were not forgotten; the names - both victims and perpetrators - could be recited. The distant past was glorified, revered. The future was constructed on idle dreams (to be drunk or smoked or set to music) and a few delusions (to prop up the dreams). But it was sustenance nevertheless. The present was tolerated. When the present did not move of its own accord it was pushed on from one day to the next, on the never-ending treadmill of the human passage through time.

Each new day meant a new battle of attrition for the emotions. You had to be fit and able to fight. You had to believe your one God had a plan for your salvation. You had to have total faith in your family and close friends. You dared not lose the will to survive: the alternative was to slowly shrivel up, or sink. In earlier times cheap lives had been hollowed out and left to rot. Now times were better, the optimistic would argue, they were simply left to simmer.

In the Ghetto time moved at the same plodding pace: you could not run ahead; you dare not fall behind; you could not out pace it, outsmart it. All you could do was stay with it and count it, second by silent curious second; with the danger of going slowly mad always hanging over you. In here the physical world was both primitive and complex. There was still love and hate, loyalty and loathing; idleness and insolence; wishful thinking and verbal energy. In here beautiful moments were prolonged, as were beautiful thoughts. In here everything worn was worn to the limit, and beyond. Sewing machines were vital, a godsend, and had pride of place on the table; alongside threads, needles and buttons. Curtains (recycled from beyond the grave) were often kept closed to keep out the depressing view. They only opened when the sun came out. Beauty had to be built from scrap

Section Four: Passing Out Parade

parts. It could not be purchased. Ugliness had to be disarmed. It could not be disguised. Nothing was dumped if it fell apart - only if it could not be resuscitated. Leftovers were not left on the plate. Cracked crockery was not thrown away. A broken hairdryer would be exchanged for a pair of ripped, ill-fitting trousers. The hairdryer would be returned repaired, as would the trousers, now fit to wear. You wrote on both sides of the paper. Jam jars became all-purpose jars. The little that became final, ultimate, unequivocal rubbish - that which could not be put back into the soil or burnt - ended up in an unholy hole in the ground.

When Yosef came in through the door Diza looked up, expectant. Her man looked tense. She began to worry. He was staring right into her eyes and clutching a brown envelope. Bad bad news?

"What is it? Tell me. I can take it."

He sat down opposite her, placed the envelope down on the table and pushed it towards her into her reach; like it was a loaded gun, or a capsule of cyanide, or a large diamond.

"Open it," he said matter-of-fact.

Diza took it slowly, felt it, and stared back at him with equal intensity. It felt like a thick wad of banknotes. Yes it was banknotes she decided and she rushed to open it. She drew them out and held them up to the light like pieces of gold - which for her they were, except in paper form. She nearly passed out. Only the fact that her husband started to talk prevented her from doing so.

"It's a contribution from the community. It makes up the difference. They said pay back what we can when we can. And they said talk to him. Make it clear such stupid, reckless behaviour must never happen again."

"He probably knows that already."

"I hope so." Yosef did not sound convinced.

He peered down at the dirty old notes before picking them up again to return them to the envelope for safekeeping. He had never held so many in his hand before. Now he had a good idea what it was like to feel rich; to have all worldly goods on tap; to be able to diminish their worth through overwhelming financial power.

Diza wanted to cry. She had to cry. She started to cry.

Yosef rushed round the table to join her and hold her through it. He didn't cry. He had already got past that stage - and anyway his wife did enough crying for the both of them. They could set their one and only son free. They could carry on living: they had their reason for living back. They looked at his photograph on the wall, taken when he was just a baby, in another world; on the outside when the inside did not

Section Four: Passing Out Parade

exist; when the Ghetto had just been a poor, mainly Jewish part of town.

They remembered life before the Ghetto. It had not been great but at least it had been under their control and direction, and a life with variety. In here the future was a singularity, an unavoidable finality: the same sense of nothingness lay ahead, day after day; not much different from the 'now'. You could not fight it, avoid it, bend its dark light. But as long as they had their son and he had a chance of something different ahead - perhaps on the outside - it was worth carrying on. For his sake they refused to give up.

"I'm making tea," Diza announced, forcing normality back on to the table where it belonged.

She looked at the other chessboard. "And you, you make your move."

Yosef looked at the pieces, but right now he couldn't think straight. His attack would have to wait. Later they would submerge themselves in the flood of joy and relief, and drown in the river until the river ran dry. They would prepare, put on their best clothes and go collect their precious son.

◆

Size did matter: the city stadium dazzled the mind and consumed the body. It was a powerful place where power was put on display. This immense, carefully constructed space could be filled to bursting point with all the right people, all in the right state of mind. The incentive was just one particular old man, and the life he had lived, and the mind he had set - set hard like concrete. In here, from the same cosy contrived spot, the Fuehrer had, many times, spoken to and shouted at his adoring fans. And each time, despite the repetition, his core fans had cheered as loudly as they had the very first time. There was no let up on either side. It was a total embrace. They had grown up with him, or grown old like him. The party was not allowed to come to an end. The Party ensured that. The celebrations had to continue. You were not permitted to sober up. The old man could repeat himself until he was blue in the face and still the crowd would hang off his every word, and cheer cheer cheer until they were exhausted. Some would faint. Some would fold. Few would forget. Once, on a diet and having forgotten to eat a proper meal, he had nearly fainted. Once, in his later years, he had lost his way but stumbled on. But it did no harm: it made him seem more human, more accessible. Now he had precise autocue and such dangers were past.

Section Four: Passing Out Parade

And tomorrow the Fuehrer would stand there, high up on the podium, and say much the same again; and put on his Messianic act despite the fact he had no one left to rescue. His nation had recovered it all, and more: national dignity; wealth; economic power; land and good living. There was no one left to attack. They were dead, or had fled, or were locked up, or had converted late to the cause. But attack he did. It was all he could do. It was all he could remember. And for some in his audience it would be as fresh as the first time. And for many watching him on a television screen - perhaps in colour - in private, away from prying eyes, it would be faintly amusing. But for most it would be business as usual. For a few it would be like watching the devil dictate in disguise. They were a small, reckless minority. That was tomorrow. Today the stadium was near deserted. Today the Fuehrer was present in image only, which made the place feel incomplete, waiting, wanting. The grand imposing platform stood pregnant, waiting to push out its performance of polluted persuasion. A light cold wind blew in and out, and around and around; searching, feeling its way ahead.

Today there were just the workmen, the technicians, the security and the Party organisers. They had the whole place to themselves but did not look like they were enjoying it. Stress levels were at an all time high. Cables were not properly connected. They were not delivering power. The sound system was still not fully functional. Only the cameras and their bored cameramen stood ready. If the set was not ready and right on the day heads would roll, into the basket. This was not a rock concert. This was not a folk festival. A great man's global image was at stake - though the day after tomorrow they would pull it all apart with the same vigour and speed. Everything would come together tomorrow then a day later scatter, like a storm sweeping through. And like a storm it would leave wreckage.

Senior members of both the SA and SS were here today: encircling each other, watching each other, rarely speaking to each other; each trying to out command or overrule the other. The Fuehrer loved to see them fight. It was the ultimate cock fight. It was black versus brown. The National Broadcasting Company was here and ignored them both. It took its orders from the Doktor and no one else. It knew exactly what it had to do: same as last year; same as the year before. Same next year: you could set your watch by it.

Even when empty this vast arena could suck you in and hold you down, tight, as if under restraint. On the day it would rip you apart if you didn't join in and become part of the moment - his moment. You could not refuse the energy of the crowd: it entered - engulfed - your

Section Four: Passing Out Parade

body, and electrified it. You had to release it the same way, else it would fry you. Full or empty it seduced you. The stadium enforced a ritual in which you arrived with the truth, joined a lie, and left dazed, distorted; unsure if the truth was the lie or the lie was now the truth. Either way it won the day.

Like a big satellite dish the stadium beamed its broadcast out to the world. At its centre was one particular - and strange - human being who had made it big by turning himself inside out, whilst hiding the parts which were not suitable for public consumption. It magnified him, dehumanized him. Its audience turned him into a superman. (But he could not fly.) In truth, in recent years, it had been noticed that the energy of the crowd had slackened and the passion had been lacking in places. The great man's milestone birthday would hopefully correct that decline and set the mood back on course - the course of religious compliance. The same old flags went up. The same old flags would come down. The same old tunes would be played. The same old songs would be sung. Secretly, beset by familiarity, some regular attendees high up in the Party would have to fake it.

After being shouted down out of the bus the boys were herded down a long tunnel and on into the stadium. There were other buses and other boys and other bruised brains. Those who were not in uniform received a dirty or critical eye from those who were. Today was not a day to express your individuality - or expose your laziness or absent-mindedness. They moved at speed: no time to take in the sights; no time to ask questions; no right to protest. Inside they were told to form their units and await further orders. Franz and the twins were reunited with their cell leader Gebhard Strasser. He was in his element. He looked on top of the world. Franz looked like he was buried beneath it. Today he would find it difficult to play the game. And the uniform was beginning to suck. The circus had come to town and it expected him to act the clown but Franz was in no mood for smiling or dressing up.

He looked around, and tried to take it all in. He tried to snap off the huge space in one bite but there was no give. He loved space - he had been born and raised on the stuff - but this was not his kind of space. It was fake. It would be filled. It was surrounded. He was surrounded. He wanted to be out of here as soon as possible. The stadium was empty: he had only ever seen it on the news stuffed full. It felt weird. Now he was standing in it; and tomorrow, stuffed full again, all those faces would be looking down at him. His every movement, his every facial gesture; every slip of the tongue, every hesitation, every disappointment, every regret would be captured on camera and amplified into every household across the Reich - perhaps across

Section Four: Passing Out Parade

Europe. The thought terrified him and he began to choke on his own thoughts. He could not swallow his own helplessness, or redirect it on to another poor soul.

He watched Gebhard, envious that he was taking it so well. Gebhard was restless for lack of action; striding up and down in front of his command; playing the part to perfection; hungry for orders and hungry to give orders. Franz wanted to trip him up and watch him fall. But he did not want to take his place. The twins kept exchanging looks, needing each other's support - each not giving it but each still convinced they were receiving it. The rest of the cell looked equally glum and unsettled. They all hated the waiting. And it was much the same with other cells around them. Today, here, the Hitler Youth looked tired and broken, a collection of wasted, wanting souls. None of them had better things to do but there had to be something better than this. Too much waiting around made you want to run off in another direction.

Finally a few top officials in their organisation gave the boys their undivided attention. They were lined up in formation and made to listen, at length, to instructions for the grand parade. All detail was covered at length, until it stupefied: times; meeting points; conduct; dress code; personal behaviour code; even the mindset and mask required for the big day. Roll call was taken. The cells were told how to line up and where to march; to look happy; to shout the loudest. They had to play their part to the full and make him proud. There was no getting out of it until the show was over. It gave them all one hell of a headache. Franz wanted to get seriously drunk. Gebhard Strasser wanted to get started.

It all had to work smoothly and look spontaneous. And it had to fit the television screen. The pictures would be broadcast across the entire length and breath of Europe, and beyond - even in those places where the Reich had no particular friends. The world could not help but watch - even if only a snippet - even if only to snigger. Watching a mad man grow old was fascinating.

Franz soon got fed up with being pushed around like an inanimate object. He wanted to strike out. He knew what he had to do: march; salute; cheer; go home; ride his motorbike; chase his dogs; but not get drunk with Lev. The moment Lev entered his head he looked around again: when full this was no place for the likes of Lev, and possibly no place for the likes of him. Emptiness suddenly gave him a good feeling.

Finally they were ordered to gather up their marching flags and reform into lines, ready to march around the stadium. Then they

Section Four: Passing Out Parade

marched, struggling to shout, which infuriated the officials. Difficult to shout when no one is listening. Furthermore the stop start sound of a military band warming up to practice was a distraction.

Franz did not try hard. He had to make a point, a small private protest. He faked it. He played the fool. Suddenly he was happy to act the clown. Gebhard saw it and told him off. In return Franz told him to go fuck off, which shocked some and brought smiles to the faces of others. Gebhard reported him and a furious official lectured him on his 'attitude problem'. He was shorter than Franz and hated having to look up to look a boy in the eye. (The look in his eye said it all.) Franz thought it hilarious and was glad he had insulted the insane Gebhard Strasser. He would not have the chance tomorrow.

Playing his height advantage for all it was worth, Franz took the berating in silence then apologized to the official, saying he had had a bad day, whilst trying not to grin. But the official, suspicious, had no time for him and walked away even as he spoke. He had little or no time for the youth of today. They were undisciplined. They had not suffered hardship. They had not marched to war. Fuck you, thought Franz. I'm a soldier. You're no soldier. In this odious little man Franz saw Gebhard Strasser with thirty years added on top.

Finally they were told to disperse and leave, with not so much as a 'thank you for coming'. Like most others Franz was left exhausted, his head soaked through with visual clues, sounds, detail, trepidation, and promise. It was a heady mix. It was tomorrow's cocktail. Would it be this good or this bad? Would it hurt or heal? Would he look good on television? Would he be noticed? Would Father be proud? Too many questions. Early on, a life did not deserve too many questions.

◆

Luka's little girl sat on her bed, seemingly in a trance, but kicking inside. The blanket on her bed was ancient, deep in dust, and the bedsprings refused to yield, which in her book was no bad thing. She could make them squeak by bouncing up and down. It had stopped raining. She had to find something else to concentrate on. All she had was the wallpaper: rank; damp in places; torn in others. She stared at the vertical stripes. If she stared hard enough and long enough they seemed to quiver, change shape. She could not look forward or look back. All she could do was look over her shoulder.

The house was a squalid place. There was little which was not torn, ripped, damp, badly repaired or recycled. It was a house where nothing fitted: not the furniture; not the furnishings; not the people. It

Section Four: Passing Out Parade

harboured smells unfamiliar to her. The toilet was a disgusting place. The kitchen less so. The sitting room stank: too many women squashed up close together, like sardines; mainly moaning or miserable, or trying to manage their bodies. Already they had begun to penetrate her - like the customers - so she kept herself in her bedroom. She did not want to contribute to the communal misery. The house was international, but disunited: powered by injustice and grievances, physical and emotional abuse. But there were no riots. There was no revolution, just submission and suffering. It was a place for waiting, not for living. Once inside its walls you wanted to get out.

She recirculated the same thoughts which now occupied her day on day. Dare she make friends? Would they betray her? Would they move on, leave her stranded again? Would she do the same to them? (She knew she could.) Some girls did try to be kind and welcoming. The rest were standoffish, sometimes hostile. Some looked worn down, broken. Some looked brain dead. She shared her room with two other girls: one good girl, one bad girl. One she avoided. One she was talking to.

Sleep had suffered. Sleepiness was the daytime norm. Simple talk was the comfort zone: she had yet to engage in serious talk with anyone, and at present she had no candidate. She had to survive alone, isolated, watching her back; just like before. The only time she felt good was when she was cooking or taking a long hot shower. The shower cubicle was her favourite place, second only to being hidden away beneath her bed sheet and blanket. In both places she could disconnect from her immediate surroundings and seriously pretend. She was learning fast to hold her breath; close her eyes; ignore some sounds, grasp at others; put living on hold; despise all Germans, all Poles, all Czechs, and all Slovaks.

She was stranded in a big city. It might devour her. She was a country girl. She had grown up in the slow lane. Now it was a case of no more playing with the boys; no more playing with toys. She had been tempted west, to the wicked wicked West, and had failed to heed the warnings. She had been trapped by a Pole, then a German. The streets were not paved with gold as promised, but covered in shit. She had no way back: so soldier on. Refuse to cry. Refuse to die. Hold firm. Believe in a future. The present is a lie. As a child she had been abused by a German: now she had to give them pleasure, along with anyone else who could afford her. In her home town she had been able to keep them at a distance - pretend they didn't exist. Now she would have to keep them warm and dry in her knickers.

Her outer shell she was surrendering rapidly. Her inner core - her

Section Four: Passing Out Parade

inner being - she prized even higher than before and she held on to it even tighter. It needed protection like it never needed it before. One thought cheered her up: Germans were not super humans. Kleine was a pathetic example, a well turned out monster. He thought he was magnificent. She thought he was grotesque, mental, with a heart cast from metal. Dare she dream. Dare she deny? Dare she flee? The clock on the wall was now a constant reminder that time was no longer hers to spend, to save, to assign, or to appreciate. It would be sold on at a fixed price, else snatched away.

The girl was pulled from the gutter by a message delivered in haste. Outside a young man, described as one of 'her lot', wanted to speak to her. He looked dangerous apparently. She slipped from the bed uneasy, unsure; ill-equipped to deal with surprises. She took her time to reach the front door, not wishing to arrive. When she did she saw it was the lad from the pimp's flat; the crazy one who had intervened, tried to snatch her. The pimp's brother? Her face drained of colour. Was this business? Was she in trouble? Had she forgotten an appointment? She kept the door ajar and peered out like a timid church mouse, expecting to see a cat licking its lips. Instead she saw a shy young man. His eyes were wandering here and there, up and down, rarely straight ahead at her. She took some pleasure in his discomfort, and it made her brave.

"Well, what do you want?" The girl spoke sharply in her native tongue.

Lev hunched his shoulders and kicked the ground in protest at such a difficult question.

"Don't know really. Just thought I'd call round." It was the best he could come up with. That aside it felt great to speak Ukrainian again.

"See how I am?"

"Something like that."

"How did you find me?" Stupid question she realised even as she finished speaking.

"Luka gave me the address - but I had to fight him for it."

Lev was not being rhetorical: they nearly had come to blows.

"You've seen me now. Can I go?"

Not wishing to get involved the girl began to shut the door - but not so fast that the pimp's brother could not make a worthwhile case for her to keep it open. She was willing to give him a second thought. She expected him to take it, surprise her, impress her; else piss off back to the pimp and the Germans. Lev stuck his boot out, obstructing the door.

"Hang on, not so fast."

"Well?"

Section Four: Passing Out Parade

"Well."

Lev stalled again. He had nothing worked out. He just wanted some companionship. A bit of female friendship and a reminder of home was all he was asking for right now. He wanted nothing else from her. His eyes lit up. He had a question.

"Where you from? Ukraine somewhere?"

"Lutsk."

"Gone for good?"

"Gone for good? Probably."

"And now you're living in this house?"

Living? She didn't think that was the right word to use. She declined to answer.

"Lonely?" he asked, sounding slightly desperate.

She did not want to say yes - she guessed he expected her to say yes.

"Not yet. Not been here long enough."

"Lucky you."

"Lucky me. Why you asking? You lonely?"

"Me? No!"

That sounded like a lie to her.

Lev looked up at the big grand house. It looked grubby and in a bad state of repair. Not so grand he thought, and said so.

"This place looks like a shit hole."

"It is a shit hole - look what exactly do you want? You here on business? Your brother sent you?"

Lev took a step back, slightly shaken by her sudden outburst. This girl was hard.

"No. Like I said, just wanted to see how you were. See if you were OK. You know, usual thing."

His body language backed up his claim. It carried that look of damage done by wild accusation. It began to convince her that he was being absolutely straight - something she was not used to round here, or anywhere for that matter. She decided to let him in. She could do with some company. Let him see for himself where his pimp brother had dumped her. She gestured with her thumb.

"Come on then."

Lev followed her in, wary but determined to be as polite and as pleasant as he could be. Not an easy thing for him: she was a girl and in his experience girls were difficult dogs to handle. Some could be real bitches. Unusually for him though the thought of sex with this girl - a girl from home - had not crossed his mind. He was almost playing the angel: an angel in a cesspit, as far as possible from Heaven without actually being in Hell. He kept looking around as if searching out the

Section Four: Passing Out Parade

fire exits.

She asked about the knapsack slung over his shoulder.

"What's in the bag?"

"A towel."

The answer, though strange, didn't grab her interest and she led him into the sitting room, then quickly out again - too many eyes, too much hostility. They ended up in the back garden. It was rarely populated with people. It barely rated as a garden. It lived but it did not glow. It grew wild: weeds, grass, nettles and ivy in particular. They were breaking their way into the concrete and smothering the paving stones. They were repainting the red brick walls with various shades of green. The stormy couple sat on a wasted wooden bench, each looking straight ahead, not wishing to impose. They looked like a couple awaiting bad news or two strangers who happened to have stopped to rest at the same time; side by side but in different worlds. Lev went into standby mode, knapsack at his feet, always within grasping distance. The girl went into standalone mode. She looked around into every corner of the garden and thought it a great shame. Lev didn't look much, except at the weeds. They were unstoppable. They could not be beaten. Finally she had to speak. The silence was driving her up the wall.

"You a pimp? Like your brother? You work for your brother?"

"No and no. I'm just staying with him."

"How long you been here?" she asked.

"Me?"

"Yes you. Who else?"

Lev counted on his fingers. "Six days." It felt much longer.

"You staying?"

"Suppose so. Don't know." He had absolutely no idea. Staying alive with his dignity intact was his only concern right now.

The girl returned to her key question, as if to trap him with inconsistency.

"Why did you come here?"

"Like I said, see how you are. Nothing else."

The pimp's brother sounded hurt: it convinced her that he was telling the truth. But still she held him at arm's length; ever watchful, circumspect.

"This must have been a nice garden once."

In response to her suggestion Lev scanned in its parts: its dilapidated features; the rampant undergrowth; the discarded rubbish.

"Was it?"

"Don't know." She had nothing further to say.

Restless, the girl began to boil and wriggle. She needed to get out of

Section Four: Passing Out Parade

the house, away, where his nasty pimp brother could not find her. If she was with his little brother then she could not be touched: she could blame everything on him. She refused to be a prisoner as well as a prostitute. She stood up smart and straightened her dress, smoothing out its creases.

"I want to go to the fairground."

"What?"

"I saw a poster. There's one in town. I want to go to the fairground. Don't you?"

Fairground? thought Lev. Okay. Yes, fairgrounds were fun places. Perhaps she would be fun at the fairground.

"Okay count me in."

With the deal done they left the house sharp; he clutching his knapsack; she fingering a pocketful of coins. She found the poster which had first informed her and together they headed on to the park. It was on a bus route: a few stops down. Being a weekday the fairground was not busy.

They prowled and patrolled, never touching, never holding hands: side by side yes but never together, never a pair. And as they wondered where to spend their money, never once did they allow themselves to lapse back into childhood. Each knew too much now for that to happen. The people around them did not look that happy. If they were having a good time then they were not showing it. When they reached the big wheel the girl pointed up.

"I want to go up there."

"Okay."

Lev was not bothered. He just wanted her to smile, act happy. It would make him feel happy - and perhaps smile.

They stood in line, paid, and took a seat in the big wheel. And still she hadn't smiled. Miserable cow, thought Lev, looking miserable. And then they took off, up; slowly at first, then faster; and as they rose up the ground beneath diminished and the city unfolded around them. Finally, high up, the girl burst out smiling. She could not hold it in any longer. Then shouting followed. Lev joined in and made it a chorus. And as they reached the top of the cycle they felt on top of a world which normally was out to crush them. They looked down on the city, feeling they had conquered it. But they couldn't stop there: they had to move on, down. The only way was down. Down they came until they reached the bottom, and the start of their little adventure. They were back on terra firma.

Each felt disappointed, a sense of defeat and, considering the cost, each thought the wheel had turned too fast. But at least no more

Section Four: Passing Out Parade

miserable cow, thought Lev. She thought much the same of him. Next she spotted the bumper cars. Bumper cars! She had to ride a bumper car! Lev was of the same attitude. They had to go on the bumper cars. No question.

They each took a car and chased after each other: banging, bumping, bruising; pushing each other out of the way; flying apart and coming back together; going at top speed around and around and getting nowhere. They bumped others and others bumped them. Loud music enhanced the mania, along with the screams and shouting between rivals. Electric motors were rarely this much fun. They had let the children back in. Lev forgot she was a prostitute who slept with Germans. She forgot he was the brother of a pimp who worked for the Germans. Instead they swore at the enemies on all sides. But finally that too ran its course and they had to end it. The man in charge kept remonstrating and flagging then down. They gave up the chase. They were hot, energized, sweating, but happy now to talk. The children had crept back.

Ghost train next. For no reason whatsoever it was the natural choice: on that they were both agreed. They joined an empty mock up of a carriage and watched a silly man wave a flag and blow his whistle like it was real. It made them laugh, at him. When they entered the dark tunnel she grabbed his hand, then let go. Mistake. That was too much intimacy for such an unknown quantity. They quickly came to regret their choice: the tunnel was crap; the special effects were crap, stupid. This train set couldn't scare a small child who had never left home let alone a big one who had. They poured scorn on the pathetic - and expensive - attempt to scare them. The children crept away with a raw deal. But on the plus side they were not yet dead and buried. They still had a little life left in them. Lev told the fellow in charge - Romanian, perhaps Gypsy - that he wanted his money back, that he had been conned. He was told to sod off back home. The girl spat and swore as Lev backed off, also swearing.

Seeing a rifle range cheered Lev up: a good place to let off steam. He had to shoot something, preferably something alive. Instead silly faces would have to do. He pretended one of them was his dad, aimed carefully, and fired. He missed wide of the mark, by a good six inches. Suspicious, he checked the gun sight. It had been tampered with. Trusting his skill he adjusted his aim and next time hit it, bang on. Penkin is dead! If only, he thought. Instead he had to make do with a stuffed toy. He left that to the girl. She chose a teddy bear. She had never had a teddy bear.

The last thing they did was to try and win some money back,

Section Four: Passing Out Parade

shoving pfennigs. There was a big pile of them, ready to fall right into their hands if they timed it right. They were patient. They were clever: they bided their time and watched others drop their coins without success. Somehow they thought they were better, that they could win where others had failed and where the odds were clearly stacked against them. The laws of physics were for other people, not for them. The coins were piled up against the raised lip, unable to overcome it or come over it. They thought a few more nudges would do the trick. But they didn't. So just a few more they decided. But no. The pile would not budge, it just grew. Downhearted they chucked in their remaining pfennigs and decided to escape the place: roaming the streets suddenly felt like a lot more fun and for no cost. Lev left the park gripping his knapsack. The girl left gripping her teddy bear. She would not discard it. She had to get it home.

They wandered back to the bus stop then, feeling adventurous, walked on, deciding to track the bus route home. Side by side their strength and attitude grew. They kicked bottles and stones out of their way. They didn't talk. They didn't need to talk. Not wishing to rush back they took it slow, and took in what passed for scenery. The girl hated to admit it but she felt protected. She wasn't sure if she liked it: it made her beholding.

They stopped in front of a big black poster promoting the Czech Fascist Party. It preached the benefits of cooperation and reconciliation with the Reich. 'Rejoice!' it screamed. Lev began to tear it down. The girl helped. Their actions attracted the attention of a local gang parked further on down the street. Four boys and one girl sat bored on the steps of a building. Any distraction was a good distraction. Any fight was a good fight. Prompted by their leader, the gang got to their feet, stretched, and followed him down the street. They could smell immigrants in the air, disturbing their peace. More immigrants from the East. Germans from the West. Their leader carried with him a small shiny hammer made of best steel, the kind used by geologists to crack open small rocks. He used it to crack open heads and hands.

When he got within spitting distance (and spat) Lev took notice. He saw a kid acting big in front of his mates and his senses told him to expect trouble. The numbers did not worry him: these were just kids, with attitude. The girl, clutching her teddy bear in one hand and scraps of poster in the other, moved to be close by his side. She stared back at the other girl - if looks could kill they would both be dead by now.

The gang leader was fuelled by a reservoir of hatred for foreigners, outsiders; anyone cleverer than him, better looking than him, having a better time than him. Much of this he had instilled in his gang, and

Section Four: Passing Out Parade

with it he had managed to seduce them. And with a gang to his name he entertained the delusion that he had real power to shape events. He glared down, appalled, at the fragments of poster which littered the ground and then looked at teddy bear, bemused. Feigning civic outrage he saw his opening and made his accusation - by necessity in German, the common language, which he hated.

"That's vandalism. That's illegal in our country - not that you would know that, scum."

"Fuck off," replied Lev, in Ukrainian.

"Yes fuck off," echoed the girl.

The gang leader got the gist. "No you fuck off. You fuck off out of here. Back home. We don't want your kind here."

"I'll go when I'm ready," said Lev, in German this time. He wanted the twit to understand him.

"I'll fuck off when I get the first chance," added the girl.

She raised a finger at the other girl who raised one back just as fast. They had started their own separate little war.

The gang leader was stuck. These two had not buckled. He turned to his mates, to turn it into a joke. Together they laughed and poured scorn. In situations like this they did everything in unison, at the instigation of their leader. He was their strength, their compass, their certainty. He stopped them becoming bored. He found them things to do. He articulated their grievances and desires. In return they were his credibility. (Give it a few more years and they would grow up faster than him, and see him for what he was: loud but little.) Meanwhile a slight nervousness bubbled below the surface of their smugness: these two immigrant kids did not act like they were bothered. He produced his hammer and swung it from his wrist, inviting a response.

"I should report you for that."

Lev laughed. The girl raised her eyebrows. The girl in the gang sneered. The boys in the gang sniggered. The gang leader became annoyed. Rattled by an immigrant with attitude he lost his composure and flared up.

"Show me your papers!"

Lev laughed again. "You sound like a German! You Gestapo? Or you just an arsehole?"

"Show me your papers!"

Second time round Lev took it seriously: the twit had raised his silly little hammer. The girl saw it and took measurements. (She felt sure Lev could protect her if she so wished but right now she did not wish.) With calm calculation Lev knelt down and let his knapsack slip from his shoulder. Slowly he produced his towel, much to the consternation

Section Four: Passing Out Parade

of all those around him. He was the centre of attention and loving it. The gang leader held back, confused. With his hammer he thought he had the upper hand but felt something bigger beneath.

Lev unrolled his towel and in doing so generated great mirth. He received catcalls. The girl stood back as Lev, now the star of the show, produced his pocket pistol; his Mauser; his pride and joy. He stood up, twice as tall; now the hero, the soldier, the gangster; the only one carrying a loaded weapon.

"I don't have my papers - just got this."

Lev raised his gun and pointed it at the twit who kept annoying him.

"That's not loaded."

"Oh yes it is. Is that hammer loaded?"

The twit began to tremble: voice first, with the rest of him not far behind. His gang had turned to stone. The hammer began to fall.

"You won't use that."

"Won't I? Try me. I've got nothing to lose if you report me. If I'm going to spend time in prison may as well take you with me. The Germans don't give a shit about you lot. You know Inspector Kleine of the Gestapo? He's a friend of the family."

No answer.

Lev smiled, wishing to relax now, wishing for this twit of an opponent to do likewise.

"Go on. Leave us be. You've made your point. You hate us. Go find some Germans - they're the enemy. We're just passing through."

Surprised and boosted by his own short speech, Lev lowered his gun - and realised he had left the safety catch on. The big talk impressed both girls. One wanted to hold his hand. The other wanted to rub her dirty hand through his greasy hair. The twit had a way out, and took it, pretending an outbreak of comradeship and common cause; dignity vaguely still intact. He walked away, not too fast; trying to whistle a tune; swinging his hammer; gathering in his gang and making a joke of it. They were all happy to wipe the encounter from their minds as it did not fit their universe.

The girl was greatly impressed by the odds Lev had beaten. He was hard inside and calm under pressure. She liked that. She could relate to that: it was the only way to survive. Lev stowed away his gun as if nothing had happened - inside his heart was still thumping away like mad - and suggested they get the first bus back home. He was starting to feel vulnerable on the streets of this foreign city. She felt the opposite: more secure now she knew that Lev carried a gun and was not afraid to use it.

They walked on the next bus stop - it had their number on it - and

Section Four: Passing Out Parade

waited, pumped up by victory. Spotting a snack bar Lev nipped across the road and purchased a bag of chips and a packet of marshmallows. He was hungry. If she was hungry so much the better. She was, and they shared chips both waiting for the bus and on it. Thinking alike each went for the best big chips first then, when they were gone, the best small chips. After they were gone they cleaned up the remains. When all that was left were tiny fragments or inedible lumps Lev crumpled up the paper into a ball and threw it across the floor. The girl tapped him with her foot for dropping litter but as they were alone on the upper deck she did not make him pick it up. Her scruples were flexible and negotiable.

Upon reaching her front door Lev held up his bag of marshmallows: perhaps testing her willpower; perhaps mocking her. If she let him in she could have some. It was a simple trade. She did.

They sat in the garden again; on the bench again; knapsack at Lev's feet again; except this time they had a game of backgammon set up between them. They chewed slowly and made moves slowly. The teddy bear was tucked up in her bed, with only its head in view. Despite their time spent together the girl had nothing say. Lev had little to say and while he was eating he couldn't be bothered; and afterwards, mouth empty, he forgot. If they spoke it was only to tell the other to make a move. The game barely registered in their thoughts. Neither was playing to win, just to not lose.

Killing time was the only reason for sitting there: especially as it was cold now and overhead dark clouds threatened. The sky had closed in and with diminishing daylight the garden too was closing in. Aimlessly they stared down at the board, or across the garden and up the walls; or beyond, to where they could be beyond reach; each wanting to discard the present, search out the future, and crush the past out of existence. (The past had an annoying habit of creeping back, unresolved.) Occasionally she would glance down at the knapsack. It was becoming hypnotic.

Lev's mind drifted back to times spent killing time on the rooftops in the camp; sometimes alone, sometimes with Franz; sometimes sober, sometimes drunk; sometimes happy, sometimes sad; rarely content, usually discontent; sometimes an angry young man, sometimes a stupid, stubborn boy; always a disillusioned boy; sometimes with lots to say, sometimes with nothing to say, either way rarely listening to the sound of his own voice. Were they good times or bad? Or a mix of both? Lev didn't know. Now he could not tell the difference. And what about Franz? Was he on the roll of his life now? Was he enjoying a great big party and living his dream? Was he touching the

Section Four: Passing Out Parade

heavens in his dear Reich and shaking hands with his gods? Had he got his Bridget into bed and shagged the life out of her? If they ever met up again would he recognize his friend? He recalled their last moment together. It could have gone better. Suddenly the girl stood up and disturbed Lev from his thoughts.

"It's freezing. I'm going inside." She had had enough.

Likewise Lev stood up. The game became forgotten. There was no winner.

"You have to go now."

Lev was not allowed to protest or negotiate: he was led - frogmarched almost - back to the front door. The girl held it open, looking at him; almost challenging him to complain or beg to stay. But looks could be deceptive: she wanted him gone. She wanted to be tucked up in bed, with her teddy bear, as a break from business. As he left Lev issued a stern warning: she was not to come round to the flat again - not for any reason.

"I won't allow it," he said.

She said nothing but did note the passion in his voice. She closed the door slowly and Lev was left standing in the rain which had begun to fall. He turned and made his way back to what passed for home, determined to get drunk. He had only one regret: perhaps he should have tried to kiss her when he had the chance? Had she been expecting him to try? Perhaps she felt insulted that he hadn't tried? Perhaps he should have said nice things about her - like he had done for Franz in his letters? Perhaps he simply should not have bothered.

♦

Back at the hotel Franz was looking for relief, but instead caught sight of Uncle Max entering a lift. The man looked raw, dangerous. His heart stopped. Suddenly it was all change - loose change. Franz confirmed his suspicions at the desk: yes, his parents had checked in. He made his way up to their room via the stairs, slowly, with stealth; not wishing to bump into Uncle Max. He crept up to their door and crouched to eavesdrop. A foreign maid gave him a dirty look which he returned, with interest. The angry twitching face persuaded her to move on, not get involved. She needed to keep this job. Germans could be crazy sometimes - and this was a very crazy time right now.

Franz struggled to tap into the conversation - assuming there was one. The talk was low, slow, intermittent. There were no raised voices to be heard. No surprise. No confrontation. The one dominant voice he did hear he did not recognise so it had to be that bad uncle, Max.

Section Four: Passing Out Parade

Father was saying little. Mother was saying nothing. Did Uncle Max scare them? Franz needed to be on the inside. Franz needed his mother. Franz needed to be held, to wipe away the day before the next one started. Franz wanted to report to his father the lie that all was well. Tomorrow loomed over him. Reichsfuehrer Heinrich Himmler loomed over him. The Fuehrer loomed over him. Bridget on the other hand was far away, out of reach, as was Lev. Everybody else and everything else was just getting in the way.

Driven by the determination to confront his enemy, Franz finally stood up and knocked. Mother answered the door. Overjoyed she shouted his name and grabbed him; and hugged him; and almost dragged him into the room. It was a room which smelt of cleaning fluid and human perspiration.

Mother had hold of her son. She would not let go easily. Father looked pleased to see him. Uncle Max looked uneasy, perhaps even scared for a moment, though no one except Franz spotted it: he was the only one fully focused on Uncle Max. He thought he could detect alcohol emanating from the man. He hated the fact that the man looked like his father but there was nothing he could do about it, except wish. The two brothers were seated as far apart as the room would allow. Once, long ago, they had climbed over each other for fun. Once, long ago, they had made plans together for the future. Once, long ago, they swapped toy soldiers.

"Good to see you boy."

"Hallo Father," said Franz as Mother tried to comb his hair with her fingers. She wanted to smarten him up.

Franz had to explain his grazed forehead to a fraught mother. His father was not bothered, and only asked 'did you give as good as you got?' He had to suffer too many of his mother's kisses - and give one big one back. She asked the questions. Franz barely answered any of them: she was just talking, letting off steam like she always did. Father had little to contribute right now. He just kept on smiling, relieved that his son was back. Finally Franz was able to sit down and find his composure, if only physical. Satisfied that all was well, Mother returned to her chair, alongside Father. There they sat, looking uncomfortable with the silence and without it. Uncle Max did not appear to have their attention - but he wanted it. It was winter in the room. Franz felt the cold and caught the chill. He wanted to start a fire or drop a bomb - anything to wake things up.

Prompted by his father, Franz recounted his recent activities - but excluding any mention of Uncle Max. Uncle Max was squeezed out by all three as Franz talked and his parents listened. Uncle Max also

Section Four: Passing Out Parade

listened, but only to pay lip service, and bide his time. As he talked, and rambled, and invented, Franz took in the lie of the land: Father and Uncle Max - brothers - barely made eye contact; likewise with Mother. That was a good sign. The man was isolated.

He gave them his neat, uncomplicated version of time spent in Berlin, careful to avoid any mention of his stopover in Prague. The mention of meeting the Reichsfuehrer impressed them both and for the first time that day Franz felt good about himself. This was how it was meant to be. Father wanted to know more but Mother said later. He skirted around the unsavoury aspects of his stay with the Schrimer's, instead simply stating that 'it had been good' and that 'they had been good to him'. On the subject of Bridget however he found it difficult to put on a brave deceptive face. Mother saw through it immediately.

She looked him straight in the eye. "You don't look happy when you mention her. Are things not good?"

Caught out, Franz was stumped for a reply. "It could have been better."

"Give it time," she advised. Then an awful thought struck her. "Are you two still talking?"

With that Franz caved in. The day was not yet over but already it had been a long day; a strange, torturous day during which he had been pulled apart and smashed in the head by words. On this matter he had no fight left.

"Probably not." He suddenly sounded very tired, very fragile.

His mother, alarmed, looked at his father. Her face fell. His face rippled but held firm.

"Oh I'm sorry. What went wrong?" she asked, afraid to ask.

Franz shook her off, not wishing to delve into his own black hole.

"Don't know. You know what girls are like."

Mother nodded. She did know.

"Stress?" added Franz.

'Stress' sounded like a good word, a heavy adult word.

"Stress?" asked Mother.

"Stress?" repeated Father, now wanting to be in on the talk. The last thing he needed right now was a stressed out son. He had enough on his plate.

Uncle Max smiled, for the first time since he had entered the room. Stress? I can tell you about stress.

Franz found a good answer to hold them off. "Stress. It's been a heavy week. Too much going on."

"Are you good for tomorrow?" asked Father sharply, whereupon Mother threw him a critical look.

Section Four: Passing Out Parade

"Yes. I won't let you down."

Their exchange was rapid fire.

Franz scrambled for a change of subject: he asked about the dogs, the house, the estate, and anything else he could bring to mind which related to home - even the servants, even the car. He did not take in the answers. Meanwhile, through it all, Uncle Max was shifting and bending his toes, trapped as they were inside a tough pair of old boots. He wanted to talk. He wanted to poke them all with a stick and get a reaction. His nephew had said more than enough.

When Franz ran out of steam, an awkward heavy silence descended: the same which had been struggling to take hold before he entered the room. The Helmers could have found more to talk about, but not with Uncle Max in the room. His unexpected appearance had struck them dumb. They had been forced to invite him in and sit him down, in the corner. Family could not be refused. Franz Senior thought his brother had aged badly: Max had gone to seed. Max thought the same of his brother. His sister-in-law Hilda had no thoughts, only disquiet. The brothers had an understanding, a truce. It went way back. Now, here, each struggled to understand, and the truce had become forgotten.

Max probed his brother about life back home: working the estate; being a magistrate; chasing after Russians; but not about his family. Franz Senior gave little away - just enough to be polite - and asked nothing in return. There was no hostility. There was no humour. There was no embrace. Franz Senior had no axe to grind: he simply wished that Max had not turned up; that he was gone; that he remained distant. And on this his wife Hilda stood squarely by his side. He had her total backing. Uncle Max was a very black sheep.

Studiously, while recovering his strength, Franz watched his uncle speak, his contempt providing the motor. This man had no right to be in the room. This man had no right to be family. He did not fit. He was a maverick, a criminal. He brought shame to his uniform. Franz had questions but saw no way to ask them. Politeness and family stood in the way.

"Same house?" asked Uncle Max.

"Same house," replied Franz Senior.

"But bigger. We've extended it," added Hilda.

"You still do the magistrate thing?"

"I am the senior town magistrate yes."

"Sounds important."

"It is."

"It pays well? Good money?"

"Good money, yes."

Section Four: Passing Out Parade

"No regrets then, staying out there?"

"No regrets," said Franz Senior, firmly.

"No regrets," repeated his wife, emphatically.

It could have been a game of cat and mouse, or table tennis between sworn enemies. Frau Helmer was left on the sidelines, perhaps as umpire. She looked more and more worried by each question and each answer.

"Still a magistrate - the best in town! Who would have thought it: you, on the moral high ground, handing out all that justice."

"What's that suppose to mean?"

"You know what it means."

Franz Senior did, as did his wife. Franz didn't.

Suddenly Franz Senior seemed to lose his composure. "What exactly are you doing here?"

Uncle Max looked at a loss. "You came to Berlin. How could I not look up my own brother?"

"How did you find us?"

"Easy. I just asked around."

"But how did you know we were coming?"

"Your son told me." Uncle Max looked at Franz. He had him trapped. "Isn't that right Franz."

He was causing destruction in the room and enjoying every moment of it. It was a sort of petty revenge. Franz looked mortified. Unable to remember exactly what he had said, he assumed the man was telling the truth. Finally Franz could take it no more. He attacked.

"Why do you never visit?"

Max looked at his brother for help: the cat was amongst the pigeons. Franz Senior looked down at the carpet.

"It's a long way."

Franz heard a lie.

"And I'm never invited."

Franz ignored that bit, and instead attacked again; this time with a more dangerous question.

"Why are you not married? You should be married by now. You should have children."

"That's what we're suppose to do is it?"

"Yes." Franz was emphatic.

Frau Helmer was not pleased with where this was going. "Franz what sort of question is that!"

But Max had his standard answer.

"Never met the right woman. I would only marry for love, not domestic necessity, not because it's in the party handbook."

Section Four: Passing Out Parade

Franz lost that one. He had no idea what the man meant. All he knew was that this uncle of his was violating the natural order of things. He was family of the worst kind: he could not be removed, rubbed out or replaced. Franz couldn't fathom out why Father put up with it. The situation was unacceptable. He could detect ridicule in the man's voice. He dropped his bombshell.

"That man. Why didn't you answer the door when I called. Who was that young man in your flat. Why did he look scared?"

The Helmers looked at each other, then at Uncle Max, but other than that they gave no reaction. Franz was disappointed and had to cope with his furious uncle drilling into him.

"He's a good friend. He has a problem and he came to me for advice, help. I'm his friend. You have a problem with that?"

Franz did, but stayed silent. He had had the wind knocked out of his sails. His bomb had failed to explode. It was just a spent bullet. He could only mumble one last question.

"Why did you come round then run away?"

Franz Senior looked at his son, incredulous, then looked away, shaking his head.

Now Uncle Max sounded truly angry. "I didn't run away. You didn't want to come out to play."

"That's enough Max. Best you go." Franz Senior slapped his knee in protest. He had had enough of both of them.

"What, can't stand to have me around? I've only just arrived. I thought we could talk."

"Talk? You thought wrong. We've got nothing to talk about." Franz Senior didn't like talk at the best of times.

Franz was transfixed. This was both fearsome and fun. He searched for, and found his best retort.

"We don't talk to people like you."

Uncle Max turned on him, face flushed with a level of anger he had not experienced in a long time. He was back in a war, a very personal war.

"Don't you judge me. You lot have no right to judge - me or anybody. You've all been brainwashed."

Franz Senior stood up, followed promptly by his wife.

"That's it Max. Get out."

"Please go now," she advised.

"Bad mistake coming here. I can tell." Even in the fire of such a moment Uncle Max could still whistle up a touch of irony.

Badly stung, Franz played it by the book. "You should report him Father."

Section Four: Passing Out Parade

"Don't be silly," said Mother.

"Your mother's right," said Father, to the bewilderment of his son.

Max exploded.

"Report me? For what exactly? And what about your father? You going to report him? He's no knight in shining armour you know - but then you wouldn't know would you. I'm no disgrace. Compared with your father I'm the angel in the family."

Franz Senior took a step closer in to his brother. He was prepared to thump him and was only held back by his quick thinking wife. Max was not in the least bit intimidated: in their previous lives his brother had kicked and punched him many times, and he had always kicked and punched back.

"Isn't this a great country - a man who commits war crimes can still rise to the top of the justice system, and hand it out."

Max looked his brother in the eye before leaving. "Do you still deny your past? I don't, nor my present."

His brother wanted to spit in his face. Yes, time to leave.

The backlog of things to be said were never said, and Uncle Max left, probably for the last time. He would die old and alone in Berlin, but on the moral high ground and with his soul still intact. His brother would die old, compromised; out in the middle of nowhere; never able or willing to admit his crimes.

The final outburst by Uncle Max left its chill. The air was electric so to breathe in was a dangerous thing to do right now. He was gone but he had left his mark on their thoughts, and their thoughts had them trapped. Suddenly there were ghosts in the room, ghosts in the family: some of the past; some of the future; some screaming for forgiveness; some begging for mercy; some shell-shocked. For Franz there was also the heat which came from his father. (For his father there was the coldness which came from his mother.) The look on his father's face said, quite empathically, 'no questions, no comments'. The room had a bad smell. They had to get out. As his parents seemed stuck it was Franz who took the lead.

"I'm hungry," he announced.

"I need a drink," said Father. "Let's find the bar."

"Will they serve tea?" asked Mother.

"Of course. This is a hotel. You can order anything you want woman."

His curt reply nearly caused sparks to fly. She flashed him a look which made him bite into his lower lip. But he did not think to apologize. Franz did not like what was happening between them but right now but his feelings did not matter.

Section Four: Passing Out Parade

They made their way down to the bar: father and son in a hurry; wife and mother refusing to be hurried. Their Mother grabbed a table (even though she didn't need to) while Father ordered drinks and sandwiches. Mother wanted to talk but only if Father was willing to talk, and right now he did not want to talk to anyone. A pretence quickly set in: the pretence that all was well in the family; that all was in order; that no sins had been committed; that the truth was comfortable and not a lie.

Frau Helmer watched her family sink beer and chew food ravenously, like starving lions after the kill. She looked like a fish out of water. She said nothing and that suggested everything. Franz watched his father's neck stretch as he stared up at the ceiling and searched for something to say, something to break the ice. Mother was happy to let him stew. Finally when he spoke, it was with great relief.

"Tell me about your meeting with Himmler. What was he like? Was he good?"

Good? thought Franz. Good in what way? He had to invent quickly, unable or unwillingly to retrieve much from the ten minutes of near sheer hell.

"He's like you expect, like he is in those films."

Franz paused. It was not enough. Father wanted more.

"He kept staring at me, looking me up and down."

"He was inspecting you, making sure you were good enough for him. And did you?"

"I think so."

"Did he impress you?"

"Yes."

"Did you impress him?"

"I think so."

Mother cut in. "Leave our boy alone will you."

Franz looked at his mother, surprised by her intervention, then back to his father, as if to apologize. Silence returned, this time more entrenched.

Two men entered the room, chatting loudly despite the fact they were almost shoulder to shoulder. They looked fit, robust and full of vocal energy. They belonged to the generation which had fought in the war. They flew past the Helmers with a swagger which suggested that they did not fear another fight. They planted themselves in a far corner and gestured for service with an authority which had long since expired but a flamboyance which still rang true. They had lots to talk about and no time to waste. Franz Helmer Senior could not see their faces but the sound of their voices was more than enough to persuade him that they

Section Four: Passing Out Parade

may have once served together. He looked like a child who had just seen the ice-cream van fly pass.

Suddenly and without warning he got up to go join them. Clutching his beer he had to stop himself from dashing after them: he did not want to appear needy for reinforcements. Upon introducing himself he was immediately pulled down into a spare chair. He had been captured (or had surrendered). In an instant years spent living the life of a civilian rolled back and Franz Senior was a free spirit again; released from responsibility; relieved of civilian duty and dues; ready to fight. He was back in his element while his family were left to fend for themselves. Lips pursed Frau Helmer stared blankly into the space her husband had just vacated, feeling abandoned and insulted. Franz simply felt a heavy hand lift, and the return of fresh air. Finally he could put the question which had been bugging him.

"Is he angry with me?"

"Yes."

"Why?"

"You should not have approached his brother."

Franz took note of the error of his ways: he would not repeat the mistake.

"Who's Father talking to?"

"Probably men he served with. They're here for their reunion dinner. He hasn't told you yet but we've been invited this year."

"Why's that?"

Frau Helmer looked at her son, wondering why the bleeding obvious had passed him by.

"Because of you of course. And if you go he has to invite me along as well."

Her last remark was tinged with bitterness and Franz felt a cold chill run down his back. He could not remember the last time he had caught such a bad chill - and from his own family.

"Don't tell him you know. It's to be his surprise."

"OK."

Humbled, Franz turned away from his mother to watch his father. Yes, there was definitely something glamorous and enduring about being a soldier. They had the big stories to tell. He wanted to sit with them. He wanted to listen in. He wanted to share their secrets, no matter how grim, how exhausting. Finally Frau Helmer had had enough. She could bear it no more: the raucous laughter; the slaps on the back; the lads being loud lads. She got up, saying she was returning to her room, and left her son stranded. Franz cut back and forth between his parents: one rapidly disappearing; one already distant. It

Section Four: Passing Out Parade

was no competition: he jumped up and raced after his mother, dumping the remains of his sandwich in the process. As he trailed her back up to her room he held on to another burning question. At her door, when she paused to insert the key, he dumped it in her lap.

"What did he mean when he said spoke about Father in that way, you know, about the war?"

Mother seemed totally preoccupied with opening the door: but it was just a deception to delay her reply.

"I don't know. That's between them, between brothers. Ask your father."

She sounded impatient to get inside and close the door behind her - close the door and lock the unsavoury world out. She had been tempted to add 'if you dare', only to be prevented by her distaste for theatrical outbursts.

Somehow Franz didn't think it was as simple as that. He went back to his room: to vegetate, to ponder; to try and pick apart the world he was understanding less and less, and at ever increasing speed; and to work up the courage to finally make that phone call. He needed to chat to a friend.

Franz sat on his bed as if he had been hung out to dry; trying to play the part; wishing for his parents to play the part; wishing for it to all be over; wishing to be dropped back into the boring but solid routine of home life. He stared at the telephone. It was begging him to make that call. But that might be a dangerous thing to do: he might talk too much, reveal too much; discover that Lev was having one hell of a time. But on the other hand he needed to know what Lev was doing, right now.

Holding on to his prized scrap of paper he picked up the phone and - expecting a trap - made his request to the operator before she had a chance to speak and confuse him. Methodically and precisely he read out each digit. He could have been standing up in front of class, reading out text whilst trying to hold on to dear life.

A lady's ancient but firm voice informed him that he was being put through, with the phrase 'connecting you now'; and as the line buzzed so Franz began to tremble and his solid intent began to melt. He was about to be exposed, but just as he was on the verge of running away his call was answered.

"Who's there?" It was the cold cutthroat voice of Luka.

"Franz. Franz Helmer."

Luka shouted into the distance. "It's that German friend of yours!"

The sound of the phone smacking against a wall was followed by a long wait and Franz was left hanging. He could just make out the sound of music and mad, wild singing. It sounded like the new Rock

Section Four: Passing Out Parade

and Roll noise from across the sea.
"Franz?"
"Lev?"
The sound of Lev's voice lifted him. He stood up. Suddenly he had a spring in his step and he needed to start walking as much as he needed to start talking. The fact that he was holding a telephone would stop him from doing both.
"You OK?"
"I'm OK. You OK?"
"Yeah. What's happening?"
Now Franz was stuck: he couldn't slap his friend on the back or shake his hand, or push him around. He could only speak, and he didn't know what to say. What was happening? Everything and nothing. Everything was going wrong. Nothing was going right. It was hurting.
"You good?"
"I'm good. So what's happening?" Lev had to shout down a bad line.
"Everything. And you?"
"Everything."
Their voices were creating sparks but the engine refused to turn. Lev took up the challenge.
"It's raining here. What's it like in Berlin, beautiful Berlin?"
"Cloudy - but not raining - sunny even."
"It's always sunny in Berlin."
"What?"
"It's always sunny in Berlin - isn't that what they say?"
"Right."
The attempt at humour fell flat. Lev tried again.
"How's the party, the big party?"
"That's tomorrow."
"Of course."
At that point Lev ran out of words with which to fire questions. He waited: Franz had called him so the onus was on him to take the lead. Franz grew alarmed.
"Are you still there? Can you hear me? It's a bad line."
"I can hear you."
Like any small boy Franz wanted to swoop down on the other boy's toys and see what he was missing out on.
"What's that music?"
"Elvis Presley."
"What sort of name is that?"
"American. It's Rock and Roll."

Section Four: Passing Out Parade

"I know what Rock and Roll is - it just sounds stupid."

"Well he's fantastic. And he sells like hot cakes."

Another, almost peculiar painful pause followed: until this point in time talking endlessly and at speed into each other's face had never been a problem. But distance and recent experiences had changed that.

Lev found another question, a good one. "Have you met him yet?"

"The Fuehrer? No, but I met the Reichsfuehrer."

"Himmler?"

"That's him."

"What was he like?"

"Alright."

"What about Bridget? Does she still fancy you now she's met you?"

"She's met me before."

"And she still fancies you?"

"Of course."

"Have you slept with her yet?"

"Don't be stupid. I was staying in her house remember?"

"What's that got to do with anything?"

"Her parents were watching us. We never had the chance." Franz kicked the ball back. "What about you? You got a girlfriend there?"

"Maybe. I'm working on it."

"Czech?"

"Ukrainian. Left home like me."

"Sounds perfect."

Lev was not so sure.

The conversation struggled on until it finally fell flat on stony ground. In a feeble attempt to maintain a connection they talked about 'meeting up for a drink sometime somehow', but with no idea about the how or the time. And talk was all it was. Franz was left feeling low, and hungry; still hungry for dialogue, for the sound of his friend's voice. And Franz felt he had been cheated. It wasn't the same: without seeing Lev's face it wasn't the same. Franz had pictured him in his mind as he listened or strove to speak, but in doing so had distanced himself from the conversation. There had been no intimacy, only motions to be going on with, a 'tick in the box' to be executed. For Lev the only real problem had been a bad line and a stilted, sorry sounding Franz. With a wicked sense of humour he surmised that the Nazis were slowly suffocating his friend. He suddenly sounded in a hurry.

"Sorry got to go. There's an idiot at the door. Call me again sometime."

"Bye - by the way I went to the Berlin zoo."

"Great. I went to the fair. Got to go. Bye."

Section Four: Passing Out Parade

"Bye."
And that was that. They hung up: each having said little of substance; each wishing there had been more; each wondering why the hell not.

◆

I see a Jew coming. Run for your life!
He carries a knife. He's after your money.
He's after your wife!
See the Jew, shitting in the street.
Cut off his arms. Cut off his feet.
Tie him to the bed. Cut off his funding.
Chop off his head!
See Jews over there, swimming back to shore.
Never enough money, always after more.
Jews in the bedroom, under my sheets.
Jews under my feet. Jews watching me eat.
Jews in the bathroom, taking a leak!
Jews on the inside, in the woodwork, in the pipes.
Jews on the outside, out of touch, out of sight.
Jews up the chimney. Jews in my hair.
Jews in the boardroom. Jew steals the chair.
(Jews in the middle. Oh how I despair!)
Clever Jews, stupid Jews. Jews without a name.
Big Jews, small Jews. Each is the same.
Rich Jews, poor Jews, driving me insane.
Jews in on the secret. Jews never taking sides.
Jews hands me my change, taking me for a ride.
Jews make me scratch. Jews make me bite.
Jews make me angry. Jews make me fight.
Jews with attitude cover me in lice.
Jews bearing gifts, pretending to be nice.
Jews in the bushes. Jews about town.
Jews up a tree, refuse to come down.
Jews to the left. Jews to the right.
Jews steal my milk in the middle of the night.
Jews chew my meat. Jews bite my bread.
Jews in my soup. Jews in my head.
God listen to me! Jews will be the death of me.
God don't you see the trouble I'm in?
I'm willing to confess if it's a matter of sin.

Section Four: Passing Out Parade

Can't see no Jews. Have they all died?
Jews can't hurt me. So why do I cry?

Skin thicken, lips tighten, and stars attached, Isaak's parents were now ready to venture outside. Outside was a different story. Outside you tiptoed through life. You did not speak unless spoken to. You kept your head down or looked away. If you did exchange looks you did so in a way which did not invite trouble. If you were addressed you let the idiots set the tone of the conversation - and win the argument. You did not question the question. You did not argue the result. You played the part prescribed: you acted miserable, under the thumb; you made yourself out to be a loser. And if you did all that you could still come out on top. Outside you temporarily divorced yourself and engaged reality as if a broken soul. On a good day they took pity on you. On a bad day they poked you with a stick to make you squeal. On a really bad day they took pleasure in simply beating you up. Back on the inside you could reunite yourself and pretend it hadn't happened. Unfortunately that didn't always work.

Isaak's parents arrived at the police station on borrowed bicycles and out of breath. They had been pedalling hard, on stomachs made hungry by a light lunch. Bicycles gave them speed which gave them the cover to fly through town without be recognised for who they were, for who they dared to be, for where they dared to be. It was difficult to spot yellow stars flying through the air. It was difficult to throw an insult at someone who was out of earshot even before the foul words left the foul mouth. Bicycles made life easy.

They chained their bikes up against a lamppost and took time out to calm themselves before heading inside. They stood impassive; at their most polite, most vulnerable, least capable. The young policeman who loitered nearby with a cigarette did not. Even without raising an eyebrow he threatened - and he knew it. Each knew what they had to do: Yosef had to play it dumb; Diza had to play the broken mother and expose her vulnerability. Diza needed her son back. Even more she needed her child back: children were the vital ingredient - the medicine - which kept them sane and the ghetto healthy.

They were dressed as if for dinner. On the outside appearance was everything, second only to perception. Appearance was something they had control over. Perception was not. Diza brushed her yellow star to ensure it was clean, then rubbed it flat, to check it was secure. Yosef voiced his disapproval.

"Leave it." He spoke sharply. "Come on, let's get this over with so we can go home."

Section Four: Passing Out Parade

She followed him inside, trying to keep up.

The desk sergeant looked up, and upon seeing two yellow stars knew exactly what they had come for. He made them wait, refusing to be rushed. It was important that Jews knew their place. They sat on a wooden bench, eyes down, not wishing in any way to look impatient, or agitated, or a threat in any way. Finally, when he could find nothing else to fill his time, the sergeant told them to up and follow him - and to mind their manners. Yosef had his standard response to that instruction and Diza hoped that he would not use it.

He led them to the office of his chief and thumped on the door. The chief was a big chief. He had his own private office. He had a special uniform and a special cap which he adored because it set him apart. He had awards for long service and bravery lined up along the shelf behind his desk. He socialised with important Germans. They had pinned medals to his chest. The Germans liked him. He liked the Germans. Most of his older officers despised him. His younger officers feared him - or feared his stupidity. This sergeant simply put up with him and his tantrums, his inconsistencies, his childish outbursts, his pomposity, his corruption, the pleasure he took from the pain of others. It was a local disease.

The big chief was leaning back in his big chair, feet up, staring out of the window; killing time; bottle in hand. Nothing interesting had happened so he was bored. The big chief liked to spin in his chair. Despite repeated attempts he had never made it full circle. 360 degrees eluded him. This failure left him feeling unfulfilled: such was his imagination and motivation these days.

Hearing the call to duty he dropped his feet, sat up and swivelled his chair to present his best side to his audience. He screwed the cap back on the bottle and placed it on the floor out of sight. Satisfied that he looked like a man in charge he shouted out permission to enter. It was his desk sergeant, hopefully with something to interest him. When the man told him that he had two Jews outside and that they had come to collect their son he waved them in, as if he was doing them a favour (which he was). This would be interesting. This would be a bit of fun.

With the sergeant barking orders the Jews were hustled in and made to stand before his desk. Without prompting they stood to attention, side by side without even an inch of space between them. The big chief looked the Jews up and down, like he was checking cattle for signs of disease. The male was clutching a brown envelope to his tight stomach whilst trying to conceal it beneath his folded hands. The big chief knew what it contained. The female clutched a small bag. It had something in it like a small box or a parcel. That did confuse him - and

Section Four: Passing Out Parade

he hated being confused by things.

"What's in there?" he grunted, pointing.

Diza reached in and produced a small cardboard box held together by string. She tried to smile.

"It's a cake." She tried to smile again. "For you? Just to say thank you for giving us our son back?"

She had used up all her brown sugar to bake it.

"Are you trying to bribe me?" Suddenly the big chief sounded dangerous.

Yosef jumped to his wife's defence.

"No please, nothing like that! It is simply a friendly gesture, nothing more."

Yosef was able to smile as he quickly invented a line.

"My wife loves to bake cakes. Any excuse."

The big chief was stupid enough not to recognise a stupid lie. His sergeant was not and strained to keep a straight face.

"What is it?"

"Carrot cake?" replied Diza, hoping that the man liked carrot cake. "Do you like carrot cake?"

For maximum effect the big chief inhaled deeply and took his time before responding. He objected to Jews asking questions, especially those of a personal nature. Intimacy of any kind was a headache: it made it harder to hate someone.

"What I like or don't like is none of your business. And I cannot accept gifts as it would be construed as bribery. Do you think I can be bribed with a homemade cake?"

Bewildered, Diza shook her head. Yosef thought he could.

The big chief pointed at a filing cabinet - a filing cabinet stuffed full of hated paperwork. On some days he hated paperwork second only to Jews. On other days he hated paperwork second only to his immediate superior, a stupid German.

"Put it over there."

Diza did as she was told. Quickly but gently she laid it down in its new resting place like she was handling a new born baby. She returned to the same spot alongside her husband, doing her best to look grateful and subservient. She found that easy to do whereas Yosef struggled: his impatience and resentment were beginning to boil. Cut to the chase and hand over my son: that was his dominant thought. He had the money. Cut the crap.

The big chief looked up at his sergeant. "Remind me, what are we holding their kid for?"

"Driving without a licence. Driving a stolen car - though he didn't

Section Four: Passing Out Parade

know it was stolen to be fair. Outside without a night permit."

The big chief crossed his arms and leant back in a display of contrived outrage.

"That's quite some charge sheet. That could send him down for years."

"You said pay the fee and we could take him home."

The big chief lurched forward: arms on desk; hands folded; a very serious look on his face.

"How dare you say that. I didn't say that. A member of my force may have said that but not me."

A crack appeared in her world and Diza, distraught, turned to Yosef; who in turn looked to the desk sergeant for help; who in turn was trying to not look at anybody. He didn't want to be part of this developing farce. The big chief smiled at the enormity of his joke and thumped the table.

"You know the problem with you Jews?"

Tell me, I'm dying to know, thought Yosef.

"You have no sense of humour."

Diza, sure that Yosef wanted to punch the man, clawed at her husband's rib cage as if somehow that would calm him, contain him.

"Put it on the table."

Smartly Yosef did as instructed. Ripping opening the sealed envelope he methodically counted out the notes as he laid them down on the table. The big chief noted progress, brain counting. He liked money. He loved money, especially when it was cash. But he did not like to be seen grabbing it, milking it, or degrading himself in dirty business transactions for small gains. He liked easy money as much as he loathed Jews and their ability to acquire it no matter what obstacles were put in their way. He loved to take money off the Jews because it hurt them so much - and also because ripping off his own people was harder to get away with.

When Yosef had finished counting he licked his lips and stood back, back on his spot next to his wife. He was finding it difficult to breathe, impossible to speak. Inside his throat was bone dry. Outside, his skin was breaking out in a sweat; here, there, and everywhere. He watched with well disguised contempt as the poor excuse for a policeman ran his hands through the paper money - as if to be sure that it was not a trick, a Jewish trick.

Diza clutched her husband's hand and squeezed, passing him a calming message of hope and deliverance. They both locked eyes on the big chief, the man who held the destiny of their wayward child in his hands. Yosef's patience began to wane as the man stayed silent. He

Section Four: Passing Out Parade

was saying nothing only for the pleasure of seeing how it effected them. And when he did speak it was a shock. The big chief sneezed and wiped his runny nose across the back of his sleeve, pausing to check his handiwork. He looked gruesome.

"Not enough," he declared casually.

"What?"

Yosef could barely mask his fury. Diza wanted to slap the man for being a monster then almost collapsed to the floor. Yosef gripped her tightly around the waist and held her up. He wanted to snatch his money back: no son meant no money. The look on his face said 'kill' but luckily the big chief was still looking down at the notes. Like Yosef the sergeant struggled to contain himself.

"You deaf? I said not enough. For what he's done it's not enough. I don't know why my man fixed this price but it's not enough."

Diza began to sob, pushing out words to join her flood of tears.

"We can't get any more. There is no more. It's all we have. That's the truth, the honest truth. Please, he's our only son, our only son. Please."

Yosef refused to plead. He refused to cry. He refused to go down on his knees and beg. He would not give this man the benefit, the pleasure. He made a fist but did not shake it. He was still, just, in control of himself.

"I thought we had an agreement. I was wrong." He managed to remain calm as he spoke.

For a fleeting frozen moment in time the Jew and the Ukrainian policeman glowered at each other across the void. They locked horns. The big chief saw a broken Jew; a man who had to be kept firmly in his place; a man without a future, unlike himself. Yosef saw a cretin; a man fuelled only by his own inflated self-importance; a man who ate too much; a man living beyond his means or abilities; a man propped up by a uniform; a man without a shred of moral fibre. The big chief had a reputation. Yosef had his humanity.

The moment passed, but not without incident: the conviction and truth in the statement stung the big chief. He did not like being criticized, put in his place - and by a Jew! He slammed the table. (His sergeant was not impressed. He had seen it and heard it all before.)

"Know your place Jew! Know your place!"

Diza jumped to her husband's rescue.

"Sir my husband meant nothing by that. He - we - are just desperate for our son back, our only son. He's all we have. He's all we have to live for. Apologise Yosef."

Yosef stared blankly into the face of the enemy and apologised. It

Section Four: Passing Out Parade

was an apology stripped of all emotion. He kept his eyes fixed on the floor when in return he took a verbal battering from the big chief: a man who thought he was the most important man in town second only to 'The Colonel', or the most important Ukrainian in town second to no one. (He was in fact neither, despite the uniform.) The big chief was one to never pass up the chance to launch a tirade of abuse against a Jew. Both his father and grandfather had taught him to distrust them, despise them, avoid contact with them, blame them; but if forced to do business with them tread carefully and check the small print. The high point so far of his nasty, miserable little life had possibly been the day when the Germans had rounded up all the Jews, stuffed them inside the newly declared Ghetto, and locked the gates. For shear excitement and relief nothing had yet bettered it - not even getting married - not even his promotion to station chief as that had involved a big bribe and a lot of grovelling in German. His promotion had been expensive and hard work, not a nice surprise. Still, at least the communists had been destroyed, and Stalin - that evil monster who had starved his people to death - was dead - shot in the back of the head by one of his own generals so the story went. Good riddance to him. Rot in Marxist Hell. That said, the issue of 'Germans versus Russians' still confused him: he was never sure who he hated more. It all depended on how much or how little he had drunk, and who with.

The big chief savoured the moment when these two particular Jews, hopes cruelly crushed, were led out of his office. He returned to his bottle and avoided looking at his financial gain, pretending to himself that it was not important. Not much later he would scoop up the notes and fold them away for safekeeping. A few he would hand out - like sweets - to keep his troops happy.

Outside Diza collapsed into a chair. She had no energy left: she could not stand, talk, think, sink or swim. She was traumatised. Yosek wanted to grab the sergeant by the collar and shake him, and demand his money back. But he couldn't do that. He was just another Jew. The sergeant was apologetic.

"Leave it to me. I'll have a word when the time is right. Come back tomorrow, with whatever extra you can lay your hands on. I'll sort it out."

"Why? Why should I trust you?"

The sergeant returned an icy stare and for a moment he became the big chief's little chief, with all his faults.

"Because you have no choice."

The force of the answer consumed both Yosek and Diza. They waited with baited breath for his next pronouncement. Yosek had been

Section Four: Passing Out Parade

put firmly back in his place. Diza had never left it.

"Now listen. Chief is just stringing you along, playing it out for a laugh - that's his wicked sense of humour. He doesn't want to hang on to your kid. Too much hassle. He'd rather have the money."

Diza thanked him for all his help as he lead them to the door and saw them out - an act for which he received dark menacing looks from passers-by who did not take kindly to seeing Jews being treated with respect by one of their policemen. Unruffled by this he made the point of watching the pair cycle away out of sight before stepping back inside to light a cigarette. He would bide his time and wait for the best moment to work his magic on the fat stupid oaf who was his boss.

Diza cycled as fast as she could, sometimes overtaking her husband. He was elsewhere; lost inside his own head; barely able to steer a straight line. He was still smarting from the treatment he had received: there was no honour left in the world; the world had gone to the dogs. She wanted to get home before it got dark - and rip off her yellow star, and feel like a complete human being again.

Meanwhile, inside, the chief was feeling very happy with himself, very satisfied. He loved getting one over on the Jews; outsmarting them; denying them their due. He regarded it as a sport - and being fat and unfit it was the only sport he could play, and play without risk of losing. The suggestion that he might have an inferiority complex never once entered his head. He was too stupid for such self-reflection.

♦

Franz, paid up member of the Hitler Youth, fought to kill time while wearing his uniform. He stood. He sat. He walked up and down and around the length of his room. Nothing worked. To make matters worse his uniform felt uncomfortable, irrelevant; worse still felt stupid. He had outgrown it but he could not remove it. He had to dress smart for dinner, be in uniform; to please Father. He felt he had put on somebody else's skin.

The telephone rang and he picked it up expecting it to be him. Instead it was the reception desk. There was someone to see him. He slammed it down, horrified, and stood back: he was trapped again, under fire again, as events (again) threatened to overwhelm him. He paced back and forth with nowhere to go, nowhere to hide, no plan of action, no escape; shell-shocked and under fire.

Fixing his sights on the door the obvious suddenly struck him: he pounced forward and locked it. He withdrew to the far end of the room, secure but still trapped. Then it happened, just what he had been

Section Four: Passing Out Parade

expecting: the knock on the door. He froze, unable to move, breathe or think. Herr Schrimer called out his name and demanded to speak to him. Franz pretended not to hear. The door handle turned and turned again; driven by force and frustration but producing no result. Franz watched its every turn. Logic told him it could not open the door but his imagination screamed otherwise. Worse still the locked door could keep Herr Schrimer out of his room but not Bridget out of his mind. He cursed her for causing him so much trouble.

"I know you're in there Franz Helmer. Speak to me. Please."

Franz saw a trap. He covered his ears and played it deaf, dumb and blind. It worked. Herr Schrimer gave up and walked away. He waited for what felt like an eternity (but which was in fact barely five minutes) before edging towards the door, unable to stand it any more. He pinned his ear up against the door and listened out. Nothing. Next he turned the key in the lock, followed by the handle; both slowly; inviting a reaction. Nothing. Taking a deep breath he opened the door and peeked out. The coast was clear. The devil was gone. He could smile. He could laugh. He could relax. He did none of these things for a shocking thought struck him: Herr Schrimer might go talk to his parents. He rushed down the corridor and up the stairs where, at the top, he crept forwards, on the lookout for the enemy. There was no sight of the man. As before he ended up outside his parents room; listening in; snatching at pieces of conversation. Yes Herr Schrimer was in there and it was turning loud and nasty. He would hear everything but accept nothing.

Mother was the louder, the more defensive, the more aggressive, the more passionate, the more protective of her son. She defended her son to the hilt. She simply would not accept such accusations from a stranger - a stuck up German from the big city who used fancy words. Father was playing it down and trying, unsuccessfully, to be more conciliatory. (Privately he knew that what he was being told was probably, mostly true.) His parents were fighting for him, dissecting him. He was the centre of attention, which made him feel important. Right now Mother made him proud whereas Father was proving to be a disappointment.

When he heard his father refer to him as 'a kid' Franz wanted to correct him, push him aside. Franz wanted to defend himself - he didn't need help. He wasn't a kid. And cruel? I was never cruel. Honest, yes, but never cruel. I never made her cry! She wanted to cry, to make me feel bad! She hurt me not the other way round! I never touched her where she didn't want to be touched, or when she didn't invite me to. She was asking for it. She ordered the alcohol not me! Rude? How

Section Four: Passing Out Parade

dare you! Frau Schrimer was the rude one, and in bloody French! Herr Schrimer was spreading malicious lies about him in a most unGerman way and Franz felt powerless to stop him.

Then he remembered that it was his birthday tomorrow - the thought had not struck him for days - and he would officially be a man. Unofficially he felt the moment had already arrived and he stood up, sorely tempted to storm in. But then he heard his father say he would go get his son and 'sort things out, get to the truth'. He panicked. He crept away as fast as he could without making a noise. When the door opened he spun around, 180 degrees, and began walking, acting the part brilliantly. He looked like an innocent bystander, without a care in the world. At school Franz had always been a good actor: fooling boys, girls and teachers alike. He looked up feigning surprise - then truly was surprised: it was Herr Schrimer, not his father. Unconsciously he decided to let the uniform say it all, or say nothing. Either way he hid behind the uniform.

Herr Schrimer was equally surprised. Then his surprise turned to anger but before he could say a thing Herr Helmer appeared, equally surprised to see his son standing before him. He was wearing his old uniform, medals included, and he looked unbeatable - but lost for words. Herr Schrimer ended up sandwiched between them. He finally spoke when it became apparent that neither Helmer was willing to.

"Another Helmer in uniform. You Helmers, you love the uniform."

Franz disagreed. Franz Senior didn't.

"How many Russians has your son shot yet?"

None, thought Franz. But just watch me. Franz Senior just shrugged, baffled by the odd question.

Satisfied by his own poetic outburst Herr Schrimer walked away, giving Franz a wide berth. He wanted the Helmers out of his life and that of his family. Father and son watched him disappear down the stairs; still up for a fight; feeling victory had been denied.

Good riddens, thought Franz, thinking he was in the clear - but then his father spoke.

"Come inside, now."

Herr Helmer sounded very angry and he wiggled his index finger, as if at a ten year old. It was a bad sign and a habit which had come to irritate Franz for many years now. Inside, the look on his mother's face offered no way out, no protection. She was very upset but holding herself in and giving nothing away. Franz, clutching at theatricals in the hope of making his audience laugh, wanted to throw his arms up in the air in an act of surrender and yell 'Shoot me! I deserve it! I messed up again!' But he didn't: his parents had little in the way of a sense of

Section Four: Passing Out Parade

humour. He wanted to laugh the whole thing off. Is this what hotel rooms in Berlin did to visiting families?

"Wipe that smile off your face. You have let us down, seriously. Shame on you."

Franz didn't think he had any sort of smile on his face and wished to protest, but sensed that would be catastrophic. And as for 'shame', shame on him? He looked towards Mother for support but she remained tight-lipped - always her perfect defence mechanism.

"Sometimes I think you don't deserve to wear that uniform."

Fine, thought Franz. I'll take it off then. Sod it, he thought, and spoke out.

"Shall I take it off then?"

"What!"

"Nothing. Just a joke."

"A joke? You think this is a joke? That man wants to report you for assault! You think that is a joke!"

"Will he?"

"Probably not. I think I persuaded him it would not be a good idea right now."

Thought not, thought Franz. Tomorrow I'll be very very special and no one will be able to touch me.

"Tell me the truth. Did you try to have your way with her against her will?"

"No. She had drunk too much champagne. She flirted with me. She confused me."

"Champagne? Who's idea was that?"

"Hers. She ordered it."

"And that's the truth?"

"That's the truth. Ask the staff."

Herr Helmer appeared placated if not satisfied. Franz was not: he had been put on trial by his own father. He felt like a Jew - a victim - except he was guilty. Punishment was to never see her again, to never write to her again. Franz had no problem with that: so no way back, only onwards. Fine by him. The past and the present was rapidly falling apart, so onwards.

He wanted to get back at his father, be his equal, exert his new state of manhood. He wanted to flee the room. He wanted to get out of the stupid uniform and into a better one, one with true status and power. He wouldn't be pushed around: he would march to the beat of the drums yes, but he would not be somebody else's silent, polished symbol. He did not want to sit like a puppy at his father's side. Except of course he knew he would. He had to. What else was there? It was the only party

Section Four: Passing Out Parade

in town. As he left the room he cast a last look at his mother, and got the gist of her final conclusion - or condemnation. 'Just like your father.'

Back safe in his room Franz had cause to cry, and wanted to cry, but try as he might he could not cry. Crying was for girls. And he could not hide: not under the bed; not up a tree; not behind a big girl's skirt; not amongst a gang of boys. Life was more complicated even though complicated things he had always tried to avoid. He couldn't just kiss a girl on the cheek and run away. He couldn't just salute the flag and walk away, empty-headed.

◆

> In front of the mirror the Perfect Nazi reflected passion but no compassion.
> In front of the mirror the Perfect Nazi reflected the glory of his sacrifice but never the sacrifice of his glory.
> In front of the mirror the Perfect Nazi was never moved to tears – though others, far removed, would tear at the image, if only they could summon the strength.
> In front of the mirror the Perfect Nazi saw only his carefully crafted image – conspiracies contained, wistful thinking restrained.
> Despite the mirror the Perfect Nazi never saw beyond the end of his nose.

Franz Helmer Senior stood tall before the full length mirror, in uniform; using it to stamp out the years, to reintroduce an electrified past to a stale present. The uniform reequipped him, amplify him, enabled him to pretend that he was that other, younger Helmer who had always been in the middle of some great adventure. They could never take any of this away from him: his uniform, his rank, his service record, his medals, his heroics, his very private thoughts. Though a more complicated, stressful day-to-day existence, his war service had been a simpler life with rules which never needed to be questioned as they did not bother the conscience. Its moral code had been carefully constructed and nailed into place; never to unwind under any circumstances, not even under fire.

Franz Helmer Senior had more power now, more authority. He carried extra weight now but felt more powerful back then, almost superhuman, supported as he was by likeminded individuals - all young, male, fanatical and driven by a single cause. In the nation's mission to carve out a bigger piece of paradise he had been given a

Section Four: Passing Out Parade

mandate to hand out the gift of life, or snatch it back. With it he had dealt out death according to his own, sometimes devilish design. Back then he was told what to achieve but rarely how to do it. Now he had to follow the rules and fill in the paperwork, and be polite to inferior beings - some of them German. The energy which had flowed through him was missing now. Now he had to generate some poor substitute day after day, until the day he died. And through it all he had to pretend, invent: that life with his wife, and with his son; and all he had built; and all he ruled over with absolute authority, and at times even with sincerity, was something much better than -

The curse of negativity was creeping up on him again and Franz Senior took a step back in mind and body. He adjusted his uniform for the last time then turned away from his less than comfortable reflection to go meet his comrades in war. He wanted to see the other soldiers; hear them speak; touch their past lives; brush aside then revitalise the present. They would excite him. They would reignite him, just like last time. And he was hungry.

Hilda Helmer had been waiting patiently, watching the clock else watching her husband being a thousand miles away. This side of him she had experienced before, and each time she had failed to break through and be a part of it. Cut out many times, she had given up trying many moons ago. Instead she licked her ageing wounds and thanked God for what she did have - mainly her son. She looked very presentable, good for her age, and would make any husband proud but she lacked the enthusiasm to impress, which she hid well. She was acting the perfect wife despite the imperfect husband. When it came to suffering her husband in uniform, Hilda Helmer had still not made her mind up. It brought back good memories and bad, a true Helmer and a fake.

Outside, sulking, simmering, and suffering by the lift, Franz was forced to wait and still wait. He needed escape from his current demons. Right now he needed a war - even if it was second-hand and twenty years old. He wanted to see the other soldiers; hear them speak; touch their past lives; brush aside then revitalise the present. And he was hungry.

Reunited, the Helmers took the lift down to the lobby. When it landed and the doors slid apart the Helmers burst out, back into the public eye; as if being bottled up together was too much to bear and went against the forces of physics. The three of them were a distinct family unit again, except now the bonds were weaker and the rules of engagement were up for criticism and renegotiation. Its parts, pushed together, were tending to pull apart the moment there was space to do

Section Four: Passing Out Parade

so. Franz Senior stormed ahead and ordered a taxi for the short ride to the banquet hall. His loud, impatient voice embarrassed both his wife and son. His uniform felt threatening to the young foreign worker who dealt with his request.

The Helmers flew through the streets of the capital, conscious that the next day would be a very different kind of day. The journey took so little time that no one settled down or warmed up enough to break the ice which had spread suddenly. And Berlin in the dark kept them in the dark. Occasionally there was the flicker of red flag to remind them who was in town, and still in charge: theirs were little lives; to be lived out on his stage, to his script and to his music. Upon arrival at the banquet hall everything changed - and it would never change back to what it was before.

As the Helmers entered the building they were scooped up and swept along: by the splendour, the splash, the brash bold personalities who welcomed them; by the big stories of recent history begging to be heard at the earliest opportunity. Now Franz Helmer Senior was Hauptsturmführer Helmer again and he had fallen in love again. He was in his element as he recognised fellow comrades and they recognised him, and old connections sparked. There were other wives, but no girlfriends, and like Frau Helmer they were perfectly presented. Franz was the only child of a former soldier present, and hence the youngest in the room. He looked around for others like him but quickly realised that he was alone - and the only one wearing short trousers - stupid short trousers. He was in uniform but out of it. He was Franz Junior again. Part of him wanted to flee, back to his hotel room - a place he now found to be a comfortable retreat. The rest was determined to soldier on: here was a good time to be had, he felt sure of it. Something was begging to happen, he just didn't know what.

The flags and symbols of the Schutzstaffeln, the Party and the state were out in force, grabbing attention in all directions. And there were decorations and trophies representing all the glory of the 2nd SS Panzer Division. You could not take it all in without passing out. The swastika and the double runes were scattered here and there, as if like confetti: on walls, tables, people's clothing; perhaps even inside people's heads. Here the imagery fought for prominence over actual human experience. No matter how hard you had fought, no matter how many times you had put your life on the line, you remained secondary to the cause, to the Schutzstaffeln, to your country. You were never allowed to get too big for your standard issue boots. Here Fascism was a calculating creed and a collection of perfect souls. It was the reason to celebrate, the cause to consume. It defined you beyond your limits.

Section Four: Passing Out Parade

But do the wrong thing and it would hang you out to dry, or die. You didn't need to understand it you just had to worship it. And all those present to eat and drink themselves silly did exactly that, in the smartest uniforms possible.

In the crowded bar waiters were rushed off their feet as the guests from another universe gathered for their feast. For some it was a holy gathering. There the Helmer unit disintegrated. As Hauptsturmführer Helmer shook hands and was shaken up, and was pulled back to an earlier time, so his wife and son became forgotten, superfluous to requirements. At first he remembered to introduce them - but only once - before the excitement engulfed him. Frau Helmer quickly peeled away and joined up with other ladies suffering the same. The wives formed tight circles, impossible to breach. Their talk was subdued, serious, almost sober at times. Franz saw a bunch of mothers mothering: it reinforced his decision to follow his father.

When the right faces locked in place and sweaty hands shook something ignited and both sides struggled to take in air. There was so much to say, so much that needed to be said again and again and again, even if it had been said at previous reunions. A few of the wives experienced the same interaction but with a completely different agenda. Theirs was the talk of marriage and raising family, and hanging on in there. Theirs was never the talk of fighting battles, saving lives, and losing lives.

Franz hung on, trailing behind his father; trying to listen in; trying to experience the vibe; trying to imagine himself as one of these soldiers - a soldier with sharp memories of a war decisively won. Everything was here on a plate, accessible, for him to pick at and chew over, perhaps even swallow: the highs; the hate; the victories. There were stories here, keen to be heard, and Franz wanted to hear them all, and bear witness. The present was shifting back to the past and he had to run to keep up but he had nowhere to run to. And he began to watch the clock: soon he would be eighteen and his own man. The shorts began to burn his legs and he wanted to yank off his tie.

Franz gave as much attention to the dress as he did to the grand talk. These veterans of the 2nd SS Panzer Division were hard, as hard as nails. They had never been beaten. They were an elite class who had fought the war and won it, single-handedly in their view. They had won the East for National Socialism. You did not argue with their version of history. A few times he became the object of attention - but even then Hauptsturmführer Helmer did the talking, showing off his son proudly but not expecting him to speak. Franz just smiled, stiffly, and at times felt required to salute - but each time he managed to stop

Section Four: Passing Out Parade

himself acting like a twit.

There was one retired general in the ranks. He resided in his own special bubble of respectability and superiority. Lower ranks swarmed around him, attracted by the heat of his special glow. Hauptsturmführer Helmer was hoping to be introduced - reintroduced after so many years - and at times worked the crowd towards that objective. But the summons to dinner scuppered his progress.

Come the bell and the call to arms a landslide of uniforms engulfed the vast dining hall. It was a bubbly, floating mass of black and grey. It shifted here and there. It broke apart and reattached like some giant intelligent creeping, consuming mould. Across its dark surface flickered splashes of white and red - shapes tailored to express power and oppression. It generated its own power, its own narrative, its own warmth. Historical facts had to fit, else they were excluded. They were the armour - the bullets - which executed a self-certified ceremony. In here all soldiers were heroes. All kills were justified. All action was decisive. All failure was forgotten else reduced to a useful learning lesson.

With quickening pace conversations were cut short and the guests went searching for their seating arrangements around the big circular tables. The quick-witted rule breakers ganged up and swapped name cards to hijack tables for their own exclusive use. Hauptsturmführer Helmer found himself sharing a table with people he did not know: wife on his right, chatting privately to another wife on her right, oblivious to him; son on his left, saying nothing unless prompted, and then still saying little. Fine: as long as each knew their place and kept it, fine.

A toast was made, then another, then another, to the gods who ruled over them and to the comrades who had fallen. The crowd was kept on its feet for ages. With some pain Franz remembered standing in front of the Reichsfuehrer while the man peered at him through his little round glasses. He did his best to toast him with total sincerity and admiration but it was difficult: this man was no god despite being at the heart of a religion. Some of the women floundered. Others played the part to perfection. As for the Fuehrer: a toast to him was easy, the natural order of things, almost cathartic; a replenishment of the soul. To drink to his health was to drink to the health of one's own self. His spirit lived in your spirit. He could pull your levels without you knowing.

No matter what Himmler thought, or how hard he pushed, his army would always be loyal to the Fuehrer first and foremost. Both were worshipped with equal measure and might, equal vice and spice, but

Section Four: Passing Out Parade

one was always the senior and always had the last word. Himmler would always have to accept second place. He knew that and was comfortable with it most of the time: sometimes it would rankle in his sleep but he always managed to shake it off. The Reichsfuehrer was totally loyal to his Fuehrer. It went with the job.

While Hauptsturmführer Helmer ate and drank himself to excess he instructed his son to limit his drinking. 'Don't get drunk!' Franz decided to ignore him and do exactly that. A hangover was exactly what he needed to face the next day. After midnight he would be eighteen and he could anything he liked - except bow out of the parade. While he ate and drank, and ignored some of the now repetitive chat, he searched around, trying to pick out one particular face from the seated crowd: fleetingly his father had spoken with a fellow officer who knew him well. Franz wanted to speak to him, ask about his father, dig up old bones. He vowed to see it through before the night was out. And he kept watching the clock to see if it was turning.

The food was excellent and no one wanted to talk while they filled their faces with all things delicious. When the courses ran out and guests were left holding their drinks - willing now to chat - the band struck up, inviting couples to leave their chairs and enter the space which served as a dance floor. The general led the way, quickly followed by other senior ranks. Slow, and often out of step, they failed to do the music justice. Hauptsturmführer Helmer sat bloated, exhausted, and never thought to ask his wife for a dance. That suited her fine. She quietly slipped away to chat with her female friends: some already known to her (if only long distance); some newly acquired; all with something in common. An ex-sergeant stumbled past on a bad foot. He recognised Hauptsturmführer Helmer and slapped him hard on the back, greeting him loudly as he brushed past. Hauptsturmführer Helmer, pricked, twisted in his chair, but the man was gone.

Following in his mother's footsteps Franz also slipped away, back to the bar; for a little personal freedom, and to listen. This was where the real action was warming up. There he found his man: Strecker, his father's close comrade in war. He introduced himself and Strecker, also a retired Hauptsturmführer, bought him a stiff drink - with the sole intention of getting him drunk. This time the voices were louder, rougher, unrestrained; and the egos escaped, to exert themselves, to push outwards to fill the space between the bodies, to grab attention. The lighter, sweet tones of female voices were gone - something which only seemed to registered with Franz. The lack of women made him more determined to muscle in and climb into the pit. And still the clock

Section Four: Passing Out Parade

was not turning fast enough.

As alcohol flowed into bodies standing close and swollen by too much food their noise and heat began to ferment its own particular stew. The men were pagans again. God was a beast again, with a cause to crush again. Their minds were drawn to blood and guts, stone and mud, bark and bush. Tongues loosened, then wagged, and undesirable facts and opinions began to leak out: some harmless; some irritating; some intentionally confrontational; some just plain stupid. Unfinished, unsavoury business began to seep out from the cracks which were appearing in the ranks. Loose talk began to dig it up. Some of it was welcomed, positive and embracing. Some of it was divisive, threatening. This was a stage where brains, inflamed and galvanised by alcohol, could argue over the method and the means but never the mission statement. Question that and you would soon find yourself on the outside looking in and feeling lonely. Up to now there had been no talk of bombs, bloodshed, broken bodies and busted limbs; of toil and tears, flight and fear; only 'the good old days', 'the good times', 'the day we grabbed Stalin by the neck and squeezed until he choked to death'. Up to now war was a wondrous thing, without casualty of mind or body; just the expansion of political and social boundaries under duress, to the advantage and satisfaction of the victor.

Strecker interrupted the thoughts of Helmer's boy with sharp observation and a blunt question.

"Impressive aren't we."

"Yes."

"And we know how to talk - you can't stop us."

"No."

"You want to be part of it?"

"Yes."

Suddenly Franz felt himself in serious conversation - and with an expert. He looked up at the clock - still not eighteen, but getting closer - and swallowed more of his drink; to prove a point or to spite his father or to forget his uniform, or all three. He hated the uniform touching his skin, here, now. Tomorrow would not be so bad: tomorrow he could use it to hide in the crowd of brainless, witless school children. And the day after tomorrow? Perhaps it was time to throw it away.

"You look shattered."

"Do I."

"What are you doing tomorrow? Watching the show?"

"Not watching it no, marching in it, in the parade."

"Really?"

"Really."

Section Four: Passing Out Parade

"Your father must be proud."
"Of course."
"He didn't mention it earlier."
"He didn't need to."
"You sound just like Franz."

That last remark ripped Franz right down the middle. Half of him wanted to sound exactly like his father. The other half wanted to sound like himself, whatever that was.

"And will you march with your head held high?"
"Yes."
"And if he asks you will you march to war?"
"Yes. As a Hauptsturmführer, tank division, in my own Tiger Two."
"So you want to be an officer of the Schutzstaffeln?"
"Yes."
"They only take the best."
"I am the best."

Strecker slapped him on the back.

"You know what, I believe you! Come let me buy you another drink - let's drink a toast to your great father!"

Franz wasn't sure but he thought there was a whiff of sarcasm in the man's voice. Either way he was happy to accept another drink. At the counter he took the initiative.

"What was the first Tiger like? My father commanded one. Did you?"

"Yes I did. Proud to. Loud, slow, heavy but a beautiful machine, but a real gas guzzler. It blew everything out of the way. It turned those T-34s into mincemeat."

"Were they any good?"

"The T-34? Yes to be fair they were. They fought well in them - just led by crap generals."

Franz jumped to another place. "Will it be hard, officer training?"

"Hard? You haven't got a clue - Franz? It's Franz isn't it?"
"Yes."

Strecker rotated the glass in his hand and chose his words wisely.

"Well Franz, from day one they will try to break your balls, and under fire. Build you up. Break you down. Build you up again, break you down again. And so on, until you disintegrate and run home with your tail between your legs, or prove to be indestructible and totally loyal to the cause, and the one man."

"The Fuehrer?"

An unexpected pause produced a diplomatic answer.

"Probably."

Section Four: Passing Out Parade

Franz looked confused and Strecker had to smile to reassure him.

"Just a bad joke."

Franz didn't view it that way and made that very clear. Hitler Youth, thought Strecker. No bloody sense of humour.

At that point they were joined by another veteran, one ex-sergeant Brandt. He cut into the conversation, releasing the flare up of tension, though at a price: he would later inject his own, stronger toxic mix. The smell of alcohol on his breath was strong. Despite his limp he waded straight in, targeting the younger Franz much as he used to target the older. He could not resist a poke, a shove, a stab, a sharp reminder.

"So you Helmer's lad. Helmer owes me two hundred marks."

Floored, Franz looked to Strecker for guidance but Strecker just shrugged. He knew Brandt the crass comedian.

"What are you doing these days Brandt?"

"Building business in Slovakia, and a bit of import, export."

"And you Franz, Sumy isn't it? What is Sumy like?"

Franz turned back to Strecker. This Brandt guy had a disconcerting edge.

"Mostly flat. Mostly boring. A few Germans. A few Jews. Lots of Ukrannies."

"And your father owns most of it?"

"I wouldn't say that. We have a large estate outside town - very large. It's got villages - and we run a factory."

"And he's king?" asked Brandt.

"I suppose so, yes."

"That makes you a prince."

Franz didn't respond to that. It sounded plain stupid. He glanced at the clock again, needing to see the hour hand. It had barely moved because each minute had to have its say.

"Helmer is a magistrate now Brandt."

Franz quickly corrected Strecker. "Senior magistrate."

"Senior? Top dog."

"He must love that, still shouting orders, still controlling lives. Just like a Russian warlord," said Brandt.

Franz was miffed. "No he's not like that. He takes the job seriously."

"Just pulling your leg."

Well don't pull my fucking leg, thought Franz.

Brandt continued to it.

"Always knew he would do well for himself. Always looked after number one - knows the right people."

"What do you mean?"

Section Four: Passing Out Parade

Brandt smiled and tapped Franz on the shoulder.
"Nothing, don't you worry about it."
Franz wanted to kick him. Frustrated, he tried to reclaim the conversation. He spoke to Strecker and tried to pretend Brandt didn't exist.
"How many Russians did you kill?"
"Me? Lost count."
"Not enough," said Brandt.
"Did you fight any women?"
Brandt giggled and Strecker gave him a dirty look.
"Russian women?"
"Yes."
"No - but I fought alongside a few women."
Strecker smiled at his own joke and Brandt laughed at it. Franz didn't get it.
"We had women in the front line?"
"No. The Russians did but not us."
"Unfortunately."
"Unfortunately."
Franz looked at the two retired soldiers: sometimes they were dead opposites; sometimes they were mirror images and blended into one.
"What were the Poles like?"
"In battle? A pain in the arse."
"They still are."
"True. Too fucking civilized for their own good."
"We gave them the easy bits."
"And still they fucked up."
Strecker and Brandt laughed. Franz tried to join them.
"Did you meet any Japs? Or Chinese? Could you tell the difference?"
Strecker shook his head. "They're at the other end of Asia, in Siberia and God knows where. Why would we?"
"Oh yeah, forgot." Franz carried on quickly. "What was the food like?"
"Standard Wehrmacht stuff was crap. But ours - Waffen SS - that was good."
"We were the best so we ate the best," added Brandt. "Any Russians where you live?" he asked Franz.
"No, we tend to catch them all, or the Ukrainians give them up."
"He probably shoots them all."
"No. Only if they resist, put up a fight. We patrol the border."
"What, you included?"

Section Four: Passing Out Parade

"Yes. It's something we Helmers have to do."
"Tough is he, your dad on border patrol?"
"Yes. He's always tough."
"And how many Russians has he shot there?"
"Shot? A few I suppose, never asked. Don't know about killed."
"And are you tough enough to shoot to kill?"
"If I had to, yes."

Brandt's next remark was aimed exclusively at Strecker. "Spoken like a true Helmer. He must be proud of his boy."

"He is - and I'm not a boy."
"No of course you're not."

Suddenly Strecker delivered a double punch.

"You listen to that American Rock and Roll shit?"
"Yes." Franz feared the next, obvious question. Would he say yes or no? He didn't know. But it did sound good.

"It does your brains in - how you going to kill the enemy with your brain scrambled by that shit?"

"He won't. His lot can't. They're going soft in the head."
"I'm not soft!"

"That's enough Brandt. Give the kid a break." Strecker sounded tired.

"I can look after myself."

Franz sounded stung but Brandt had no intention of stopping.

"Happily married, your dad?"
"Yes."
"So not one for the girls anymore."

Franz refused to be drawn by someone who sounded like a git. Strecker found a good question to change the mood.

"Franz, you tell me, sum up the war in one word, or two."

Brandt laughed. "Or three."

Franz thought hard, determined to produce the best answer.

"Tough adventure?"

"Good try, but no. 'Fucking ridiculous' is the better answer."
"Or 'fucking bollocks'."

Franz looked at them both: two retired, decorated soldiers both suddenly looking very sceptical, cynical, beaten even.

"I don't accept that."

"Well you should," said Brandt. "What do you know?"
"Leave him Brandt."

"I know what I've been taught, what I've read, what I've seen at cinema."

"And what your father told you?"

Section Four: Passing Out Parade

"Yes, and others, like the colonel."

"The colonel?" Brandt looked around. "Which one?"

"The colonel back in Sumy, our garrison commander."

"I see."

"And the Ukrainians."

"Don't believe them. They're just lying bastards. Tell you anything you want to hear to get an advantage."

"They're not all like that. Some are just like me."

Strecker and Brandt exchanged looks, and a private joke, and perhaps a private concern. Brandt handed out a cigarette to Strecker, then offered Franz one.

"Here you want one?"

Franz grabbed it. "Thanks."

Brandt lit it and watched, wondering just how far he could push the only son of Hauptsturmführer Franz Helmer. The kid was a target he could not ignore.

Franz puffed on his cigarette and addressed another question to Strecker.

"How easy was it to beat them?"

"We had to pull out all the stops, grind them into the ground."

"We had to beat the shit out of them, even when they had their hands up - ask your dad Helmer, he'll tell you all about it."

"About what?"

Strecker jumped back in before his partner in crime could respond.

"There were no rules."

Brandt could not resist another sharp poke. "No rules, not even for your father."

Franz flipped and flopped back and forth, like he was watching a double act; but with no comedy to it, only troubling exchanges. Feeling uneasy, he shifted his weight from one tired leg to the other. His discomfort spread to Strecker.

"No rules?"

"Depends what day it was, how the campaign was going."

"And how drunk we were - your dad knew how to drink! And if they were POWs or civilians."

"Civilians? What happened to them?"

"Shit," said Strecker, and he walked away, leaving Franz to the dogs.

"You really want to know?"

"Yes."

"You really want to know what we did in the war - what Helmer did in the war?"

283

Section Four: Passing Out Parade

Franz didn't want to pause but he had to: he was at odds with himself. Finally he beat himself back down.

"Yes."

"We pissed on their heads - I remember Helmer pissed the longest and the loudest. Your dad was very good at smashing people's heads in with the butt of a rifle - seemed to have a knack for it."

With those words Franz fell into a temporary trance. The alcohol spared him the worst. The raging words sounded distant, blurred. It was easy to let them pass over him. And this Brandt was simply the worst kind of git. How did he ever get to join the glorious Schutzstaffeln? A delicate question pulled him back.

"You said you killed lots of Russians - did you torture any? Tell me, I want to know."

"Some, yes, we had to, especially those fucking partisans."

"And my father?"

"Of course. Goes without saying."

"What did he do?"

"You really want to know?"

Brandt was keen to tell him and would do so, regardless of his preference. With Strecker out of his hair he had a free hand.

"Yes." That said, Franz wasn't sure.

But the alcohol and the long day would not let him work out the right answer. He looked towards the clock again. This time he saw it had moved, and that cheered him up.

"Did he ever tell you about our game 'shoot the runaways'? He always got the highest score, being the fastest shot with a rifle."

They were interrupted by the sound of glass shattering followed by that of a silly, giggling female voice. It was out of place and broke the rhythm. Franz turned towards its source, only to see his father striding towards him; negotiating his way around static bodies at speed and trying to appear sober. Franz now dreaded what was on his mind. Hauptsturmführer Helmer was in a great hurry and did not look like he was enjoying the party. Possibly for the first time Franz saw a complete stranger, a man who had invaded his home, and one he had to keep at arm's length while he tried to piece together the pieces which defined him - and puzzled Franz. This man, his father, Franz Helmer Senior, had yet to be revealed.

Hauptsturmführer Helmer knew exactly what he wanted to say.

"Stop drinking and stop smoking."

"I'm eighteen in under two hours."

"But not yet - you need to be on best form tomorrow."

Franz froze and looked his father straight in the eye, refusing to back

Section Four: Passing Out Parade

down. He wanted to say 'fuck you'. But the look his father returned slowly ground him down, until he was forced to back down. Habits of a lifetime - even a short lifetime - were not easy to break. He dropped his cigarette and stamped on it, then took one last sip from his glass before returning it to the bar counter. There he quickly took two more sips and tried to scratch his balls before turning to face the music. Brandt had a silly grin on his face again. His father simply looked dissatisfied.

"When you're eighteen you can do what you like."

"Can I?"

"Within reason - and when the time is right."

Great, thought Franz.

And still Brandt would not let go.

"Your dad did what he liked without reason as far as I remember. Isn't that right Helmer?"

"Don't know what you're on about."

"Oh but I think you do."

Franz recognised the bad sign: Father was not looking at the man he was speaking to. He pushed himself awake a little more. Things might get interesting.

"Why are you talking to my son? Filling his head with shit?"

"It's a free country. It's what we fought for isn't it?"

Like his son before him Hauptsturmführer Helmer tried to disengage and pretend that the man wasn't there.

"Your mother's not feeling well. She's taking a taxi back with another lady."

"Remember my foot Helmer? You shot it."

"It was a stray shot." Hauptsturmführer Helmer repeated himself to his son. "Stray shot. Close quarter fighting. It happens."

"You did it on purpose!" declared a furious Brandt.

"Rubbish man!"

Franz wasn't listening. He had recognised the 'your mother' moment and wanted to ask a question. He didn't, and instead rushed off to find her while he still had the chance. Outside in the freezing cold air he saw her stumble her way into a taxi. A lady already seated inside was helping her in - like she was a cripple, thought Franz. Mother looked unwell, unhappy. Mother was suffering something and Franz didn't know what it was which would make him suffer. She didn't see him. He didn't wave. He didn't call out. He didn't want her to know. He didn't want her to be hurt. He wanted her to be gone. And above all he wanted her to take him home. He rubbed his stomach, then his throat, then the back of his legs, then felt his face. He felt awful, run down,

Section Four: Passing Out Parade

used up. He felt feeble.

Back inside, the warm air smacked his exposed skin and the cold snap was driven off. He rushed to return to the source of his pain, wishing to miss nothing while wishing it was nothing. The two men were enraged, exchanging insults as one attacked and the other defended. The moment was unfolding like some trial of past criminal misconduct, to reveal a rotten body and painful questions which deserved answers. Franz was relieved that his mother was not seeing this side of his father, oblivious to the well-concealed, neatly buried fact that she had, many times, in an earlier life. He saw an explosion of emotion but heard no dangerous words - they had dried up when he arrived back on the scene. Hauptsturmführer Helmer grabbed Brandt by the neck but Brandt simply smiled as Helmer wondered what do to next. Here and now there were limits, and witnesses. Franz watched as out of the blue Strecker stormed in to separate the two.

"You still owe me that money Helmer, to keep my mouth shut - remember?"

Hauptsturmführer Helmer stuck one finger up. The number of times Franz had seen him do that he could count on the fingers of one hand. His father was suddenly looking very uncivilized, very 'peasant like'.

Strecker apologised as he forcibly removed Brandt. He didn't want another war with Helmer. Brandt threw one last remark over his shoulder as he limped away.

"Screw you Helmer."

"Screw you Brandt."

Satisfied that he had had the last word, Hauptsturmführer Helmer turned away, to be stopped in his tracks by his son staring at him, and calculating. For a few seconds - and a few seconds more - they switched their traditional roles: Franz Senior was the lesser, Franz was the greater; Franz Senior was the child, Franz was the man; Franz Senior floundered in emotional turmoil, Franz retreated into calm reflection. But it couldn't last and Franz Senior took back control.

"Forget him Franz. That man has always been an arsehole."

"I know."

On that they were both firmly agreed and for awhile they were back on the same side, reunited. It gave Franz the confidence to speak out.

"He said a lot of nasty stuff. Dishonourable stuff. Any of it true?"

The backlash was brutal.

"How dare you! How dare you speak to your father like that!"

But Franz held firm, helped by the alcohol which stopped loud words hitting his head hard. Like what?

"It's a reasonable question - put by a reasonable son."

Section Four: Passing Out Parade

Like his father before him, Franz was finding it easier to refer to himself in the third person. Somehow it made it less awkward, more imperious. He went all the way.

"For example did you torture anybody?"

Franz Helmer Senior - sometimes Hauptsturmführer Helmer - stepped forward, beyond furious, as if to grab his son by the neck. His son was now a threat. He managed to stop himself just in time. This was his son. He could not hurt him. He could not dismiss him so easily. He could get mad with him but only for a brief moment before the madness deflated, having nothing to feed off. It had been the same with his wife when she had been weaker and the war had been closer. He walked away, no longer a soldier, with no idea where he was going; throwing out one last announcement on his way.

"We have to go. It's late."

"I have to go to the gents."

"Well hurry up. I'll order the taxi."

In the gents room Franz bumped into Strecker who greeted him in the manner of a doctor who truly cared about the state of his patient. He tried to reassure Franz that it was just one bad night; that things repeated often got distorted; that Helmer was, at heart, a good man. Franz took a piss as he spoke, as did Strecker. As they washed their hands afterwards Franz put a clear cut question.

"Did you really know my dad in the war?"

"Enough. I knew him enough."

"He wasn't a bastard was he? A torturer? An evil man? Just doing his duty?"

Strecker wanted to give a clear cut 'no', but could not go so far as to adapting the truth to meet the need. There was simply too much truth.

"We were all bastards for a time. But it was a short time. And we didn't do anything for our own gratification. It needed to be done. We could never let them get up again."

Franz accepted the answer on Strecker's terms. He dried his hands on a towel and fled the scene. It was a bullshit answer, almost worthless, and the words 'at heart' refused to leave him alone.

Loaded down with aching questions he would never dare to ask and shame he would never admit to and ambiguities he would never resolve, Franz went looking for his father. He found him back in the banquet hall, seated at a table, sipping water and looking humble. Two tables away the general sat with other officers - closer friends now - in a tight circle as they chatted and debated in private. Hauptsturmführer Helmer was not in the circle. He was Franz Helmer Senior. He was half watching them and vaguely trying to listen in - and not sure if he

Section Four: Passing Out Parade

really wanted to. His son stood in the doorway and saw a vulnerable, wasted, almost sad man. He saw a lesser man than the one he had grown up with. He wanted to assist his father, help him out of the hole which had opened up - but he was also in that hole. He could not provide a helping hand. They were both stuck. It was a hole made of history and hurt.

Franz looked around for a clock and saw one. Not long to go now. He didn't know it but son resembled father: son too looked vulnerable, wasted, and definitely sad. He looked around at all the flags and all the red; and in particular all the swastikas; as if they were trying to tell him that everything was fine, that his place in their world was set, that theirs was his to inherit, warts and all. There and then Franz wanted to jettison his definition of his father, Franz Helmer Senior, and start again with a blank piece of paper. But he had no idea, no clue as to how to do it; not even how to start dismantling the old. And as it would prove impossible to 'unlearn', to deny fresh facts and new clues, so doing nothing was no option. His mother knew: he only had to ask her.

When Franz Helmer Senior saw he was being watched - by his son of all people - he shifted his weight and stood up, and adjusted his uniform as he shook off the trance into which he had allowed himself to drift. He was being spied on - by his son of all people - and he didn't like it. He was being studied like an animal in a zoo - by his son of all people - and he didn't like it. With nothing to say to each other they took a taxi back to the hotel. Both were the worse for wear, alcohol and food. Franz Senior could cope. Franz could not.

♦

In the back of the taxi they still said nothing, each pretending to give the drive back their full attention. The ride was a form of release, though short-lived. Franz felt his stomach roll. He felt giddy. He felt ill: here he was stuck in a confined space with a bad head, a bad stomach, bad thoughts and a bad dad who was now avoiding him. He took to the window: staring into the darkness else chasing the flashes of light which flew past - street lights and decorations.

It became unbearable, not being able to speak to him, as did the state of his stomach. He felt he was about to pass out. Then the taxi drew up in front of the hotel. Before it came to a full stop Franz threw open the door, leant out, and threw up over the pavement. Franz Senior - who had thrown up many times in his life, and often in full public view - looked away in disgust. He got out quickly and apologised to the driver as he settled the bill. The driver said 'no apology required' but Franz

Section Four: Passing Out Parade

Senior didn't agree. Impatient, he had to wait for his son to recover his composure. He did not help him out of the car. He followed him into the hotel, much like a guard escorting his prisoner, where they were forced to share the lift - a worse denial of personal space than the back of the taxi. In there the perfect father told his imperfect son to drink lots of water before going to bed, and to tell Reception to give him a wake up call. (Even as he said it Franz Senior decided to do it himself - but would then forget an instant later.) Franz replied yes, yes, yes to all his demands. He escaped the lift with his sanity barely intact.

Back in his room, Franz staggered to the bathroom and let loose a massive stream of hot piss, one which seemed to go on and on and out for ever and ever. He tried to brush his teeth, but gave up. He drank water from the tap and spat it out. It tasted like pond water. Back by his bed he was more successful with a bottle of spring water, managing to drink half of it before his stomach threatened to explode. Climbing out of his clothes proved another exhausting hurdle. The buttons drove him mad when they refused to cooperate. Left in his underpants he fell onto the bed, stretched out, and passed out. He left everything behind - comfortable or uncomfortable, real or invented, rational or ridiculous - as his brain powered down and fell in on itself. For now it demanded total rest - nothing less would do - but it would not be long before the bad crept back in to fill all the available space, leaving nothing for the good.

Franz Senior crept into his room as quiet as an elephant. He blew wind, and belched, and stumbled around the unfamiliar room in the dark trying to find his bearings. The wife, now no longer dangerous, was lying on her side, curled up and facing towards the wall. As he negotiated his way into the bed and under its sheets he looked her over. She looked asleep but he knew she was pretending - and she probably knew he was watching her. (Each knew things about the other that the other wished they did not - but that was the downside of marriage.) He stared up at the ceiling as he started to drift off, confident he had cast out any demons which had come back to haunt him this day. But he was fooling himself: they were still lurking, still able to stir things up, still refusing to lie down and let him be.

Franz clutched his, trying to strangle them as they in turn tried to strangle him. It would be a fight to the death in the back of beyond without rules, without result, without religion. Franz Senior pretended his were gone, or didn't matter. For both father and son, the memories which stirred during the night would demand re-evaluation and resolution, whilst causing new conflict and confusion - despite being nothing bold, nothing new.

Section Four: Passing Out Parade

Sleep for all three of them was a ragged, restless affair. For Hilda Helmer it was her well practiced but deluded attempt to shut herself off and push away all the unsavoury aspects of her married life - a life spent far away from home in a desolate place where she was expected to be a model wife, mother and German. For Franz Senior it was a respite, a kick-start, a period of reconstitution. It was peace and quiet, and respite from all those who demanded his time and consumption. For Franz it was simple more of the same and a chance to rest his body, but not his mind.

> Beat the drum. Curse the sound, a dreadful noise.
> Stand in line. Hang around, with the boys.
> Cheer the speech. Consume the cause. Hurry to please. No wish to pause.
> Hear the call. Dress to kill. Check the gun. Repeat the drill.
> Raise the flag. Salute the lie. Watch women weep. Make children cry.
> March off to war. No enemy in sight. Bird has flown. Still looking to fight.
> Tired and hungry. Set up camp. Write that letter. Lick that stamp.
> Piss in the well. Scorch the land. Take all the food. Eat what you can.
> One last push. Stop to toast. Finish that letter. Forget to post.
> Lose a father. Lose a son. Blow the whistle. Damage done.
> Pollute the peasants. Grab their land. Crippled by victory. No helping hand.
> Music must be heard. The beat must resume. Heads might roll but the body will consume.

As he fell into deeper sleep and had to wrestle with memories now not so familiar, now not so accommodating, so Franz became Little Franz again. And one floor up, in an identical bed, Franz Senior became Young Franz again. Each slipped back through time, to re-experience the past, to replay it - to repel it - whilst looking for clues, or escape, or some sign that what it suggested was false. Sharp, broken pieces of the past punctured the present until it surrendered and the past unfolded for yet another spell of re-examination. It would not let them sleep easy. It carried a mean sting. It made them sweat.

Stepping out of the car Father looked mean and miserable. A raised hand seemed ready to strike. A loud voice began to hurt. Lev was shouting too much. Aneta was smiling too much. Bridget was protesting to much. She popped up, played up, protested her innocence

Section Four: Passing Out Parade

and looked cheerful for no reason. If he tried to push her away she pulled him in closer. If he tried to pull her back she pushed him away. She was looking at him like he had done something wrong or had not done enough. She was dancing around him like a monkey. She was making him the monkey - talking at him in stupid French. The music was too loud. The girls were screaming. He wanted to flirt. He wanted to fight. He could not keep up with the dogs. He could not keep up with Lev. He paused: Lev was throwing up into a bucket. He watched: to see if the bad boy missed. The bad boy didn't. Lev never missed the target. Lev was perfect, the perfect peasant. He watched a drunk Lev move his body with precision and clear intent whilst he on the other hand, Franz, a German of good stock, would fall over and pass out. End of pause. He could not hang around town. He could not keep out the girls. He had to march when he wanted to run. He had to run when he wanted to sit. He had to sit when he wanted to shit. He was running into the sea, screaming with joy. He fell over in the sand, but picked himself up. He had a bucket. He had a spade. He had glorious sunshine. He built himself a castle and watched it fade. He climbed a sand dune and looked out to sea and up to the sky: both bewildering and bursting with blue. Mummy forced him to stand still. She combed his hair. She covered him in clothes. He hated it. He wanted to play with his soldiers. He had to be the chief. He fell from his bike and was bleeding. He slipped from his saddle and was seething.

The beer hall was packed to capacity with military men - all pretending to be real men through and through – swaggering and swaying, and stamping their boots; and shouting, and sweating; and shifting in the sand of garbled, gross conversation; and all ready to march in the direction ordered. Some had never learnt how to think for themselves. Some had forgotten how to think for themselves, and the few women present were taking full advantage of that fact. The celebrations were heading towards bedlam and the pounding of ferocious, sometimes false dictums masked the lack of substance in anything which was shouted out in the crossfire. Tempers flared. Everything caught fire. Nothing was wrong. Everything was right. Nothing was broken. Everything had been fixed. Nothing went to waste. Everything had a purpose. Nothing could be questioned. Everything was to be believed.

Slipping on ice. Sinking into sand. No diesel. No ammo. No helping hand. Tank track snapped. Lips cracked. Loitering with intent in an unmapped land. Frozen butter and stale bread. Alcohol for the buzzing in the head. Mud and manure and mouth ulcers. Shit and

Section Four: Passing Out Parade

urine and dreadful underpants. The Russian was laughing at the knife when he should have been begging for his life. It was held to the neck but the scum was showing no respect. She was showing no respect. She was suppose to be loyal. She was suppose to be his wife.

There was a cottage. Smoke was rising from the chimney. Young Franz rushed forwards and turned the handle. It was locked! Outrageous! He kicked the door hard. It refused to budge. Fiendish! Young Franz kept on kicking, again and again, until it flew open. Success! He rushed in looking for the enemy. A man was quivering behind a table. The man was reaching out to grab something. Danger! There was no time to think. There was no time to ask. There was no room to manoeuvre. Necessity demanded that Young Franz shoot. He fired off some rounds, spraying the room. The man fell down dead. Chest blown open. Job done, by the book. Young Franz felt vindicated.

He heard a noise upstairs. More danger! Clutching his weapon tight Young Franz bounded up the stairs, with an enthusiasm to kill. Another door, behind it the sound of movement. Young Franz kicked it open. He saw no one. He moved on in, gun pointing forwards. There was a sound to his right. Danger! Young Franz turned and pulled the trigger. A woman dropped to the floor, wounded, not dead. Mistake? So what. This is war. He drew his pistol and finished her off with a single clean shot. He was doing her a favour. Job done. Young Franz stared at her lifeless body and decided - there and then - that it had never had a soul. Hiding was a stupid thing to do. All she had to do was call out and surrender. Her fault.

Young Franz heard another noise, this time coming from inside the wardrobe. Danger? He moved forward, gun pointing forwards again. Something was in there. He opened it up, to see a small boy inside: tearful, trembling, petrified; unable to move; wetting himself. Danger? No. But a witness? Yes. Danger! Better to not have a witness. Shoot! Young Franz shot the boy dead and retreated. Job done. This was war.

Young Franz stumbled back down the stairs and fled the cottage. It has been neutralized. Job done. Back to the war. Tough luck if you hang around in the middle of a battlefield. You're bound to end up dead. The man only had himself to blame. He resisted. He fought back. The woman only had herself to blame. She should have surrendered. And as for the kid? What kid? There was no kid. Back to war.

Franz Senior rolled over as the sequence replayed itself, refusing to go away, refusing to calm down. It played out in his head in real time

Section Four: Passing Out Parade

while he battled to change it. So the man definitely had a gun. Shoot! And the woman was about to attack him, perhaps with a bread knife. So shoot! And the kid? What kid? Forget the kid! Franz Senior rolled over again. They want you dead! Shoot! Shoot them before they shoot you! That's your job. It's tough being a frontline soldier.

Little Franz was sitting on the stairs, exhausted, stomach bursting with cake and cream and fizzy lemonade. The party was over. His friends - some not so friendly - had been collected and escorted home. Little Franz was sitting on the stairs in his usual place, ten steps up, by the tear in the carpet. He was sitting waiting for something to happen and, seeing that no one was watching, he began to pick his nose. It badly needed picking. Little Franz was in uniform for the first time. He was as proud as punch. He was dressed like Daddy. He had a swastika armband and a peaked cap. He could go to war. He had his wooden gun. He could fight like Daddy. Then something did happen. Little Franz heard shouting. Mummy and Daddy were talking loudly at each other in the party room. Little Franz clutched his knees and waited for it to stop. It always did. Startled by the sound of breaking glass he stopped picking his nose and watched the door.

Mummy appeared. She was flushed and in a rush. Little Franz stood up and saluted her. She looked up at him. She did not smile. Instead she looked puzzled and moved on, still in a rush. She was escaping to the kitchen. Little Franz sat down again, wishing she had stayed. But then Daddy appeared and things felt good again. Daddy looked jolly, like he was still enjoying the party. Daddy was definitely smiling. He called out after Mummy, joking. But she didn't want to hear him. She was gone. His face fell back to earth. He looked unhappy, like he had been insulted. Little Franz decided to cheer Daddy up. He stood up and saluted. Daddy turned and Little Franz grinned but no smile appeared on Daddy's face. He saluted again but Daddy did not salute back. Instead he waved his little Franz down and walked off, out through the front door and onwards, looking for a fight. Little Franz watched him go then sat back down again and gripped his knees again. He wanted the party to begin again. He would have to wait.

Young Franz found her lying there, nameless, suffering but looking good while he was suffering and looking bad. War was making him suffer. The enemy was making him suffer. Was she the enemy? Yes. Let her suffer. Pay back time. Depravity beckoned. It was irresistible. In the heat of battle Young Franz could do anything - just as long as no one saw, no one recorded, so that no one had to judge. She was sweating. Young Franz was sweating. The war made everybody

Section Four: Passing Out Parade

sweat. The war made everybody stink. She had been raped they said, by Brandt they said. Her fault he thought. She had been weak, looking too good for her own good. He could not afford to be weak. This was war. He was not permitted to be weak.

I'm only human. I need sex. I haven't shot her. I haven't hurt her. She owes me. If she's nice to me I'll let her go. Come on, smile. Be nice. Smile damn you! Be nice you bitch, don't turn away! I'm not disgusting! You're the disgusting one! Look at you, in the dirt, covered in muck. I'm willing to give you a lift up, get you out of here. I'll give you money. But you have to look at me first. Look at me bitch don't turn away! Fuck you! Fuck you! Brandt was right. Fuck you!

She was tempting him by not running away. Young Franz had no choice. He had to show her who was boss, who was the victor, who was the German. He held her down. She needed to be taught a lesson - another lesson, like the one before. She refused to cooperate so he wouldn't be nice about it. The war had not been nice to him so he could not be nice to her. Quick now. No time to waste. Get it over with, quick. There's a war to be fought. She didn't scream. She had run out of breath, just as she had run out of fight, attitude, steam and strength, and almost all awareness. She wanted to sleep, forever.

I've earned this. She owes me one. It owes me one, this damned desolate, alien place, a million miles from civilisation. It owes me one. She's the one. There. Done. Now leave me alone. I'm done in. But I need to keep fighting. There's a war to be won. Wars don't win themselves. Back to the job in hand.

Franz Senior tossed and turned. She had not left his head. Troublemaker. Go away. Go away now. She didn't move. So he kicked her, again and again, to make her get to her feet and be gone. Only she didn't. He didn't see her face then. He didn't see her face now. Look away. Look away. Don't see her face. Push it away, into the long grass. Make her look away. Look away. Don't see my face. He couldn't get to sleep. Afraid he might wake his wife - and sometimes afraid of his wife when she was awake - he slid out of bed and went and sat on the sofa. Then he laid out on it, feet sticking out. Then he fell asleep. He saw the girl again but this time imagined himself walking on past. Brandt was the monster, not him.

Little Franz was up the tree, watching the world go by. The view had not changed but he had: he was bigger now; his thoughts lasted longer; his questions were more demanding; his patience was wearing thin. Everything he could see would be his one day. He would rule it like a king. Everyone would have to follow his orders. Little Franz was up the tree and feeling very tall. He could see but not be seen. He

Section Four: Passing Out Parade

could see over the wall. He could spy on that Penkin. The branch was hurting his backside and he couldn't scratch his arse but it was worth it to see Penkin sitting, drinking from a bottle, getting drunk when he was suppose to be working for his dad. Despicable. He didn't like him. He didn't trust him. He was an idiot. He wanted to report him. But Lev might not like that.

Little Franz heard voices approaching - Germans. Yes it was Father and someone who sounded like a soldier. All soldiers sounded the same to him: sharp voices, short sentences; speaking at speed; never listening; know-alls. Yes he could see them now. Father was showing an army officer around his estate. He called him 'major'. They both look golly, extra happy. Had they been drinking too? Little Franz watched Penkin struggle to get to his feet. Go on you can do it. Oh no stupid you just dropped your bottle. Clumsy sod. They've heard you, you idiot! Better run Penkin better run. But you can't because you're drunk. You've just been caught red-handed. Quite right too. Hope you get sacked.

Herr Helmer rounded on Penkin and pinned him up against the wall, shouting furiously. It made Little Franz shiver. The major picked up the bottle and read the label before tossing it to one side. Little Franz held on tight, afraid to make a sound, straining to catch the words. Penkin tried to stand steady as his boss berated him. Penkin tried to negotiate his way out of trouble but that just made things worse. He was giving lip. He was assuming special rights and privileges. When the major joined in Penkin answered back, which sent the major into a rage. He drew his pistol, aimed, then handed it to his host, telling him to shoot. Shoot the peasant. Yes he was drunk.

Herr Helmer felt the weight of the gun and hesitated while Penkin tried to laugh it off. His boss would never shoot him. Would he? When he saw his father finally take aim Little Franz held his breath. He had never seen a peasant shot before. He had never seen his father shoot someone before. Shoot him, he thought. I want to see what it's like. Let Penkin die. He's a no-good peasant.

Penkin began to shiver and shake. His eyes locked on to the barrel of the gun. Sobbing, he begged for mercy. Having made his point Herr Helmer lowered the pistol and handed it back to its owner, apologizing for time wasting. Penkin's relief was short-lived: the major pointed his pistol and pulled the trigger. Penkin nearly had a heart attack. Little Franz nearly fell out of his tree.

Click. No bullet fired. The major laughed and slapped his host on the back before putting his gun away. Together they walked away, revelling in the cruelty they had inflicted on their victim. Penkin

Section Four: Passing Out Parade

looked exhausted, vacant, wasted. As his master and the soldier - a new enemy to add to his collection - walked away, Penkin spat out his disgust and retrieved his bottle. But it was empty now. He threw it away and staggered off in the opposite direction. I should report you, thought Little Franz.

Slowly the Dead, still dressed for battle or flight, rose to surface as the living dug them up. The stench of decay advertised their coming. They had more than a bone to pick, more than time to kill, but less than a fighting chance. With the aid of his spade the remains of the first body appeared, and then there were more, all around, not far under ground. The state sanctioned killers had done their work well. There were no ghosts to haunt, no spirits to bless, no souls to lament; only bone and hair and teeth, fingernails and fabric, the traces of rotting flesh, and tougher attributes. And there were the personal affects: a rusty watch, unable to keep time; a limp leather belt, its buckle broken; a bullet lodged in the back of the skull.

The Dead were dispossessed of their yesterdays but could not claim for damages: the right to raise family ripped away; the chance to comfort a loved one squashed; music, dance, good food and wine, dialogue and debate - all these delights denied. The Dead had yet to have their day in court while the living still denied their yesterdays: but inch by inch, as second by second time rolled on, these days were creeping up on the present, to become nasty little creatures – little creatures with a big nasty sting - little creatures let loose amongst the living.

♦

Lev sat sipping tea and reading a book he had salvaged. To fill time he had decided to read. He was bored with cold beer and thirsty for mental stimulation. This was not his home. He did not feel settled in: he was clinging to the small piece of space he could call his own, namely that occupied by his body and nothing more. He had to fight hard to hold back the feeling of disenchantment which was slowly crawling towards him. Progress had stopped. He was not moving forwards.

Lev rarely looked up. If he did it was just to check up on what his brother was up to, which seemed to be much the same: shuffling around, checking out stock; moving it around; sometimes talking to himself else coughing with a cigarette in his mouth. They had barely spoken to each other all evening for nothing had happened which demanded any exchange of words. Lev couldn't help but see their

Section Four: Passing Out Parade

father in him. It was a frightening thought: Luka was slowly turning into their father. God forbid his brother became another Penkin! Did he really want to hang around to see that happen? He had no other choice. He had to make this place work as his home. He returned to the book. It was a tourist guide to the Czech Republic. When his brother did speak to him it was to say he was 'just slipping out awhile, might be gone all night'. He was off to see 'some girl I know'.

Isaak looked up, as did his cellmate. A rattling key had startled both of them awake. The door was being unlocked. It opened and a guard stepped inside the cell. He was grinning. He had a severe twinkle in his eye and a crooked smile taped to his face. He held out his hand. In it was a paper napkin. There was something wrapped up inside the paper napkin.

"This is for you."

"What is it?"

"Cake. It's a piece of cake."

Cake? The guard had baked him a cake? Was this part of the service? Isaak, dumbfounded, gave the guard a look of curious disbelief. The guard, sensing the confusion, quickly made to clear up any misunderstanding.

"I didn't make it. Your mother left it, for you."

"My mother? She's here now?"

"No, they're long gone."

"When are they coming back?"

"Don't know that they are. Don't think they are. Just left a cake."

The guard wasn't being malicious, he was just ill-informed.

Isaak stared at the slice of cake. Yes it was her usual carrot cake but he couldn't bring himself to touch it. To eat it would be to seal his fate. No, if he didn't eat it Mother would come back to ask him why he had refused her best cake. It wasn't a logic approach based on facts, or even faith. It was just desperate means. He waved it away.

"Give it to him. I can't eat it."

The guard shrugged and held it out to the other prisoner. He jumped up and grabbed at the chance to eat some nice cake. It had been a long time since he had eaten something so sugary, so sweet, so tantalising. He had been a child; still smiling, still happy; still innocent of the misery and damage grownups could inflict on the vulnerable, the needy, the destitute, anyone who got in their way. Isaak watched his cellmate tear into the slice and devour it in less than a minute. Nothing went to waste. He even swept all the remaining crumbs into his wide open mouth. Good for you, thought Isaak. That's the way to survive.

Later that night, as the enormity of his new predicament sunk in,

Section Four: Passing Out Parade

Isaak sat huddled up and began to rot from within. He could feel his flesh beginning to fall away - it was creeping away, leaving him stranded. Unable to sleep he stared out of the window and up at the stars - as and when his neck muscles allowed it. He feared he had slipped too far now down a big black hole, and there was no way back. He felt his situation was final: no way out; he was heading towards extinction, to be left for dead and broken up for scrap. He suddenly went from being nineteen to being ninety. He had lived his life: there was nothing more to come. From now on he was living on borrowed time. He was stuck in time and space - a confined space of four walls and no sense of time passing - with nothing to look forward to and little to look back on. All he could do was look out at the blackness - not only a lack of light but also a lack of humanity - and question the world in which, for someone like him, a Jew, the act of living was designed to be nothing less than a miserable balancing act on the precipice of sanity and humanity; and never anything more than that. It was a balancing act on the blade of the sharpest knife. The situation was impossible. Life was impossible. How was that possible?

His cellmate, caught by his mood, did much the same. He wished to console his new friend but was unable to. He did not have the mental agility required. He could only stare. Together they sat like corpses, waiting to die, not caring if the sun came up.

Franz woke up smart and looked at the clock. It was gone midnight. He was eighteen now, time to do something, time to act. He got up, smart. No time to celebrate. He had his mission. He got back into uniform, not caring which uniform it was. This one would do for now. It didn't look right but no matter: he could hide behind it. He attached his holster and checked his gun. Still that one bullet. He would need it for his mission. He opened the mini-bar and looked inside. Too much choice. He could not decide. He had a change of mind: drink was bad; drink was the devil. Let it be. He stepped out of the room. No one in sight. No one to stop him. No one to question him, judge him, dictate to him.

He called the lift, waiting with intent. When it arrived he looked around one last time - as if it was to be the last time - before stepping inside. Still no one was watching. He stepped out into the lobby - deserted save for one old man sat behind the desk, legs up, hidden behind a newspaper. Useless, thought Franz. The old guard. You are not fit to do the fighting. You cannot win my war. I must do the fighting now. While you, sitting there, idle, grow old and die. I am eighteen now, you must get out of my way.

He headed for the door, one hand on his gun, pausing only as a

Section Four: Passing Out Parade

telephone caught his attention. He could call Lev. But why bother? He had nothing to say. And Lev was too busy to be bothered to answer. Good old Lev was busy making a life for himself. Lev had no time for the likes of him. Lev could go to hell. The security guard lowered his newspaper and took stock before raising it again; vaguely suspicious that something was up; vaguely satisfied that all was well. He would rather get through his paper than get involved in anything real happening around him.

Franz stepped outside, into the freezing cold of night. It felt like a slap in the face but he would not be deterred. He began to shiver. He held on tight to his one key thought, which was to complete his mission. He had to fight the world. But before he could do that he had to fight the heavy fog which threatened to descend and swamp his now electrified, pulsating mind. He had his mission. He had to see it through. He was a Helmer, through and through.

He looked around. The street was empty - no, correction, there were two men approaching, in black uniforms. Were they drunk? Why always black? The two were talking - in English? They were struggling to hold a straight line. They were disturbing the peace. One whistled at him. The other sniggered. I should shoot them for insubordination; for insulting my fine country with their drunken, loutish behaviour; for their lack of respect for me, a future soldier and hero of the Third Reich. But no, he stood back and allowed them to pass. They were not the enemy, just irritants from a far off place. They were even allies of sorts. They were unwelcomed family.

He looked around in vain for the enemy. Nothing at first. He was alone, holding the fort, defending the front line. And then he saw them, here and there; once hidden but now revealing themselves as they emerged from the gloom: agents of evil with evil eyes and nasty features. They carried a grievance. They were all focused on him - Jews and Peasants. They wanted to kill him as soon as look at him. He was outnumbered but he was not afraid. He reached for his gun. He had one bullet. That would be enough to kill one and make the rest run for their lives. They began to point - the Jews and Peasants were pointing at him, laughing at him! Showing no respect! Even Lev! Even Lev was laughing too! Not drunk but sober! Sober and laughing at him, his best friend and his best chance of protection. What was the world coming to?

And as for that one Fräulein Bridget Schrimer. Who was she now anyway? A pain that's what she was, a let down, defective goods. She didn't know the concept of loyalty. She didn't know how to please him. No, best be shot of her. No way was he going to have those Schrimers

Section Four: Passing Out Parade

as family. They were not good Germans. They were fake. One of them spoke French, not German. They listened to black music. He would only marry into a good German family. That was what good Germans did. No, Bridget Schrimer could go to hell. Shoot her, and her parents. No, that would be going too far.

He shivered and shook as the cold drained his body of warmth. Some foul malignant force was slowly draining him of energy and intent. But still he held firm. He had his mission. He would not let anyone down: not his family; not his party; not his Fuehrer. He looked around. The Fuehrer was nowhere in sight. Where was his leader when he needed him? He did not want to let anybody down but he was feeling let down - by his friend, by his family, by his party. He had only the Fuehrer for support. But right now the Fuehrer was nowhere to be seen.

He had his mission. But first he had to identify the enemy target. Amongst all these Jews and Peasants and Foreigners - some French, some English - he could not find an enemy. He had no one to attack. He wanted a clear, unambiguous target; something to shoot at; something which could not shoot back. He felt a severe headache coming his way.

A firm hand touched down on his shoulder and a gentle voice told him to put his gun away. It was an old man in an ancient uniform. It was the hotel guard. Franz did as instructed. Following orders: it was the natural order of things. The old man led him back inside, back into the light and warmth. Franz looked behind him one last time: they had all gone; the Jews and Peasants had all gone. They had retreated back into the darkness; back to their homes and families; back to their peculiar little lives and their peculiar little dreams; back to something he possibly didn't have. He wanted to do the same: go back home; back to the house he knew inside out; back to the dogs who adored him; back to the motorbike which thrilled him; back into the family as it was, the one he had grown up with. But before he was allowed to do that he had to march, march until he was exhausted, march until he went mad; and beat the drum until he was bonkers, or bad; and salute the Fuehrer until the Fuehrer was glad.

The old man was speaking. He seemed to be asking him for identification, just like in the army, or the Schutzstaffeln. He wanted to know his name and number. Franz wanted to cooperate but he had no number. What number? I have no number yet. I have yet to sign up. But I am eighteen. I will fight for my country.

"No, room number," said the old man, now terribly baffled. "Tell me your room number."

Section Four: Passing Out Parade

Finally Franz got it and told him what he wanted to hear. The old man confirmed his details in the guest book and, satisfied, called the lift. When it arrived he guided Franz into it, telling him to go back to his room and get some sleep. Get lots of sleep. The boy looked like he needed a good night's sleep.

"But what about my mission?" asked Franz.

"What about it?" asked the old man.

"I must complete my mission."

"Complete it tomorrow," said the old man. "When you have slept on it, when you are wide awake."

But Franz, with a flash of recognition, wanted to correct him.

"Tomorrow is now, today. Today is tomorrow. They are both the same. I must complete my mission today, now, before it's too late, while I'm still eighteen."

"No," said the old man, now impatient. "Go to bed and sleep. Forget your mission. Forget them all. Just sleep. Sleep well. Have good dreams."

He hit the button and allowed the doors to close, sealing the boy in and sending him on his way. In the lift, alone again but warm again, Franz felt his mission slip away. Perhaps it would come back in the morning, perhaps not.

Lev, restless, did not sleep well that night. Isaak fell asleep only because his body forced it upon him. Total, absolute exhaustion meant he got a good night's sleep even if it was in a bad place and at a bad time.

♦

The Greatest Germany awoke to face the Grand Parade. Heads were filled with expectation. There would be no room for doubters. Dissent would not be tolerated. It was a national celebration of the triumph of will. It was a day for reputations and good manners. It was a day for trimming the famous moustache, and rehearsal. It was a day for glorious repetition of a hard hitting combination of sound and colour. It was a day for snuffing out accusations and evicting evidence from minds tempted to enquire. It was a day when foreign diplomats would be forced to shake hands with undesirables. It was a day when grown men would scream and shout and kick up a fuss like school children, and school children would delight in their day off. It would be a day of pensioner parades, boy bands, machine gun marches. Attention spans, stretched, would snap. Attention seekers, wretched, would snake their way to the front of the crowd. It would be a day for celebrity fashion.

Section Four: Passing Out Parade

It was a day for icons. It was a day when differences of opinion would not be tolerated. This public arena demanded total enthusiasm, total exhaustion, total meltdown.

    It was the perfect day to salute the Nazis.
    It was the perfect day to make an arrest.
    It was the perfect day to send dogs packing.
    It was the perfect day to beat one's chest.
    It was the perfect day to seek out a lover.
    It was the perfect day to kiss the wife.
    It was the perfect day to hand her flowers.
    It was the perfect day to jack the knife.
    It was the perfect day to orchestrate mind games.
    It was the perfect day to act one's best.
    It was the perfect day to fix the TV screen.
    It was the perfect day to fake self-respect.
    It was the perfect day to slice the sandwiches.
    It was the perfect day to cut the cake.
    It was the perfect day to meet the neighbours.
    It was the perfect day to turn up late.
    It was the perfect day to bag the best table.
    It was the perfect day to wear a silly hat.
    It was the perfect day to clap and cheer loudly.
    It was the perfect day to smell a rat.
    It was the perfect day to dump the dishes.
    It was the perfect day to eat a lot.
    It was the perfect day to drink a little.
    It was the perfect day to drink a lot.
    It was the perfect day to treat the children.
    It was the perfect day to bake them bread.
    It was the perfect day to serve them pudding.
    It was the perfect day to let it be said.
    It was the perfect day to snatch a milkshake.
    It was the perfect day to steal a toy or two.
    It was the perfect day to sit on sister.
    It was the perfect day to raise ballyhoo.
    It was the perfect day to call it a day.
    It was the perfect day to put them to bed.
    It was the perfect day to stoke their dreams.
    It was the perfect day to let it be said.
    It was the perfect day to wash down brandy.
    It was the perfect day to sing Lucy in the sky.

Section Four: Passing Out Parade

It was the perfect day to silence the critics.
It was the perfect day to question an eye for an eye.
It was the perfect day for profiteering.
It was the perfect day to raise the rent.
It was the perfect day to sell the dollar.
It was the perfect day to take a percent.
It was the perfect day to tease the cripple.
It was the perfect day to make him cry.
It was the perfect day to round up radicals.
It was the perfect day to watch them die.
It was the perfect day to sit in judgement.
It was the perfect day to scowl and spit.
It was the perfect day to swallow heroes.
It was the perfect day to be full of shit.
It was the perfect day to engage the enemy.
It was the perfect day to settle old scores.
It was the perfect day to sedate the savage.
It was the perfect day to end all wars.
It was the perfect day.

Franz rolled over, opened his eyes and took in the face of the clock. He was eighteen now. He was eighteen now! What now! Now what! He fell back to sleep, too exhausted to even want to wake up. Later, half asleep, half awake he switched on the television set and hooked himself to what was coming out of the screen. He blinked in rapid succession when in danger of nodding off.

He saw Alois and Klara stare down lovingly into the eyes of their new born baby son. They would name him Adolf they agreed. It was a good name, a strong name. They would raise him to be a good Austrian, a good German, a great man.

"Our empires will need men like him," said Alois to his beautiful young wife. "There is change on the way."

"Change?" asked Klara, suddenly fearful of the future and what it had in store for her son.

"Yes, change my love. Europe will change. The old way is on the way out. Empires will crumble. Kings will be kicked out. Germans will suffer terrible hardship. Austria and Germany will need a new generation of strong men to take up the challenge - men with modern ideas."

"Will our son be strong enough to take up the challenge?"

"We can only hope my love. We can only hope. But we must do our best to make it so."

Section Four: Passing Out Parade

Alois took his wife's hand and gripped it tight. "With God on our side I am sure that we can."

That was enough to convince Klara and she began to rock her baby gently. Right on cue the baby began to giggled into the camera. He was a sweet little thing, without any thoughts to load him down.

Franz watched a little Adolf running off to school, eager to learn everything there was to be learnt. He saw him sitting at the front of class, thrusting his hand up high and impressing the teacher with the depth and gravity of his answer to the question. Little Adolf had the rest of the class enthralled. His classmates were under his thumb. Franz wished his time in the classroom had been a similar experience of total supremacy. Franz nodded off for five minutes or so - staying alive was too much like hard work.

When he next awoke he saw Adolf the wild young artist sitting on a window ledge, pencil in hand, looking down at the street below and the people passing along it. Adolf watched them living their lives in a rush, without direction or purpose, oblivious to the fact that he was watching them - watching over them as far as Franz was concerned. The young Adolf was bathed in the soft sunlight of the afternoon, and the look on his face was that of someone in deep thought; the look of someone searching for the big answers to the big questions, and the next big challenge. There was a twinkle in his eye which could not be ignored.

Adolf popped his head up above the trench. He held Franz in his grip with his smile and that same twinkle in his eye. The Great War - which he was in the process of winning all by himself it seemed - was turning into an excuse for changing the world, and transforming it into something closer to his heart and desires. His imperial moustache was bold and eye-catching. His slim face gave no hint of a future fanaticism and arrogance. (But then it was the face of an actor.) He bounded forward under fire with a swagger and intention to save some souls and fix the world. It left Franz fixed to the screen, amazed and utterly impressed.

Suddenly Adolf the war hero was in Munich, watching the crowds who were watching the political extremists who were on the march, begging to be seen and heard - and taken seriously. He was watching everybody and missing nothing. And still he had that twinkle in his eye and an attitude which had so enthused a young Franz. The moustache had changed into something smaller, sharper; something far less glamorous but which carried far more punch. Adolf was witnessing the nation tearing into itself and the look on his face of fiery, mischievous innocence was in the throes of being replaced by one of furious intent. It was plain that he was determined - duty bound - to put things right, to

Section Four: Passing Out Parade

put the greatness back into Germany, else die trying.

Franz saw that, and felt it, and wanted to say thank you. He did not turn away from the screen despite a body begging to close its eyes and fall asleep. Then there were the beer halls; the orchestrated battles with the evil left; the loud, passionate speeches which brought audiences to their knees and made women weep. The journey had began and Franz was determined to keep up.

It was dramatic reconstruction which had polished the truth until it shone with poetic beauty; and it was a story which transfixed Franz, just as it had before, and before that. And each time Franz had never dared to put the question 'when will this ever change?' Change was not allowed. It was not a concept to be explored. Everybody was stuck in the groove and had to remain stuck in the present which was also the past. (And in the meantime Franz was stuck in bed when he should have been up, and downstairs, and tucking into a big breakfast with a smile on his face in anticipation of the great day ahead.)

Adolf, now slightly older and looking wiser, more thoughtful, more statesmanlike, was sitting in a luxury prison cell as the special guest of the state. There he received visitors and cemented his political ideology and vision for the future of Germany. He had an acolyte type it out. And while he dictated his struggle the twinkle in his eye was gone. And then he was free again; back on the streets again; mean looking again; doing mean things for the greater good through his bunch of mean henchmen; and selling his mean message of salvation to the masses. In this reconstruction however the meanness was not to be seen: it had been replaced by righteous almost religious conviction. And Franz loved it, thinking that what he was seeing was how it had been. And all the sinners who surrounded the Fuehrer were saints and all his victims were deserving.

Franz watched a more mature Fuehrer standing in the back of a truck, flirting with the women of Germany: they adored him; they strained to touch him; they nearly fainted when he shook their hand or patted them on the head. Franz hoped that one day, when an officer, he would have the same effect on unmarried women. And then the Fuehrer was sworn in as chancellor, and shook the president's hand. Franz saw the Fuehrer wave from a balcony. He looked tough, energized. He looked ready to take on the world as chancellor of a reborn Germany. Franz wished he had been there. He wished he had been his father - the young version of his father.

Franz saw an older, bolder Fuehrer lead his troops into war against the Russian threat; standing majestic over a map of Eastern Europe; explaining his strategic military goals and offering advice on tactical

Section Four: Passing Out Parade

imperatives. Franz watched the field marshals and generals look on in awe and humility as the commander-in-chief of the armed forces told them how to do their job and conduct the 'necessary, noble war'. Franz wished he had fought in that war. He was resolved not to miss any coming up.

Victory secured, Franz watched the triumphant Fuehrer stand bold but battle weary in the centre of Red Square. Arms folded, he stared across at the Kremlin, in his view a monumental monstrosity. Surrounded by his military escort he carried an expression of satisfaction for a tough task completed well with minimal loss of life. Classical music soared around him. There was not a Muscovite in sight - cut to him sitting patiently, hands clasped, at a massive table; waiting for the dregs of the Soviet leadership - Stalin long gone - to take their places on the other side, read the writing on the wall, and sign up to peace. The Fuehrer sat saintlike, above it all, as a rabble of wild, scruffy malcontents were pressed into signing the document of surrender by a gang of top German and Polish generals. Franz thought he could see the twinkle in his eye again.

Suddenly there was tapping at the door. It was Mother's tapping. It was Mother, in a mood, talking loudly while refusing to shout. Why wasn't he downstairs? Was he awake? Get up! Quick! Franz jumped out of bed and switched off the television and said whatever he had to say to get her off his back. She told him to be downstairs in five minutes 'or else'. To be honest, the 'or else' no longer scared him like it used to. I'm eighteen, thought Franz. That has to count for something.

At breakfast the three Helmers barely sat as a family, barely ate as a family, barely talked as a family. Herr Helmer was in uniform but the previous day was not mentioned. It was off limits. The day ahead was barely discussed: it had all been said, repeatedly; they were here now; it was here now. Now their son just had to perform and the Helmers would cheer. And then they could all go home, back to their private kingdom over which each wielded control - some absolute - in their own special way. It was the big day and the big day was in danger of squeezing them all out of existence.

Frau Helmer tried to sound upbeat as she handed her son his birthday card. She failed: her time spent in Big Berlin with its Big People had been too much of a wrench. Franz thanked her, and his father - who struggled to smile - and found a key taped to the inside of the card. He held it up for examination. It woke him up.

"It's a car key?"

"We've bought you a car," explained Mother.

"It's waiting for you when you get home," added Father.

Section Four: Passing Out Parade

"Thank you. Thank you both." Franz was truly astonished, overwhelmed. Now he was wide awake.

What warmth was generated immediately evaporated when his father began a tough line of questioning. It came out of the blue, as if the man was under fire and felt duty-bound to check one last time that all was well and ready. Though the questions were tough Franz found then easy to answer.

"Are you ready?"
"Yes."
"You will give it your best?"
"Yes."
"You won't let us down?"
"No."
"Are you hung over?"

Today Franz could not lie to his father - and hoped that his father would not lie to him. His silence betrayed him.

"Go to your room. Drink lots of water. Lie down and wait to be called."

Mother took the key. "I'll look after this for you. You don't want to lose it."

"Thank you."

"It was your father's idea."

"Thank you Father." Franz spoke without looking up. He stood up, which made him feel sick. "I have to go to my room now."

"We understand," said Mother graciously.

Father didn't, and never would.

♦

The old man awoke from his secret world, into another - real but still full of secrets. Grudgingly he let slip from his mind the often revisited memories of old battles and past glories, and re-entered the land of the barely living. He looked small, frail, insignificant in his big four poster bed, in his big bedroom, in his big house, surrounded as he was by the big beautiful perfect people who were his household staff. His body was stiff, like his mind. His remaining hair was thin, grey and limp but his eyes were still sharp, still piercing, still on the lookout for threats and opportunities. The old man was an inflexible stick of rock, through which ran the constant signature of a thug, a racist, a manipulator of crowds, a frustrated artist, and a born fantasist.

He swore at the mattress. It was hurting. It was not showing due respect. The old man, forced to put his best thoughts to bed,

Section Four: Passing Out Parade

immediately fell into his customary bad morning mood. He had forgotten that this day was different and rang his bell, repeatedly, for his breakfast in bed. It was late, very late. He only stopped when somebody appeared, flustered. This time it was the young man whose name he could not, and cared not to remember. The servant looked harassed, stressed, which was how the old man liked it: keep them on their toes.

The old man demanded to know why there was no tray, no breakfast. It was intolerable. Somebody deserved to be fired. The young man, pale but smartly dressed in his valet's uniform, stood to attention and sweated profusely, terrified as he was whenever the old man lost his temper or sense of reality, or both. He fumbled through his words as he explained that he had been instructed to prepare no breakfast this morning as the Fuehrer would be dining with guests instead. The old man, never one to admit a mistake, or defeat, waved him away with an order for one cup of strong coffee. The young man clicked his heels, smartly turned, and rushed out of the door, glad to be out of there. The old man struggled out of bed: help was available if he commanded it but vanity meant that it was to be the last resort. He slouched on the end of the bed, remembering now, in slow motion, that yes, today was his birthday; that yes, today they would celebrate him; that yes, he would have to make an appearance, entertain, give a speech. The thought of the day's coming pleasures was digested much like a heavy meal.

Suddenly the old man wanted to see all the main newspapers. He wanted to see what they had written about him. He grabbed at the telephone and yelled his order down the line. Somewhere in another part of his grand mansion, newspapers were hurriedly gathered together, folded, and rushed to the front, to join up with the coffee on its way. Though the old man now lived at a slow pace, often with slow thoughts and slow reactions, everything around him happened in a snap, at speed; triggered by his sudden whim and impatience for an immediate result or gratification. It was a perk which went with the job.

The old man sat up with a sharp in take of breath and a bolt of lightening to his head. Today he would make a speech of fire (again). He would revisit the past (again), and reiterate the future he expected his people to make (again), and leave them exhausted (perhaps). He would show them, again. The old man's mind could still race around the circuit, but the circuit went nowhere. When he could think straight the old man held his extreme beliefs tight inside his head, lest he dropped them. They were like favourite toys: he dare not put them

Section Four: Passing Out Parade

down for fear of never finding them again.

The old man sipped his coffee. It tasted funny. So he became angry. Excuses to get angry were hard to come by these days so he never stood up an opportunity. His rage had been caged by the requirement to act at all times like the polished, noble leader of a powerful civilized country. His rages were reduced to sporadic outbursts over trivialities. He had been muted by success and old age but he could still roar when it suited his displeasure. The old man looked around at the four walls. He had seen this wallpaper for far too long now. It had to change, today: new wallpaper for a new year of his life. The old man yawned. He still felt tired. He was tired but he had to get up and perform. The German people expected it of him. He looked at the clock. Today was his birthday, again; his 75th. What now? Another round of handshakes, that's what. Another parade. Another speech. So be it.

There was a gentle tap at the door and the soft voice of his personal assistant asked when he would be ready for his breakfast appointment. All the guests had now arrived and were waiting. The food was ready to be served. Make them wait, thought the old man. It will do them good. The old man shouted down the phone: send in the valet, he was getting dressed. He had a big day ahead of him. He had to be extra big today, and big-headed. He had a twinkle in his eye. With meticulous attention to detail he washed and dressed, dismissing his sudden affliction of insecurity with childish rebuke. But the genius of twisted thought was gone. All havoc had been wreaked. There was nothing left in the pot to burn: just a hollow existence and the crushing weight of boredom and loneliness.

The old man hated sharing his breakfast time. He preferred to dine alone, which was best for all considering his state of mind first thing in the day. Instead he had to share it with some so-called special guests. (One of them was there because they had won some competition.) He only had himself to blame: he had agreed to the idea as a neat piece of propaganda. He was expected to be witty, passionate, even entertaining. He tried his best - which was not much - but not for very long before calling out to be helped up from the breakfast table. He walked out to the consternation of his guests and the disappointment of his loyal staff.

The old man became irritable, tired, confused as sycophants and protective, caring staff explained the lengthy, detailed agenda for the day. He repeated himself. He asked which 'world leaders' would be attending to pay him due respect. His mind wandered back again to the best of past rallies. He felt he was being 'readied' for the big event like

Section Four: Passing Out Parade

they owned him. When dealing with official papers, he lost his temper and sent them flying across the carpet. The old man wondered where Eva was, then he remembered that she was dead. Must go see her today, he told himself, before I forget. He missed his wife, but not that much. (She had always fitted in, like a well-trained dog.) He missed his first dog, but not much more. (His dogs were always called Blondie and they were always German Shepherds.) He missed his mother, no question. He didn't miss his father.

With Blondie at his side the old man ordered that he be driven to the burial ground of his beloved Eva. The spontaneous decision for a visit to her grave - always with his dog - threw his staff into confusion. It was not on today's very tight, precisely planned schedule. (He had done it on purpose: to upset their meticulous planning; to show them who was still the Boss.)

Blondie, happy and affectionate, paced around the site, sniffing and checking the place out while the old man stood, leaning on his stick, staring down at her tombstone and asking himself the question he always asked when there. Had he used her as an opportunity? Had he truly loved her or simply adopted her as a useful accessory, for show, to prove to the critics and unbelievers that he was perfectly normal, perfectly human? His personal guards stood at a respectful distance; neither here or there; always in the shadows; always armed; never seeing anything. The old man hated to admit it - and he never would - but now, finally, he wasn't missing her. By the end she had worn him out with her fluffy lightweight conversation and vacuous commentary, her lack of logic, her wish to always party, her willingness to squander private time best spent alone by inviting over friends. She had never really understood him - and had never tried - as he had never really understood her - and had never cared to. Alone, he denied his loneliness.

An anxious assistant, conscious of time, finally persuaded him to leave, leave her be. Truth be told the old man was glad to leave, but disguised it by resisting calls and then dragging his heels. He didn't want anybody to think he had become cold-hearted.

> Is there anything left to live for Adolf?
> Is there anything left worth denying?
> Is there a place in your heart for the boring old fart whose existence you could not conceive?
> Are you fragile now Adolf or still hard as rocks?
> Are you up for the fight which is part of the job?
> Have you sown your seed? Have you encoded your creed in a way which

Section Four: Passing Out Parade

forbids extinction?
Your dreams make for dire drama. Your memories are so complex that your taste for theatre deceives you leaving your actors somewhat perplexed.
Stomach ulcer? Blood too thin?
Indigestion now you've taken them in?
Now you've captured the crowd and settled the crime do you sit on a pin?
Be warned, the dead are waiting to greet you.
They are sad and extremely distressed.
Perhaps you can take the time to remember in the time it takes to confess.

♦

It was mid-morning in Luka's flat and the telephone rang to disturb the peace. For a change Lev decided to take the call. It was Kleine, and the last person he wanted to speak to was Lev: that he made abundantly clear. Luka, glaring, snatched the phone away but his younger brother was not prepared to give ground. Striking a pose and gesturing, Lev made it quite clear what he thought of Kleine the corrupt policeman. The detestable German had a hold over Luka. He had him over a barrel.

Lev heard girls names being spoken, traded. Sex was being sold, at a discount. He tried to catch the sound of one in particular. Luka, cornered, turned his back on his brother, stretching the telephone cord to its limit. But Lev refused to back off. It had been a long time since they had been so physically close, so tense in a situation of their own making. Suspicions roused, Lev pushed in and tried to hijack the conversation, wishing to tell the great Inspector Kleine to go to hell, go back to Germany. Luka kicked him away but he kept coming back, like a mad dog; one which had spent too long a time in a cage too small to accommodate its existence. Luka apologised to Kleine and slammed the phone down. And then they came to blows.

As in their previous lives they fought over a point of principle; one which neither actually supported or opposed, but one which gave them an excuse to fight for right; and then they just fought. They fought for space, for gratification. They fought over old wounds. They fought for the pleasure of inflicting pain and exercising muscle. They fought over broken toys, stolen sweets. They fought because fighting made them feel good. They fought for the hell of it. They stopped when they realised it was beginning to hurt more than that which they were

Section Four: Passing Out Parade

prepared to bear: neither wished to inflict serious damage on the other. They were after all brothers.

With nothing changed, yet everything feeling much worse, Lev skulked out and wandered the streets - streets he now found easy to hate and difficult to dominate. Fearing the worse he headed off towards the house of the only girl he knew in town. He wanted to be a hero. He wanted to save a life. He wanted her to say thank you, show gratitude, be beholden to him. He did not want to live an honourable life. He just wanted to be seen sometimes doing the honourable thing. And he wanted to stop a German from always getting his own way - his German way.

♦

The double doors were swung open for the old man and heads turned. The old man paused, resting on his stick, trying not to stoop. He looked in, and beyond; and waited for the shop talk to stop, for the gossip to be shelved. There they were, the old and the new, the best and the worst of his inner party. Their salute was a joint venture. They were all waiting for him to say something. He knew exactly what they were thinking. Why was he still here? Did he still have the magic? Was he still in control? Why would he never discuss retirement? He waited to see which one would race forward to greet him first. It was Himmler of course, never one to miss a trick, and as nimble and slim as ever, unlike that fat buffoon Goering.

Himmler firmly shook the old man's hand and forced him to smile, before he proceeded to make some long boring announcement which went in one ear and out the other. The old man pushed on into the room, determined to dominate, even though his thoughts were cloudy, his passion dulled, his energy waning. He had to put up with Goering slobbering over him and Hess overexerting himself into a dangerous mental frenzy with too many theatrical, emotional outbursts. His mind is going, thought the old man. He's losing it again.

The old man stuck to his stick as he accepted endless praise and congratulations; and reminders of his greatness and standing in the world, and how important he was to the state, to the people, and to the Party; until he was forced to sit down and look up at them. He hated having to look up at Himmler or Goering. As always Hess did the honourable thing: he sat down beside his Fuehrer and offered to hold his glass. Hess was still his most loyal fan. The old man declined. He was not a cripple. He was still capable of holding a glass. He looked around at all the dull colours of the uniforms: brown, black, grey.

Section Four: Passing Out Parade

Nothing had changed. They still mostly hated each other. At best they put up with each other. And he liked it that way: it kept them on their toes. It was like a visit from bad family. There were no angels here, only arseholes.

The old man caught Himmler out of the corner of his eye. As usual the righteous Reichsfuehrer had retreated a little from the mob, to take up a better position from which to watch all the others. He wants my job, thought the old man. Well you can't have it yet. It's still mine! He did his best to avoid one Bormann. That Bormann bored him. And as for Reinhard Heydrich: he was only loyal to Himmler, not to him; and he was a stuck up aristocrat who looked down on everybody, even Himmler, though Himmler was too short-sighted to see it. The golden boy of the Schutzstaffeln could do no wrong, and the look in his eyes dared anyone to say otherwise. It dawned on him that Doktor Goebbels was nowhere to be seen. He asked where his doctor was - which at first caused alarm amongst some - and was told that the doctor had a problem with his foot. That made the old man laugh. They kept reminding him that it was his 75th birthday. That turned him sour.

The old man wanted to make a little speech but could not find enough words, so instead he had to put up with those made by others. As usual the Reichsmarschall was the loudest with the least to say. Speer? Where was Speer? With Speer he could have a serious conversation. The old man banged his stick: he had just remembered that Speer was dead. Died in a car accident the stupid man! He was not ready to die yet. That would be too convenient. Let them wait. Let Himmler wait.

The old man sat and stewed. He had no enemies left to pursue, to devour. He had already devoured his few friends. That left only himself. And he didn't realise he was doing it. He was too old to notice where his fire was being directed. The old man became bored. He wanted to fight new battles. He wanted to win another war. He wanted to keep on rebuilding his cities. The old man had never had it so good - so good that it left him vacant. In moments of wishful thinking he sometimes wished that the war had gone on longer; that there had been tougher battles to fight; that he had pushed his armies harder, to the limit and beyond. (The Poles had proved to be a pain. He should have crushed them, not indulged them.)

The old man wanted to live it all again, start the fight again; from the beginning again; young again, with his loudest voice, his loudest ideas; and win their hearts all over again; and feel the passion now as he had then. He missed a good fight, a good punch up, a total annihilation of his enemies. He wanted to hear the clap and crash of

Section Four: Passing Out Parade

thunder as communism collapsed. He wanted - needed - a dangerous, unhinged world to need him. But he didn't want to be reminded of Jews.

There were still Jews left in the far corners of his Reich. He should have been more thorough, when no one was watching. He should have let the vicious little Himmler loose on them. He thought of Himmler's anointed successor, his deputy Heydrich, and as he thought of him the old man laughed - his thoughts turning to the young American president: he was a sanctimonious idiot - image, nothing more. The man was a fake, a piece of marketing; too young to run a country. At least his generation - and his next - had proved themselves in war. They were tough, zealots, as hard as nails. The Americans, the English, the French: they could never stand up to him; they never had the guts for war. The old man puffed out his chest. He still had plenty to say, just no way to say it. When he had had enough of his party line Party chat he said he wanted to walk his dog - until he was reminded, gently, that he already had.

The old man was pulled from some spurious thoughts by a Party attendant whispering in his ear. There was the invitation to meet two important Englishmen: the Duke of Windsor and Sir Oswald Mosley. They were in another room, wishing - waiting - to meet him. The old man delayed, wishing to make them wait until it hurt. (Apparently the Duke was growing tetchy with the lack of courtesy and the leader of the BUF was beginning to march up and down like a restless dog.) One of these Englishmen he regarded as an oaf; pushy, always self-promoting, full of fluid bluster. The other he regarded as a shambles; stupid, vain, conceited. He did not recognise any similarities with himself. Duty calls, the old man told himself, as he allowed himself to be raised up and moved on. Let them share his limelight.

As always Sir Oswald was here to talk politics, and get funding (which would tire the old man out); and the Duke was here to be seen, and to talk about very little except himself, his wife, Paris, and the weather (which would bore the old man to death). If Sir Oswald was not in his face all the time then it was waffle about wonderful Paris, a wonderful wife, a wonderful life. (The old man remembered being shown a list of all the women the Duke had ever slept with - some single, some married, some possibly related.) And still the duke had that annoying accent. The old man caught the tension between the two Englishmen: one a brainless aristocrat, of the best royal stock; the other a tough street-fighter, also of good breeding. That provided for some entertainment. In his younger days he would have stirred it up for all its worth, just to see what might snap. These days he lacked the energy.

Section Four: Passing Out Parade

The meeting did not last long. Little was exchanged much beyond pleasantries. Well-worn, crinkly hands were shaken until wrists threatened to sprain. Tongues wagged. Official photographs were taken of fixed poses with smiles all round. The politician was still tough, sharp, energized beyond social norms. The duke was vague in the extreme. He was losing it. Sir Oswald wanted to talk politics but the old man would not reciprocate. This was his party. After an adequate amount of time spent with his guests the old man excused himself: duty called; tight schedule to keep to. There were no hard feelings on the part of the English. (As usual on such occasions the French were not there and the Polish generals were, in force.)

You should have come to me first Adolf.
I would have held your hand.
Your toys were never big enough.
Your plans were all too grand.
You said you loved your mother Adolf.
Did she take you in her arms?
Did she shake away the playground blues?
Did she mend you with her charms?
You took your father's fear
and promoted it.
You soaked it in blood and tears,
and exploded it.
You pushed her too hard. You made your mother ill.
You shouted into a sweat.
You marched them up to the top of the hill.
You made their sons see red.
Were you the sinner Adolf
or were you sinned against?
You found favour with the butcher,
the baker, the banker, and the rest.
They all had familiar faces,
and a yearning to persist,
and fraudulent family values
which catered for the beast.
You sent the politicians packing.
You made the civil service stink.
You gave them money, an intellectual feast.
Saying Grace you silenced all the priests.
The march-past was fake expression
of nostalgic reaffirmation.

Section Four: Passing Out Parade

You judged their grand procession
without a tear in your eye.
You took my name in vain Adolf.
You sold it as a drug.
You made the mindless mutiny.
You made my Youth your thugs.
Did you tell your mother?
Did you tell your father?
Did you hang your ego out to dry?
I don't think so Adolf.
I think it's time to die.
Wash your mouth out Adolf.
Brush your teeth now Adolf.
Say your prayers now Adolf.
Sweet dreams Adolf?
I don't think so Adolf.
I think it's time to die.

◆

The telephone cracked its whip and Franz jumped awake. It was time. It was time now. He was made to slip into uniform by the combined force of compulsion and circumstance. The hotel lift gave him no way out except down. His parents pushed him on to the minibus and waved him off - after he had been kissed to death by his mother and inspected for faults by his father. There he sat, still weary, brain busted, at the back; almost solidified; watching his parents still waving and wondering why he couldn't bring himself to wave back. Their images hung on inside his head: one unable to release him; the other still protesting his innocence. Franz was off to war. He didn't want to think too much about it, just get through it, survive. He folded his arms tight and closed his eyes. No one else made a sound. They were about to enter another man's world, in a dream.

Franz was a prisoner under escort. He was being transported unseen, towards something still out of sight and out of mind. The bus was taking him towards the absolute totality and the point of reckoning. It was a meeting point of a thousand other threads, all part of the woven fabric. It was a point still evolving into existence. Soon it would explode charges of pomposity with a devious, addictive reality. All manner of interest, self-interest and detachment would hang on the one point in time when the presence of Adolf Hitler - his stature, his voice, his body language, the gleam in his eye, the expression of absolute

Section Four: Passing Out Parade

conviction, his predictable salute – would bring things together, and transfix; and all would be forced to be with him and all the things that he ever intended to be would be forced to remain so, forever more, 'amen'.

Amen?

Amen.

The traffic increased and intensified as the bus approached the stadium. The roads were becoming jammed and the human traffic was swelling but the bus cut its way through: with its official markings and special cargo of youth it had right of way and a parking space reserved. Now Franz - now everybody - was on the edge of their seats. The whole world was here, queuing to be entertained, and an army was gathering to satisfy it. Duty, Franz reminded himself. I have to do my duty. There will be a crowd, the size of which I have never seen for real and will never see again. But I must do my duty. He was the last to tumble out of the minibus. And when he did he struggled to breathe.

There was a circulation in the air of something heavy, something crude, something perspiring. It was the distillation of fifty thousand souls hanging on a moment. It stung unbelievers and comforted all others with the promise of sweet salvation, and more. Heavy with history it suffocated the easily led and swallowed them whole. It would leave in its wake burnt out brains and worn out bodies. The stadium had filled to beyond capacity. It was bursting at the seams but not with opinions; not with the dialogue of a crowd in motion; not with a proliferation of lifestyles, beliefs or aspirations. The gang of the old guard congregated on the high platform, their gestures manicured; some watching the others; some thinking politics; all playing to the crowd. The only poverty in the event lay in the absence of true history. All across the Reich ordinary people, proud to be ordinary, rose to the occasion and temporarily reinvented themselves.

When he was reunited with his cell Franz was not surprised to find them equally subdued, equally shell-shocked by the enormity and gravity of what lay ahead; even Gebhard. Even Gebhard Strasser was keen to get it over and done with as quickly as possible: yesterday had been an excuse to show off, exercise command; today they had to get it right, in front of the whole nation. Millions would be watching and they had only the one chance to get it right. Failure was not an option. Gebhard told them so, unequivocally, and they all agreed with him. Even Franz was one hundred percent behind him. The cell was working as one, as one cell should.

Surrounded by other bewildered boys they waited; shifting nervously; watching other formations of men, women and machinery

Section Four: Passing Out Parade

lead the way. There were the Teutonic Knights in shining armour with their maidens on tap. There was the flash of steel and heavy metal. They squeezed the juice out of the rumour that they would get to meet the Fuehrer himself. (That they could deal with.) And then suddenly it was their turn to perform, to turn heads, to impress all. They were the next generation and they had it coming.

♦

Lev turned up at the house of Luka's little girl with his trademark knapsack. He looked lost, homeless to someone who didn't know better; and he looked wanting for friendship. The television was on, loud. It was screaming. Somewhere in Germany it was celebration time but there were no celebrations to be heard inside this particular house. There was instead just the exhausted, pacified audience of an underclass. Lev knocked, and kept knocking until he was heard. A young skinny woman with spots answered the door. She was smoking a cigarette and was defensive: alert to danger she did not like talking to strangers - boys or men. Lev made a request to see 'his friend' and was told to wait. The door was slammed shut. It opened again a minute or too later and he was allowed to come in and go on up to her room.

Lev knocked on her bedroom door. The girl said come in, though she could barely be heard. Upon entering Lev was thrown off balance. He saw a teddy bear sitting upright on the pillow and a baby in her arms. It was that old teddy bear and some new baby. The girl explained that she was baby-sitting, giving the mother a break. Lev didn't understand why a mother needed a break from her own baby of all people. He looked around the room and was unimpressed. The girl didn't say sit. She didn't take in the famous knapsack. She just continued to look down at the baby, and smile with loving care. Lev was left to stand and watch Luka's little girl cradle some baby. Not your baby, thought Lev with a streak of clumsy jealousy. Finally, fed up, he took a bold step and crashed down on a spare bed, just to watch her watch the baby. He felt forgotten. But he had got used to that.

Luka's little girl sat with a baby which she made her baby, her future. She was a big girl now. She was really kicking inside. She had switched off from everything around her except the baby she held in her arms. The baby stared back up at her, secure but slightly confused. She did not talk to her baby. She did not need to. She simply watched it smile and grin and be content. Occasionally sudden noise from the screen drama below would reach them: a lot of people somewhere were having one hell of a good time. And then Lev remembered: it was their

Section Four: Passing Out Parade

fucking Fuehrer's birthday. And then he remembered more: Franz was there, in the thick of it all; having a great time; being a typical German. Still, Lev wished him luck. All in all he considered Franz to be a good German.

After awhile Lev forgot he had been forgotten and began to find the stationary situation relaxing, almost therapeutic. He didn't want to spoil things by trying to talk - not that he had much to say - and he didn't want to mention that word, 'Kleine'. Keep Kleine out of it. Keep Inspector Kleine away. At the front door he had briefly entertained the desire to squeeze a kiss out of her: just one kiss from the little girl would do a lot to put things right. He had been short-changed last time. But with a baby there amongst them that desire had evaporated. The baby was on its way but in the way.

Somehow - he didn't know why - Lev took great pleasure in simply watching the baby being happy in her arms, without a care in the world, and she, likewise, being equally happy. Was he happy then? Was this happiness then? Lev didn't know. The girl obviously didn't want to talk to him. He didn't mind that. But she had invited him up? He didn't understand that - not that it bothered him much: that was in the nature of women. Women kept doing things their men didn't understand. Suddenly Lev shifted uneasily: that was Penkin speaking. He didn't want to be reminded of Penkin. He made a silly noise and the baby searched for its source. It tried to giggle. The girl didn't look up but she did give an extra wide smile. The baby had become the loudest person in the room with the most to say but no way of saying it. And it had the strongest grip: able as it was, without even trying, to pull them both in towards it.

Suddenly it was all about to change.

There was a series of sharp knocks at the door - which they didn't hear - then two loud bangs - which they did, just about. Lev was instantly put on alert. Next he heard the sound of heavy boots stomping their way up the stairs, almost with calculated precision. Kleine. It had to be Kleine. The girl barely registered the fact. She is not expecting him? thought Lev. Or had she simply given up on resisting anybody and anything which smashed into her?

Momentarily frozen in his thoughts Lev woke up and broke free. He jumped up and rushed towards the door, just as Kleine banged on it and announced himself; like he was the most important person in the world. That did it: the girl took note. She held her breath. She clung to her baby. The baby was her lifeline. She wanted a baby - her own baby - now, before it was too late. She didn't want to but she had to look up. The monster was on the other side of the door. The monster was after

Section Four: Passing Out Parade

her body. The monster wanted to drag her away to some place awful - or perhaps some place really nice, clean and tidy. She looked hard at Lev for the first time. Would this boy come to her rescue? Would he run away? She looked down at her baby. It was the only place to look now.

Kleine called for the girl to come out, to join him; just for an hour; somewhere 'nice'. All had been arranged, he said, as if that would make the whole experience acceptable. The girl looked at her baby as the monster on the other side of the door began to breathe fire. The baby had heard a strange commotion. It tried to look around and get an answer but the girl would not allow it. She hugged it even closer to keep it safe from her danger. Kleine tried to force the door open. He was confused. It did not want to open. His girl had not uttered a word, not protested in any way, but she was holding the door closed with brute force. That was not possible. He kept pushing and swearing until finally it gave - and that was when it all made sense. It was that bloody kid.

Like a monster Lev glared back, ready to fight the devil. Kleine laughed - badly - and pushed him backwards into the room. Being a policeman he looked up, around and down. Old habits die hard. He was visibly disgusted by what he saw. His initial reaction to the inside of the house had been to turn his nose up. Now it was turned so far up it was in danger of snapping off. There was a teddy bear on a pillow. It made him look away: he did not want to be reminded of children on a day like this. He looked down at the girl and the baby she was holding for all her worth. The sight of them disturbed him. He even turned to the bloody kid for an explanation. Why was she ignoring him? It was like she had totally switched off.

"She's baby-sitting," explained Lev, reluctantly. He hated exchanging words with Kleine. He wanted to keep things at a distance, on the level of fists only.

Kleine looked down again, at the baby again; unable to place it, ignore it or arrest it. It simply didn't fit into his world. He backed away slightly before turning his attention - one hundred percent - back on to the damn peasant kid. He had had more than enough of that kid even though it was, in sum total, very little. In no uncertain terms Lev told him to get out, to leave them alone, to be gone. For Kleine the outburst was pure comedy. His reply, also in no uncertain terms, was to tell Lev to get out of town before he busted him, or him and his brother.

The girl watched them tear into each other, and hugged her baby close, and tried to cover its ears. The baby was not liking all the noise: in its tiny world this was deafening. She didn't have the nerve to tell

Section Four: Passing Out Parade

them to keep quiet. Terrified, she watched one try to throw the other out of the room.

Lev resisted well which sent Kleine wild. They grappled, but at a level which made them both look strangely incapacitated, or under restraint. It was the baby. In both their minds violence in a room where there was a baby was not permitted. It was an absolute no no. Kleine tried to pull Lev outside by his shirt. Lev slipped free, long enough to grab his knapsack, before turning the tables and pushing Kleine out of the room. Kleine staggered backwards, clutching Lev. They didn't speak or shout. They had no words left for each other: it was all about the fight, physical superiority, finding closure. Kleine tried to grab the rucksack but Lev held it tight and close: like girl and baby he would not be separated. (She was still on her bed, hoping they were both gone for good.)

Kleine got the upper hand and kicked the infuriating peasant boy down the stairs. They had an audience: female heads stuck out from the rooms below. This was real entertainment. Someone - possibly someone very stupid - was attacking a very important German. At the turn in the stairs Lev paused to recover himself. He took in the situation, but not to analyse it. He just wanted to react to it. With a furious fuming, red-faced German staring down at him and contemplating victory Lev ripped open his knapsack and torn into the towel inside until he made contact with cold hard metal. To the roar of the crowd on the television he produced his Mauser pistol. The crowd was seeing weapons raised in abundance.

Kleine stood, legs spread, hands on hips, like a general surveying the battlefield after victory (or before battle). He poured scorn, in buckets, on the kid's pathetic attempt to scare him.

"You won't use that you little shit. Loaded is it?"

"Yes."

Kleine stuck out his hand. "Hand it over now if you don't want to spend the rest of your life in prison having your balls broken."

Lev didn't want that to happen but he did want to shoot at least one German in his lifetime; especially this one, one of the worst. He didn't have any time to weigh up his options: the German devil was stepping down the stairs; pausing on each step, as if treating Lev like a joke, as if teasing him.

Kleine repeated himself. "Hand it over. Give it to me."

This time the order was delivered in his signature flat, ice cold chilling voice.

Lev gave up on living, and gave it to him. One shot rang out. Somehow it was a form of release. The bullet struck Kleine in the

Section Four: Passing Out Parade

shoulder. Stunned, Kleine put his hand up to cover the entry point. The look of incredulity on his face said it all - searing pain had yet to engulf him. The peasant boy had not read the script. Slowly Kleine eased himself down on to the stained disgusting carpet, to try and think things through while he could still think. Being shot, here, in this sordid place, by an alien would not look good. Things like this were not suppose to happen to him. People did not dare shoot him - not even hardened criminals. His mind could not sort out the mess before the blood began to flow. He began to shake as on TV some guns fired a salvo and the crowd roared their appreciation. On a day like this Kleine wished he was stationed back in Berlin.

The girl appeared, still holding the baby. She too could not take it in. She was still absent. She would not allow their hatred to affect her baby. The baby began to wail. Those who had been watching freaked out and retreated back into their rooms, slamming doors shut as if to barricade themselves in; as if thinking they could simply disconnect themselves from the incident. Lev turned and fled, wishing he had killed the German. His survival instinct drove him at full speed in just one direction. He didn't give Luka's little girl one last look - as if to say sorry, or farewell, or 'what went wrong?'. He just fled the house. And she was left holding the baby.

◆

Time has ceased to function for Isaak. He was neither here nor there, nor waiting for an outcome. When he was asleep he was awake and when he was awake he was asleep. He was completely drained of energy and emotion and deep thoughts. He had rotten away, leaving only a shell of a man who had not even begun to live life. When he could he tried to dig up memories of moments in the Ghetto: those which had been restful, or playful, or enticing. His cellmate snatched at moments in the woods, under the stars, up a tree, under the hot sun, in a field of fully grown wheat. They were not dead but they were not aspiring to staying alive. They were just making do with breathing air in and out, beating blood, blinking, repeating the same second in time. Most of the time they laid still: it was good practice for what corpses did.

A guard unlocked the cell door and beckoned Isaak to step outside. The severe, impatient look on his face did not bode well. Isaak dragged himself up off his bed and tried to reengage with the land of the living. He had once entertained the idea that this particular guard was a decent fellow. Now he was not quite sure. Every thought his mind now

Section Four: Passing Out Parade

released was fraught with uncertainty and immediately recalled. Had he done something to upset this man? Had he not died soon enough? He was being taken from his cell at an unusual time of the day. This was not part of his natural rhythm now and it scared him. His cellmate saw the fear and was infected. Isaak looked behind him to check on his cellmate - and perhaps because it might be for the last time. His friend did not look good.

"Where are we going?"

"Never you mind."

No hints, no clues: the guard was milking the situation for every last drop of pleasure. It was what you did to Jews in these parts. (There was after all little else to do in way of entertainment.) He handcuffed Isaak to his own wrist - an entirely unnecessary action and one which had not been done before - and led him out to the front of the station. Isaak, weak in mind and body, walked like a dead man, a zombie even. Was he going to prison proper?

There it all changed. The world shifted. It was a different universe - one in which Isaak rediscovered hope, and rediscovered himself. He saw his mother and father, and was electrified; as were Diza & Yosef when they saw their son, their only son. On making eye-contact Isaak's sense of worth soared to new heights, almost all the way to heaven. So high, it was in danger of not falling back to Earth (where it was most needed). The joy on all their faces sparked like a lightening strike. Even those watching felt it - even the guard still handcuffed to his prisoner - and felt they were missing out on something worth having. Suddenly for Isaak the world was OK again - no better than that: it was absolutely perfect. Diza shouted his name and rushed forward, and grabbed her boy, and hugged him, and squeezed him, and kissed him, and forgave him for causing her such agony. Mother had her son back. She would not let go easily. Isaak welcomed all his mother's kisses, and gave one big one back. Yosef looked on, relieved, satisfied and feeling superior to all those watching their family drama (free of charge). The guard began to feel rather silly in his situation and scrambled to remove the handcuffs. He wanted to be free of the Jew as fast as possible.

"You paid it then?" asked Isaak.

"Just about," replied Yosef.

"Was it a lot?"

"It was enough. But worth it I suppose."

Father and son smiled at each other. A joke, thought Isaak. That was always a good sign.

There was plenty to talk about - and the three wanted to talk - but

Section Four: Passing Out Parade

not here, not in this demeaning, sometimes wicked place which pretended to enforce a fair law for all. They began to walk out, each parent embracing one arm of their only child. From a distance it looked like Isaak was still under arrest.

"I've got a taxi waiting," explained Yosef.

"Expensive?"

"Of course. For us everything is expensive. You know that by now."

"Yes, sorry." Isaak suddenly felt very sorry for all the trouble, financial loss and heartache he had caused his parents.

"I'll pay it back."

"We'll see. Just don't do it again."

"I won't, I promise."

His father believed him.

"And thank you for the cake Mother."

"They gave you some cake? That was nice of them."

"You didn't bring me any cake?"

"Not exactly. It was meant for the chief of police."

Thanks mum, thought Isaak. Suddenly he halted at the main entrance; like all the joints in his body had seized up and were refusing to operate; like old machinery which had blown its final fuse. His mother nearly fell over.

"What is it now?" she asked as she recovered her balance and composure.

"I'm not leaving without my cellmate. I have to go back and get him."

Diza & Yosef looked at each other with misgivings. They both had questions - much the same questions.

"Cellmate? What cellmate? Did you not get your own cell?"

Isaak gave his mother a funny look. "No."

"Some criminal?" asked Yosef.

"No."

"What's he done?"

"He hasn't done anything. He's innocent, just lost. He needs a home."

Isaak slipped from his parents firm embrace and left them standing looking hard done by. He confronted the guard and made his request with force and determination, before being quickly reduced to begging as his attitude and attempt to show authority fell on deaf ears. The guard watched his performance at being a strong man and was amused. Isaak tried to put his hand on the man as he said please, repeatedly, but the guard was having none of it. He did not want to be touched by a

Section Four: Passing Out Parade

Jew. Yet, somehow, he finally succumbed to exercising a bit of basic humanity.

"Wait here. I'll go and check with the chief."

Isaak did as instructed - a rather pointless instruction in his opinion - while his parents delayed nervously, suspended; Yosef with one eye on the taxi; Diza with both eyes on her son. The taxi was beginning to cost a small fortune.

The guard reappeared, jangling his set of keys as if it was party time. He nodded towards Isaak.

"Come on."

"He can leave? He is free?"

"Yes. He's all yours says the chief."

"Thank you."

"Don't thank me. Thank him."

That was something Isaak did not care to do if he could help it. When the cell door was yanked open again its remaining occupant jumped up in alarm. There was no Isaak coming back in. That freaked him out. He retreated to one corner of the cell and tried to hide, by shrinking down to a point or becoming invisible. Now he definitely wanted to die. But then his cellmate, his new friend, popped his head into the cell. He was smiling and he held out his hand.

"Come on. You can come with me. You're free, like me."

Free. The word 'free' would take time to sink in. The word free meant, what? Climbing trees again any time he liked? That conundrum could wait. For now he just had to follow his friend. He could trust his friend. That's what friends were for. He took his friend's hand and immediately it calmed him back down. Before leaving Isaak snatched up his few possessions which had served him so well. The dirty underwear needed washing - a job for mother.

Diza & Yosef turned with a gasp of relief to see their son reappear; and now looking even happier; and now holding the hand of a fragile young man, and his old bag. He too looked very happy. Suddenly it all made sense to them.

"He doesn't have a home?" asked Yosef.

"No. He was living wild, in the woods, abandoned. No parents."

"What's his name?"

"I don't know. He doesn't know."

"We'll have to give him one then - come on let's all go home."

"It might be a tight squeeze in the back of the car," warned Diza.

Yosef smiled first, then Isaak. The cellmate tried to follow suit and nearly pulled it off, unused as he was to smiling.

Business complete and a line drawn, the four of them squeezed into

Section Four: Passing Out Parade

the taxi and headed back to the Ghetto. Isaak was on his way home, back to his island of escape. Unbeknownst to Isaak, Diza & Yosef had one last trick up their sleeve: waiting for him back home was a party. Friends and family would all be there. His liberation had to be celebrated.

♦

> You dare not ask him the reason why.
> You dare not laugh. You dare not cry.
> You dare not think to intervene.
> You dare not ask him where he's been.
> You dare not think to consider him wrong.
> You dare not sing another song.
> You dare not think to consider him vain.
> You dare not think that he's to blame.
> You dare not delay or fall behind.
> You must sign up and fall into line.
> You watch him closely, just in case.
> You salute his picture. You fear his face.
> You know you'll never shake his hand.
> Yet you stumble to reach his land.
> He has that look you cannot deny.
> It makes you weep. It makes you cry.
> He makes true that which was a lie.
> He lets some live. He lets some die.
> He dares you to look him in the eye.
> He dares you to fake or compromise.
> He holds a loaded gun to your head.
> He's there at night when you go to bed.
> He has the charm. He has the wit.
> But he has to piss. He has to shit.
> If he has a heart, he keeps it chilled.
> If he has a spirit, it's just a thrill.
> If he has ever loved, it was a waste of time.
> If he handed out hate, he committed no crime.
> He's in your heart. He's in your head.
> He's around the next corner. He's streets ahead.
> He's heaven and hell. He's dirt and dust.
> He's everything possible. He's nothing just ...

On the way to the stadium the old man could smell the waiting crowd

Section Four: Passing Out Parade

long before he heard it or saw it. His stick was hidden away out of sight. The route to the stadium ran like a river of red fed by red waterfalls from the rooftops. Crowds - some near crazy, some beyond crazy - filled every position which commanded a clear view. There was no room for the individual, only the herd; pushing to the front; maintaining the mania by squeezing out those who did not contribute to the same degree. The old man tried to revive hard memories of past parades, mass rallies and mass adulation. But it proved too much of a drain. It could have all been a dream.

The old man was let loose right on time. When he appeared at the balcony, less his stick and stoop, a great roar rolled out and rippled around the stadium. The old man was in his element. These were his people. He had forged them into his new nation. He had no time for any others. The expectation of his people energized him, but not for long. The old man could not produce the energy. He wanted to give another explosive performance and blow them away with his fireworks but all he could do was wave. So that was all he did.

Franz was locked in a dream. He fell into line, like a robot. He sucked in as much air as his lungs could handle, stared no further ahead than the back of the head in front, and swung his legs into action. He picked up the tune and tempo as instructed. He headed out into the arena as directed, head held high, heart beating like a drum to the sound of real drums, and immediately he was assaulted by the sights and the sounds. They engulfed him. He was in a crazy dream. Somewhere in the crowd Mother and Father were searching him out: they might find him in his crowd but he would never find them in theirs, nor did he wish to. He dreamed that he would see his Fuehrer, and see that his Fuehrer had seen him, and that would put things to right.

He wanted the Fuehrer to see that he had not changed, that he would never fail him, never fail to do his duty. And yet even as he thought it, and postured, so denial tried to creep up on him and take control. He hid behind and within his uniform, as all the boys did. It released them from their personalities. Set in stone they marched, some beating drums to death. Franz refused to panic. He refused to be afraid. He stamped his boots and moved with the music. There was some safety in numbers: he could hide in the crowd when the crowd was identical - boy soldiers, toy soldiers, heroes and villains; all made identical.

The crowd roared, like a mindless monster, whose only cause was devour all other moving, living creatures. The boys had to keep moving, moving to the beat of the drums. Franz did not want to stop until he was marching back out of sight and away. Forget the crowd. Forget family. Forget friends. For now, even forget the future. There

Section Four: Passing Out Parade

was only the Fuehrer. All he asked was that the Fuehrer recognize him and forgive him for any weakness, any doubt. The Fuehrer would help him up and out. The Fuehrer would see him through his extended moment of misery. The Fuehrer would set him free from the torments life threw at him.

A sharp pain shot down one side and abruptly curtailed his public appearance. The old man was whisked away, to be checked out by his doctors, to be rested. The old man was cut loose.

It was the right time. Now was the time. The time was right. Franz looked up at the balcony and scanned its length, dismissing all other famous faces. There was only one which mattered. Nothing. He could not see him. He was not there. The Fuehrer was not there. Franz was trapped in a very confusing dream. Stony faced the boys gave the salute and received some back. But it was not the same without the Fuehrer's salute.

Franz snapped and lashed out. The Fuehrer had no time for him, Franz; Franz Helmer of Sumy; Franz son of Hauptsturmführer Franz Helmer of the Waffen-SS and war hero. It was an insult. And then he recoiled, in shame, hating himself beyond measure for such a reaction. Arm still extended he had to keep marching. He had no choice. He was still in uniform. He could not take it off. His head began to cave in. His thoughts melted away. He could make nothing add up. He could see nothing of value. He was chasing contentment, old certainties. And he was abandoning them. His state of flux was sending him beyond giddy. He blanked it out. He blanked out. He began to fall, to the sound of the drums. He didn't want to go to war if this was war. He didn't want to go home. He didn't want to stay in uniform. He didn't know what he wanted - just that it be good and wholesome, like Christmas Day.

> I have left one place and reached another.
> The air smells sweeter but the land is the same:
> little worth, little gain; same pleasure, same pain.
> One face looks much like another:
> I see fathers; I see mothers.
> I even see sisters, some with brothers.
> The anger is altered and the smile is subtle.
> The land is the same but I am in trouble.
> I am out of place. I am lost in the crowd.
> I dare not scream: I might scream too loud.
> If God is my land then I am disconnected.
> If God is my land does he know my name?

Section Four: Passing Out Parade

> If God is my land will he explain?
> Adrift at sea I look out for land.
> Then I discover there is but sand:
> between my toes; beneath my feet.
> I stand up straight and pause for breath.
> I look inland. I am out of my depth.
> But the land is the same.

Sturmhauptführer Max Helmer and his lover sat cuddled up together on the sofa. Max held his lover's hand. He brushed some loose hair and dandruff from the shoulders of his lover's gorgeous uniform. They had the television on. In broken black and white they watched the screen: both fascinated and fearful they refused to be beaten. They could not easily ignore him: that old man who had caused them so much hardship. Grief had yet to come.

The Schrimers dissected the images and sound, the messages and the mania, until all that was left was a nasty taste in the mouth. Their daughter, wounded, just sat, still mixed up: sometimes stunned, other times impressed; overwhelmed then under whelmed then overwhelmed again; for then against; sometimes thinking the best of Franz, sometimes the worst; sometimes trying to, sometimes not. But whatever her state of mind she could not stop looking at the screen. The event was simply too big to be ignored. It had the girl totally in its sights. Three times the Schrimers looked across at their daughter: Herr Schrimer to check that she was alright; Frau Schrimer to check if she was still pure. All in all they stayed inside their own heads, where it was safe.

The colonel sat proud, like a lump, on his way to getting drunk; already acting loud while his wife laughed loudly. The colonel saw what he expected to see, nothing more, nothing less. He thought what he wanted to think, being incapable of nothing more, nothing less. He was easily impressed by the more powerful, and hard to dissuade. His wife would clap for no reason, which irritated him.

◆

In blind panic Lev called his big brother from a telephone box - dropping the phone twice before finally dialling correctly and getting a connection.

"Get back here, now. Don't wait. Don't stop. Don't think just do. Don't draw attention. Make sure no one follows you."

Clear precise, firm instructions: exactly what Lev needed right now.

Section Four: Passing Out Parade

And it came out of the mouth of his big Brother. There was no better place for it to come from. As he ran up the stairs to the flat the door opened and there was Luka, ready to whip him inside in a flash. The door slammed behind them. In seconds flat Lev was made to explain what, why, how. The when was obvious. Luka drew no conclusions; made no comments; passed no judgement. Instead he told his distraught younger brother to pack the essentials, nothing else. They were getting out, fast.

Luka did not panic. Lev did want to panic, fly off the handle. He was expecting Kleine to burst in at any moment and shoot him. But big brother Luka knew Kleine well: he would go home first; get medical help, in private, off the record; only then would he turn his attention to revenge, and a visit - perhaps late at night when it was dark and there would be no one around; no witnesses to anything he might care to inflict. Sharing that knowledge calmed Lev back down, until he was able to cope.

Lev was surprised and impressed by his brother's secret 'survival pack': a stash of money in various currencies; a wide range of travel and work documents; best of all the best fake IDs. Something for a rainy day, explained Luka to a wide-eyed Lev. They were the perfect brothers again: one leading; one following, trusting. Quickly and expertly, with kit he kept tucked away from prying eyes (like Inspector Kleine), Luka transferred Lev's photo across to a new ID and reapplied the official stamp. They were both old men made new.

They took time to drink coffee and stuff themselves full with the best food to be had lying around in the kitchen. Some they packed: cheese, ham, bread and biscuits; and the best chocolate. Luka had no intention of going hungry. While packing Luka grabbed some high value items which were dear to his heart: bottles of pills; Cuban cigars; jewellery; and a few important photographs.

"These little pills are worth a fortune."

"Why?"

"For the experience."

Luka's final act upon leaving was to spit into the room, then lock the front door, then kick it. It was a ritual born of a life lived in danger and disgust.

"Fuck this place. Fuck Kleine."

With that they were both free of the flat and the disgust which went with it.

Luka led the way to the main bus station where he intended to catch a bus to Warsaw. He had a few 'mates' there, business contacts. It was then that Lev, reinvigorated by a new adventure and having got his

Section Four: Passing Out Parade

breath back, made his move and surprised his big brother. (Though Luka would not remain surprised for long: after all his brother was just like him.) Lev wanted to go south, to the Med, to the sun, sea and sand. Luka did not try to dissuade him. He wished him luck. He only warned him that down there, outside the Reich, he really would be forced to live a dog's life; underground, never a legal citizen. Lev didn't care. He had to give it a go. He knew the odds were stacked against him: if he came back with his tail between his legs then so be it. Luka handed him a contact number in Warsaw.

"Give it a week at least before you try calling," he advised.

Lev thanked him and tucked it away securely.

"Visit me when you find your feet."

"Of course."

Each sounded like they didn't really mean it when in fact they did, deeply. Family was all they had. They didn't hug. Their eyes stayed dry. There were no speeches, no last words, no final reflections, no promises. And when the first bus pulled into its parking bay, one did not wave as the other boarded. Waving was for weaklings and neither was weak. They were hard, as hard as nails when the situation called for it. It was the only way to survive. They did not say goodbye they just kept looking.

On arrival back at the gate Isaak was saddened to see no one waiting to greet him, inside or out. No one could be bothered to welcome him back from Hell. There were just two guards, and one of them was asleep. No family. No friends. It was then that Diza confessed and Yosef twitched at her indiscretion. Everybody was waiting inside to throw Isaak a party - nothing big she warned. Diza did not want to create an anti-climax in her son's possibly fragile mind. Yosef said she had spoiled the surprise. Diza retorted that the surprise was getting their son out of jail. Isaak said she had spoiled nothing: it was a great day, a wonderful day.

They rushed to get back inside: Isaak leading from the front; his ex-cellmate trailing but trusting. Yosef paid the taxi driver. No tip was given and none was expected as the price was already too high. Isaak wanted to see his room again; walk the streets again; run around again; feel free again. He wanted to beat his father at chess again. The guard who could be bothered let them through one by one while the other, now partially awake, watched the show through one eye. The exception was Isaak's ex-cellmate: he had no ID, no yellow star. When Yosef and Isaak explained the poor man's predicament the guard was more relaxed, but still stuck.

"I can't let him through. He needs to be registered. I could get in

Section Four: Passing Out Parade

trouble."

"But your police chief doesn't give a damn. He wants him gone, out of his hair. That's why he gave him to us to keep."

"You sure?"

"Absolutely. Go check with him. He's there, now."

Argument almost won, Yosef took the guard to one side and offered a deal which might tip the balance. Over a period of time Yosef would supply him with a trickle of cash, food and drink. But not straight away. He had just paid a fortune to get his son released. Yosef even offered to sign a contract - at which point the guard waved him away. It was all getting too complicated, too heavy.

"Take him. Lose him in there. He's free to go. If the police don't care, take him. Just keep the idiot inside."

Yosef smiled, glad that the guard had dismissed his offer. "We will."

'Free'. Isaak's friend heard that word again and wondered what was in store. Would he be free beyond the gate, inside there? He rushed to catch up with Isaak - he was well on his way to a party. Isaak looked behind him once. He had no wish to step outside again for quite a long time but knew he had to. That was where it was all happening.

Two were alive to the world and its way of working. One was dead to it, or in denial: he was in a strange kind of sleep. For Lev it had come to a sudden stop and now it was a sudden start again. For Isaak it continued, much like before. Only he was a wiser man with a bigger heart. Tomorrow could be the last day, so live today someone had said, possibly as a joke.

Franz was laid out on a stretcher, though he did not know it - nor did his parents yet. They were still enjoying the show, Father much more than Mother. He was surrounded by others who had also been overcome by the heat of the moment, or had suffered injury. Some had sprains to wrists and ankles. Some had cuts or bruises. Some had tripped or got smacked in the face by some nasty object. Some were just old. Like nuns a few nurses glided back and forth, lost in their own tight little world of professional serenity and emotional detachment. They did not need to worry, just attend. Let the well paid doctors of the Schutzstaffeln fuss and diagnose and take the stress.

His agitated state had been calmed and countered with a drug. Now he was in an artificial state of peculiar unconsciousness; still sweating; lost in a void of his own making; all at sea again without his boat again. That said, it was a good place to hide, to not deal with the world, to just delay. But over time the drug would wear thin and Franz would have to return to the land of the living; and nothing would have changed; and

Section Four: Passing Out Parade

he would have to go home, where all was the same; and carry on, perhaps a hero. His life was about to change - military service beckoned - and he might change with it. Or he might stay the same. Either way the odds were stacked against him.

There was a prison cell, sometimes open, sometimes locked. Sometimes you could walk in. Sometimes you could walk out. Sometimes you were stuck.

God is my land
but he drew a line in the sand,
in a place where the devil may care.
It grew and drew close - was this a dare?
I was not drawn to be moved, to look over the edge,
but there was a whisper of secret regret.
Cross the line and you bleed they say.
It cuts no ice that I can walk away.
It cuts no ice when I stick my head in the sand.
I shook my head. I held back.
I hold to the principle that black is black.